The Bessie Blue Killer

Also by Richard A. Lupoff

RICHARD A. LUPOFF

The Bessie Blue Killer

A Hobart Lindsey/Marvia Plum Mystery

St. Martin's Press   New York

This is a work of fiction. Names, characters, places and incidents are either
the product of the author's imagination or are used fictitiously. Any resem-
blance to events or persons, living or dead, is entirely coincidental.

Design by Basha Zapatka

Library of Congress Cataloging-in-Publication Data

Lupoff, Richard A.
   The Bessie Blue killer / Richard A. Lupoff.
     p.   cm.
   ISBN 0-312-10425-1
  I. Title.
  PS3562.U6B47   1994
  813'.54—dc20   93-43652
                                  CIP

First edition: March 1994

10 9 8 7 6 5 4 3 2 1

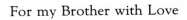
For my Brother with Love

Introduction

Jane Langton

A SUSPENSE NOVELIST SOMETIMES CARVES OUT a special niche, a personal space, by sticking to one subject or setting.

Tony Hillerman writes about crimes on Indian reservations in New Mexico, Emma Lathen about shady manipulations on Wall Street, Jonathan Gash about hanky-panky among dealers in antiques.

Richard Lupoff's bailiwick is all his own, the world of the nostalgic collector. His protagonist, Hobart Lindsey, works for International Surety, an insurance company that must shell out when the valuable collectibles it insures are stolen—rare comic books or classic cars or antique airplanes. Lindsey does his best to save the company enormous sums by tracking down the lost articles himself. Along the way, the reader is treated to fascinating lore about Batman and the Human Torch in *The Comic Book Killer*, a parade of glamorous automobiles in *The Classic Car Killer* and a succession of Zeros, Focke-Wulfs and B-17 bombers in *The Bessie Blue Killer*. Of fabulous value and heavily insured, the comic books and the magnificent cars and the heroic war planes vanish or are threatened, and International Surety sends Lindsey on the road to find out what happened. Like any ordinary hard-boiled private investigator, he must work his way past many a dangerous obstacle before tracking down the clever deceiver at last.

Along the way, bobbing up in Lindsey's mind during his pursuit of lost valuables, are remembered fragments of the pop culture of the thirties, forties, fifties and sixties. Walking into some villainous bar or sleazy hotel, he is reminded of old movies with Victor Mature and Jane Russell, or Jack Webb in

"Dragnet," or the music of Miles Davis, or the jingle of Gary Cooper's spurs as he saunters into the Last Chance Saloon.

> There was a TV set above the bar. It looked like something out of the Lyndon Johnson era. It was silent and dark. Maybe they'd left it up as a memorial to the Great Society.

Swift images like these enliven the action, evoking layer upon layer of time. The sense of a superimposed present and past is not easily come by in a thriller. Most of the characters in a mystery novel inhabit a flickering now. Lupoff's have histories that sometimes coincide with our own. We too remember Billie Holiday. The intersection of the reading self with the invented one brings the fictional person sharply alive.

Another specialty of Lupoff's, part of the niche he inhabits, is the setting, his home territory, the California cities of Berkeley and Oakland. Hobart Lindsey moves in a landscape that rises vividly around us as we follow him—the sun falls behind the East Bay hills, fifty thousand people roar in the Oakland Coliseum, the morning fog descends on Berkeley, kids mill around on a dangerous street in downtown Richmond, a gray cat strolls down a gangplank to a wooden pier on the Oakland Estuary.

> He drove to Oakland . . . and found the Embarcadero. Roberts' address was in a block of modernistic condos opposite a railroad track and an industrial slum. But the condos themselves looked expensive, and with the estuary on the other side, it seemed a safe bet that the occupants wiped the sight of the factories and warehouses from their minds when they got home at night.

This is more than pleasant description, it's social commentary, evoking a complex image in depth, reminiscent of the way Raymond Chandler writes about Los Angeles.

The landscape isn't merely a background against which events happen. Rather it has an organic relation to the story, which grows out of it like a strangling vine wrapping around the legs of Hobart Lindsey and Morton Kleiner and Aurora Delano and Desmond Richelieu and Lieutenant High.

Something else that sets Richard Lupoff's stories apart is his profound interest in the color of his characters' skins, his close examination of a multiracial metropolis. It's not simply his white protagonist's love for Marvia Plum, an attractive and brilliant black woman. It's his keen depiction of the interaction of black and white at every level.

A poignant example is the moment when Lindsey introduces Marvia to his mother on the last page of *The Comic Book Killer*. Throughout the story as it unfolds we have become familiar with Mother, lost in a dreamworld of the 1950s, completely out of touch with the present. Through her son's concern and sympathy we too are committed to her welfare. It is all the more shocking when she greets Marvia as if she were the new cleaning woman:

> *"You must be the new girl," she said. "I try to keep up with the house but it's such a problem with a little one underfoot and my husband away at war. It's hard to get a good colored girl to clean up. I hope you'll work out better than the last one we had."*

It hurts. There's a real pang. And pangs are few in detective fiction, in spite of the proliferation of murders as we flip the pages.

Lost collectibles, nostalgia, Berkeley and Oakland, race relations—these are all part of Lupoff's special niche. But the principal occupant is Hobart Lindsey himself, a man of stature. As a character, he is both real and good, no mean trick. Lindsey moves through Lupoff's chapters cautiously, making his way thoughtfully from point to point, carrying no gun:

"Well, what about your pistol permit?"

"Don't have a permit. Don't have a pistol. Don't know how to use one. Don't want to learn."

"That's the trouble with you minimalists. Nothing we can

threaten to take away from you. How are we supposed to keep you in line?"

Unarmed, his courage is the greater, if more wary. Inevitably, he is attacked. Violence swirls around him, and he goes down. When he gets up, he doesn't reach for the gin and leap into his car. He has a terrible headache. But his limited strength is balanced by intelligence and a politely ironic view of the world. His likableness grows on us, turning into admiration. Lindsey, we discover with gratitude, is a man of compassion. For instance, after learning that a child has been killed in Richmond:

> He gave it up and turned off the TV and climbed into bed and stared at the ceiling some more.
> Eventually, God sent morning to make things better.

All the more satisfying in contrast with Lindsey's humanity is the ghastliness of some of the other characters. It's always a pleasure to read about a genuine bastard:

> Lindsey got himself an English muffin and a cup of coffee. Mueller ordered bacon and eggs up and a prune Danish, and proceeded to dip the Danish in the egg yolk . . . He hadn't shaved and a yellow blob adhered to the stubble just below his lip . . .
> Lindsey wanted to limit the conversation to business. "Look, fill me in on Bessie Blue . . . "
> "Bessie Blue? Name of a B-17. I don't know what the name means. Ask a jig and see if he'll tell you."
> Lindsey felt his jaw clench. "Please, Elmer."
> . . . "Oh, right. I keep forgetting what a good liberal boy you are, Hobie. Don't ask a jig." Mueller looked at Lindsey with something that might have been an impish grin. "Ask an American Africoon."

The opposite of a good hate is a good love. Sex pops up frequently in Lupoff's novels. But just as his violence is tempered with pity, his bedroom scenes are laced with tenderness.

They are not slipped in merely to titillate. They advance the story and deepen our commitment to two admirable human beings.

It's trite to say that people read mysteries because the real world is a confusing and chaotic place, and that in these books, at least, order is restored, justice handed down and evil vanquished. Indeeed, in Lupoff's novels the world is plentifully bad, but in the person of Hobart Lindsey simple integrity lends a saving grace, along with a naiveté, a doggedness, a masculine kind of graciousness and even the love of Mother.

In the words of Lindsey's lover, Berkeley Homicide Investigator Marvia Plum, "We can't let the haters win."

More power, then, to the good guys, in fiction as in life. Sometimes, perhaps, they are one and the same. Is Richard Lupoff really Hobart Lindsey? If so, it would support my Niceness Theory of Literary Authorship: good books are written by good people, because only they have the gift of empathy, of understanding others, of writing with sympathy. The actual character of writer Richard Lupoff backs up my theory brilliantly, since it is just as superior as that of his creation.

Unfortunately my theory breaks down altogether in considering the entire history of literature in the English language, since so many great works of fiction were written, as everyone knows, by really rotten human beings.

The Bessie Blue Killer

One

You only dream in black and white.

You only dream in black and white, but that was okay with Lindsey. The B-17 lumbered through the early morning skies, its four 1,000-horsepower Wright Cyclones droning steadily at 2,300 rpm, the French countryside slipping away almost five miles beneath the Flying Fortress's belly.

Somehow he knew he was dreaming but he didn't wake up, he kept dreaming. In black and white.

It was one of the 918th's deadliest missions. The 17s were keeping formation, their P-51 Mustang escorts diving and zooming like a bunch of motorcyclists cutting in and out of a heavy truck convoy. The air was cold and Lindsey's electric flight suit did little to help.

It was easy going as long as their course lay over Allied-held territory, but once they crossed the frontier into German airspace, the Messerschmitt 109s came roaring up to meet them and the 51s broke away to knock them back down.

Lindsey crouched over his single .50-caliber machine gun, scanning the sky for attackers. There was no way the 51s could stop all the Messerschmitts, and once the enemy broke through the fighter escort, the Flying Fortresses would have to defend themselves. It was strictly fight or die, and Lindsey had seen too many B-17s die, too many of the big bombers lose engines, lose wings or tails and spiral down to explode in flame, or simply blow up in midair and rain onto the French or German soil in a shower of metal and rubber and human flesh and blood.

A Messerschmitt was coming at the Fortress. Lindsey didn't need the message that came over his helmet radio. He swung the .50 at the Messerschmitt. He could see the flashes of the 109's wing guns as they spit lead at the Fortress. He pressed the trigger and felt his machine gun buck as it spit back at the Messerschmitt. He followed the path of his tracers as they sizzled into the 109.

A puff of black smoke bellied away from the Messerschmitt. Lindsey felt a surge of adrenalin that made his heart pump and his scalp tingle, but the Fortress's aluminum skin was no match for the Messerschmitt's deadly rounds. Metal projectiles ricocheted inside the fuselage. Lindsey felt an impact, a solid thump against his flight boot.

International Surety had done it right for once. Hobart Lindsey had spent his career working for the company, starting out as a trainee just weeks after he got his degree from Hayward State. And how long ago was that?

He sat up in bed. Cletus Berry was pounding him on the bottom of one foot. The TV set in the corner was still playing, tuned to a cable station rerunning an old series. In black and white. "Twelve O'Clock High." Not even the Gregory Peck–Dean Jagger movie. The TV spinoff. A second-rate imitation of a first-rate re-creation of a long-ago reality.

Lindsey rubbed his eyes. Back in the room to dress for dinner, he'd put his head on the pillow and fallen sound asleep. Taking an afternoon nap at his age.

He sat on the edge of the bed and calculated his years of service with International Surety. Not that he needed to work it out. He knew all too well. Still, he'd got his B.A. during the short-lived Presidency of Gerald Ford and here it was almost twenty years later. And he was sitting on the edge of a bed in the Brown Palace, the oldest and most prestigious hotel in Denver, Colorado, pulling on his socks and getting ready to attend a graduation dinner at the Broker, one of the city's finest and most expensive restaurants.

He blinked at Cletus Berry. Berry was black and Lindsey was white. International Surety was not going to run afoul of civil-rights legislation.

Lindsey hadn't done so badly for a small-town boy. If you

could call Walnut Creek, California, a small town. It had been a small town when he was growing up there, caring for his widowed mother, learning in painful increments the true story of his father's death. Lindsey's father had been killed in a MiG attack on the destroyer *Lewiston* off the coast of Korea early in 1953. It was just weeks before the end of the war and just weeks before Hobart Lindsey was born.

He had never known his father, never seen him except in a few snapshots that Mother treated as holy relics. A pudgy young man in a sailor's uniform, grinning happily, his dark, curly hair worn a little longer than Navy regulations allowed. But he had never had to answer for that breach of discipline.

The ship's anti-aircraft batteries had picked off the two incoming MiGs. One of them plunged into the Sea of Japan but the other crashed onto the *Lewiston*'s deck sending a wave of flaming jet fuel roaring into the battery.

"Better get a move on."

Lindsey snapped out of his reverie.

"Don't want to keep the Duck waiting, Bart. You know what a stickler he is."

"Right." Lindsey pulled up his socks, pushed himself upright and looked for his shoes. He'd sent them out to be shined, a rare indulgence for him, and he wore his best suit for the occasion. You didn't graduate from a course like this every day. In fact, a third of the people who'd started it were back at their former jobs—or out of the company—already.

International Surety had splurged, putting up its employees at the Brown Palace during the seminar. But it had also put them two to a room. Class was all very nice, as the corporate brass were forever reminding their underlings, but International Surety had to preserve its resources, and one person didn't need a room all to himself. Not when he was attending workshops all day and struggling with study assignments and papers every night.

Come to think of it, it wasn't too different from living in Walnut Creek and attending Hayward State, except for not having a room to himself.

Lindsey and Cletus Berry walked the five blocks to the Broker. A couple of their classmates had been mugged on Seventeenth Street the week before, but they had decided not to let themselves be intimidated, and that was final. But they kept their International Surety name badges in their pockets until they reached the restaurant. They pinned them on when they entered the marble lobby.

The Broker was in an old bank building, and its decor was calculatedly Wall Street. Clearly, International Surety had chosen the location to make a point.

Happy hour was subdued. Lindsey and Berry drifted apart as soon as they arrived. You had to mix at this kind of corporate function. You never knew who was going to be your boss someday, in a position to do you good or harm.

And Lindsey had already crossed his boss, Harden at Regional, more than once. He'd done a lot of good for International Surety, saved the company plenty of bucks in earlier cases that he'd handled. A claims adjuster didn't just shuffle papers and authorize checks. It was his job to get the facts, to track down the truth when a claim had a peculiar odor to it. Especially if it was a big claim.

Trouble was, when Lindsey saved the company six-figure amounts on stolen collectibles, he outshone Harden. Ms. Johansen at National was aware of Lindsey's work and of the fact that he'd done it despite Harden's obstructionism.

Harden had managed to squeeze Lindsey out of the district office and had replaced him with the odious Elmer Mueller. Now Lindsey was completing a training seminar for International Surety's corporate troubleshooting team. They gave it a fancy name—Special Projects Unit/Detached Status—and a funny logo, a russet potato with SPUDS lettered across it. Everybody in SPUDS got to wear a little cloisonné potato on his lapel.

Still, Lindsey knew that the team had been the graveyard of careers.

Lindsey found himself standing next to a thin, pale woman from Grant's Pass, Oregon. She'd hardly spoken during the course and had sat far from Lindsey. He let his eyes flash to her badge.

4

Aurora Delano, right. Beneath her name, her home town. Practically a neighbor. Behind her, a white-jacketed bartender was doing slow business.

"So, Hobart, you had enough of this? Eager to get home to California?"

Lindsey grunted. "This is too much like being back in college. And I'm a little worried about Mother. She . . ."

The bartender caught Lindsey's attention. Aurora Delano was holding an empty glass, Lindsey noticed. The bartender flashed a question with his eyes. Lindsey said, "Aurora, would you like a . . ."

She turned toward the bartender and held up her glass. "Refill, sure."

"And you, sir?" the bartender asked.

"The same. I'll have the same as the lady."

The bartender made Aurora's empty glass disappear and placed a clean one on the bar. He turned both glasses upside down, wet the rims and dipped them in a bowl of salt. He reached under the bar for a jug and ran a blender of greenish liquid and crushed ice before filling both glasses. Lindsey paid for the drinks. International Surety ran a no-host bar.

Aurora said, "We never got to talk during the course. I don't mind Denver, but I'll be happy to get out of here."

"And go back to Oregon. How do you feel about working in SPUDS?" Lindsey asked.

"No way I'm going back to Oregon. I only went there because my ex's work was there. I'm a Southern girl."

Lindsey was surprised. "I would have guessed New York."

Aurora smiled. Her long, thin face was surrounded by a wash of auburn hair. Definitely the Katherine Hepburn type. "A lot of people think that. I was born and raised in New Orleans. That's why I took the SPUDS job. Get out of Grant's Pass. Get out of range of my ex. I talked Ducky into sending me back to Louisiana."

The way she said it, it sounded like a little girl's name. Like *Lucy Anna.*

"And your ex is going to stay in Oregon?"

"I hope to hell he does! Besides, SPUDS will be a change. It gets pretty dull paying body shops to pound out dented fenders and replace broken windshields. Not to mention comforting grieving widows and greedy offspring with checks.''

Lindsey smiled. He raised his glass. Aurora did the same and they touched rims. Lindsey took a sip. He tasted the salt from the rim and then the drink itself. It was bitter and pulpy. Grapefruit juice. ''This what you always drink?''

''Around International Surety, you bet it is. On my own time, that's something different.''

Music oozed from concealed speakers, something totally unidentifiable and equally undistinguished. Lindsey's musical tastes had grown in recent months, largely due to the influence of a Berkeley police officer he had worked with on a couple of his more interesting cases.

Now the music—Lindsey decided it was a Gershwin medley played on a soupy synthesizer—was interrupted by a polite chiming. It was the signal to proceed to the dining room. Lindsey hoped that the meal would be better than the usual corporate mass-feeding.

Inside the private dining room Lindsey found his assigned seat. Happily, Aurora Delano was to be his dinner partner. He spotted Cletus Berry at another table and recognized the others in the room from the classes and work groups of the past weeks. The music had resumed. Either Lindsey had been mistaken or the tape had segued from Gershwin into Jerome Kern.

The food was not as bad as Lindsey had feared, although not quite up to what he had hoped. Aurora Delano was an interesting conversationalist, going on about her ex-husband and how they had climbed the Himalayas, rafted down the Snoqualmie, explored the Great Barrier Reef. It took her a while to get around to the reason for their split.

Lindsey didn't have to say much. As quiet as Aurora had been during lectures on coordination with local probate courts and investigation of motor vehicle registration records and IRS involvement in insurance claims, she had plenty to say over the lamb chops and watercress.

There was even wine on the table. The SPUDS in their dark suits, male and female, were at least allowed that pleasure.

Survival tactics now ruled in the corporate world. No more drunken revels. Now you stayed as sober as a judge. If you didn't, you might let your guard down for a moment and that could be fatal.

"Well, he was a great guy, my ex." Aurora sipped her wine. "He was a great guy. He designed nuclear triggers for a living, and he was good at it. Made a nice paycheck, too. Then the bottom fell out of the market for nuclear triggers. Blooey. No more Evil Empire. No more money. All of a sudden, instead of the headhunters sniffing after him, he had to start sending out resumés."

Lindsey didn't have to ask a question. He popped a fork full of lyonnaise potatoes into his mouth and followed it with a sip of ice water.

"He was hot stuff as long as the money kept rolling in. Those guys make a lot of money, you know. Nuclear trigger designers. Get treated like royalty. President of the United States comes around to the shop. Puts on a white lab coat. Gives the boys a little pep talk. Serving the cause of freedom. Making the world safe for our children and our grandchildren. Holding the forces of tyranny and oppression at bay."

"I've seen the clips," Lindsey said.

"They start to believe it themselves. You know that? Those Stepford Husbands with their sports cars and their big houses and their pert little wives with the big station wagons."

"You drive a station wagon?"

"The Red Octopus dies and Uncle Sam doesn't need all those weapons factories anymore and they have to start looking for an honest job."

Lindsey didn't pursue the station wagon.

"You know what?" Aurora put down her glass, picked up her fork, speared a piece of lambchop and chomped down on it. Lindsey couldn't tell whether she was nodding in agreement with some thought she'd had, or if the motion of her head had to do with chewing the piece of lambchop. "All of a sudden, nobody wants nuclear trigger designers. And there's not much positive transfer of the skills."

"What did he do?"

7

"He had a couple of offers from universities. For about a quarter what he was making."

"What did he do?"

"He called some of his old buddies. You know, they network, those nuclear trigger designers. I don't know what went wrong. Maybe he wasn't as popular as he thought with his old buddies. Maybe they didn't like him. Maybe there's just no work out there."

"So what did he do?"

"He took it as long as he could."

"Yes."

"Then he couldn't take it any more."

"Yes."

She picked up her glass again and looked at Lindsey. The pastry baskets were empty. The waiters were clearing away the dinner plates. At the head table, a major corporate bigshot, Ms. Johansen from National, was looking around. Clearly, she was getting ready to make a speech.

Lindsey asked Aurora, "What did he do?"

The spotless white linen tablecloths were still spotless. International Surety people ate carefully at corporate banquets.

Desmond "Ducky" Richelieu, the director of International Surety's Special Projects Unit/Detached Status, was on his feet, waiting for the room to quiet so he could introduce the distinguished guest.

The murmured conversation dropped to a dead silence. Huh, maybe it was Cole Porter, not Gershwin and not Jerome Kern either.

Aurora Delano said, "He came home from a job interview. I knew it had gone badly and the poor lamb was so upset, he had to do something. So he broke my arm."

Two

THE INTERNATIONAL SURETY SUITE was in a glittering office tower just off Speer Boulevard. The receptionist had a sign on her desk. MRS. BLOMQUIST. She wore her hair on top of her head like a Gibson Girl. Lindsey could not remember ever seeing a woman with skin that looked so pale and powdery. He wondered what she had to do to make it look like that, and why she did it.

The thin air made for a snappy May morning, but Lindsey had packed his topcoat and taken a cab. He wore a medium-weight gray suit. He usually dressed more casually than this, but he was on his way to visit his new boss and he didn't want to look like a California swinger.

Mrs. Blomquist made Lindsey wait while she buzzed Mr. Richelieu, then made him wait some more. Lindsey browsed through the *Rocky Mountain News*, looking for stories with California datelines. He could care less about scandals in the Colorado State Legislature, shakeups in the Denver Police Department, new real estate developments in Arapahoe and Elbert Counties, or the hopes of the Colorado Rockies for a better season than last year's. He was eager to get home.

Richelieu stood up when Lindsey walked in. The sign on the inner door said simply, DESMOND RICHELIEU. Nobody called him Ducky to his face. He wore a neatly trimmed moustache and rimless bifocals that glinted in the sunlight that poured through his office window. He looked like a steel engraving of a French cardinal Lindsey had once seen in a high-school library edition of *The Three Musketeers*. There was even a shadowy suggestion of the cardinal's dark, pointed goatee. He gestured Lindsey to a seat.

"I always like to have a chat with each of our graduates before they head out on their first assignment. I imagine you'd heard that."

Lindsey nodded. He had carried his attaché case with him and placed it carefully on the carpet beside his chair.

"The way the chief used to do it when I worked for the Bureau." Richelieu made a barely perceptible motion with his head. His hair was very black with just a tuft of pure white above each ear. Richelieu had combed his hair with some sort of pomade that made it look like glossy corduroy.

Lindsey followed Richelieu's gesture with his eyes. A tastefully framed, diploma-like document stood out against the elegant paneling. Beside it hung a blown-up glossy of a boyish Richelieu shaking hands with a dumpy, bulldog-faced man in a double-breasted pinstriped suit. The picture was cropped so neither man's feet were visible.

"It's a funny thing," Richelieu said. "The FBI is like the Mafia. Once you're in it, you're never really out." He shook his head sadly. "But once John Edgar was gone, the Bureau was never the same. Mixed up in Watergate, White House interference. They never got away with that when the chief was alive. He took on everybody. The Kennedys. Everybody. But once he was gone, why, it was never the same."

Lindsey had heard that J. Edgar Hoover had been sensitive about his height, habitually standing on a box for photo-ops with his underlings. Bureau photogs knew that they had to keep the focus up and not show the box. Agents knew that they had to keep their eyes up and not see it, either. Failure to comply could cost a man his career. He wouldn't get tossed out of the Bureau, but he was likely to reach age 65 counting pencils in the Fargo, North Dakota, branch office.

Richelieu leaned forward on the glass top of his desk. The glass was polished to a perfect sheen. There was nothing beneath the glass but polished mahogany and nothing on top but Richelieu's spotless sleeves. "When Harden at Regional recommended you for SPUDS, he said you were reluctant to take the job, Hobart. Is that true?"

Lindsey hated his first name. He preferred Bart, didn't mind Lindsey, hated Hobart. "Yes, sir."

"That's all right, a lot of my people join up reluctantly. What happened to your job in Walnut Creek?"

Richelieu didn't have Lindsey's personnel folder on his desk. He must have studied it before Lindsey was admitted to the inner sanctum. Lindsey said, "I was hospitalized."

"Yes. Shot in the shoulder, wasn't it?"

"Mr. Harden brought someone else in to run the office. I thought Ms. Wilbur could handle it until I got back, but Mr. Harden brought in Elmer Mueller instead. When I reported back, Mueller had my job and I had a plane ticket to Denver."

Richelieu leaned back. Lindsey half expected a flunky to run in and polish the glass. Richelieu said, "You've doubtless heard that we have a high rate of attrition in SPUDS."

Lindsey nodded.

Richelieu kept on going. He had not waited for the nod. "Well, we do. You'll get tough cases. Some people think SPUDS is International Surety's own little Gestapo, or its own little Gulag. Neither of those is true, Hobart. We're not police. We don't torture anybody. We're very law-abiding. We are a bit like detectives, but then I understand that you like to play Dick Tracy. Is that correct?"

"No, sir. I just try to do my job, sir. I'm a claims adjuster, that's all. Somebody's store is burgled, we pay for the loss. Somebody's car gets stolen, we pay fair value."

"Yes, yes. But if you can recover the stolen goods, you can save International Surety a lot of money. You've done that, haven't you?"

Lindsey nodded. The man was playing cat and mouse with him. He had to know that Lindsey had saved the company a fortune in rare 1940s comic books and an even bigger fortune on a stolen 1928 Duesenberg. Each case had involved a murder, as well. But the company paid him to save money, not to catch killers. He did that on his own time, and Harden had used it against him more than once.

"I'm not going to spend a lot of time reviewing material that you learned in your seminars," Richelieu said. "If you do a good job for me, you can make a good thing out of SPUDS. You'll have lots of freedom. I understand you have a penchant for breaking rules, Hobart. You should be very happy working for me."

Richelieu swung around in his heavily padded leather chair and gazed out the window. Lindsey followed Richelieu's glance. The sunlight glinted off Cherry Creek. Lindsey wondered if he would see Perry Mason pacing regally beside the waterway, a black Burberry jacket concealing his girth, a polished walking stick in his hand. TV shows and motion pictures, magazine covers and record sleeves. Mother had kept him tied to her for so many years. While other kids grew up riding bikes and playing ball, he had lived a life of media images that permanently formed his perception of the world. Sometimes it was useful, sometimes frustrating, but there it was.

"I think I'm ready for my first assignment," Lindsey said.

Richelieu whirled back. The eyes behind the rimless bifocals flashed. Clearly, he did not like having anyone else take the lead in a conversation. Last night at the Broker, he had deferred to Ms. Johansen but, as Lindsey knew, she represented the corporate structure. Richelieu had saluted not the man—or woman—but the rank. And Richelieu outranked Lindsey and expected Lindsey to acknowledge that relationship.

Once upon a time Lindsey would have quivered and apologized for his faux pas.

Now he stood up and said, "I have to catch a flight for Oakland. If there's nothing else . . ."

A smile flashed across Richelieu's lips so rapidly that Lindsey would have missed it, if he hadn't been watching for a reaction. "Sit down, Lindsey." That was an improvement! "Mrs. Blomquist can phone Stapleton and change your flight if you need to. Harden is still running Regional and Mueller is running Walnut Creek, but you're working for me now. For me. You get that?"

Lindsey hesitated for a moment before slipping back into his chair. This wasn't the FBI, despite what Desmond Richelieu might think. And it wasn't the Army and it wasn't the Mafia. It was a corporation, for heaven's sake, and if Lindsey decided to walk out of here, there was nothing that International Surety could do to stop him.

Richelieu smiled. "This is your first assignment for SPUDS, and I'm going to make it a nice easy one for you. Just to help you get your feet wet. You understand?"

Lindsey nodded. If he answered verbally, even grunted, Richelieu could turn away and still continue the conversation. But if Lindsey spoke only in body language, Richelieu would have to stay focused on him. It was a subtle tug of war. Maybe it was something in the Rocky Mountain air that was changing Lindsey. Maybe it was his encounter the night before with Aurora Delano.

What kind of man would break his wife's arm because he had lost a job? A common enough type, if the TV feature stories about battered women were to be believed. Was that the kind of man who ran the governments and corporations and families of the world? What kind of man was Hobart Lindsey? What kind of man had he been since Hayward State, and what kind of man was he becoming?

"Make it a good one," he said.

The ghost-smile flickered across Richelieu's lips again. He reached under the edge of his desk. Lindsey assumed he was pushing a button to summon Mrs. Blomquist. Lindsey wondered whether Richelieu had a telephone in his office, or a computer, or any of the tools of a modern corporation. Maybe he let Mrs. Blomquist deal with machinery.

The door opened behind Lindsey and he swung around to see Mrs. Blomquist enter carrying a folder. Lindsey chewed the inside of his lips. He had lost a point to Richelieu. He followed Mrs. Blomquist's progress as she carried the folder to Richelieu and laid it on his desk. Lindsey didn't follow her as she retreated to the outer office. He figured that he had got back maybe a quarter of the point he had lost. It was really getting complicated when you had to calculate in fractions of points.

"This is practically in your backyard," Richelieu said. He hadn't opened the folder, just left it lying on his desk. "Elmer

Mueller has written a special policy for a film company that's going to shoot some footage at the Oakland Airport. You can stop and check this out on your way home today, Lindsey."

"How much is involved?"

"Ah, this is a big policy. Cost of the aircraft, indemnity to the Port of Oakland, personal liability, life coverage of people involved in the film."

"Why didn't the movie company set up its own coverage?"

Richelieu tapped the tobacco-brown cardboard folder with one fingertip. Richelieu's fingernails were perfectly manicured and coated with clear polish that caught the sunlight bouncing off Cherry Creek. "It's an odd situation. Not a commercial studio. Somebody got a line on a bucket of foundation money and put together an ad hoc organization to make a film."

He ran a polished fingernail over his neatly trimmed moustache.

"I don't understand. Is there a claim on the policy?" Lindsey asked.

Richelieu shook his head. "If there were it would be Mueller's problem, not mine. This is a risky operation. We're getting a nice premium out of it, but if we have to pay off, we'll be in a deep hole. We're covering their aircraft, the flight crews, ground crews, passengers, the film crews, bystanders, physical plant—the works."

He pulled his rimless glasses down his nose and peered at Lindsey over their tops. "What if a plane crashes and takes out a school yard full of kids? Or an office building? You had a light plane crack up in a shopping mall out there, didn't you?"

"I remember it," Lindsey said.

"Well, what if . . . say, what if one of these people pancakes into the ballpark out there during a baseball game? Can you imagine the claims? It could cost us millions. It could put us out of business!"

"And you want me to go out there and baby-sit these people? Make sure they run a nice, safe operation? Is that it?"

"That's it," Richelieu said.

"I'll need to study the file," Lindsey said.

"Take it." He shoved the tobacco-brown folder across his

desk. Lindsey peered at him questioningly. Richelieu said, "It's all photocopies."

Lindsey locked the folder in his attaché case and stood up. This time Richelieu didn't try to stop him.

Mrs. Blomquist hadn't changed his reservations, but he caught a United 737 as planned and was in Oakland in time to face the afternoon rush hour on the way to Walnut Creek.

Marvia Plum had offered to pick him up at the terminal, if she could clear her schedule with the Berkeley Police Department. But Lindsey had promised Mother that she could come out to the airport. She had been staying in the present most of the time, a slow, steady improvement over her condition in recent years, and he wanted to reward her for staying connected.

He didn't think it was her fault, the way she strayed through time. He hadn't understood when he was little, and she had managed somehow to cope with everyday realities. But as he had grown up, Mother had got more and more disconnected from the calendar.

Her point of reference was always that dreadful day in 1953, the day she had received word of her husband's death in the Sea of Japan. Sometimes she knew what year and day it was and connected with people around her. Other times, she thought Jack Kennedy was in the White House, or Harry Truman or Ike. Most often, Ike.

But as Lindsey had grown away from her, as his relationship with Marvia Plum had ripened from a professional partnership to a friendship to a troubled and intermittent romance, Mother had somehow regained her grasp on the reality of time. She was still young enough to build a new life for herself, and Lindsey wanted to do all that he could to help her.

Now he made his way down the airport's faux terrazzo corridor. He carried his attaché and flight bag. No dealing with luggage carousels! He spotted Mother, a thinner, older, female version of himself. But not very much older. She had been a young bride, just a teenager, when her husband had died and her son was born.

With her was Joanie Schorr, their neighbor. Joanie baby-sat

Mother when Lindsey had to go out at night. Mrs. Hernandez came during the day. Lindsey stayed with Mother most nights and weekends. But Joanie had been a real lifesaver. Even today, she had driven the Hyundai from Walnut Creek. With a start, Lindsey realized that little Joanie was as old as Mother had been when she had given birth to him.

Both women waved.

Attaché case in one hand and flight bag in the other, Lindsey couldn't wave back. He hoped they could see his smile. He wanted to climb into the Hyundai and head for home.

ner's wagon. The body might still be in place. Lindsey had never seen a fresh murder victim. He shuddered at the thought.

He felt his heart pounding and his blood pumping through his body. This had to be an adrenalin rush. He'd been involved with murders twice before. There was nothing like the excitement they produced. He was getting addicted.

He parked the Hyundai in a square clearing behind an aircraft hangar. At first the surface looked like blacktop, but then Lindsey realized that it was an old dirt-and-gravel lot, where they sprayed a layer of oil every now and then to keep down the dust. Talk about poisoning the earth!

The police cars were parked near the hangar. At the end of the line was an old Cadillac. The area lights that illuminated the parking lot were bright enough for Lindsey to read the vanity plate on the Caddy. SURETY-1. That had to be Elmer Mueller's car.

The hangar's huge rolling doors were closed and only a small metal door, the size of a house door, stood open. A uniformed Oakland policeman stood outside the door. He looked Asian and was big enough to play a bad guy in the World Wrestling Federation. He stopped Lindsey. "Can't go in, sir. Crime scene."

Lindsey tried to talk his way past the cop. He flashed his International Surety ID. Insurance credentials usually got him past cops. This one chose to be difficult.

Twenty feet away inside the hangar, a figure in a brown tweed jacket and slacks paced back and forth. He looked down, studying the hangar floor. His hair was thick, dark, curly and unkempt.

Lindsey kept trying to talk his way past the cop. The cop raised his voice.

The rumpled man turned, startled. He recognized Lindsey at the same time that Lindsey recognized him. He headed for the doorway, put his hand on the officer's arm and said, "Let him in, Walter. This is Mr. Lindsey. He helps us out sometimes."

Walter touched one finger to the bill of his uniform cap and let Lindsey pass.

"Walter Chen," the smaller man said. "Good young officer.

Bright future. How are you, Lindsey? You don't mind if I call you that? I feel as if we're friends, after that Duesenberg case. We put you through a lot on that one. But it all came out in the end, didn't it? It always does. Well, not always but usually. You're here because of Mr. McKinney?"

"I don't know. I . . . It's nice to see you again, Lieutenant High."

"Doc. I'll just call you Lindsey. You like that better than Hobart, I recall. You call me Doc, right?" The two men shook hands, then Doc High patted the pockets of his tweed jacket, looking for his forbidden pipe and tobacco pouch.

Lindsey smiled.

"Caught me, eh?" High grinned sheepishly. He was several inches shorter than Lindsey and a few years older. Beside the blue-uniformed Walter Chen, he looked tiny.

"Is Mr. McKinney the, uh, victim?" Lindsey asked.

"Looks like it. Name on his coveralls, ID tag with a photo and his name. Leroy McKinney. Resident of Richmond. Come on. If you want a look, you'd better look now. The coroner's here and the technicians are almost finished. Mr. McKinney will be leaving in a few minutes."

He took Lindsey by the elbow and steered him across the oil-stained cement floor. The hangar was cavernous and old. North Field was the oldest part of Oakland International, dating from the daredevil era when Earhart and Hegenberger flew out of Oakland to make their Pacific hops, back in the days when airplanes were exotic machines and aviation had the charisma of professional sports or MTV stardom.

The body lay face up, presumably where it had fallen. The forehead was caved in and brains and blood had filled the unnatural cavity, forming a horrific triangle with staring eyes. The brains and blood looked like scrambled eggs in dark ketchup. Lindsey's stomach lurched and he turned away.

"You all right, Lindsey?"

Lindsey pulled a folded handkerchief from his trousers and mopped the cold sweat from his brow. He felt uncomfortably chilly. He shoved the handkerchief back into his pocket. "I'm okay. It was just . . ."

"Understand. You'll start taking it in stride after you've seen your first few hundred."

"I don't want to see that many. I've seen enough."

"You don't want to look at Mr. McKinney? Up to you, but you never know what you'll notice. Sometimes . . ." He gestured vaguely.

Lindsey turned back and looked at the body. The technicians had marked its position with white tape. The dead man was black and elderly. His short hair was mostly gray. His head was tilted slightly and one hand rested against his cheek. Lindsey could imagine this old man years ago, a sleeping child lying with his cheek nested against his hand. There was a startled expression on his face. His other arm lay outstretched, his elbow bent so the hand lay palm up, even with his face. The fingers were horribly deformed, claw-like.

Lindsey shivered. The hangar was chilly. An old-fashioned woodstove did little to dispel the cold and damp of the previous night. North Field was built on marshy flatlands, and men had died in the cold that crept in from the Oakland Estuary and San Francisco Bay.

"You have to pay a claim on this fellow?" High cocked his eyebrow at Lindsey like Groucho on "You Bet Your Life."

"I don't know. That, uh, that would go through Walnut Creek. I don't know if we carry a policy on him."

"I meant to ask you about that," High said. "Thought you ran your company's office out there. What's this fellow Mueller doing in your job?" He jerked a thumb toward an overdressed individual seated at a makeshift desk near one wall. A mug of something that steamed invitingly sat on the desk in front of him. He was filling out papers attached to a clipboard.

Behind Mueller, a metal door led to a smaller room, an old-style office complete with filing cabinets, girlie calendars and a hot plate. A black man in civilian clothes, a gray-haired woman and a uniformed sergeant hunched over a metal desk. Lindsey could see only the woman's back. She wore a heavy quilted vest over a plaid shirt. The male civilian was talking and the sergeant was writing. From time to time the sergeant looked up, obviously to ask a question, then down again to write when the man answered.

"I guess I should talk to Elmer," Lindsey said. "He's got my old job, Lieutenant . . . Doc. I've been sort of kicked upstairs. Working out of Denver now."

"Just like Perry Mason!"

Lindsey smiled. He handed High one of his new business cards. It was the first one he had ever used.

"Special Projects Unit," High read. He looked up at Lindsey. "Very impressive. Congratulations. They paying you a lot to do this?"

Lindsey shook his head.

Elmer Mueller looked up from his clipboard. He didn't appear surprised to see Lindsey at the murder scene. Their eyes caught and briefly held. Lindsey nodded. Mueller returned to his papers.

High steered Lindsey away from Leroy McKinney's cadaver. "Can't say I like your Mr. Mueller too much, Lindsey. He used to run an insurance agency in Oakland."

"I know."

"Never quite got in trouble with the law. Certainly never got into my bailiwick, Homicide. But a lot of the boys at Broadway and Sixth know him. Boys and girls, excuse me. Men and women. Martians. Too many times over the years we'd get involved in something messy and shake hands with Elmer."

Lindsey grunted. He didn't like Mueller either but he didn't want to run down another International Surety man.

"Well, before we get back to the case at hand," High said, "if Elmer is your company's man on the spot, what can I do for you, Lindsey? You're not here just out of curiosity are you?"

"Hardly. As a matter of fact, I just started this new job and I'm in trouble already. I was supposed to prevent losses on this project. *Bessie Blue*. You know about *Bessie Blue*, Doc?"

"Just a little. I expect I'm going to learn a lot more about it."

"International Surety wrote an umbrella policy for *Bessie Blue*. Anything goes wrong on the project, mechanical failure, equipment loss, public liability, we have to pay."

"Just like Lloyds of London."

"Close enough."

"I guess you're in trouble, then, with Mr. McKinney."

"I don't know. I'll have to study the case folder, then get together with Mueller. What happened to the victim? And what's the matter with his hand?"

"What happened, almost certainly, was a monkey wrench. Come on over here."

The wrench lay a few yards from the body. It had been marked off with white tape. The wrench was made of some dark metal, maybe cast iron, and its head was covered with the same red goo that had seeped into the cavity in the middle of Leroy McKinney's forehead.

"It'll be bagged and taken away and tested," High said. "If we're lucky, we might get some useful fingerprints off it. And we'll compare the blood from the wrench and from the victim, run a genetic scan just to make sure. But I'd give big odds that we'll get a match."

"Do you know . . ." Lindsey asked half a question.

"What? Who, when, why, how? You know us, Lindsey. There's not much difference between a detective and a newspaper reporter. Speaking of which, the Oakland *Trib* was already here, reporter and photog. And Channel Two. Ask me an easy one."

"Okay. Who found the body?" Lindsey asked.

High nodded toward the office where the uniformed sergeant and the civilians still huddled over the metal desk. "Mr. Crump and Mrs. Chandler."

Lindsey studied the trio as best he could. The male civilian was wearing a leather jacket like a World War II aviator. He was gray-haired, like the murder victim, and was nodding and gesturing in response to the police sergeant's questions.

"Did they do it?" Lindsey asked.

High managed a small laugh. "That would make things easy, wouldn't it? I don't know who did it. My guess is, somebody who was known to the victim. Look at that. Hit him right between the eyes. No sign of a struggle. How could somebody get that close, with a heavy wrench in his hand, without the

23

victim trying to fight back or escape, or even putting his hands up to ward off the blow?"

Lindsey forced himself to look at the corpse again, then waited for High to resume.

"The body was already cold and rigor had set in when our kids got here. So McKinney had to be dead several hours when Chandler and Crump found him. Unless they killed him and stood around for five or six hours before they phoned it in. Which, I'll admit, is not impossible. We'll have to check their whereabouts. There's not much security around here, like there is over at the passenger terminal. But I think we're looking at a third party."

Lindsey peered through the glass at Chandler, Crump and the police officer. "Still, who are they?"

"He's our movie star. Lawton Crump. One of the original Tuskegee Airmen. You ever hear of the Tuskegee Airmen?"

Lindsey moved his head uncertainly. "Might have seen something about them. I think it was on PBS. I don't watch much PBS."

"Yeah. World War Two outfit," High said.

"He's still got his jacket."

High grinned. "Hardly any Negro combat troops at the start of the war. Mostly the government used them for service troops. Cooks, laundry, mechanics. You know. There was a lot of agitation to let Negroes fight. We had a whole Nisei brigade, and the Japs were the enemy. The blacks had been here for hundreds of years. Why couldn't they fight for their country?"

Lindsey shook his head. "You tell me."

"Somebody even got the cockeyed idea that Negroes could learn to fly airplanes and go into combat. So the government set up a segregated training base in Alabama and pumped out whole units of black fliers. Called them Tuskegee Airmen. Now they want to make a movie about them. Times change."

"And Mr. Crump was one of the Tuskegee Airmen?"

"That pleasant, soft-spoken elderly gentleman of the colored persuasion . . ." High nodded toward the office again. Through the windows, it appeared that Crump and the uniformed police sergeant were concluding their business. "He flew everything we had. Or so I'm told. It was before my time, Lindsey."

"And the woman?" Lindsey asked.

"Mrs. Chandler? She's from Double Bee Enterprises. They're the outfit making the movie."

"I don't see any cameras. Or any airplanes, for that matter."

"They haven't arrived yet. You'll have to get the details from Mrs. Chandler or Mr. Crump. She's the producer. He's the technical adviser. In fact, I think the movie's pretty much about him. But they're merely the advance party. McKinney was a janitor here. We have to find out what he was doing in this hangar. The maintenance boss vouches for him . . . that he's legitimate. But he wasn't scheduled to be working in this building. The signs are that he was killed here, not just brought here and dumped. So what's the story?"

Lindsey grinned. "You're the hawkshaw, Doc. You tell me."

High shrugged. "I'll tell you this. Mrs. Chandler and Mr. Crump found him. They arrived at the building together. Crump spotted the body first and got a good look at it. Then he called us. He's really upset."

"I don't blame him." Lindsey shuddered.

Inside the office, the sergeant and the two civilians rose and headed toward the door that led back into the hangar. At the same time, a coroner's squad lifted the remains of Leroy McKinney onto a folding gurney and headed out of the hangar.

Four

MOTHER SOUNDED NERVOUS AND LINDSEY apologized for leaving the house without telling her, but all in all, she handled it well. No hysterics, no confusion, no allusions to Lindsey's long-dead father as though he was alive and expected home at any moment.

Lindsey explained that he had been called out of Walnut Creek by a work emergency and that he would be home in a few hours.

Mother told him she had dressed and breakfasted and was waiting for Mrs. Hernandez to come and take her shopping. She was so happy her son was home from Colorado that she wanted to make a big dinner just for him.

Lindsey told her that he had promised to have dinner with Marvia Plum in Berkeley.

"Oh, that nice colored girl. Well, she can come and eat at our house. She can sit right at the table with us."

Lindsey pressed his hand to his forehead. He was phoning from the desk where Lawton Crump had given his statement to Sergeant Finnerty. The evidence squad was packing its gear, preparing to leave the airport. Mr. Crump was gone. Doc High was gone. And Lindsey was going to have the pleasure of breakfasting with Elmer Mueller, while they went over the contents of the *Bessie Blue* case folder.

Mueller insisted on driving his Cadillac to the main terminal.

They found a table in a snack shop full of commuters headed for LA or San Diego or Seattle. Lindsey got himself an English muffin and a cup of coffee. Mueller ordered bacon and eggs up and a prune Danish and proceeded to dip the Danish in the egg yolk.

Mueller had the peculiar quality of always looking slightly dirty and a little bit greasy.

"So, how you like SPUDS?" Mueller bit off a gob of egg-covered Danish. He hadn't shaved and a yellow blob adhered to the stubble just below his lip.

"It's all right." Lindsey wanted to limit the conversation to business. "Look, fill me in on *Bessie Blue* and this McKinney fellow. Lieutenant High showed me what happened, but what's really going on? What does it mean to International Surety?"

Lindsey still had the case folder in his attaché case and still hadn't had a chance to read it. He should have studied it on the flight from Denver; he was annoyed and promised himself that he would clear a couple of hours and examine the paperwork thoroughly.

"*Bessie Blue?* Name of a B-17. I don't know what the name means. Ask a jig and see if he'll tell you."

Lindsey felt his jaw clench. "Please, Elmer."

Mueller looked up, surprised. "What?"

Lindsey lowered his voice. "Jig."

"Oh, right. I keep forgetting what a good liberal boy you are, Hobie. Don't ask a jig." Mueller looked at Lindsey with something that might have been an impish grin. "Ask an American Africoon."

Lindsey shoved himself to his feet and left. All the way to the exit, he heard Elmer Mueller laughing. He took a cab back to North Field and climbed into the Hyundai. He was entitled to desk space at the Walnut Creek office and to administrative support, meaning that Ms. Wilbur would handle his mail and keep him posted on company gossip. But he wasn't going in today. There was a chance that Elmer Mueller would show up.

He drove to Oakland's Lake Merritt and parked near the Kleiner Mansion. The mansion was closed at this hour so he found a bench on a grassy bank and opened his attaché case. There were joggers and dog-walkers on the footpaths and ducks on the lake.

The *Bessie Blue* folder was in standard International Surety format, with plenty of paperwork. The company had computerized its operations in recent years, but cautious heads still insisted on keeping hard copies of everything. And a series of computer virus scares had left the corporate structure in a state of electronic paranoia.

The umbrella policy was made out to Double Bee Enterprises, as Lindsey had expected after talking to Lieutenant High. The policy covered all equipment, personnel, and operations of Double Bee and all its officers, employees, consultants, agents and independent contractors engaged in lawful activities in behalf of the company in the course of the development, production, post-production, promotion, distribution and exhibition of the film tentatively titled *Bessie Blue*.

The coverage included the insured's operation at Oakland International Airport, all grounds and facilities thereof, travel and transportation to and from, and other related movements and taking place at any location throughout the entire universe.

Lindsey laughed. A jogger in spandex and a headband stared. Lindsey turned to the policy appendixes. Double Bee Enterprises listed the airplanes it planned to use in *Bessie Blue*. A Stearman PT-17, a North American AT-6, a Lockheed P-38, a Bell P-39, a Curtiss P-40, a Republic P-47, a North American P-51, a Boeing B-17F, a Messerschmitt 109, a Focke-Wulf 190 and a Mitsubishi A6M2 Zero.

There were photos of the airplanes. Wonderful machines packed with character. They were like something from another age and were as real to Lindsey as suits of armor or Roman catapults would have been.

Where in the world were they going to get a fleet of fifty-year-old warplanes in flying condition?

Study the folder, study the folder. They had taught him that from his first day with International Surety, and they had drilled it into him all over again during the SPUDS seminar. Desmond Richelieu would be proud of him.

Right. Aircraft to be provided by the National Knights of the Air Historical Association and Aerial Museum of Dallas, Texas. One more question answered.

There were signatures from all sorts of corporate officers at

Double Bee and at International Surety. Every item in the policy carried a separate dollar value. The whole policy faced out at $100,000,000.

Lindsey's ears rang.

He shook his head, placed the airplane photos, the appendixes and the policy back into the folder inside his attaché case and snapped close the brass locks on the case. He locked the attaché case in the Hyundai and found a restaurant on Grand Lake Boulevard.

A late breakfast by himself was a lot pleasanter than his abortive early one with Elmer Mueller.

When he phoned Oakland police headquarters, he was able to reach Lieutenant High. He had the number of High's private line and avoided the Broadway bureaucracy. High agreed to see him. Lindsey headed across town.

There was even a visitor's badge ready when he hit the front desk. Upstairs, High greeted him. "You should have come over earlier, Lindsey. You missed the show."

Lindsey asked what show that was.

High grinned. "You could have attended the autopsy on Mr. McKinney. You're following up on that, of course. Have you ever attended one?"

Lindsey shook his head.

"Always interesting. Always the same, yet always different."

"Coroner must have been in an awfully big rush."

"Well, yes. We don't usually get to postmortems this fast, but Sergeant Finnerty had an interesting theory about the McKinney killing. The evidence squad hasn't brought in its report yet, so we don't know about that. But I thought we should get the PM report on the victim as quickly as we could."

Lindsey grunted. He was sitting in a hard-backed chair next to High's battered desk. Homicide in the Oakland Police Department worked out of a crowded, fluorescent-lit bullpen that would have driven Lindsey crazy if he'd had to spend his days there. Maybe that was what kept the detectives out on the job. Maybe it was a deliberate device intended to discourage them from lounging at their desks.

He didn't believe that for a minute. "What theory was that?" he asked. "Sergeant Finnerty's theory."

"Narcotics."

Lindsey closed his eyes. "Every story in the paper seems to be about narcotics."

"Right." High picked up a ball-point pen and stuck the tip of it between his teeth. He studied the pen for a moment, then laid it carefully on his desk and sighed. "You think that tobacco craving will ever go away? Or maybe the headshrinks are right, pipe smokers just want their mother's breast."

"Narcotics," Lindsey reminded him.

"Well, we get pretty close to a homicide a day in Oakland. That's no match for L.A. or Chicago. Half a dozen cities beat us, but then we're not nearly as big a city as they are. Most of the homicides are related to narcotics. Not the users. Well, sometimes we'll get somebody so strung out, he'll kill for a fix. But not often. Mostly it's the dealers. It's turf wars, just like Prohibition. God, I wish I could smoke my pipe. First the doctor gave me hell and now they've started passing laws about where a peaceful, law-abiding citizen can smoke his pipe."

Lindsey nodded vigorously, willing High to get back to the point. Eventually he did.

"Most of our gang activity is organized around the drug trade. Some of our enlightened citizens still have this image of young idealists in tie-dyed shirts and long dresses smoking nature or taking pills so they can see God."

He shook his head.

"The reality is crack houses and Uzis. Toss-ups. You know what a toss-up is?"

Lindsey said no.

"Lowest form of prostitute. We get young women—and I mean really young, twelve, thirteen, even younger—young women so desperate for crack that they stay in the crack houses. They live there. They don't have any money. They have sex with the customers for a hit of the stuff. Most often they perform oral sex because it's quicker and they don't have to get undressed or lie down. They get lesions in their mouths and throats from the hot crack smoke. Then they give some user a blow job, and the semen gets in the lesions, and they wind up with HIV. God, I wish I could smoke my pipe."

"Sergeant Finnerty thinks that's what happened at the airport, to Mr. McKinney?"

"We had one woman a few weeks ago . . . a couple of crack dealers were fighting over who got sidewalk rights in front of her house. She went out and tried to chase them away. They killed her. Right there, on the spot, just pulled out their automatic weapons and killed the poor woman."

"Finnerty's theory?" Lindsey said.

"These old airplanes are coming up from Texas for this movie they're making here in Oakland. Most of the stuff comes up from South America. A lot of it comes via Mexico. Most of the heroin still comes from Asia, but crack is a cocaine derivative. You knew that, right?"

Lindsey nodded.

"Right. I knew you knew that. The coca grows mainly in South America, and they bring a lot of cocaine in by air. If they could get it as far as Texas, Sergeant Finnerty thought, they could load it onto those old airplanes. Nobody would think they'd be carrying cargo. They're museum pieces. They're just going to be here for this movie, right? So why not use them to carry the cocaine? Who would suspect?"

"Sergeant Finnerty?" said Lindsey.

"Right."

"But none of the planes has arrived yet?"

"No. I think they're due in tomorrow. Mrs. Chandler would know that. But Sergeant Finnerty thinks that Mr. McKinney might have been involved. So we were really eager to see the postmortem on Mr. McKinney. Just in case he's a user himself. Most of the dealers aren't users, especially at the higher levels. They're too smart to get hooked on their own wares. But at the lower levels . . . Well, Sergeant Finnerty thought Mr. McKinney might be a user. So we rushed the autopsy."

"And?"

"He was pretty clean. Coroner found a little cannabis in his bloodstream and a little alcohol. My guess is that Mr. McKinney was not a happy individual. Well, look, a man in his sixties, seventies. He's lived all these years and worked all these years. He feels as if he's paid his dues. He's entitled to some kind of recognition, some kind of payout. Am I right? What do you think, Lindsey?"

"Okay."

"And here's Mr. McKinney, sweeping up a hangar and swabbing out urinals at the airport. I can understand his wanting to start the day with a little fortification. A little something added to his morning coffee. A joint before he leaves the house. Then down the freeway, it's just a hop, skip and a jump from Richmond to Oakland. And it's another day, another dollar."

"What about the crack?"

"Nothing to indicate he was involved at all."

"But those planes are coming in from Texas tomorrow."

High smiled. "We've already talked to the Feds. They're all over those airplanes. Even as we speak, Lindsey, even as we speak. You didn't think I'd tell anyone about this now, do you, if we were going to wait until they arrived to check them."

"Of course not," Lindsey said. "Certainly not."

High pushed himself to his feet. "Come on, Lindsey. I'll treat you to a cup of Oakland's finest legal stimulant." He led the way to a coffee machine. He held up his hand. "My treat." He fished a coin from his pocket and slipped it into the machine. "I forget how you take it."

Lindsey pushed the buttons himself. When the machine had made his coffee, he took a sip and moaned.

"You ever read Jim Thompson?" High asked. "Used to write paperback books. He wrote a book once about a deputy sheriff who tortured people by making them listen to clichés for hours on end. *It isn't the heat, it's the humidity.* He'd say that as if he'd just thought of it, as if it was some kind of profound discovery. *The child is father to the man.* He used to torture people that way."

"I don't think I ever read him," Lindsey said.

"I always thought that deputy sheriff missed something. He should have offered his victims machine-brewed coffee. *Too many chefs spoil the broth.* That kind of thing. And treat his victim to a cup of this oily tasting muck." He looked at Lindsey with soft, watery eyes. "Did you say you had another appointment, Lindsey?"

Lindsey said, "Actually, I have to make a phone call." High started to say something, but Lindsey headed him off. "No, it's all right, thanks. I'll use the pay phone in the lobby."

Five

LINDSEY HEADED FOR WALNUT CREEK and the International Surety office after all. As he crossed the threshold he felt a wave of emotion sweep over him, a feeling of homecoming mixed with a sense of loss.

Ms. Wilbur sat behind her desk, the same as ever. Seeing Lindsey, she let out a glad cry. She came around her desk and wrapped Lindsey in her arms. She planted a kiss on his cheek. She was a few years older than Lindsey's mother.

He started to fend her off, then changed his mind and returned the kiss.

They separated, laughing.

"I thought you were too high and mighty to come and see us anymore."

He shook his head. "I missed you. I'll still be working out of the office. You'll see me around." He took her hands. "How's it been?"

"You mean since Mr. Mueller took over here?" She made the title an epithet. "He's out of the office this afternoon. On business, he says. I think he's looking after those real-estate interests of his in Emeryville."

"Not good, eh?"

"I have almost enough years in for retirement. My husband is still working. My kids are grown up. I'm a grandmother, Bart. I think I'll just be a housewife and a grandma for a while. I think I'll enjoy that."

Lindsey plopped into a familiar chair. "You going to do it?"

Ms. Wilbur exhaled loudly. "I don't know. I think so."

"That bad?"

"You wouldn't believe it."

"Yes I would. I had breakfast with the man today. I mean, I tried to."

Ms. Wilbur grinned. "Don't tell me, he was stewed."

"No. Just obnoxious. I couldn't take it, and I realized that I didn't have to. I've never enjoyed missing a meal so much."

"And what are you doing for International Surety now? Ever since you went off to the mysterious SPUDS, I've been wondering."

Lindsey told her about *Bessie Blue* and Double Bee Enterprises and about the murder of Leroy McKinney.

Ms. Wilbur shook her head. "I'll take a look and see if we have life coverage on him." She called up the file of policyholders on her computer. "No policy. You don't think they're going to try and claim a death benefit under the umbrella policy, do you? He wasn't even working for Double Bee, was he? Wasn't he some kind of maintenance man or janitor or something?"

"That's right. No, I'm only afraid that the investigation is going to hold up the project and Double Bee will come after us with an indemnity claim. If we could clear up this killing, it would be a big help."

Elmer Mueller strode into the office. He had cleaned the egg off his chin but had some on his tie. He wore the same stained black suit he had worn at Oakland International. He dropped his briefcase on his desk. "Lindsey, Harden says I have to let you use this hole. I guess he's sucking up to Ducky Richelieu. God knows why. But I want you to remember who's the boss here now. I am. Get it? You're supercargo."

He turned and pointed a finger at Ms. Wilbur. "As for you, Mathilde, if you don't have anything better to do than gossip with visitors, maybe we should see about cutting your hours."

Mathilde! Lindsey had worked with Ms. Wilbur for more than a decade. She was a gray-haired, elderly woman. She'd helped him learn the ropes of International Surety. Mathilde! He had never even thought of calling her by her first name.

Lindsey sat down at a spare desk and began writing up his notes on the day's work. He had been back in California for only a matter of hours and was already involved in another murder case and an intracompany mess.

He shot a covert look at Ms. Wilbur, feeling like a schoolboy and expecting the teacher to scold him at any moment for not concentrating on his textbook. All he could see was the back of Ms. Wilbur's neck. It was flaming red.

He booted up the computer on his desk and called up KlameNet. Ms. Wilbur hadn't found a policy in the name of Leroy McKinney, but Lindsey knew the umbrella policy issued to Double Bee had to show. He called up the full text of the policy and verified that it contained a moral turpitude clause. If Double Bee suffered a loss through its own illegal or immoral conduct, the coverage was void.

Not that he believed anyone from Double Bee to have killed the janitor. Ina Chandler was with Lawton Crump when Crump discovered the body. Still, it wouldn't hurt to have a talk with Mrs. Chandler. Or even with Mr. Crump. Sergeant Finnerty had already questioned them, but Lindsey would approach the pair from another angle, a skewed angle. Sometimes that made a difference in the response. Sometimes it made a very big difference.

He phoned Berkeley police headquarters and reached Marvia Plum. Now that she was a sergeant in Homicide, she was spending more time at her desk and less time in the field. She complained about it. Doc High made the same complaint. Lindsey hardly knew Sergeant Finnerty, but undoubtedly he would grumble out the same gripe if he had the chance. They all worked for promotion and then complained that they weren't in the field anymore.

Lindsey would pick Marvia up and drive her to Walnut Creek for dinner. That way she couldn't go home afterwards by herself. He would have to drive her back.

"You're a schemer," she said. She laughed. The sound was like a hot jolt that ran through his body.

When he arrived at Oxford Street one of Marvia's housemates let him into the restored Victorian house. She was a heavyset, orange-haired woman. "Well, if it isn't Mr. Suburbia. Back to grace the land of peace and progress with your presence?"

Lindsey managed a polite banality before racing up the stairs two at a time. He reached Marvia's turret apartment gasping for breath.

Marvia had showered and was standing before a full-length mirror in her underwear drying her hair. There was a fireplace, but the only heat in the room came from the evening's warmth. Lindsey crossed the carpeted room and wrapped his arms around Marvia. His hands rested on her naked arms. She shut off the dryer and turned to him.

There were still a few drops of water on her chest.

He bent and kissed them off. "I missed you. Denver was okay, but I really missed you."

She said, "I love you, Bart."

He sat on the edge of her bed, on the Raggedy Ann quilt. She stood before him, barefoot and half-dressed, holding him. He pressed his face against the blackness of her belly, between the whiteness of her brassiere and the whiteness of her panties. "I love you, Marvia."

She finished dressing, and they drove to Walnut Creek, fighting the thousands of commuters struggling home from San Francisco and Oakland to the bedroom communities of Contra Costa County.

In the car Lindsey said, "Mother's doing well. She's making dinner. But we can't expect too much. I mean . . . we can't expect too much."

"Does she still think I'm your football coach's daughter?"

"I don't know what she thinks. I told her you were coming for dinner and she said something like, 'Oh, that nice colored girl.' I don't want you to be hurt. When you are, I feel it too. I know I can't feel it the way you do, but I can see it and . . . "

Marvia put her hand on his thigh. They'd left the classic Mustang that Marvia's brother had restored as a gift for her, at Oxford Street. She said, "I have some vacation time coming up. I've been saving my days. You think we could get away for a little while?"

37

"I'd love it. What about Jamie? You don't mind leaving him with your parents?"

"We could do that. Or maybe we could take him with us. I thought we might go down to Monterey. He's interested in fish. He'd like the aquarium."

"As soon as I wrap up this case!" Lindsey wanted to jump out of the car and dance on the freeway.

Amazingly, dinner went well. Mother served a simple pasta dish. It wasn't gourmet fare. But for a woman who had been almost helpless a few months before, it was an achievement.

After dinner, Mother served coffee and ice cream and chattered about a wonderful movie she had watched on cable while Lindsey was away. She enjoyed it so much that she got Mrs. Hernandez to take her to Vid/Vid/Vid to buy a copy. Now she watched it everyday.

It made her think, she said.

At first it had confused and upset her, but toward the end of the movie she started to understand it better.

Now, after watching it so often, she understood a lot of it. And every time she watched it, she understood more.

Lindsey asked what movie it was.

Mother said, "It's called *Sunset Boulevard*."

Lindsey exchanged looks with Marvia.

"Have you young people seen it?" Mother asked. "I'm sure you've seen it. Haven't you?"

"I know the picture," Marvia said. "Gloria Swanson and William Holden and Erich von Stroheim."

"Yes." Mother's eyes were shining. Her expression was gleeful. "Gloria Swanson. And Norma Desmond, don't you see? And this other picture I've seen, where Janet Gaynor is Esther Blodgett and then she's Vicki Lester. But who is she really?"

She held her hands to her cheeks. She was getting agitated. Marvia started to move toward her, but Lindsey put his hand on her wrist to stop her. "She's all right. She's . . . " He stopped.

Mother went on.

"But Norma Desmond. She was an old-time movie star, but she was Gloria Swanson, but she was really an old-time movie star. An actress playing an actress. A silent star. But she couldn't bear it. Everything changed, and she couldn't bear it. She lived in this huge mansion with a butler and just pretended it was the old days. But it wasn't, don't you see? Everything was changed. Everything was changed. Everything was changed."

She took a paper napkin from the table and wiped her eyes. She buried her face in the napkin, in her hands. Lindsey held her by the shoulders. She looked up, looked at him, looked at Marvia and said, "Everything was changed."

After a few minutes she said, "Well, if everyone is finished with their coffee, I'll clear these cups and saucers away."

A little later she said, "Hobart, if you and your friend want to go on, I'll just clean up a little and go to bed. I'm so glad that you're back, but I'm a little tired."

Lindsey stood holding her hands, studying her face. "You're all right, then, Mother? Is Mrs. Hernandez coming in tomorrow?"

She said, yes.

"Then I may stay over in Berkeley. I'll phone you in the morning. And Joanie Schorr is right next door, if you need her. You're sure you'll be all right?"

Again she said, yes.

When they reached Marvia's home and climbed to her apartment, Marvia put on a CD and knelt to light the fire. She was wearing a loose shirt and dark jeans.

Lindsey sat in an easy chair, watching Marvia and listening to the music. A woman sang to a judge, pleading guilty as charged. The fire flared up with a crackle, sending Marvia's shadow dancing around the circular room. She stood up, fetched wine and glasses, filled the glasses. She gave one to Lindsey and raised the other. "Welcome home," she said.

She settled onto his lap. He put his free hand on her back, gingerly at first. Then he tugged the tail of her shirt loose and ran his hand up her spine, feeling her skin. She rubbed her head against his, like a cat claiming ownership of a man.

Lindsey said, "That's a blood-curdling song. That's a murder song. Who's singing it? Is that new?"

Marvia laughed. "That's Bessie Smith. She's been dead since 1937. It's a great song. 'Send me to the Lectric Chair.' "

> *I caught him with a trifling Jane*
> *I warned him 'bout befo'*
> *I had my knife and went insane*
> *And the rest you ought to know.*

Lindsey sipped the wine. It was red and dry. He rubbed his cheek on Marvia's and ran his free hand around her waist underneath her shirt.

Bessie Smith sang,

> *I cut him with my bilo*
> *I piqued him in the side*
> *I stood there laughing over him*
> *While we wallowed 'round and died.*

Lindsey said, "What's a bilo?"

Marvia opened Lindsey's belt and slipped her hand inside his trousers. "It's a corruption of 'Barlow.' It's a kind of knife, like a Bowie knife. A double-bladed dagger, very nice. Some people say it wasn't really named for Barlow, but that bilo comes from bilobated. I found that in the dictionary myself. Cops know everything."

"What happened to Bessie Smith? That was an amazing song. I like this next one, too. How did she die?" Lindsey asked.

"She was hit by a cab," Marvia said. "They rushed her to the nearest hospital. She might have survived, but they refused to treat her there. It was a white hospital, you see. So they took her to a black hospital, but by then it was too late. She was forty-two years old."

Bessie Smith was still singing, a song called "Take me for a Buggy Ride." She sounded happy.

Lindsey and Marvia finished their wine and climbed into bed. The fire cast moving shadows on the walls and ceiling. Her room was in the turret of a restored Victorian, the kind of room where you would keep a crazy aunt.

Lindsey held Marvia's hand in his own and brought it to his face. He closed his eyes and used his face as an organ of touch, feeling Marvia's palm and fingers. He ran his tongue between her fingers, feeling and tasting her skin.

Six

THE OAKLAND TRIBUNE AND THE *San Francisco Chronicle* both ran stories on the Leroy McKinney murder. The *Chron* gave it a couple of paragraphs on an inside page. To the San Francisco papers events in Oakland were by definition minor stories. The *Trib* gave it a banner above the logo and a top position on page 3.

Included with the *Trib* story were photos of the crime scene. One photo showed the taped outline of McKinney's body on the hangar floor. The monkey wrench, surrounded by its own outline of tape, was visible in a corner of the picture.

The *Trib* photographer had also gotten a picture of the body. And he had somehow managed to shoot a close-up of McKinney's ID badge photo, which the *Trib* had blown up to column width.

Leroy McKinney in life had looked little different than he had when Lindsey saw him in death. The pool of jellied blood and brains was missing from his forehead, and his eyes had a look of life to them. But there was no mistaking the man.

The story in the *Trib* gave McKinney's address in Richmond and quoted the usual reactions of family and neighbors. McKinney had been friendly and outgoing, had kept strictly to himself, he'd been a wonderful man, nobody knew much about him, he was a pillar of the community, everyone loved him, he was a victim of society.

And so he was.

Next of kin seemed to be a young woman named Latasha Greene. After reading the story, Lindsey wasn't quite sure whether she was McKinney's daughter or granddaughter or niece. She was described as distraught but calm, prostrate with grief and bearing up courageously.

A memorial service was planned.

Marvia's Toshiba clock radio had popped into action with an early-morning show on KJAZ and the news that a popular and innovative trumpeter was hospitalized but making good progress. Marvia made a pot of coffee. She was on the day shift and left Oxford Street early for police headquarters. She had her own caseload. Lindsey hadn't burdened her with the Leroy McKinney killing, and she hadn't unloaded any of her cases on him.

He read the newspapers over a second cup of coffee and a stack of pancakes in a hole-in-the-wall restaurant on Shattuck Avenue. This was the older downtown Berkeley. It survived, but barely, in the shadow of Telegraph Avenue with its frequent riots and demonstrations and its near monopoly on the trade of 30,000 University of California students.

Lindsey phoned Mother and assured her that he was all right and that he would probably be home for dinner. Mother was expecting Mrs. Hernandez.

He borrowed a pair of scissors from a muscular woman decked out in army fatigue pants, a blue denim shirt and a 1940s-style waitress cap. He clipped the *Trib* and *Chron* stories on the hangar killing. The *Trib* ran a jump that butted against an aerial photo of the *Abraham Lincoln* at sea. It didn't look like the Love Boat, but Lindsey could think of worse ways to spend a few weeks. When Lindsey finished his breakfast, he walked to an instant printing service and made copies of the stories on the killing and extra blowups of the ID photo of Leroy McKinney. The dot pattern of the newspaper photo didn't enlarge too well, but the pictures were recognizable.

The instant printer was called the Gandharva/Ganesa Copy Center.

The Gandharva/Ganesa Copy Center. Lindsey looked around for the Amon-Ra Laundromat or Jesus Jives CD Headquarters, but they must have been on another street.

* * *

Latasha Greene's address was on Twenty-third Street in Richmond, just off Nevin Avenue. Lindsey had spent some time in Point Richmond, a hilly spur of land stretching into San Francisco Bay, populated by a mix of wealthy recluses and executives from a nearby oil refinery. But downtown Richmond was a very different kind of place.

He found a parking spot between a rusted-out Corolla and an ancient Buick the size of a gymnasium. Before driving to Richmond he had gone home, checked on Mother and Mrs. Hernandez and showered and changed his clothing. Working for Ducky Richelieu certainly had its compensations.

He'd passed kids skateboarding on the sidewalk, groups gathered around ghetto blasters practicing their rap moves, some derelicts slumped in vacant doorways, paper bags in their laps, their eyes as vacant as the doorways they made their homes.

Latasha Greene lived in a 1930s frame-and-stucco bungalow. Once it might have been a pleasant little house. But now it looked as though it had not seen a paintbrush or a carpenter in decades. The paint had faded to a nondescript tan, the wood was cracked and there were holes—they looked like bullet holes—in the stucco. Several windows were cracked and patched with cardboard.

Well, at least they were patched, although it looked as if the cardboard had been in place for months if not years.

The lawn was strewn with litter. On either side of the house were vacant lots, overgrown with weeds and scattered with old tires and trash.

The kid pointed his weapon as Lindsey turned from the Hyundai and started to slip his keys into his pocket. He said, "Drop the tachy case, gringo, and reach."

He had pale, almost albino features marked with blotchy freckles and frizzy blond hair. He wore his baseball cap sideways. He must have been wearing some kind of clothes, but all Lindsey could focus on was the gun in his hands. He couldn't tell whether it was an Uzi or a Raven or an Intratec. He didn't really know anything about guns, but they were in the news so much lately that he had picked up a few names, almost against his will.

He gasped. His hands started to shake. He dropped his attaché case as the kid had ordered.

"Too slow, gringo!"

Time froze. Lindsey could see the gun clearly in the kid's hands. He identified it. That would be a big help. He could see three or four more kids behind the one with the gun. They couldn't have been more than 12 years old. They all wore baseball caps with the visors over their ears and plastic straps hanging onto their cheeks. One wore a Chicago Bulls jacket. One wore a Georgetown Hoyas jacket. Lindsey's eyes moved back to the kid with the gun. He wore a Los Angeles Raiders jacket.

In his last moment of awareness, Lindsey thought, *what a pity the Raiders moved away from Oakland. They were always a source of civic pride.*

The kids behind the one with the gun were all grinning, all baring white teeth in black faces.

The kid with the gun yelled again, or maybe his words just hung in the air or maybe Lindsey's brain was stretching them. " . . . s-l-o-w, g-r-i-n-g-o!"

The kid's finger tightened on the trigger. Lindsey felt his knees buckle. He saw the stream of water coming from the muzzle of the gun. He heard the kids burst into hysterical laughter.

He hit the ground, tearing the knee out of his trousers and scraping the flesh beneath. He saw the kids running away, all except the one with the gun in his hands. The kid stood over Lindsey, looking terrified. Lindsey thought the kid was ready to cry. The kid said, "I was only joking, mister. It's only a water gun, see?"

He held the gun in front of Lindsey and pulled the trigger again. A stream of water squirted from the muzzle and puddled on the lawn near Latasha Greene's house.

"I didn't mean to tear your pants," the kid said. "I don't got any money. I don't know how to . . . Don't tell my grandma. She's kill me if you tell her. Don't tell . . . "

Lindsey said, "No, it's all right. It was just a joke, right?"

"That's right," the kid said.

"I won't tell," Lindsey said. He grasped the attaché case with one hand and braced the other against the passenger's door of the Hyundai. He rose to his feet and managed to steady himself. "Do you know Latasha Greene?" he asked the kid. "Is this her house?"

The kid nodded three or four times. "That's her house all right. You gonna visit her? She's all broken up. Mr. McKinney, he got offed. *Wham*, some sucker got him with a lead pipe. I saw it all on TV. *Wham!* Right in the face! Must of been some sucker he knowed. Right in the face!"

The kid grinned, turned around, ran off in the direction his friends had gone.

Lindsey climbed three rickety steps and knocked on the door. After a while he heard the latches opening. There were a lot of them.

The short man who opened the door had the blackest skin Lindsey had ever seen. His hair was cropped short around his ears; the dome of his head was hairless and shone as if it had been polished. A pot belly pushed out beneath a dove-gray clergy suit. "I'm the Reverend Johnson. Did something happen to you?" He was looking at Lindsey's soaked jacket and his wrecked trousers. Lindsey realized that his face was dirty as well.

Lindsey said, "I ran into some kids outside. They didn't mean any harm, but . . . " He felt more embarrassed than anything else.

"That's too bad," Reverend Johnson said. "But why are you here? This is a house of grief today."

Lindsey pulled a handkerchief from his pocket and wiped his face. "I know. I'm very sorry. I hoped I could talk with Miss Greene. I represent International Surety." He fumbled for a business card and handed it to Johnson.

Johnson took the card. He studied it for a long time, then slipped it into a pocket. "An insurance man."

"Yes, sir." Johnson seemed to think that Lindsey was here to arrange a payment. Let him think it. People talk to you when they think you're going to give them money. "It's about Mr. McKinney." He managed a note of detached sympathy. If he hadn't been an insurance man, he would have made a good undertaker.

Johnson said, "Come in, young man. I expect that Miss Greene will receive you in the parlor."

Inside the furnishings were shabby and the air was musty as if the house hadn't been aired in years. The front room contained a huge television set with a round screen that reflected a dead, pale-olive image of the room. The TV must have been built in the Truman era. On top of it stood a portable color set. Images of angry black faces alternated with those of violent gestures and sexual posturing. The sound was turned off.

Johnson disappeared through a dusty, rust-colored curtain. Lindsey heard him speak softly. "Latasha dear, there's a man to see you. It's about Grandfather's life insurance."

Latasha Greene was tall and brown. She wore a T-shirt with a picture of a brown-skinned Bart Simpson brandishing an assault pistol, faded jeans and wooden clogs. She balanced a baby on her hip.

She said to Lindsey. "What happened to your suit?"

"Some kids outside. It was just an accident."

Latasha said, "What kids?" She seemed distracted, only partially present, and asked her questions in a remote voice. Lindsey described the kids in their baseball caps and team jackets. Latasha said, "Oh, that's just Ahmad. That little pale-skin nigger. Mrs. Hope's grandson." She blinked. Then, as if she had just wakened, she said, "What about my Grandpa?"

Lindsey extended another business card. Latasha looked at it for a long time. Then she sat on the couch. Lindsey slipped the card back into his pocket. The Reverend Johnson sat on a reversed, chrome-and-plastic kitchen chair. Lindsey looked around, found a faded, overstuffed easy chair and settled uneasily on it.

He said, "I was very sorry to learn of Mr. McKinney's demise. He was your grandfather, then, Miss Greene? By 'Grandpa' you didn't just mean . . . "

"He was my Grandpa." Latasha nodded and asked again, "What happened to you?"

Lindsey said, "I fell. Nothing serious."

"Grandpa had insurance?" Latasha asked.

"We have to find out. I don't know whether he was covered or not under the circumstances of his death."

Reverend Johnson said, "Now wait a minute, mister! You mean you're trying to weasel out of paying off?"

"Not at all. We just have to ascertain . . . You see, Mr. McKinney was not directly covered. But there's an umbrella policy, we may be able to . . . " He let it go at that. He hated to mislead them. It wasn't his job to pour out International Surety's funds but to preserve them. He clenched his jaw to keep from saying the wrong thing.

"Just what do you need to know?" Reverend Johnson asked.

Lindsey turned to Latasha. She had lifted the bottom of her black Bart T-shirt and was nursing her baby, watching the baby with a look of unreadable concentration. "I'm trying to find out something about Mr. McKinney. What kind of person he was. What kind of life he led," Lindsey said.

Johnson said, "I don't see why you need to know that in order to pay off his insurance."

Lindsey said, "I'm sorry. He didn't have any insurance. At least, not with our company. I thought I'd made that clear. But if we can find some way to get benefits under the umbrella . . . "

Johnson frowned.

Lindsey turned back to Latasha. He managed to catch a portion of her attention and smiled encouragingly, willing her to talk to him.

She said, "My Grandpa was a great man. He was a hero." She looked away from Lindsey to her baby. She smiled at the baby. The baby's eyes were closed, but it was making little smacking sounds with its mouth. Lindsey lowered his eyes to his notepad.

"He was a war hero. He killed a whole machine-gun nest of Japs in the Philippines. And he saved two Americans. He was a pitcher, too. He should have been in the major leagues, but he never got a chance. And he ran a nightclub. He made people famous and rich, and he never got nothin' for it."

Lindsey was trying to keep track, jotting notes as fast as Latasha spoke. He wished he had a tape recorder. Maybe he'd buy one of those little portables and charge it to SPUDS. Richelieu was going to buy him a new pair of pants after today, he might as well spring for a piece of necessary field equipment. He said, "Pardon me, please slow down. You say your grandfather was a war hero?"

She nodded.

He jotted, "Verify military service record—Dept. Veterans Affairs."

She carried her baby out of the room. While she was gone, Lindsey looked over his notes. Reverend Johnson said, "How much is your company going to pay?"

Lindsey said, "I don't know that we're going to pay anything. That's why I have to get all the facts."

Johnson said, "This is a very needy family. I should think that a certain humane consideration would be appropriate."

"Insurance companies don't work that way." He couldn't think of anything else to say.

Latasha Greene came back into the room. She had left her baby elsewhere. She resumed her seat on the couch. She looked past Lindsey and fixed her eyes on the TV screen.

Lindsey said, "About Mr. McKinney's military service . . . "

Latasha said, "He was in the Marines. He fought all over the Pacific. He was on Iowa Jima. He hurt his hand there. He was working in a ammunition bunker, and a Jap fire-grenade landed and it would have blown up the ammunition and killed everybody. Grandpa grabbed the grenade and threw it back at the Japs and it wiped out a whole machine-gun nest of Japs but it burned up his hand so bad, it was never any good again. It was so ugly, it was like a claw. I used to be afraid of it when I was little and I always made him cover it up when he came on my bed or I'd start to scream."

Lindsey said, "I never heard of fire-grenades."

Latasha said, "You don't know anything about it. My grandpa told me. He used to sit on my bed at night and tell me stories. After he hurt his hand he still drug two men to safety who would have died. He saved their lives. He was a hero."

She set her jaw angrily, but her mouth was quivering and her eyes looked wet.

Reverend Johnson said, "I heard those same stories, Mr. Lindsey. I knew Leroy McKinney for many years. Latasha isn't making them up."

Lindsey said, "I wasn't suggesting . . . "

Latasha said, "I even have a picture of him. And a newspaper."

She brought a tattered San Francisco *Call-Bulletin* from the other room and a yellowed snapshot with tattered edges.

Lindsey said, "May I take these with me? I'll photocopy them and return them to you." He waited until she nodded absently and then put the newspaper and the photograph in his attaché case. Latasha's eyes were fixed on the silent TV set. Lindsey said, "Do you have his Marine Corps discharge papers? Or any of his military records? Did he go to a veterans' hospital at any time? Was he receiving a disability pension?"

Latasha was staring at the TV screen. Even though there was no sound, she must have recognized the video they were showing because she was moving her lips silently to the unheard lyrics and swaying to the silent beat.

Lindsey looked questioningly at Reverend Johnson.

Reverend Johnson said, "I asked Leroy about that. Many times. He never got anything from the government. There was some mix-up with his records. He never did get his discharge papers, disability payments, anything. He never got anything at all. I urged him to take it up with our congressman, but I could never get him to do it. He was a very embittered man. He's in his glory now. Even if there's no justice in this world, there surely must be in the next, and Leroy is in his glory now."

Latasha Greene was involved with her TV. Lindsey said, "I guess I'll be going now. I'll send back the newspaper and the photograph. Or maybe bring them." He started for the door.

Reverend Johnson said, "I was just leaving myself."

Seven

ONCE THEY WERE OUTSIDE THE HOUSE, Reverend Johnson's mien brightened. He stopped Lindsey before they reached the sidewalk. He put his hand on Lindsey's elbow. He said, "What really happened to you?" He nodded at Lindsey's torn trousers.

"Some kids." Lindsey looked around. They were nowhere in sight. "Neighborhood kids. I thought they were going to kill me. Boy had an Intratec 9S."

Johnson's eyebrows bounced up. "You know your weapons."

"At first I thought he was going to rob me. Then I thought he was going to kill me. But all he had was a toy. A water gun. It looked real, but it was just a water gun."

"Won't be that much longer before he has a real Tec. Or something equally bad. Guns are flooding into the community, Mr. Lindsey. Who's pumping them into the community and why, do you have any idea?" He cocked his head inquiringly. Lindsey wasn't sure whether he was really asking a question or making a hard point.

"I don't know who's doing it, Reverend."

Johnson reached inside his clergy suit and extracted an old-fashioned cigar case. It was either mother-of-pearl trimmed with gold or a good plastic-and-brass imitation. Johnson said, "Cigar, Mr. Lindsey?"

Lindsey shook his head.

Johnson extracted a nearly black cigar from the case and a tiny device that looked like a miniature guillotine from his trousers pocket. He made a ceremony of clipping off the tip of the cigar and throwing the pellet of tobacco on the weed-run lawn. He returned the guillotine to his pocket, then pulled out a lighter and ignited the cigar. He turned away briefly and sent a plume of gray smoke into the air.

"Come," he said, "let's stroll a bit. Maybe we'll find the miscreants responsible for your misfortune. And maybe we can exchange some more information while we're at it."

They walked to the corner and rounded it onto Nevin Avenue. They headed toward a bar and a pool room in full swing even though it was not yet noon. A cluster of young men standing outside the poolroom stirred at Lindsey and Johnson's approach. The young men were passing something around. It disappeared and there were murmurs of "Rev. Mornin', Rev." Lindsey felt hot stares on the back of his neck as he and Johnson passed the young men.

Lindsey said, "What about Latasha's story, Reverend? The part about Mr. McKinney's being a baseball player."

Johnson drew on his cigar. Between puffs, he didn't keep it in his mouth. Lindsey had half expected Johnson to hold the cigar clenched in his teeth the way FDR held his famous cigarette holder in old news photos. Instead, Johnson carried the cigar in his fingers, a cross between a baton and a scepter.

"I can only tell you that Leroy was very convincing. I wasn't there. I didn't see the things he claimed to have done. But he told the same stories year after year."

He stood still, frowning. "Just a moment. He once did show me some old baseball programs. He visited me at the church. He was sorting through a batch of old papers, and he found some scorecards or programs. He was very proud of them, and he was afraid they would be lost after he passed, so I promised to keep them for him. I haven't even thought of them in years, but they must still be where I stored them for Leroy."

Johnson stood facing Lindsey. He said, "Come with me. The church is nearby. Let's see if we can find those scorecards."

They crossed Nevin and walked past a row of abandoned storefronts. Lindsey was worried. Johnson read his mind. "Don't be afraid, Mr. Lindsey. You are in no danger."

Lindsey decided it was still a good idea to keep an eye out.

Johnson said, "Yes, I was quite a baseball enthusiast in my day. Are you a baseball fan, Mr. Lindsey?"

Lindsey admitted that he didn't follow the sport closely. He dreamed about the bomber crashing at an A's game, but he didn't really follow the sport.

Johnson sent a plume of cigar smoke into the air. "Wonderful game, Mr. Lindsey. I was a shortstop once upon a time. You wouldn't believe it, would you?" He patted his ample paunch. "That was before I received my calling, of course."

He grinned ruefully. "But Leroy McKinney. Now, he used to tell wonderful baseball stories. He played in the old Negro National League. I suppose you've never heard of that, but we used to have our own teams, our own National and American Leagues, our own Negro World Series and our own All-Star Games. I saw the Negro East-West Classic in 1948, Mr. Lindsey. I watched the game from the upper deck of old Comiskey Park in Chicago. I was a very young man then, but it was a day I shall never forget."

They had reached Johnson's church. It was better than a storefront but not much better. The building stood on a small lot between a weed-covered field and a Chinese take-out restaurant. There was a single stained-glass window in the front of the church. The glass in front of the announcement board had been broken out and the letters rearranged into misspelled obscenities.

Johnson hurried Lindsey inside the building. It was musty inside. Again Johnson said, "I shall never forget that day. Every team was represented. The Homestead Grays, the New York Cubans, the Philadelphia Stars, the Memphis Red Sox. I don't suppose you've ever heard of those teams, have you, Mr. Lindsey?"

Lindsey shook his head. "About Mr. McKinney," he started, but Johnson was on a roll.

"Forty-two thousand fans were in attendance, and that was down from previous years. We'd started playing in the major leagues by then, Jackie Robinson and all that. I didn't oppose the idea then. I still approve of it. But the fact is, integration rang the death knell of the Negro Leagues."

He smiled and drew on his cigar. "Bill Powell of the Birmingham Black Barons, pitching for the West, defeated Rufus Lewis of the Newark Eagles for the East, three runs to nothing. Three runs to nothing. It was quite a performance, although Powell was relieved by Jim LaMarque of the Kansas City Monarchs and Gentry Jessup of the Chicago American Giants. But it was Powell's triumph, yes indeed."

Lindsey said, "I'm sure it was."

Johnson shook his head. "I could not tell you who won last year's World Series. Followed it like a hawk, but I've forgotten already. A sign of advancing years, Mr. Lindsey. You can conjure the distant past in every detail, but you cannot recall what you had for breakfast. Now." He ground his cigar in an upright smoking stand like the ones William Powell used in the old Thin Man movies. "Let's see about those scorecards of Mr. McKinney's."

Lindsey said, "Yes, please." He checked his Seiko. It was after two o'clock. Now that he was in SPUDS it might be worth his while to look into a better timepiece.

The sacristy of the Reverend Johnson's church was a musty storeroom full of choir robes, battered hymnals, piles of collection plates and stacked corrugated boxes of files.

Johnson riffled through the boxes, muttering and shoving cartons aside. Lindsey checked his watch again. Four minutes had passed. He said, "Maybe you'd send them to me."

Johnson looked up. He was perspiring, his dome shining beneath the fluorescent light. "I'm sure they're here. Just a minute."

Lindsey shifted his weight from foot to foot. He checked his watch again. Six minutes had passed.

Johnson said, "Here they are!" There was a note of triumph in his voice. He waved a couple of five-by-seven sheets of light cardboard at Lindsey. "1942," Johnson said. "That was Leroy McKinney's last year as a ballplayer, or so he said. After that he went into the service. And after the war, of course, he couldn't pitch anymore. Not with his injured hand."

He spread the scorecards on the top of a cardboard file box. Someone had marked the scorecards with an old-style fountain pen and the ink had run and faded, but Lindsey could see the lineup printed in splotchy black ink. The team was the Cincinnati Buckeyes and Leroy Mickinney was listed as a pitcher.

Mickinney. Not McKinney. Someone had made a typographical error in 1942.

Lindsey found a folding chair and started to sit down. The chair was covered with dust. He looked at it, began to clean it, then realized that it didn't matter. Not with his trousers in the condition they were in.

He opened his attaché case and slipped the programs into the *Bessie Blue* International Surety folder. He said, "It's really hard to understand, Reverend Johnson. I mean, with all the advocacy groups, veterans' associations, civil-rights organizations, that Mr. McKinney never received any benefits."

Johnson shook his head sadly. "No benefits. No recognition. No appreciation. I don't think you quite understand what conditions were like, Mr. Lindsey." He changed his direction. "If you can do anything with those old documents—the newspaper Latasha gave you, the photos, the baseball scorecards— please do so. But, once you have made your copies, please be sure to return them. I'm certain that they will be precious mementos."

Lindsey said, "Sure."

Reverend Johnson said, "If we were a wealthier congregation, we'd have our own office facilities, including a copying machine. But you can see that we serve the needy not the greedy."

Lindsey said, "Sure."

Ms. Wilbur gaped. "Bart, what happened to you? You look as if you'd been mugged."

Lindsey managed a painful grin. He had thought of going home from Richmond and cleaning up, but instead he'd come to the office to catch up on paperwork. And he would phone Mother, too, and make a joke about falling, so she wouldn't scream when she saw him.

He explained about the twelve-year-old bandits and the water pistol.

Ms. Wilbur clucked sympathetically.

Elmer Mueller had observed the exchange between Lindsey and Ms. Wilbur. He said, "Harden and Richelieu have both been on the horn. I don't know which one is having a bigger fit. You better get back to 'em fast. You're really going to have your tail in the grinder after this fiasco, Hobie-boy."

Lindsey ignored the name. He dialed SPUDS in Denver and Mrs. Blomquist quickly put him through to Richelieu. Lindsey got as far as "Mi—" before Richelieu cut him off. "Welcome to the hardball game. What have you done to contain this *Bessie Blue* matter?"

Lindsey started to tell him about visiting the airport, working with Doc High and interviewing Latasha Green and Reverend Johnson.

"Are those airplanes in California yet?" Richelieu asked.

"I don't know. They were flying in today. Going to fly in today. I've been in Richmond all afternoon and . . . "

"I don't want an opera in five acts with full orchestra and chorus. Where are the airplanes? What's the status of that movie? We're standing in as de facto completion-bond guarantor, and if somebody whacks a damned janitor on the bean, frankly my dear I don't give a damn. I give a damn about that movie getting made, so we don't have to shell out millions of dollars."

"Yes, sir."

"Well, where are the airplanes?"

Lindsey swallowed hard. "I don't know for sure."

"You mean you don't know, period!" Lindsey could see Richelieu twisting his moustache, the high Colorado sunlight glancing off his rimless glasses. "Get into gear and report back to me in twenty-four hours, Lindsey. Good heavens, man, what do you think we spent all the money to train you for? What do you think we're paying you for?"

Lindsey held the receiver away from his ear, waiting for Richelieu to slam down the telephone. But all that came over the line was a gentle click.

Lindsey laid the receiver in its cradle.

Elmer Mueller was grinning at him. "Sounded like you handled that gink pretty well, Hobie. Now it's time to chat with Harden at Regional, right?"

Lindsey said, "Harden at Regional can . . . " He stopped. He was not going to lower himself to Elmer Mueller's level. He breathed deeply until he was calm, then he called home and told Mother that a funny thing had happened today, and not to be upset when he got home looking messy.

Mother said, "Did you fall in the playground? Did the nurse look at you? Maybe I ought to come to school and bring you home."

"Is Mrs. Hernandez there?" Lindsey asked.

"Yes, dear, we were just shopping. Is there something you don't want to say to me? All right, dear, I'll put her on."

Before Lindsey could say a word, Mrs. Hernandez said, "She's just a little confused, Mr. Lindsey. She's really all right. You can come home now. She'll be all right."

When Lindsey got home, Mother was settled in front of the TV set watching one of her old movies, a cup of hot chocolate in her hand. She barely noticed his arrival. Lindsey went to his room, showered and put on fresh clothing. He looked at the suit he had worn to Richmond. A total loss. He hoped SPUDS was prepared to replace it for him.

Mrs. Hernandez reassured him that Mother's confusion had been a minor lapse. The doctors had said that her improvement, after years of disorientation, was remarkable but that Lindsey had to expect setbacks from time to time.

He loved that phrase.

He thanked Mrs. Hernandez and she left for the day.

Lindsey stood watching the TV screen. Mother was completely absorbed in her old movie. Lindsey recognized the film. Mother hadn't even had to tinker with the TV controls, the movie was already in black-and-white. It was *Whatever Happened to Baby Jane*. Lindsey watched for several minutes. Davis and Crawford were either awfully wonderful or wonderfully awful. He couldn't tell which. But as far as Lindsey was concerned, the bloated, mincing Victor Buono stole the show.

Mother set her cup on its saucer with a clash. She turned toward Lindsey, pointing back at the screen where a frightening image of an elderly Bette Davis costumed as Baby Jane pranced and sang, obviously mad.

Lindsey started forward, reaching to switch off the movie and calm his mother.

But she said, "You see, Hobart? It's like that other one, like that one with Gloria Swanson. Only this one is different. Norma Desmond really thought it was long ago, but Baby Jane only wants it to be long ago. She wants to make it be long ago, but she can't do it."

Lindsey didn't know what to make of it. What should he say?

Eight

First thing Friday morning, Lindsey called Oakland Police Headquarters. Doc High took Lindsey's call and told him that the DEA had approached the National Knights of the Air, et cetera, et cetera, and the National Knights of the Air, et cetera, et cetera, had agreed to its aircraft and museum being searched and had come up clean. "Clean of drugs," High added.

Lindsey frowned. "Wait a minute. I think you're playing with me, Lieutenant."

"Doc."

"What about it?"

Even across the telephone line, the sigh was audible. "Thought I could get away with it first thing in the morning. You're too sharp for me, Lindsey. Well, the drug kiddies went in there with their dope-sniffing doggies and their little chemical analysis kits. They didn't turn up anything you could put up your nose or shoot in your veins and get a thrill from. But they found themselves a miniature zoo."

"A what?"

"A zoo. Some of these old-airplane people seem to have a fondness for rare animals. Uncle Sam has been getting down on illegal importers of endangered species. Mostly South American birds, a few primates, a couple of rare breeds of cats, even some snakes. It's quite a list. And you know what happens when you tell people they can't have something, whether it's dirty pictures or homemade atom bombs. That's what they want."

"So are the planes in Oakland?" Lindsey asked.

Doc High said, "I don't know. There's no indication that

they were planning to fly the animals out here on this jaunt. The people at the museum claim they don't know anything about the illegal livestock. Some employee, whatever. They're quaking in their cowboy boots that Uncle Sam is going to bring a RICO action against 'em and seize their precious old warbirds."

Lindsey held his head. "You think that's going to happen?"

"I doubt it. But you can never tell with the Feds. Tell you what, I think your best bet is to ask Double Bee."

High was a nice fellow. He gave Lindsey Double Bee's local phone number without requiring a writ of mandamus.

Double Bee had taken a suite at the Parc Oakland Hotel, a glittery establishment on Broadway not far from police headquarters. It was the company's temporary office and housing for visiting personnel.

Lindsey had expected to visit the airport again in order to track down Ina Chandler and was surprised when he located her at the Parc Oakland. After explaining his job to the production secretary a few times, he was put through to Mrs. Chandler.

She opened the conversation. Her voice was soft and she spoke with what sounded like an Alabama accent. But her words were more modern career woman than Southern Belle. "I'm very busy. This production is top priority. We haven't even started shooting yet and we've already had a fatality. The airplanes aren't here, we're behind schedule and running up bills every hour, and you want to sell me life insurance. I don't know why that idiot put you through. The answer is no."

She whacked the telephone down with a sound like colliding funny cars.

Lindsey had to go through the whole process again to get back to her. This time he headed her off at the pass. This time he planned the call before he placed it. This time he wasn't the old stammering, diffident Hobart Lindsey.

"Shut up and listen to me," he opened. "I'm from International Surety and I'm going to save your movie for you unless you stop me. And if you do, your ass is grass."

Was that the right expression? He frowned.

60

It must have been a good choice. He heard her gasp, "What?"

He said, "The police are in charge of the murder, but I'm in charge of the insurance. I'm going to straighten this thing out and save your movie for you. You're in the Parc Oakland now. I'll be there in half an hour. Don't leave."

She murmured, "All right."

He hung up before he could do anything to ruin the conversation.

He took the elevator up to the Double Bee suite. A dozen people lounged around looking miserable. Most of them wore plaid shirts and blue jeans, but Lindsey spotted a couple of bright blue satin jackets with a *Bessie Blue* logo on the back. The logo featured a picture of a round-faced black woman in a beaded dress and feathered headband. Other than the jackets, there wasn't much of the Hollywood glitter that Lindsey had expected to find.

There must have been a dozen different telephone conversations in progress. That would work out even. Half the Double Bee people were talking to the other half.

He located the production secretary and was directed to Ina Chandler. Despite her gray hair, Mrs. Chandler had the figure of a younger woman and knew it. Lindsey wondered if there was a Mr. Chandler waiting in a cozy cottage somewhere, or if Ina had shed him somewhere along the way. Or buried him.

She was sitting at a wood-patterned table with a tray of donuts, a pot of coffee and a yellow pad. There were cartons under the desk with newspapers scattered over them. She took Lindsey's card and waved him to a straight-backed chair.

Lindsey had finally read the *Bessie Blue* file and had the salient data in his mind. He didn't want to risk losing the documents that Latasha Greene and Reverend Johnson had loaned him, so Ms. Wilbur had locked the case folder in International Surety's safe.

A digital clock on Mrs. Chandler's makeshift desk had apparently lost and regained power at some point. It simply flashed "12:00, 12:00, 12:00," but nobody in Double Bee seemed to care about hours. Fair enough, neither did Lindsey.

Mrs. Chandler shoved the donut tray toward Lindsey. She said, "Have some sugar."

He found a cup and a paper napkin and took some coffee and a frightening pink glazed donut.

She said, "I thought Mueller was handling this for your company. What's the story?"

Lindsey said, "Elmer works out of our local office. He authorizes payments for legitimate claims." He emphasized the adjective but just a little. She didn't take the bait. "I'm from Special Projects. I work out of Denver."

Mrs. Chandler looked unimpressed but she waited for him to continue.

"We'll be a lot happier if we don't have to pay off, and I don't mean we're trying to weasel out of our obligation. I mean, I'm here to try and help you get your cart back on track. If we can do that, you'll be happier and International Surety will save a load of dollars."

He looked at her. Well, at least he had her attention. They had made eye contact. Okay! "Now, what's the story on your fleet of aircraft?"

Her eyes darted to the yellow pad before her. She was fiddling with a metal pen shaped like airplane fuselage with suggestions of wings and a tail in the proper position. She said, "They're coming in tomorrow. At least, that's the plan. So we're two days behind schedule. And that's our best case."

"Are you all set up with the airport? Tower controllers alerted? Oakland Police informed? All cleared with the Feds?"

She nodded.

"Lieutenant High didn't seem to know your plans."

"When did you talk to him?"

"Less than an hour ago," he said.

"I got off the phone ten minutes ago. Do you know what happened in Texas?" she asked.

"The zoo?" He felt like Jack Webb in a late-night rerun of "Dragnet." The dialog was enough to make him look for Harry Morgan. He hoped he wouldn't develop a jerky-jerky Joe Friday walk.

"First thing that happened, the DEA wanted to wash their

hands of the matter. Customs Service got involved, Department of Agriculture came snooping around, Environmental Protection sent a couple of their spooks, the local Humane Society got into the act. The Knights are going to be in court for years on this thing."

"But there's no RICO suit. The airplanes can fly."

"The airplanes can fly. They'll be leaving at dawn tomorrow. My stars, what day is it?" She fumbled around for a newspaper under the table and came up with an Oakland *Tribune*. "Tomorrow's Friday. You get so you can't keep track after a while."

My stars. She'd actually said *My stars*. Maybe there was some Southern Belle left inside the Chandler after all.

"Leroy McKinney was not employed by Double Bee. Is that correct?" Lindsey asked.

"That is correct."

"You didn't know him. You and Mr. Crump found him when you arrived at the hangar yesterday. Is that correct?" The sugar from the donut was making Lindsey's teeth ache. He took a mouthful of coffee and tried to swish it around without being too conspicuous.

"That is correct." Mrs. Chandler looked at Lindsey with an odd expression. "Are you all right? Are you in pain?"

He swallowed the coffee. "Not at all, no." He picked up the remnant of his pink-coated donut, stared at it for a moment and put it down on his paper napkin. "What time was this?"

"Five-thirty A.M."

"Is that your normal practice? That's very early."

"We thought the planes were coming in yesterday. We had a lot of work to do at the airport before they arrived. We work long hours in this business. Movies aren't all shiny cars and wild parties. In fact, there are hardly any shiny cars or wild parties, not that I've seen."

He tried to read her expression, but failed. "Was there anyone else in the hangar when you arrived?"

"No."

"Had there been? I mean, of course there had to be. Mr. McKinney was there. I mean his body was there. And whoever

63

killed him had been there. Could you tell? Did whoever it was leave behind, oh, a sandwich wrapper or a coffee container or some cigarette butts?"

"Nothing." She paused. "Oh, well the stove was going. It was pretty low, but there were still some flames."

"Right. It was still warm when I got there. Not warm enough, but it was better than nothing." He frowned. "What time do you expect the airplanes tomorrow?"

"We want to film them arriving. They fly at different speeds, so the slowest planes will leave Dallas first. The controllers will time the other takeoffs, so they'll assemble over San Jose and fly the last forty miles in formation. We're expecting them around 4 p.m."

Lindsey jotted that down. "Let's get back to yesterday. You and Mr. Crump got to the airport at five-thirty. What time did you leave the hotel?"

"Five o'clock."

"Together?"

"Of course together. Why should we take two cars to drive from the hotel to the airport?"

"You were both staying here in the hotel?"

"Yes."

He picked up his cup, sipped some coffee and put it down.

There was a silence between them. All the other conversations in the suite had stopped, or maybe everybody just happened to pause for breath at once.

"I'd like to know why you're asking these questions. You claim you're here to handle the insurance side of *Bessie Blue*, but you must know that you're acting a hell of a lot like a cop."

"I'm not a cop, believe me."

"I didn't say you were a cop. I said you were acting like a cop. Dumb, among other things."

"I happen to know some pretty brainy cops, but never mind." He inhaled deeply. Was the all-business Mrs. Chandler wearing perfume? He wasn't sure. He said, "Okay. You left here at five o'clock, yesterday morning. That was Wednesday."

"Right."

"In whose car?"

"Double Bee company car. Actually a rental."

"Mr. Crump was with you."

"Right."

"Why didn't he just meet you there? The insurance file has him on the list of covered people. It indicates that he lives in San Jose."

"Holy City."

"What?"

"Some real estate developer's nutty notion. Lawton Crump lives in Holy City. On Call of the Wild Road, no less."

Lindsey tried not to laugh and nearly coughed up his pink glazed donut. "I thought developers named new streets after their wives or daughters. Rhoda Road, Della Street and Lois Lane. At least this guy was original. Okay. Still, Crump would have to drive all the way *up* from San Jose or Holy City or wherever and then ride all the way *back* to the airport with you. Why not just meet at the airport?"

Mrs. Chandler exhaled, sounding exasperated. "He stayed here at the hotel the night before. Are you trying to stave off an insurance claim or pry into people's personal lives? It's Lawton's business where he spent Wednesday night, not yours."

The conversation was going nowhere. "When will you know if the planes are on time?" Lindsey asked.

"They'll be in constant communication with ground controllers all along their flight path. This isn't any routine trip, you know."

"I know," Lindsey said, and asked, "Where's Mr. Crump now?"

"Back in Holy City. Sorry to disappoint your prurient interest. If that's what it is. Nesting with Mrs. Crump, his Nellie, his bride and the companion of his life for the past forty-odd years. As he never misses a chance to remind me."

Lindsey picked up his attaché case and set it on his lap. Before he rose to go he asked, "Mrs. Chandler, do you have any theory? Any idea that you think might be of help in this matter?"

She looked up at him, leaning forward so that her plaid shirt buckled. "Back to playing Sherlock Holmes?"

"I guess you don't."

On his way out of the suite, Lindsey stopped for a good look at the *Bessie Blue* logo on one young functionary's jacket. "I guess that's Bessie Blue herself, right? Was that her name?" Lindsey asked.

The young person, a vaguely androgynous individual who was really quite pretty if she was female, said, "Not the foggiest." The voice was also of indeterminate gender.

Nine

LINDSEY PHONED LAWTON CRUMP'S HOUSE from the lobby of the Parc Oakland. Mrs. Crump answered the phone and insisted on knowing Lindsey's identity and business before she would put him through to her husband.

When Crump took the call he said, "You'll forgive my wife. She gets protective. And after what happened to that poor fellow at the airport, I'm afraid I've been a little bit upset myself."

"I understand. If I could have just a bit of your time, though . . . " He left it there.

"All right. I presume you have credentials to prove your bona fides?"

"Of course."

It was a relief to drive from Oakland to San Jose when it wasn't rush hour. The freeway passed between the Coliseum and the airport and the image of a bomber heading for the stadium and crashing into a deck full of spectators flashed through Lindsey's mind. He shook away the image and steered the Hyundai between a roaring chemical truck and a bright-red Dodge Shadow. He thought about trading in the Hyundai.

Holy City was southeast of downtown San Jose. Lindsey had a harder time finding it than he had expected. Holy City was a development of split-level homes. The houses stood on large lots. The newly planted trees wouldn't provide any shade or beauty or support children's swings for decades. Either the homesteaders planned to live a long time or they had faith in future generations.

Lindsey pulled into the driveway and parked behind a shiny

Jeep Grand Wagoneer and a dark-green Oldsmobile sedan. The sedan could have come straight from the showroom except for the traces of reddish dirt and the residue of oil that clung to the side.

The Crumps' lawn was immaculately edged and trimmed. An intricate pattern of red and yellow roses lined the front of the house. Lindsey felt a pang of guilt when he thought of his own casual landscaping in Walnut Creek.

The front door was painted Chinese red. Mrs. Crump opened the door for Lindsey. She wore a tan blouse and slacks, nearly the color of her skin. Her hair was only partly gray. She appeared to be close to her husband in age. But if they had been married for forty years, she would have to be.

She led Lindsey into the living room. It was furnished in teak. The couch and chairs were covered with dark-brown leather. There was a flagstone fireplace. The walls were of dark-stained, knotty wood. Old photos hung on the walls. Several were group portraits of uniformed men, many of them standing before World War II aircraft.

Lawton Crump was clad in khaki trousers and a patterned sweater. He wore an iron-gray moustache that extended beyond the edges of his mouth. At first Lindsey thought the pattern on his sweater was abstract then saw that it was a picture of clouds and birds. A picture of aerial peace.

Crump shook Lindsey's hand and offered him a seat. Lindsey had seen him at North Field being questioned with Mrs. Chandler, but they had not actually met. Crump waited patiently while Lindsey showed his International Surety credentials. "Don't mean to sound suspicious, but you can't be too careful," he said.

"You must be very excited about this film, Mr. Crump."

Mrs. Crump sat quietly, watching them.

"I was very excited. Underline *was*. Wednesday's incident has put a damper on it for me. Perhaps I'll regain my enthusiasm."

Lindsey tried to place Crump's accent and speech pattern. He sounded Southern, but not the way Ina Chandler sounded Southern. Maybe they were from different parts of the South, or maybe Southern blacks and Southern whites spoke differently. At least those of Crump's generation.

Lindsey tried to explain his involvement in the case. In fact, he wasn't quite certain himself of where he was headed. If he could clear up the McKinney killing and get *Bessie Blue* back on track he would save International Surety a lot of money, and that was his official task. Ina Chandler had hammered at him that he was not a cop, and she was right. But seeing Leroy McKinney flat on his back, the puddle of brains and blood in his forehead, the frightening claw of a hand upraised, and the old woodstove from another era, had had an effect on Lindsey.

Maybe Doc High was right. After you had seen enough corpses, maybe you took it in your stride. But Lindsey was not taking it in his stride. He had to resolve the case for the sake of his own peace of mind.

"Are they going to cover your whole life, Mr. Crump?"

"Not a chance. Film isn't really about me anyway. I'm just an exemplar." He grinned.

"You flew in the war, though. The Second World War."

"I most certainly did. Best thing that ever happened to me. Sounds terrible, doesn't it?" He didn't wait for an answer. "Going up into the air in 400-mile-an-hour machines to kill other men flying 400-mile-an-hour machines for the sake of my country and the honor of my race. Escorting other men in giant machines carrying iron eggs full of TNT to drop on cities, blow up factories and schools, and kill thousands of men and women and children. Very heroic."

"But if we hadn't—I mean, if *you* hadn't—you and all the others . . . Hitler would have won the war."

Crump nodded solemnly. "Don't get me wrong. It certainly was necessary. I'll never deny that. And it was good for me. Very good. Still . . . " He looked at the rug, his eyes shining.

Mrs. Crump stood up. "Would you like a cup of tea, Lawton? Mr. Lindsey?" She left the room.

Crump gestured toward the mantel. Over it hung a painting of a young black man in officer's gear *circa* 1945. A captain's twin silver bars glistened on his shoulders. His eyes were raised as if he was scanning the skies for approaching airplanes. He was standing in front of a bomber. Lindsey recognized it as a B-17. He wondered if it was the *Bessie Blue*.

"Recognize me? We were full of ourselves in those days, I'll tell you that. Soon as I could afford to, after the war, I had that painted. Artist used a photo for background. I posed for him in my old uniform. Didn't look so different then than I had in Europe. You wouldn't recognize me now, would you?"

"I think I would," Lindsey said.

"You're too kind."

Mrs. Crump returned with a tray. There was tea and there were little rounds of melba toast. It was a huge improvement over the food in the Double Bee suite at the Parc Oakland.

Lindsey took out a notebook and his gold International Surety pencil. "If you don't mind answering some questions, Mr. Crump . . . "

Crump shook his head. "If I weren't willing to answer questions, you wouldn't be in my house."

"Well, let's start with Wednesday and work backwards. Will that be all right?"

"I answered Sergeant Finnerty's questions on Wednesday."

"Yes, sir. Lieutenant High—he's Finnerty's boss—Lieutenant High and I have cooperated before. He's providing me information on this case. But if you don't mind, sir, I'd rather hear it directly from you. If you don't mind."

Crump nodded. Lindsey saw his eyes flash to the military portrait before he spoke. It reminded him of the way Latasha Greene's eyes had flashed to the silent TV screen at her home in Richmond. As if the here and now were unsatisfactory and unreal. As if there just might be a way out of here and into that other, better reality. But Crump was far more focused than Latasha had been.

"Mrs. Chandler's company is paying me quite well for my services as technical adviser. They wanted me at the airport early Wednesday, so I stayed in the Parc Oakland on Tuesday night. Mrs. Chandler and I drove out to the airport early Wednesday morning. She had a key to the hangar, but the door was open when we got there. I thought that was strange so I insisted on entering first."

70

Lindsey shot a questioning look at Crump.

"Call me old fashioned, but a gentleman places himself in harm's way to protect a lady."

Lindsey looked at Nellie Crump. She was listening intently.

"In I went. There was a fire going in that old wood stove. I called out, 'Anybody here? Anybody here?' "

He didn't pronounce the *r* in *here* and the word came out sounding like *he-ah*.

"I flicked on the lights. There was a switch near the door. The hangar was very dark. The wood stove gave very little light. Or heat, for that matter. The sun was just rising and the hangar was cold."

Lindsey nodded.

"There he was. Lying on his back. At first I thought he was just unconscious. Then I saw that his forehead was caved in. And I saw that claw, that deformed hand. The poor fellow. Just a janitor. He never had a chance."

"I want to make sure of this. You didn't know the victim, didn't recognize him at all?" Lindsey asked.

"Never laid eyes on him before that moment."

"All right. You'd breakfasted with Mrs. Chandler before leaving the Parc Oakland?"

"Restaurant wasn't open that early in the morning. Nor room service. We brewed up some instant java in the Double Bee suite. That was all the breakfast I had. After I saw the body, I didn't have an appetite."

"No." Lindsey crunched a melba round and washed it down with some excellent tea.

Crump walked across the room and leaned against the mantelpiece, unconsciously—or maybe not unconsciously, Lindsey thought—posing before the portrait of himself as he had been half a century ago.

"What else do you want to know?"

"Tell me about *Bessie Blue* and the Tuskegee Airmen."

Crump rubbed his chin between his thumb and forefinger. "How old are you, Lindsey?"

"I was born in 1953, sir."

"Huh. You wouldn't remember what it was like, then. I'm a child of the old South. Born in 1924."

"I understand. They had segregation back then." Lindsey was determined not to go into his relationship with Marvia Plum. Not at this point.

Crump's reserve slipped. "Segregation!" he roared. Nellie Crump jumped out of her seat and started forward, then settled back again. "Segregation was nothing! There were white schools and black schools. So what? I'm talking about lynchings, sonny boy! Blacks hauled out of their beds in the middle of the night. Shot, hanged, burned at the stake! You don't know about that, do you? Black women at the mercy of white men. My mother used to make herself look stooped and ugly, so white men wouldn't want her. Many of our beautiful women did that in those days. Negro families were broken apart by stresses you could not comprehend. Institutions were wrecked or nipped in the bud to prevent their development."

He turned and stared at his younger self, posed heroically before the warplane. "Segregation was nothing. Eleanor Roosevelt could deal with segregation. She knew nothing of lynchings."

"But Tuskegee. The Air Corps," Lindsey said.

Crump strode back and picked up his tea cup. The act seemed to calm him. "Air Force, sir. United States Army Air Force! Let's get the designation right. The former U.S. Army Air Corps became the Air Force on 20 June 1941, well before I entered the service."

"Air Force. Yes, sir." The old man was picky.

"Even the Air Force wasn't colorblind. That was why our units were entirely Negro at the lower ranks. The higher you rose, the more white faces you encountered. You know what else they did? Any Negro soldier who could fight. I mean with his fists . . . " He held up his hands. They were heavy, strong, callused. Even at his age, Lawton Crump looked like a man who could hit like a pile driver.

"They summoned an assembly of Negro recruits and told us they were going to put the real fighters into a ring. We were to have a free-for-all. Tear each other to bits, they didn't care.

They'd be all the happier for it. Last surviving man to get fifty dollars and a weekend pass. The rest would be confined to barracks."

Lindsey went pop-eyed. Every time he thought he had seen or heard everything, he discovered there was more to learn.

"What did you do?"

"I would have no part of it. Some of the others did. With the carrot and the stick, Mr. Lindsey, you can get people to do anything."

Lindsey nodded. "My friend Eric Coffman—my lawyer— talks about Jewish prisoners working in the crematoriums at Auschwitz. They knew that they would be murdered eventually, but they could get another day of life that way. And another. Maybe they were hoping that the war would end and they'd still be alive."

"But we made it," Crump said. "We had our own leaders, our own heroes. And we finally got our own commander. Did you ever hear of General Benjamin O. Davis? A great man. First Negro general in the U.S. Army. And his son, Benjamin O. Davis, Junior. One of our first Negro pilots. He was a captain when he received his wings, Mr. Lindsey. By the time I knew him, he was a major. In time, he, too, won his stars. I worshipped that man. I would have flown into the jaws of hell for him!"

Crump's face had a faraway look. Then he shook his head and said, "Let us turn to a cheerier subject than war. I always loved airplanes. A fellow in our town owned a little puddle-jumper. You wouldn't remember, but aviation was a very different matter back then. No jets, no radar, everything was smaller in scale. And it was informal. Very informal."

He smiled. "I used to hang around this fellow's place. He kept the plane in an old barn. Flew out of a pasture. It was an old Consolidated PT-1. PT for Primary Trainer. He maintained the plane himself. He'd flown in the first war and he knew everything there was to know about flying machines. He let me hang around and watch him, hand him tools, run errands."

"Black?"

"What?"

"Was he a black man?"

"No, sir. He was a white man. Where would a Louisiana black get an airplane in 1930? I worked for that man for twelve years. Started when I was six years old. Worked for him 'til 1942. I learned how to maintain that airplane. I doped the fabric, tuned the engine, changed propellers, repaired the landing gear when it got banged up. Which it did frequently, believe me, landing and taking off from a pasture."

After a deep breath, he announced, "And I learned to fly. That man never paid me a nickel, but I became an airplane mechanic and I learned how to fly. He never charged me anything for the lessons, so I guess I got a pretty good deal."

Nellie Crump refilled their tea cups. Lindsey wondered how many times she had heard her husband's story and whether she was proudly reliving those days with him or just being polite.

"Came the war," Crump resumed, "everything changed. People going into the service, people moving to the North and West to work in factories. Everything changed. Everybody had to register for the draft. Most of the boys in town wound up going to boot camp as buck privates. Couple of them thought they'd outsmart the system and went and joined the Navy instead. Didn't do them much good."

The house was silent for a moment. So silent that Lindsey could hear the sound of a skateboard competition outside on Call of the Wild Road.

"Mr. Wagner—that was my mentor's name, and I never called him anything but Mr. Wagner in all the years I knew him—he went to bat for me. Took me up to Baton Rouge . . . "

"Baton Rouge?"

"I didn't tell you? My home town was Reserve, Louisiana. Still there. But you'll need a good map to find it. Wagner took me up to Baton Rouge, talked to an Army Air Force recruiter. They were starting the Tuskegee Program, and Mr. Wagner got me into it." He nodded.

"Yes, sir. Tuskegee, Alabama. Some of those Negroes from the North, they didn't like going down South to train. Conditions were not ideal. Not much to do on base and less off. Most of our officers were black, though, which was a novelty. The higher you went, the smaller the percentage. But still, we learned that we could rise. They were delighted with me. I had to learn to use modern aircraft, of course, but they still thought I was hot. Here I was a qualified mechanic, and I also knew how to fly a plane! Didn't have a pilot's license, but I could take a trainer up. We used PT-17s, Stearmans. Good, sturdy little biplanes. There are still a few of them around. I could take a ship up, fly around, bring her back and land her. That put me way, way ahead of the game."

"I can imagine," Lindsey said.

"It was truly wonderful. We went on to Texans. Those were the advanced trainers that we used. Sleek, metal-bodied monoplanes. Sweet aircraft. And after that, why, after that we moved on to fighters so we could travel to North Africa and thence to Europe. We were trained to become useful. We learned how to kill people."

Ten

LINDSEY LEFT HOLY CITY FULL of war stories. Talking to Lawton Crump—or rather, listening to Lawton Crump talk and asking him an occasional question—was like spending the morning in a time warp. It was wonderful yet disquieting. Was Crump another sad temporal nomad, a man whose glory days were long gone and whose present and future must be lived in the ever-fading glow of the receding past?

A late spring storm had moved into Northern California and gusts of cold wind swept sheets of rain across the freeway. The Hyundai's windshield wipers struggled to hold the water in check.

Lindsey got back to the office with his head still buzzing. He wrote up a progress report and faxed it to Richelieu in Denver. Ms. Wilbur and Elmer Mueller were both in the office, pointedly ignoring each other. No doubt about it, the old order was on its way out.

Even after writing up his notes and faxing his report to Denver, he had trouble concentrating. He phoned Doc High's office and got Sergeant Finnerty. Finnerty had some information for him. The crime scene unit and the forensics gang had worked over the North Field hangar and had learned a couple of things.

First, the monkey wrench with which Leroy McKinney had been killed was smeared with dirt and grease. Whoever had committed the crime had seen to it that no useful fingerprints remained.

Second, the team had analyzed the contents of the woodstove and had found wood and paper ash, some bits of metal that turned out to be staples or paper clips, a few lumps of a sticky, gummy substance, and charred shreds of heavy fabric that had barely survived incineration.

After due deliberation, Forensics had determined that the gummy substance was rubber that had been tossed into the flames, had melted and partially burned. Some of the residue had survived and recongealed, producing the blackened sludge.

"Rubber?" Lindsey asked. "As in condoms? You think there was some hanky-panky out there? Maybe the poor guy had a girlfriend. That could be important. That could be a major break."

"No such luck. I thought of that too, but it was the wrong kind of rubber. As in rubber gloves."

Lindsey grunted.

"Yeah. Looks like the killer really knew what he was doing. Put on a pair of gloves, picked up the wrench and brained poor McKinney. Messed up the wrench, printwise. Dropped the weapon and burned up the gloves. Smart. You know what else we found?"

"What?"

"There were some blue smudges on the stove. On the door, just below the handle."

"I don't get it," Lindsey said.

"The killer didn't want to leave prints on the stove, especially after being so careful not to leave prints on the wrench. So he used a ball-point pen to open and close the stove. We could try and analyze the ink and trace it that way, but there are hundreds of millions of ball-point pens around and I don't think we'd have a chance. Although it's up to Lieutenant High," Finnerty said.

"Huh." Lindsey pursed his lips.

"Listen, Mr. Lindsey, can I tell you something? Strictly off the record?" Finnerty asked.

"Sure," Lindsey said.

"If you think you have a shot at unraveling this mess, I think you ought to go for it. We'll cheer. We'll help as much as we can. But frankly, sir, just between you and me and the baseboard, I don't think OPD is going to do much more on this case."

"Why not?" Lindsey asked.

"We only have less than a dozen investigators in this department. And this is a boom year for homicides in this town. I mean, just look at your morning paper. There's a big drug war going on. They're bringing 'em in in droves. If this was a baseball team, we'd be winning the pennant. Doubles and triples every day. Yesterday we set a record. A triple and four singles."

He must have been looking at a report on his desk. He muttered, "Jesus. Seven."

"I understand." Lindsey said. "It's terrible. But . . . "

"So we're about ready to write off McKinney as an isolated incident," Finnerty said. "We'll put the folder in the permanent open file and see if anything comes to us. Sometimes you'll get a confession or an implication from some guy in a plea bargain. Can be years later. We never give up on a murder. But I don't think we're going to put much more manpower into this one. That's off the record, Mr. Lindsey. All right, sir?"

"No, I'm not so sure that it's all right at all. Maybe I ought to take this up with Lieutenant High," Lindsey said.

Finnerty hesitated. "Actually, sir, it was Lieutenant High who told me this."

Lindsey phoned Marvia Plum's office and got a voicemail greeting. He asked her to call him back.

He wanted to talk this thing over, talk it out with someone he trusted. Mother wouldn't be able to handle it, and he wouldn't know where to start with her. Eric Coffman was a possibility. He tried Coffman's office, but Eric was in Sacramento representing a client at a state commission meeting and wouldn't be back until late tonight. Ms. Wilbur might understand, but the office tension was too severe to bother her. And, of course, Elmer Mueller was out of the question.

Lindsey went home and found Mother preparing dinner and watching TV at the same time. An old movie, *The Las Vegas Story*, starring Victor Mature and Jane Russell was just starting. Mother pointed at the studio logo, a huge radio tower beaming out signals from what looked to be the top of the world. "You see that little building, right there underneath the tower?"

Lindsey did.

"I always wondered who lived in that little building. It's right at the North Pole. I used to think Santa Claus lived there. Then I thought maybe your father was there and that he'd come back to us in the little airplane."

"Little airplane?" Lindsey asked. He wasn't paying much attention, still distracted and only half following the dialogue.

"Oh, that's at the beginning of those other pictures. Lots of those old movies have that little airplane flying around the world at the beginning. I thought maybe the little airplane would bring your father home from the little building at the North Pole."

Lindsey couldn't think of anything to say.

"But I don't think so any more," Mother said. "I think they're just toys or models or something. I don't think your father is there. Poor Hobo. Your father is dead, you know. He's been dead a very long time."

Lindsey held Mother's hand until she pulled it away and concentrated on the task of preparing dinner. "You can turn that off, if you want to," she said. "I'm busy with dinner."

What a difference. Lindsey was grateful. For years it had been a losing battle with Mother, one step forward and two steps back, as she wandered slowly but steadily deeper into her mental maze, seldom knowing what year it was, seldom knowing what world it was. But lately it had been two steps forward and one back. She still had her bad days, still slipped now and then, but her direction was toward reality, toward the present. If Lindsey had believed in miracles, he would have called this one.

Not that the meal was great, but Mother had made it from scratch and served it, something she was increasingly capable of doing. Afterward, Lindsey helped her clean up and settled her in the living room. She was reading a copy of *Newsweek* from April 1973, paying more attention to the ads than the articles.

After his meeting with Lawton Crump, Lindsey could understand Mother's condition a little better. His own mind was filled with images of Mustangs and Thunderbolts, Messerschmitts and Focke-Wulfs. He hadn't lost his grip on time. He knew what year it was, and he knew that World War II had been fought half a century before.

But the images that Crump had conjured up for him were so vivid and the sense of place and time so powerful that it seemed more real than reality. It wasn't like watching *Twelve O'Clock High*. It was like being six miles above the ground in a machine that could annihilate an enemy or carry its own pilot to his death, all at the whim of fate.

His reverie was interrupted by the telephone. Marvia had gone directly from work to her parents' house on Bonita Street in Berkeley. She had eaten with her parents and her son, Jamie, and then headed home.

Lindsey told her about his day, about visiting Mrs. Chandler at the Parc Oakland and Lawton Crump in Holy City. He asked if he could come to Oxford Street and talk it over with her.

"You white boys are all the same. You just want to get laid, don't you? Y'all think ah's easy jes' 'cuz ah's black?"

"No!" he said angrily.

"Bart, you have to learn to take a joke," she laughed.

"I'm sorry. I just wanted to talk," he said.

"Oh, so now I'm losing my appeal. I should have known. Once they have their way with you, they toss you aside and go on to other conquests."

"Give me forty, forty-five minutes."

"I'll put a candle in the window."

It was raining steadily, and he drove carefully. Still, he was there in thirty-five minutes.

She was wearing a lacy outfit that looked like Rita Hayworth's nightgown in the famous World War II pinup. Music was playing softly. "That's really nice," Lindsey said. "What is it?"

"That's Sonny Rollins. An old Jerry Kern tune."

"Sonny. Sounds talented for a kid."

Marvia laughed. "That's just what they call him. He's one of my great passions, so I looked him up. He was born in 1929.

Just a few days before the Stock Market crashed. Welcome to the world, Sonny.''

He put his arms around her and gave her a long kiss. He kicked the door of her apartment shut behind him. He was turning into a regular Lothario.

They lay together listening to the music until the CD ended. The rain slashed against the windows. ''What about this case of yours, that you're so excited about?'' Marvia asked.

''It's the man who found the body that interests me. An old-time fighter pilot. He found the body in a hangar out at North Field at Oakland Airport. He lives in Holy City, near San Jose. I spent part of today with him.''

Marvia waited for Lindsey to continue.

''I don't know if this is even going to tell me anything about the murder. I'm trying to understand the dead man, too. I visited his granddaughter yesterday, up in Richmond. But this old pilot, Lawton Crump. Did you ever hear of the Tuskegee Airmen?''

''Teach your grandma to suck eggs,'' Marvia said.

Lindsey laughed. ''Sorry. He told me about going up to Tuskegee. He was from Louisiana. How they trained him, sent him over to fight. He flew fighters in North Africa. Said it was really an experience, seeing Africa with his own eyes. He expected to see jungles and mountains and waterfalls, all the Tarzan stuff. Instead, all he saw was deserts and Arabs.''

Marvia put her hand on his chest and rubbed gently.

''Then he was moved up to Italy and flew ground support and escorted bombers into Germany. Some of his friends were killed. Some were shot down, and he saw them again after the war. I asked him how many German planes he shot down, but he wasn't sure. Three or four, he said. You know what else he told me?''

She waited for him to continue.

''He said, 'Back then I thought of them as 109s and 190s. When I got older, I thought of them as men I'd killed. I used to dream. At first I dreamed about airplanes and knocking them down. Then I started dreaming about the pilots.' ''

"That was a long time ago. What did he do with the rest of his life?" Marvia asked.

"He told me that after the war he went back to Reserve, Louisiana, because that was home. His mother was still there. He had a brother, too. His brother was in the Navy. But he couldn't stay in the South. He wanted to keep flying, but he was pushed out of the Air Force and none of the airlines would hire him."

"I know."

"But he got a job as mechanic. First he went to college under the GI Bill, then he got a job as an airline mechanic. He worked for Pan Am. He worked for them for the next forty years or so. Worked on everything from the old DC-4s to 747s. Wound up as a bigshot in their maintenance operation at SFO. They kept trying to retire him, but he wouldn't go. When he was finally ready to retire, you know what happened? Company went belly up! Some fun."

"And now he's going to be a movie star."

"Well, almost."

"How did he react to finding the body?" Marvia asked.

"It was really hard to tell. He seemed, well, uncomfortable talking about it."

"Don't blame him."

"No. But he was upset. He told me he'd lost his enthusiasm for the movie. For *Bessie Blue*. Oh, that was another thing. I asked him what that meant. He said that they named a B-17 after Bessie Smith. You remember, you were playing that music of hers for me. They didn't want to just call the airplane *Bessie Smith*. They thought that was too plain, so they called it *Bessie Blue*."

Marvia had snuggled her head into the crook of his shoulder and was running her fingers down his belly. He rubbed her head. He loved the feel of her short-cropped hair against the palm of his hand. "I'm really lucky, Marvia. I'm amazed. I don't see what you see in me."

She spoke with her lips against the side of his neck. "I'll tell you some time."

82

Eleven

SATURDAY. SITTING IN MARVIA PLUM'S BED, he phoned Mother. She was puttering happily around the house. She wasn't zoned out in front of the TV. She was reading this morning's Contra Costa *Times*. Of course she would be all right, she said, she had a lot of things to do. She didn't need him at home.

A miracle.

Marvia pulled back the curtains. The storm had passed, although another could follow bringing desperately needed rain from over the Pacific. Perhaps the storm had drenched the *Abraham Lincoln* and kept her jets and choppers stowed on the hangar deck, Lindsey thought. What if the denizens of sunken Mu decided to surface and take over the world? It was something to worry about, but for now the sky over California was a sparkling blue.

Lindsey phoned the Parc Oakland and reached Ina Chandler at the Double Bee suite. She told him that the air fleet had left Dallas–Fort Worth Airport, the Flying Fortress first and then the smaller, faster planes: a twin-boomed Lightning, a rare mid-engine Airacobra, a stubby Thunderbolt, a sleek Warhawk, and the king of fighter aircraft, the Rolls-Royce powered Mustang.

The problems over the illegally imported animals would take time to resolve, but the flight was going without a hitch. The Feds had not stopped the Knights of the Air from taking off, which was all that Mrs. Chandler seemed to care about.

The Flying Fortress had been designated *Bessie Blue*. Lindsey asked Ina Chandler if it was the original *Bessie* or simply another B-17 decorated for the movie. Mrs. Chandler was in an expansive mood, obviously relieved that the flight had finally got under way. The Knights of the Air insisted that the bomber was the original, she said, and she was ready to take their word. Besides, Lawton Crump's imprimatur on the production was all that mattered.

The B-17 was carrying a flight crew of Knights of the Air and a film crew from Double Bee. She had landed for refueling at Sky Harbor in Phoenix even though, in theory, *Bessie* had enough range to fly nonstop from Dallas to Oakland and back.

Double Bee had alerted the media along the way, and newspapers and TV stations had sent camera crews up in helicopters to escort *Bessie Blue* and the fighters into Sky Harbor. The airport was crowded with aviation buffs and curiosity seekers. There were interviews and photo-ops. CNN was there. *USA Today* was there. It was a press agent's dream.

The fleet was expected at Oakland's North Field by mid-afternoon. Double Bee would film the whole event. In addition to the camera crew aboard *Bessie Blue*, the old camera mounts in the fighter planes had been refitted with modern gear and the pilots had been rehearsed in taking footage during the flight.

Lindsey ran his hand along Marvia's leg. "I think I'd better be there, Mrs. Chandler."

Mrs. Chandler didn't object.

"I hope it's all right if I bring a homicide officer with me," Lindsey said.

"Lieutenant High already knows about this. I expect he'll be there. I'm heading out to the airport myself, in a few minutes," she said.

"What about Mr. Crump? He going to be there?"

"You bet."

"Okay. I'll see you at the airport." He hung up the telephone and turned to Marvia. "This is your day off, right?"

"Am I wearing my uniform?"

"Want to see the air show?" She was wearing a midnight blue nightgown with spaghetti shoulder straps. He was toying with one of the straps.

"Later," she said.

Later he reminded her.

Still later she said, "Jamie would love it. Could we bring him?"

They took the Hyundai; it had more room than the Mustang. Jamie had never been in it before. Lindsey asked if he approved. "Better than Uncle Tyrone's taxi," Jamie said.

Double Bee had closed off the hangar and runway area at North Field. Lindsey flashed his International Surety credentials to get them in. Marvia didn't use her sergeant's badge. This was Oakland and she was Berkeley. And she was unofficial today.

The Double Bee crew seemed to have multiplied. Cameras on tripods, handheld cameras, lights, sound booms were everywhere. Why did they need lights in broad daylight? And what chance did even directional mikes have of picking up approaching airplanes?

Lindsey spotted Ina Chandler surrounded by a flock of earnest teenagers—that was what they looked like—earnest teenagers with clipboards and walkie-talkies.

The field might have been closed to the public, but several hundred aviation buffs had found ways to get in. The battery-powered camcorders outnumbered the professional cameras. Few of the spectators looked old enough to remember World War II no less to have fought in it. Lindsey had an insurance man's eye. He pegged them as mostly upper middle income, mostly professional and mostly thirty to forty-five. A few affluent retirees. A few scruffy machinery lovers whose taste ran more toward the skies than the freeway.

The professionals bustled around, while the spectators buzzed and swayed with expectancy. Every distant droning, every bright reflection in the sky, caused a stir.

"Mr. Lindsey!" He whirled. There was Lawton Crump, but no sign of Nellie. Lawton wore a leather jacket, bomber style, and khaki trousers. A white baseball cap with the *Bessie Blue* logo on its front panel was cocked rakishly over his ear. Lindsey wondered how long it would take the cap to develop fifty-mission crush.

Marvia looked at Lindsey. "That's Mr. Crump, the man I

told you about." Crump seemed to be waiting for Lindsey to respond. "Want to meet him?" Lindsey asked Marvia.

"Love it. And Jamie would, too." Jamie was holding her other hand, watching the crowd with suspicion.

Lindsey introduced them. "Marvia Plum. Jamie Wilkerson, Junior. Mr. Lawton Crump."

The older man looked at Lindsey, then at Marvia, then at Jamie. He shook hands with Marvia and muttered, "How do you do." Then he squatted in front of Jamie and stuck out his hand. Jamie shook hands solemnly with Lawton Crump.

"How do you do, sir."

"A pleasure, young man."

Jamie pressed against Marvia's leg, holding onto a belt loop with his free hand.

"Fine boy. Wilkerson," Crump said.

"My ex," Marvia said.

"Ah," Crump said.

"We thought Jamie should learn something about the Tuskegee Airmen." Marvia had said as much in her apartment.

Crump nodded. "Well, young man, this was all a long time ago. Half a century ago. Before you were born." He looked at Marvia. "Before your mother was born, young fellow."

Lindsey thought he saw a question in Lawton Crump's eyes.

"Yes, that's right," Marvia said.

Crump started to tell Jamie about the Airmen. At about the point in the story where young Lieutenant Crump saw his first Arab on a camel, a rustle went through the crowd, then a wave of pointing hands. Crump stood up, but Jamie had already transferred his free hand to Crump's. Lindsey saw a broad smile on the old man's face.

"Mrs. Crump and I were never blessed with issue," he said softly. He seemed to direct the statement to Marvia, but Lindsey caught it as well.

Like spectators at a tennis match, the crowd swung to the right. If the air fleet had assembled over San Jose as planned, it would most likely have headed northwest to pass over San Francisco. That would provide more spectacular footage for the media. A B-17 winging over the Transamerica Pyramid, a formation of glistening fighter planes circling above Coit Tower.

Like the work of some 1930's muralist, caught by the spirit of Futurism, capturing images for generations to come.

They would cross the bay and come in over water to approach the airport.

A flash of sunlight bounced from the fleet's aluminum and Plexiglas as it approached, and the crowd cheered like spectators at a baseball game.

The B-17 appeared first. It was the largest plane in the fleet, four engines to the one or two of the others. The fighters boxed the B-17, above and below, in front and behind, starboard and port.

As the airplanes passed over the runway the formation spread out. The planes swung away, then approached a second time, then a third. The cameras whirred, the spectators gaped.

Lindsey watched Crump and Jamie. Crump's eyes were fixed on the *Bessie Blue*. His jaw trembled and a tear fell.

Jamie's mouth was open and his eyes were huge.

Marvia ignored the airplanes, watching her son. Lindsey put his hand on her shoulder. She moved closer.

The flight circled the field again. On this approach, the B-17 touched down, its wheels sending up clouds of dust as they hit the tarmac. The fighters swooped away.

The engines' roar was not what Lindsey anticipated. He knew that the piston engines' sound would be different from the whoosh of jets, but it wasn't at all like the engine sounds Lindsey had heard in dozens of old movies.

A cold shiver ran through him. Betrayed by video!

The B-17 slowed, then veered ponderously to the edge of the runway, and rolled to a stop. A hatch opened in the lower fuselage and the pilot dropped to the ground. He turned toward the nearest camera crew and waved. He wore a leather jacket, helmet and flight gloves. His goggles were pulled over his eyes. Lindsey wondered why he needed the goggles in a closed cockpit. It was hard to tell at this distance, but Lindsey was pretty sure that the pilot was white.

"That's where we cut to footage of Mr. Crump."

Lindsey whirled. Ina Chandler was scurrying by. She winked at him. "Oh, right," he said.

Lawton Crump pulled a handkerchief from his pocket and wiped his eyes. He grinned proudly at the *Bessie Blue,* then smiled down at Jamie Wilkerson and then back at the bomber. Jamie's mouth was still gaping open and his eyes were bigger than ever. If that was possible.

Crump bent and lifted Jamie so their faces were on the same level. Marvia looked happy. Crump pointed and Jamie followed his gesture.

The fighters were approaching the runway, still in formation.

During the first pass of the fighters, a P-40 Warhawk touched down. A tiger's mouth and ferocious teeth were painted on its engine cowling. The pilot pulled the plane into a turn, revved the engine once and then cut it. He—no, she—bounded from the cockpit, waved cheerily to a camera, and slipped gracefully to the ground.

Jamie cringed at the roar of the engine but otherwise remained awestruck by the show. There were a number of children who looked equally enthralled among the spectators.

On the next pass, the P-39 Airacobra set down on its tall, tripod-like landing gear. Crump offered a running commentary on the aircraft, gesturing as best he could without setting Jamie back on the ground.

The twin-boomed P-38 Lightning drew the biggest gasp of admiration, the massive P-47 Thunderbolt made the most impressive roar, the sleek P-51 Mustang drew a round of applause. Once the impromptu fighter squadron had landed, the remaining planes in the flotilla followed. Seeing German and Japanese fighters marked with World War II insignia gave Lindsey a sickness in the belly.

Lieutenant High touched Lindsey on the shoulder. "Returning to the scene of the crime, Lindsey?"

"Uh, no. I, uh, Doc, you know, ah, Sergeant Plum, Berkeley PD?"

High shook hands with Marvia. "I've had the pleasure. Tried to romance her over to Oakland, but she won't budge. Loves the hippies and the wonderful community support that the City Council provides over there.''

"Yes, and if I ever decide to leave Berkeley, I thought I might get work as a prison guard," Marvia said.

High's eyebrows flew up.

"On Devil's Island."

"Very funny."

"But if they turned me down, I might think of Oakland."

"In all seriousness, we're in a budget squeeze but I could always swing an opening for someone with your talent, Sergeant Plum," High said.

"I appreciate the offer," Marvia said.

"Not really an offer. Bad policy to poach."

"Right."

"But just in case you ever think about making a move . . . ''

"Right."

High turned to Crump. "See you've made a new friend there."

Crump grinned. "What a boy. I think he's learned a lot about these planes already. Absorbed everything I've told him." He handed Jamie to Marvia. She lowered him to the ground.

"He's too big for me to carry around anymore."

"I understand. My pleasure," Crump said.

"You were proud of your service, weren't you Mr. Crump?"

Crump smiled. "May I call you Marvia?" She nodded. "Marvia, those were my salad days. They were the best of times and they were the worst of times. But, chiefly, they were the best of times."

Twelve

THE DAY'S FILMING ENDED BEFORE SUNDOWN, and a chosen few were permitted onto the field to inspect the airplanes. Lindsey recognized the TV crews and the newspaper professionals by their gear and nonchalance.

Another half-dozen amateurs were included in the group, each clutching a camcorder or still camera. They raced to the aircraft, jockeyed for position, scurried from plane to plane like a nest of ants confused by the sudden arrival of a honey rainstorm.

Ina Chandler appeared and put her hand on Crump's arm. "You're welcome on the field, Lawton. We'll have you set up for press interviews in a little while."

"I'll try and give 'em what they need. Now, I think I'll go take a peep. I want to see if that's really *Bessie* or just a reasonable facsimile."

"Does it really matter? The Texas people swear it's an authentic B-17F."

"It is that. See those little cheek emplacements near the nose? And the clean bottom, no chin turret. That would be a dead giveaway of a G model. And the gun windows on the fuselage. It's an F all right. But is it really *Bessie*? Does it matter? Just sentiment, I suppose." Crump turned and said, "Marvia, may I take young Jamie for a look see?"

Jamie was clutching Crump's hand as if he were Santa Claus. "Of course."

They headed across the tarmac.

"What do you think of Mr. Crump?" Lindsey asked.

"We need more heroes," she said. "Kids like Jamie especially need more heroes." She held Lindsey. "Bart, I've been keeping something from you." Without pausing for breath, she said, "Jamie's dad called me."

"Captain Wilkerson?"

"Major now. He was in Desert Storm then helped plan for the Somalia relief mission. He was into aviation when we were in Germany, and now he's a helicopter pilot. He did something special at the battle of Basra. I don't know what, but he got a medal for it and a parade, the whole thing. A hero. You must have seen it on the news. Personal handshake from Colin Powell. Who could ask for anything more."

"I think I saw that. I'm not sure. I forget so fast."

"Well, he got what he wanted. His career is taking off. Who knows what he's got his eye set on now. Maybe he wants to be President.

Lindsey couldn't figure out where Marvia was going with this. He decided to leave that to her. "Good for him. I don't see what it has to do with us, though."

"Well, he's coming out here."

Lindsey looked away. Crump and Jamie were standing beside the Flying Fortress. Crump was pointing at the *Bessie Blue* painting on the bomber's nose. He took off his baseball cap, adjusted the strap and put it on Jamie's head.

"James has remarried," Marvia said.

Lindsey realized he had been holding his breath. He let it out. "Then he doesn't want you back. I thought he wanted you back."

"He did, for a while. He got over it."

"Then what's he coming to California for?"

"Well, he has an excuse. He got interested in military aviation, American heritage, black heritage. He went out and learned how to fly some of the old warplanes. Claims he can fly a P-38, and he wants to watch them make this movie."

"He can't just stroll onto the set. Or the, what do they call it, the location. He can't just walk in like that," Lindsey said.

"He's a black aviator, a hero of the Gulf War. Don't tell me they'll turn him away. Not with press all over the place."

Lindsey grunted. "I guess it could make for a strained encounter. But we can get through it. Especially if he isn't trying to get you back."

Crump lifted Jamie in his arms. Jamie twisted and waved to Marvia. Lindsey could see his happy expression beneath the white cap's visor. Crump boosted Jamie into the airplane, then pulled himself in after the boy. He was a strong old guy, Lindsey thought, that he definitely was.

"He doesn't want me, not with another wife in his bed." Lindsey wondered if Marvia sounded bitter. "But he wants Jamie."

"He can't have him. He didn't want him when he was born. You told me that. All he wanted was to be rid of you both and get on with his career."

"Times change, Bart. And people change. He's Jamie's dad. And he's a successful African-American male, an Army officer, a decorated hero. Jamie needs a model. Living with his grandparents . . . "

"He's doing fine. Your parents are wonderful people. And you're a hero to him."

"I know, I know. But I have to think of my baby. My big boy. You don't know what it means to grow up like that. He's a black child with a single mother, living with his grandparents. Do you know the odds that he'll ever see age twenty-one? You know that the leading cause of death for black males under twenty-five in this state is murder? That drugs are second? And AIDS is gaining fast? I don't particularly want Jamie to be an Army brat. I've seen how those kids get shuttled around every couple of years. It's not a great life, but at least those children don't die like flies. I want my son to live."

She dragged Lindsey with her along the edge of the tarmac. They halted behind a temporary barrier. They could have crossed easily. Marvia and Lindsey had credentials and Ina Chandler wouldn't have stopped them. But they stayed behind the barrier.

Lindsey heard a child's voice. Jamie was halfway out the waist-gunner's window midway down the fuselage of the Flying Fortress. He was waving. He looked thrilled. Crump held him under both arms. There was no way Jamie would fall. Marvia Plum managed a wobbly smile and waved back at her son.

On the way back to Berkeley, Jamie played in the backseat of the Hyundai. His *Bessie Blue* baseball cap was pulled low on his forehead. From out of nowhere, Crump had produced a scale model B-17, complete with wartime insignia and *Bessie Blue* logo, and given it to Jamie. Maybe there was a secret stash of the models aboard the big airplane. Jamie was completely absorbed, flying the model through complicated maneuvers. He'd heard the piston engines of the air fleet just once but was doing a splendid job of imitating the sound.

Marvia looked over her shoulder, then turned back toward Lindsey. "I thought you'd want me to give Jamie to his dad. You know, then we could be married. If you still want that," she said in a quiet voice.

Lindsey ground his teeth. "I want that. But you mustn't give him up. He's your child."

The freeway curved past the grim walls of the fortress-like Oakland City Jail and swung northward along the Bay. Lindsey took the first Berkeley exit.

Marvia clutched his hand. "Thank you," she whispered. She pressed her head against his shoulder. He could feel her body. She shuddered.

"*Bessie Blue* to little friends, *Bessie Blue* to little friends, bogie at twelve o'clock high," Jamie yelled.

At Bonita Street, Marvia said, "I want to be with my parents and with Jamie tonight. You won't mind, Bart, please."

Lindsey drove back to Walnut Creek. When he arrived the house was empty. He checked every room, then stood in the foyer, confused. Before he could panic, he heard a key in the door. Mother entered. She held a bag of groceries in her arms.

"We needed a few things. Would you help me put them away? The young girl at the store was nice. You help me with this, little Hobo, and then I'll cook us dinner. Won't that be pleasant, just the two of us? I got your favorite kind of pasta and that Frank Sinatra sauce. It's so silly. You have to decide between Frank Sinatra spaghetti sauce and Paul Newman spaghetti sauce. If they're going to name spaghetti sauces after movie stars, shouldn't they be Anna Magnani or Sophia Loren?"

Lindsey took the bag and set it on the counter. He took his mother in his arms and rocked her.

A miracle.

It was a miracle.

He sat in his makeshift study with the *Bessie Blue* file, which Ms. Wilbur had carefully guarded and returned to him. He made notes and studied the documents. One thing about SPUDS, you didn't have to work from nine to five, Monday through Friday. No. Lucky SPUDS get to work all hours of the day and night, every day of the week.

He couldn't tell whether he was getting anywhere. He was learning plenty, but he didn't feel closer to an answer in the death of Leroy McKinney. His last conversation with Finnerty had indicated that the Oakland Police Department wasn't pursuing the case. They wouldn't close it out, but they weren't going to expend resources on it.

But Lindsey didn't answer to the police. He had to answer to International Surety and to his own conscience. His career might well rest on working this thing out. Surely, his peace of mind did.

Of course, Doc High had turned up at North Field to watch the Knights of the Air land their flotilla, so OPD hadn't totally quit the case. But Finnerty was right, Oakland was drowning in a sea of carnage. McKinney's death was just one of what would surely be hundreds before the end of the year. And it seemed unconnected to any other event.

The theory that McKinney was part of a smuggling ring—whether of cocaine or toucans—had fizzled. He probably wasn't the victim of a serial killer, or a casualty in a gang war. And the fact that he was an obscure janitor didn't do anything to bring attention to the case. He was no Marcus Foster or Huey Newton. No superintendent of schools—that killing had certainly got the attention of the police—and no headline-grabbing political activist. The newspapers and the TV stations had already forgotten about Leroy McKinney. Why shouldn't the OPD?

Lindsey put down the file. He stood up and stretched. Mother had retired for the night. The house and the street outside were quiet. On a night like this, a bedroom community for a city like San Francisco was little different from a suburb in Missouri or a small town in Connecticut.

He pulled on a warm jacket and went for a walk. He thought, *If I could marry Marvia, we'd have a dog and I'd take him for a walk late at night. He'd christen some bushes and we'd go home and I'd get undressed and climb in bed with Marvia and go to sleep.*

He thought, *I've got to do something about Leroy McKinney.* He had worked on two earlier cases involving murders and had played a major part in solving the killings. Two killers were behind bars now, thanks to him.

He thought, *I'm not a professional detective, but I'm pretty good at learning about people. If I can learn enough about Leroy McKinney, I might get somewhere with this case.*

He thought, *Understand the victim and you can understand the killer. Understand the killer and you'll know who he is.*

He stood in front of his house. The night was chilly. A fine, moist mist, half fog and half cloud, obscured the stars. The moon was bright enough to furnish some light, to make a glowing, fuzzy-edged blob in the sky.

Lindsey wished he had a dog.

He wished he had a wife.

He wished he had Marvia.

Sunday morning he took Mother to the market and she did a full-scale shopping for groceries. He gave her some cash and she handed the money to the cashier and counted her change and thanked the cashier and walked with Lindsey back to the car.

A miracle.

At noon he took some copies of the Leroy McKinney snapshot that he'd blown up from the Oakland *Trib* and drove to Richmond. He parked near Latasha Greene's house but he didn't climb her steps. He was looking for a new perspective on Leroy McKinney.

The streets were surprisingly empty for noontime on a bright spring Sunday. Maybe most of the neighborhood was still in church. He heard some of the bass thumping that passed for music, coming from a tavern. The sign outside the place announced that it was called Fuzzy's #3. He'd somehow missed Fuzzy's #1 and #2.

He took a deep breath and squared his shoulders. You entered Fuzzy's #3 through a pair of heavy swinging doors with thick panes of dirty glass shaped like half-moons. The doors were covered in heavily padded, faded red leatherette decorated with hammered-brass studs. Half the studs were missing and the other half had last been polished during the Truman versus Dewey campaign. If then. He pushed the doors open. Gary Cooper's spurs jingled as he strode into the Last Chance Saloon.

The darkness hit him first. While his eyes adjusted, he took in the sour odor and the music coming from an old-style jukebox. Inside Fuzzy's #3 the music was more complex than the rhythmic thumping he had heard from the sidewalk. There was a loud saxophone and there was some drums.

If the bartender was Fuzzy, he had taken the fuzz from his head and put it on his chin, a gray fuzz that spilled over his shirt collar. He leaned on the bar, talking with a couple of customers with half-empty glasses in front of them. Nobody paid any attention to the jukebox. Lindsey wondered why they bothered with the noise.

Half a dozen round-top tables stood unoccupied, each with a pair of unmatched chairs sitting upside down on top. The room was illuminated by neon beer signs mounted on the walls and against the backbar mirror.

There was a TV set above the bar. It looked like something out of the Lyndon Johnson era. It was silent and dark. Maybe they'd left it there as a memorial to the Great Society.

Lindsey stood near the bar, looking at Fuzzy and the customers. One of the customers wore a bandanna on his head. The other wore an old-fashioned porkpie hat.

Fuzzy pushed himself away from the bar and looked at Lindsey.

Lindsey felt overdressed in slacks and a tweed jacket, but at least he wasn't wearing a tie.

"What?" Fuzzy asked.

The two customers looked up from their drinks and observed Lindsey in the backbar mirror. Alerted by the bartender's response, they watched the world in that mirror with obviously practiced eyes.

Lindsey laid a copy of the Leroy McKinney photo on the bar. Fuzzy and the customers said nothing. Lindsey said, "This man was killed last Wednesday in Oakland."

Bandanna said, "Folks killed in Oakland all the time."

Lindsey laid an International Surety card on top of the photo. "I'm an insurance adjuster. My company may have some money to pay out in Mr. McKinney's death. But we need more data before we can act."

"Everybody knew Leroy. Not well. Didn't like people much. Kept to his self. Kept to his house. Didn't treat that granddaughter too nice," Fuzzy said.

Bandanna poked Porkpie Hat in the arm. "You know Leroy. You was buddies with Leroy."

Porkpie made eye contact with Lindsey in the mirror. Even at this distance his eyes were bloodshot and he looked as if he hadn't shaved for several days. From his odor, he'd probably been drinking right along.

"Can you tell me anything about Mr. McKinney? His background? His associations?" Lindsey asked.

"Maybe. I was one of his associations."

Lindsey waited for the man to continue.

"Hey, what's in it for me?" the man asked.

Lindsey picked up the photo and his card. He folded the photo and slipped it into his pocket.

Porkpie swung around on his stool angrily. "I told you I knew that man. I'll tell you a lot more, but it'll cost you. What can you pay me?"

"How about a round for the house?" Lindsey asked.

Fuzzy reached under the bar and pulled out a bottle. He filled the glasses to the rims before Lindsey could say anything. He held out his hand.

"How much for the drinks?"

"How much you got?" His voice was a growl.

Lindsey laid a twenty on the bar.

"Just right," Fuzzy said. He slipped the bill into his pocket. There was a cash register behind him.

"If that's all you got, I got nothing to say to you," Porkpie said.

"I have a little more cash. But if you provide useful information, International Surety will pay a lot more than I can give you," Lindsey said.

Porkpie took off his hat, wiped his face with a handkerchief and put the hat back on. He pulled it down to his ears. He picked up his drink and walked to one of the round-top tables. "Come on, insurance man," he said.

"Lindsey, Hobart Lindsey."

"Okay, Lindsey-Hobart-Lindsey. Make yourself useful." Porkpie removed one of the chairs and stood it on its feet. There was only one other chair on the table. Lindsey lifted it off, turned it over and stood it on its feet. It wobbled. He slipped into it.

Lindsey took his notebook out of his pocket and ran out the lead on his gold International Surety pencil. Might as well make this look good. Might get more out of Porkpie that way, he thought.

"This gonna cost you something, you know."

Lindsey lifted an eyebrow.

"You cross my palm with a double sawbuck and you pay for the refreshments both, or I lose interest and wander off."

Lindsey reached into his wallet and extracted a twenty. "That's right, isn't it?" Porkpie nodded and whisked the bill from Lindsey's fingers.

"Can I have your name, please, Mister . . . "

"Hasan Rahsaan Rasheed. You can call me Hasan or you can call me Rahsaan or you can call me Mister Rasheed, Lindsey-Hobart-Lindsey." To Lindsey's astonishment, Hasan fumbled through his pockets and came up with a crumpled sheet of notepaper and a stubby pencil. He wet the pencil-point with his tongue and laboriously wrote out a receipt and handed it to Lindsey. "There," he said. "You are dealing with an honest man, Lindsey-Hobart-Lindsey."

"Uh, why don't you just call me Bart," Lindsey said. "And I'll call you Hasan if you're certain all right. Is that your real name, Hasan Rahsaan Rasheed?"

"Course I'm certain. I wouldn't have said it if I wasn't certain. And that is indeed my name."

Lindsey jotted it down. "You knew Leroy McKinney?"

"For forty years." The word sounded like *foe-tea*. "Man and boy. Well, old man and young man. I'm not so young myself no more. But Leroy McKinney wasn't his real name."

Lindsey raised his eyebrows. "Really?" His pencil was poised.

"His name was Abu Shabazz."

"Abu Shabazz. Yes." He wrote that down. "How did you know him? His granddaughter said that he was in the Marine Corps in World War Two. Did you know him in the service?"

Hasan shook his head. He took a long drink from his glass, then he said, "No, I never knew him in service. I only knew him after the war." He tapped a fingernail against his nearly empty glass. "You keep this full, I'll keep talking. It go dry, so do my throat. I got a very bad problem with dry throat."

Lindsey waved to Fuzzy. Fuzzy brought the bottle over and refilled Hasan's glass. He looked at Lindsey. "You want anything?"

"Could I have some coffee?"

Fuzzy chuckled. "Sure." It sounded like *show*.

"Hasan, how did you meet, ah," he consulted his notebook, "Abu Shabazz?"

Hasan rubbed the back of one hand under his nose. "What Latasha tell you about Abu?"

"She said that he'd been a baseball player, then a hero in the Marine Corps, then a nightclub manager."

"Huh. Nightclub manager, Abu. Well, that's how I knowed him. How I first knowed him, before we was friends. Was after the war. Lot of Negroes moved up here during the war, you know. Come from the South. Georgia, Alabama, Mississippi, Louisiana."

Joe-ja, Abama, Missippi, Loozana.

"They was jobs here, lots of good jobs. I come from Missippi myself. Biloxi. I think Abu say he from Loozana. Some dinky little town, don't stop me, I'll call its name. Funny name for a town. Preserve, no Reserve, Loozana, that's it."

Lindsey almost jumped off his chair. Reserve, Louisiana. Lawton Crump was from Reserve, Louisiana. Leroy McKinney was from Reserve, Louisiana. And fifty years later and 3,000 miles away, Crump found McKinney's murdered body.

If Crump and McKinney had both been from Chicago or Atlanta, or from any big city, the odds would be more acceptable. But a speck on the map like Reserve, Louisiana?

Hasan was still talking. "We used to build ships right here in Richmond. That's what I did in the war. Builded ships. I was a welder and good at it. After the war, well, after the war the shipyards closed down. Some of us was lucky, got jobs for the Navy in San Francisco, in Vallejo, different places. Some of us got jobs in Alameda. Most of us didn't get no more jobs, not no good jobs, anyhow."

Lindsey nodded, but Hasan wasn't looking at him. He was looking into his glass. Lindsey wondered what he saw in the glass. Maybe whiskey. Maybe a window into the past.

More customers had wandered into Fuzzy's #3. Most of them sat on barstools. A few of them lifted chairs off the round-tops and settled onto the seats. Fuzzy's business was picking up. Lindsey felt eyes on him. He concentrated on his notebook and on Hasan Rahsaan Rasheed.

Lindsey said, "But Leroy McKinney, ah, Abu Shabazz, was not a shipbuilder. Or was he?"

"No way." Hasan shook his head. He tilted his glass. "After the war," pronouncing it *woe*, "most of those Negroes didn't want to go back. So a lot of clubs opened. Abu, he was a musician, you know. He was a piano player. But he hurt his hand in the war." *The woe.* "He tried to play, but he couldn't play no more." *No moe.* "But he didn't let it get him down. No way. He was a go-getter." *Go-gedda.* "He couldn't play no more, so he opened a club. He was the best. He had his own place, couple places, and he worked at some of the best."

Hasan paused.

Fuzzy refilled his glass. He held out his hand to Lindsey. Lindsey said, "Leave the bottle." They exchanged money for bottle.

Hasan smiled. "You all right, Lindsey-Hobart-Lindsey."

"Bart."

"Bart. You all right. I was a young blade then. You too young to know what a blade was. But I dressed sharp, talked smart. Dance like a snake. They called me Snake sometimes, I dance like one. Abu Shabazz, maybe they called him McKinney in the service but he came Abu Shabazz after. He worked at the Blackhawk, Hungry i, Jimbo's Bop City. I 'member Jimbo's Bop City. Not there no more. Long time gone, long time gone. Owned by Jim Edwards, but Abu he run the place."

The music from the jukebox stopped and in the distance Lindsey could hear a popping sound, a series of popping sounds, then the keening of sirens. He looked around. Most of Fuzzy's customers were men but a few were women. Fuzzy approached the table with a cup in his hand. He put it on the table and waited to be paid.

Lindsey said, "Is that—"

Fuzzy said, "Not in here."

Hasan Rahsaan Rasheed said, "Yeah, that Jimbo a good man. But Abu he my main man. Used to get me in there free. Introduce me to the musicians. They blew good music. And they had good stuff, always plenty of good stuff."

The popping sound came again. This time much closer and much louder. The half-moon glass in one of the doors of Fuzzy's #3 splintered. Someone fell against the door, swinging it open, and crashed to the floor. Lindsey flinched. The man thrashed around. Arterial blood spurted from a wound, spraying in all directions as the man writhed.

Lindsey heard sirens and then the screech of brakes. Blue-uniformed men and women crashed through the doors. The lead policeman bent from the waist and jammed a revolver against the skull of the man on the floor. The man stopped moving. The blood stopped spraying.

A second policeman—no, a policewoman—stood with her revolver drawn. She held it with two hands, the way they did on TV these days, swivelling from side to side, covering the population of Fuzzy's #3 like Joe Penny covering a gang of criminals on "Jake and the Fatman." Maybe she watched "Jake and the Fatman" every week, Lindsey thought. It had to be in reruns on some channel.

Fuzzy's customers placed their hands flat on their tables. The ones sitting at the bar turned and held their hands in the air. They had the bored look of people who'd been through all this before.

That was how Lindsey wound up sharing a jail cell with Hasan Rahsaan Rasheed.

Thirteen

LINDSEY HAD NEVER BEEN PUSHED against a wall and patted down before. He didn't like it. And he didn't like being locked up, either. It was only a holding cell and he had his own clothing—minus shoe laces and belt, just like in the movies. And he had a receipt for his wristwatch and his wallet and his pocket change and his keys. He had wanted to hold onto his pocket notebook and his gold International Surety pencil, but they took those too.

At first, on the way to Police Headquarters, Lindsey had tried to find out what was going on. The police officers were polite but firm. He'd find out shortly. Now keep still and keep quiet. He was handcuffed, with his hands behind his back, and of course as soon as he was in that predicament he had begun to itch everyplace he could no longer reach.

At headquarters, the group was told that somebody would be with them shortly. Lindsey tried again to ask what this was all about. Again he got nowhere. He asked for his phone call.

"That's a myth, you know. Everybody thinks he's entitled to a phone call," a police officer told him. "But we'll let you make one pretty soon. Probably. There's too much going on right now. Take a load off your feet. Relax. Your buddy seems to have the right idea."

Lindsey turned. Hasan Rahsaan Rasheed was sprawled on a cot, ankles crossed, fingers laced behind his head. His eyes were closed.

The police officer laughed and walked away.

Lindsey said, "You asleep, Hasan?"

Hasan opened one eye. He grinned. "Take a load off your feet, Lindsey-Hobart-Lindsey."

Yo' feece.

There was another cot in the cell, if you could call an iron rack hinged to the wall and held up by chains a cot. Lindsey lowered himself gingerly. "Hasan, you been through this before?"

"Many times, Lindsey. Many, many times."

"What happened back there? I don't understand. That man. The police. He was shot, wasn't he? Was he dead? Why were we arrested?"

Hasan said, "The walls have ears." He closed his eyes.

Lindsey stood up and paced around the cell. It was the size of a walk-in closet. It didn't take long to pace around it. He sat down on the cot once more. He counted to ten, started over and counted to 100. He looked at his watch but it wasn't there. He reached for his notebook but it also was gone.

He stood up and looked out the window. It was the size of a business envelope and the glass looked very thick and it was definitely very dirty. The window was far above his head. He could see the sky through it, and a couple of telephone wires.

He sat down.

Hasan said, "Relax, Bart."

When his teeth began to hurt Lindsey realized he had been clenching his jaw. When he heard himself exhale loudly, he also realized he had been holding his breath. He picked up each foot and looked at the soles of his shoes. There was nothing interesting there.

Hasan said, "Hell, man, relax. They nothing you can do now, so you might as well relax."

"I can't. What did I do? I can't just relax," Lindsey said.

"Okay, we talk," Hasan said and sat up on his cot. He looked perfectly at home. "What you want to talk about?"

Lindsey shrugged. "Maybe you can tell me more about Leroy McKinney."

"Abu Shabazz."

"Right."

Hasan folded his hands behind his head, leaned against the

wall, stretched his feet in front and crossed his ankles. "I tell you 'bout them clubs. 'Bout them musicians. That be interesting, that pass the time. That be all right with you, Lindsey-Hobart-Lindsey?"

Lindsey said, "Sure." He looked at his watch again. It still wasn't there. "How do you tell time around here?"

Hasan grinned. "Breakfast time when they bring you breakfast. Lunch time when they bring you lunch. Dinner time when they bring you dinner. Bedtime when they dim the lights. That how you tell time. That jail time."

Very softly, Lindsey said, "Oh." Then he said, "All right, tell me about the clubs that McKinney managed and the musicians who worked there."

"They some very nice people," Hasan said. "Some of them good family men. Some of them even women. I met Sarah Vaughan once. Sassy Vaughan, they call her. She a beautiful woman. She could sing, too. *Mmmm.* She nice to the help, nice to the customers. Nice woman. And the Lady. She on top then. Later on, they git her too."

Lindsey nodded. He knew that the less he said, the more Hasan would tell him.

"Bessie Smith, she come one time. Empress of the Blues they call her." He shook his head. "Big old woman but could she ever sing. You close yo' eyes, she twenty years old and slim like a reed."

Lindsey waited for more. It came.

Hasan said, "Now these musicians. Some of them not so very nice. Miles, he a mean man. He play that horn like an angel. He close his eyes and they nobody else in the room, just him and the horn. But mean. *Whoosh!* Wouldn't talk to nobody, wouldn't smile at nobody, had this funny voice like he always whispering or something. Didn't want nobody to know what he saying. Something the matter his throat, I don't know what. He always could play, but he couldn't hardly talk."

Hasan uncrossed his ankles and dropped his hands. He was getting into it. Lindsey would have to remember what he had said about Miles and find out who Miles was. Marvia would know. And the Lady. Who was the Lady?

"Now Bird, he another story," Hasan resumed. "Some folks think he a mean man. I don't think so. He not mean. He just crazy. He different from other people. He come and go, he miss gigs, he get mad. I saw him once, he mad at Abu. Bird, he always stoned on something, he don' care what. He gettin' ready to go on, he sitting down, start to stand up and he fall down. I don' mean he fall back on his chair, see, he fall down on the floor. You understan' me, Bart? Like, jus' *bam!* Abu, he invite me over to meet this great Bird, and I see this happen. I see it with my own eyes."

Hasan let out his breath with a *whoosh*. Lindsey waited. "I start to help Bird get back up, but Abu he stop me. He grab me with his good hand. Bird get up and pick up a fifth of gin and he throw it at Abu. Miss him, smash against the wall, glass all over. But he could blow. He could fly like a bird, that why they call him Bird, cause he fly like a bird."

Marvia would know who Bird was.

"Now Monk, he the craziest of them all. He talk to you, you never know what he gonna say. I talk to him one time. Abu invite me over. Was at the Blackhawk. I 'memers the Blackhawk. They used to have a chicken-wire fence right down the middle of that club. So's they can let kids in. Under age, you understan' me, Bart? They make all the kids sit on one side the fence, they sell them cokes and stuff. Other side the fence, they serve liquor. You see?"

"I see."

Hasan nodded to a long-ago companion. "Abu he introduce me to Monk, he say, 'This be Mister Rasheed.' Monk, he say something so crazy, I never forget it. I tell you exactly what he say. I 'memers every word. He say, 'They an ocean floor. They a secret door. They a soul in yo' breast. They a pimento.' And when it time for him to play, I 'members his band, Charlie Rouse, John Ore, Frankie Dunlop, I 'memers every one. They on the stage. Abu Shabazz, he had to lead Monk out and set him on the piano stool. He play beautiful. That man a genius. But when he finish, Abu have to lead him away again."

He shook his head. "Oh, them was some days. Some, some, some days. Some, some days." He opened his eyes and focused on Lindsey. "Abu Shabazz wrote music, you know. He could still write even when he couldn't play no more. He wrote a song for Monk. Called it fo' himself. Called it 'In Walk Abu.' Monk love that tune. Played it all the time. But he such a strange man, he fo'get the name. He call it 'In Walk Bud.' He thought it about Bud Powell. But that song really 'In Walk Abu.' Fo' Abu Shabazz."

Lindsey waited for Hasan to say more. He didn't. Finally Lindsey said, "I don't understand. If he was so successful, Abu Shabazz, if he ran these clubs, wrote music, why was he living so poorly at the time of his death? And why was he working as a janitor?"

"They rob him, Lindsey-Hobart-Lindsey. They take everything, don' leave him nothing."

The police officer rapped on the bars. "You want that phone call, Lindsey?"

"You bet." He was on his feet in the blink of an eye. As the officer unlocked the holding cell, Lindsey said, "What about Mr. Rasheed?"

The officer grinned. "He knows the drill. He'll be all right."

Lindsey looked back as he walked to the telephone. Hasan Rahsaan Rasheed was stretched out on the cot, his eyes closed.

Eric Coffman took the call at his pool. Lindsey could tell because he could hear splashing and Coffman's daughters screaming. "Happy Sunday. Eric here."

Lindsey told him where he was.

"What happened?" Coffman asked.

Lindsey told him, briefly.

"Don't talk to anybody. Don't answer any questions. Wait till I get there. You'll make a criminal practitioner of me yet, won't you?"

"Please, Eric. Just get here."

A very pleasant, very heavyset black lady wearing a pair of Reeboks and a maroon sweatsuit with a badge pinned to the shirt invited Lindsey into a plain room. She gave him a warm, motherly smile and said, "I'm Detective Hartley. And you are . . . ?"

Lindsey gave her his name.

"You're quite a fellow," Detective Hartley said. "Most white folks would be afraid to go into Fuzzy's. Most black folks would be afraid to go in there." Lindsey noticed that she was wearing a wedding band but no other jewelry.

Lindsey smiled.

Detective Hartley reached behind her, found a clipboard and started to read Lindsey his rights.

"No need. I'm not answering any questions," Lindsey said.

"Please. It's the rules," Detective Hartley said.

Lindsey shrugged.

She read the whole thing. Then she said, "Did you understand all of that?"

Lindsey nodded.

"If the answer is yes, please say yes. If the answer is no, say no."

So they were taping. "Yes, I understand my rights. But I'm not going to answer any questions. I have the right to talk to a lawyer and to have him present during questioning. I've already talked with my lawyer, and he's on his way here now."

Detective Hartley smiled her motherly smile. "Would you mind signing a statement that you have been read your rights and that you understand them?"

Lindsey ran his fingers through his hair. He held out his hand. Detective Hartley handed him a ball-point pen and a card with his Miranda rights printed on it and indicated a place for him to sign. He signed.

"Now, about this little tiff at Fuzzy's . . . "

"I want my lawyer."

"You won't talk to me at all?"

"I want my lawyer."

Detective Hartley sighed and stood up and motioned to Lindsey. She led him back to the holding cell. Hasan Rahsaan Rasheed was no longer there. Lindsey sat on the cot and waited for Eric Coffman to arrive.

When he did, he was wearing plaid shorts and a Hawaiian shirt with a quilted vest over it. He carried his attaché case, the one that Lindsey knew contained a cellular phone and fax machine. A police officer opened the lock and rolled back the bars a couple of feet and Coffman squeezed into the cell.

Lindsey jumped up. "Eric! Thanks a million. I was . . . "

Coffman said, "Shut up!" He put his attaché case down and opened it. He turned on a tape recorder. In a loud voice he said, "This conversation between Hobart Lindsey, client, and Eric Coffman, of counsel, taking place in the Richmond, California, police headquarters at approximately four o'clock on Sunday afternoon," he paused to check a pocket calendar and add the date, "is fully protected under existing rules of confidentiality and may not be used in any way, directly or indirectly, against the aforesaid Hobart Lindsey."

"Aforesaid. Great word. Get me the hell out of here, Eric. I didn't do anything. I was just trying to get some information on a dead man, trying to do my job, and I'm treated like a criminal."

"All right, calm down. Now, I want you to tell me what happened."

"I told you. Nothing."

"Certainly. Tell me everything you did today and how you wound up in the hoosegow, then."

"I told you that on the phone."

Coffman sighed. His pink dome and brown beard and ample belly seemed made for sighing. Lindsey had seen and heard him sigh many times in a three-piece suit, but he had never seen him sigh in a costume like this. Coffman looked down and said, "I didn't take time to change. Thought you'd appreciate prompt service. It's a hot afternoon in Concord."

Lindsey went through a resumé of the Leroy McKinney investigation. When he got to the point about Oakland Homicide quitting on the case, Coffman held up his hand.

"What exactly did this Sergeant Finnerty say to you?"

Lindsey repeated the statement as accurately as he could.

"And he told you this was Lieutenant High's dictum?" Coffman asked.

Lindsey nodded.

"If the answer is yes, please say yes, and if the answer is no, say no."

Lindsey groaned. "Yes."

Coffman rubbed his beard. "Might be an interesting question. You could claim to be authorized by OPD. A new kind of deputization, without benefit of oath or badge. But let that be for now. You had no prior knowledge of Hasan Rahsaan Rasheed or of Fuzzy the bartender?"

"None."

"What about the fellow who crashed through the doorway?"

"I hardly got a look at him. I didn't recognize him, but I couldn't swear that I'd never met him."

Coffman had Lindsey describe his encounter with Fuzzy, his conversation with Hasan, the exchange of cash and receipt and the shooting. He closed up his attaché case and stood up. He said, "Wait here. Don't say anything to anybody. I doubt that they'll bring Hasan back, but they might put a mole in with you. Don't answer any question, however inconsequential. You understand me?"

Lindsey nodded, "Yes."

"I said, *answer no questions. None.*"

Lindsey cringed.

Coffman said, "Sorry, Bart. Lawyer humor." He rapped a coin against the bars. A guard appeared and let him out of the cell.

Hasan did not return, nor did they put anyone else in with Lindsey. Eventually Coffman returned, accompanied by Detective Hartley. They led Lindsey back to the interrogation room.

Hartley said, "Your rights are still in effect. You understand that, sir?"

Lindsey grunted.

Hartley said, "If the answer is yes, please say yes. If the answer is no, say no."

"Yes."

Hartley laid a photo on the table. It was a standard mug shot, front and side, with the identification covered over. "Do you recognize this man, Mr. Lindsey?"

Lindsey looked at Coffman.

Coffman said, "Go ahead. I'll stop you if she asks anything improper."

Hartley shot an angry look at Coffman. To Lindsey, she repeated her question.

He shook his head.

"If the answer . . . "

"I don't recognize him. No." Abbott and Costello strike again.

"How about this person?"

It was a Polaroid of a man lying on his back. Same man. His eyes were beginning to glaze.

Lindsey asked, "Is that the man who staggered into Fuzzy's?"

"Is it?" Hartley rejoined.

"I don't know. Looks like . . . it might be. I don't know."

"How about this person?" She laid another photo on the table. It showed a child-size corpse riddled with holes and splattered with red. The corpse wore a Los Angeles Raiders jacket. Lindsey felt his stomach churn. Hartley said, "Maybe this will help." She laid another photo beside the one of the corpse. It was a close-up of a boy with African-looking features, light, almost albino skin, and freckles. The boy was dead. That was obvious.

Lindsey told Hartley that he recognized the boy. He told her about his encounter outside Latasha Greene's house with the boys and the squirt gun. She had him describe the other boys. "What happened?" he asked.

Hartley ignored his question. "What did you say the boy's name was?"

Lindsey searched his memory. "Mohammed? Achmed? No—got it—Ahmad. Ahmad Hope. That's what Latasha Greene told me."

Hartley nodded. She laid a photo of Fuzzy on the table. Lindsey identified it. She laid a photo of Hasan Rahsaan Rasheed on the table. Lindsey identified it. She showed him the receipt that Hasan had given him and the twenty dollar bill that he had given Hasan.

He identified the receipt. "I can't identify the twenty. I gave him one. I don't know if this is the same one."

Hartley said, "That's good enough." She stood up. "If you'll come with me and sign a statement that you were not beaten,

111

tortured, threatened, offered a bribe or other payment, or otherwise mistreated or unduly influenced while in custody, we'll get your belongings and you can be on your way. Sorry to inconvenience you, sir. We may need to contact you again, I hope that will be all right."

"Sure. Ah, I mean, ah, what was that all about?"

Hartley asked, "You didn't recognize Hasan?"

"Not before today. But that boy. He was just a child. I don't understand."

Hartley said, "That boy was a lookout. They pay them to serve as lookouts, runners, mules. He was just a casualty in a turf war. I know his grandma. I'll try and talk to her tonight. She's lost too many now."

"He's dead."

"Yes."

"I . . . " Lindsey started to cry. He sat down and pulled his handkerchief from his pocket. They had left him his handkerchief. He wiped his eyes. "He was a child."

"Hasan Rahsaan Rasheed, Rahsaan of Richmond," Detective Hartley said. "His real name is Luther Jones. The man who died at Fuzzy's had just killed the boy. He was working for Luther Jones. The boy was working for a rival of Luther's. Luther is absolutely clean. He was sitting in Fuzzy's talking with you when everything happened. You even gave us a receipt that he wrote for you for the money you paid him. You're his alibi, Mr. Lindsey."

Fourteen

DESMOND RICHELIEU WASN'T AS UNHAPPY as Lindsey expected. First thing Monday morning, Lindsey bit the bullet and phoned Richelieu in Denver. He had learned less about the McKinney killing than he had hoped to, and he was ready to take a dressing down for his lack of progress. But the movie was under way. That was International Surety's chief concern, the headline story. The McKinney killing was Lindsey's private sidebar.

Lindsey pulled some more SPUDS work from Denver off the fax. There were lingering problems from the Loma Prieta earthquake of '89 even though years had passed. When the Cypress Freeway collapsed, was the State of California responsible or were the insurance companies? The insurers had got together and they were trying to straighten that out.

And the Oakland Hills fire of '91 had generated a folder full of disputes. International Surety, and most of the other companies, had paid their policyholders, but the struggle now was more intense than ever. The Cities of Berkeley and Oakland were blaming each other, both of them were blaming the Division of Forestries. Everybody was mad at the press. But twenty-five people had died and the damage ran into the billions and everybody wanted somebody else to pick up the tab.

As far as International Surety was concerned, these were mostly problems for Legal and for Legislative Liaison. But SPUDS was also involved, and Lindsey found himself playing private eye, looking for lost relatives, tracking down inventories and depreciated values and making sure that nobody was in collusion with Elmer Mueller to puff up claims and split the profits.

Either Mueller was clean or he was too clever to get caught. Lindsey wasn't sure which. Mueller knew what Lindsey was doing and was furious. He kicked it up to Harden at Regional. Harden took it up with Ducky Richelieu. Richelieu backed Lindsey.

It was nice to win that one. But now Lindsey knew he had better never play poker with his back to the door.

He couldn't clear his mind of that face. Leroy McKinney's face with the jelly-like puddle in the middle of his forehead. Or that other face. Ahmad Hope with his light skin and his African features and the glazed look of death in his strangely pale young boy's eyes.

Lindsey phoned Coffman and got a portable answering machine in the lawyer's briefcase. The man never failed to amaze. He left a message and Coffman called him back during a court recess.

"Heard something from your friend Hartley?" Coffman asked.

"No. Have you?"

"Not yet. I'm sure we will, though."

"Eric, I . . . this thing is getting to me. Can I get hold of you for an hour? Just to talk about it."

"Is this International Surety talking, or is it my friend Hobart Lindsey?"

"I'm not sure."

"Well, if it's I.S. you'll have to call my office and make an appointment at the customary rate. I'm your attorney of record in the Richmond thing, unless you want to make a change. I'll be glad to hand it over to a good criminal."

"Huh?"

"Criminal lawyer, Bart. Wow, you're slow today. Criminal lawyer, some people think that's a tautology."

"I don't know. No, it's not the Richmond thing. Only if it happens to connect up. It's the Leroy McKinney murder," Lindsey said.

"Oh, I see. You want me to play Nero to your Archie or Mycroft to your Sherlock?"

"I'd just like to talk to you. As friend to friend, if we can. But if you want to charge me for it, that's okay."

"Huh, you drive a hard bargain. Tell you what, you still going with Marvia?"

"Yes."

"I really like her. She's never met Miriam and the girls. Why don't the two of you come out for dinner one night?"

"All right."

"Listen, I hate to cut you off but the judge is going to have me horsewhipped for contempt if I don't get back on time. Oh—listen—didn't you once tell me that Marvia has a youngster?"

"Jamie."

"Bring him along." Coffman hung up.

Lindsey ate dinner with Mother that night. He had decided to hold off calling Marvia until after the meal. Mother was able to discuss the day's news. She was taking an interest in the world now.

Lindsey had noticed that every time he was away, every time Mother was thrown onto her own resources, she came up stronger. Mrs. Hernandez had cut back to twice a week now and acted more as Mother's housekeeper than the companion and de facto babysitter she had been for years.

After dinner, Mother made coffee and they sat in the living room with the TV turned off, talking. Lindsey couldn't remember the last time they had done that.

"Hobart, I've been thinking of getting a job."

Lindsey's jaw dropped. He stammered half an answer and ran out of words.

"It's just the two of us. You're seldom home anymore. That's very nice. I like to see you on your own. You're a grown man now," Mother said.

Lindsey nodded, "Yes."

"And it isn't a very big house. Mrs. Hernandez takes care of everything."

Lindsey nodded again.

115

"So," Mother said, "why shouldn't I find work? You know, I used to work. When your father was alive."

Lindsey studied her face. Her eyes were clear. She was making sense.

"It wasn't much of a job. I worked as a secretary. It would be nice to have a job. I'd have friends. I'd earn my own money. You wouldn't mind, would you? I feel as if I'm a drag on you. I get your father's little pension, and you earn a nice salary, but I'd feel better if I were earning money of my own."

Lindsey lowered his cup. He didn't know what to think. If this was another sign of Mother's continuing progress, it was wonderful. But she had always been there, always been home for him. Since he was a baby. Even at her craziest. Even when she couldn't tell whether Ronald Reagan was that actor fellow in the movies or Governor of the State of California, she had been home for him.

"It's been so long, Mother. You don't know how to use a computer, a modem, a fax machine, even a copier. Everything is changed. You'd be competing with people thirty years younger."

"I want to try."

"But . . . "

"I saw an article in the *Times*. There's a group for people like me. Late-entrant and re-entrant workers. That's what they call us. Late-entrant and re-entrant. I'd be re-entrant. We can get training to get us up to date. And they have a job placement service."

Lindsey didn't say anything.

"I don't know if I'll make much money," Mother said. "Or even if I can make it at all."

"Then you can . . . "

"I have to try this. Look at me. Look at me." She stood up. "I gave birth at the age of seventeen, Hobart. I was a little girl. I'm not even sixty now. I'm not ready to die. You don't need me, I don't have a husband and I am a healthy woman. I want to work for a living. I want a place in the world."

Lindsey phoned Marvia. He told her about Coffman's invitation. She said that was fine, she would be happy to visit Coffman's home. She would bring Jamie. She hadn't heard anything further from Jamie's dad. Lindsey started to tell her about Latasha Greene and Hasan Rahsaan Rasheed but she asked him to save it until they were together.

Lindsey parked on Oxford Street and bounded up the stairs to Marvia's apartment. She had already picked up Jamie at her parents' house on Bonita. She wore a blouse and skirt, tights and high heels. Lindsey couldn't remember seeing her dressed that way. Jamie was decked out in his best superhero shirt and new jeans. Lindsey kissed Marvia and shook hands with Jamie.

When he kissed Marvia, he wondered how she would act in front of her son, but she seemed comfortable kissing Lindsey back.

They took Marvia's cream-and-tan Mustang. Small as he was, Jamie was a tight fit in the backseat. But he settled in with the miniature B-17 Lawton Crump had given him. "He hasn't let that airplane out of his grip. My dad says he even invented a way to wash his hands one at a time so he doesn't have to put it down. And he won't stop talking about his friend Mr. Crump and his big bomber. He wants to go out there again. Wants to know if Mr. Crump can take him flying."

"Maybe he can," Lindsey said.

Marvia tooled them onto the freeway and popped a cassette into the player. "Have to upgrade to CD one day. Listen to this. I think you'll like it."

Another of those wonderful blues singers Marvia played so often started to sing: *Cold-hearted papa be on your merry way.* "That's Issie Ringgold. Not very prominent, even in her day. Almost forgotten now. I like her, though. Could never pronounce her r's, but I like her anyhow." The song ended and another began. "Victoria Spivey," Marvia said. "I even love her name."

Lindsey said, "I met this fellow Hasan Rahsaan Rasheed. Rahsaan of Richmond, they called him."

"You started to tell me about that. Where did you run into this character? He doesn't sound like your type."

"Uh, a . . . " He looked over his shoulder. Jamie was absorbed in maneuvering his B-17. Was it 1944? Was he dodging flak over Saarbrucken?

Marvia said, "You can say anything, Bart."

"It was a saloon. I met him in a saloon. In Richmond. Fuzzy's #3."

Marvia burst into laughter. "Whoa! Have to stay on the road. Bless you, Bart, mad dogs and Englishmen go into Fuzzy's. You went into Fuzzy's when?"

"Last Sunday. About noontime."

"And nothing bad happened to you."

"Well, there was some shooting and a couple of people were killed. The police came. In fact, they did some of the shooting. I spent a few hours in jail but everything came out all right. I think. Eric got me out. But I'm afraid I let Hasan use me. I didn't know what was going on."

"How did Luther use you?" Marvia asked.

"You know about that. Who he really is," Lindsey said.

"Yep. Luther the Snake, Hasan of Richmond. I know."

Lindsey told her about showing the photo of Leroy McKinney and Hasan's volunteering the information that McKinney was really Abu Shabazz and the story of his career in the music business. As he wound up the story, Lindsey had an odd thought.

"Marvia, you told me that *Bessie Blue* was named for the blues singer Bessie Smith, right?"

"That's right."

"When did she die? You told me that she died, but did you tell me what year it was? I don't remember. What year did she die?"

"Nineteen thirty-seven. September 26, 1937."

"Then how could she sing at a club in San Francisco after the Second World War?"

"That's no question, Bart."

He studied the freeway traffic for a moment. Sometimes it was good to be a passenger. You could focus your thoughts. You didn't have to worry about staying alive. If some maniac crossed the median and crashed into you, there was nothing

118

you could do about it. You might as well relax and think about other things.

"He couldn't be mistaken? I mean, Bessie Smith. Smith, after all."

"No way. Plenty of other Smiths. Mamie, Ida, Carrie, Trixie, Clara. But nobody who knows blues could ever mistake Bessie. She was the Empress of the Blues. If Luther Jones saw her, he knew it. If he says he saw her in 1945, '46, whenever, he's lying."

"Okay. He lied about Bessie Smith. And if Rahsaan of Richmond was really Luther Jones, then maybe Abu Shabazz wasn't really Leroy McKinney. Or maybe he was."

Marvia laughed. "Lies are a maze of mirrors. Luther is the biggest drug pusher in this area since Felix Mitchell took a knife between the ribs."

"I remember his funeral."

The evenings were growing longer now. They had left Berkeley in daylight, but the sun had set by now, and the oncoming cars made a parade of headlights.

"I mean," Lindsey continued, "if the part of Hasan's story about Bessie Smith was a lie, maybe the whole story was a lie. Or maybe he just added a name to the list. Did I tell him I was interested in Bessie Smith? I can't remember. Maybe I did. So he told me what I wanted to hear. I've come across that before."

"Haven't we all."

"How about those other people he told me about? Would you know them?"

"Try me." A woman on the tape was singing *Papa likes his whiskey, Mama likes her gin.* "Rosa Henderson," Marvia said. *Papa likes the women, Mama likes the men.* "Bessie Smith recorded 'Barrelhouse Blues,' but this is Rosa Henderson." *Papa likes his prize fight, Mama likes the mah-jongg game.* "Those records were nearly extinct. Now they've been rediscovered," Marvia said. *Papa likes his poker, Mama's bettin' just the same.*

"I didn't get to write it down." Lindsey said. "They took my notebook and pencil from me. But I think he mentioned a priest and a Bird. No. A Monk and a Bird. And Miles. Somebody named Miles. And the Lady. Somebody he just called the Lady."

"Now that all rings true," Marvia said. She pulled around a thirty-year-old Volvo 1800. Lindsey saw the driver smile and wave at the Mustang. "Miles was Miles Davis. Bird was Charlie Parker. And Thelonious Monk. Did he say anything particular about Monk?"

"He said he was very strange. He said they had to lead him out to his piano and lead him away afterward. He said Monk told him some strange thing. I don't remember what."

"I wish you did. Monk was a genius."

"Hasan said the same thing."

"The Lady could have been anybody. Probably Lady Day."

"Doris Day?"

She gave him a strange look. "I'm almost ready to tell you why I love you, Bart. Lady Day was Billie Holiday. I know you've heard her records. I was with you. She was forty-four when she died. Luther could have seen her after the war, she lived until 1959."

"Oh," Lindsey said. "I guess this is all important, somehow, but I don't see how it ties in with Leroy McKinney."

"I don't know whether it does. From everything you told me, I was ready to go along with Doc High's theory. Just a random killing. Cops can sound pretty callous sometimes, but we have to focus our efforts. Some cases lead to big results, some lead nowhere."

From the backseat Jamie asked, "Mom, are we there yet?"

Marvia answered, "Almost, Jamie."

"I have to pee."

Marvia smiled and said, "Okay, we'll be there soon." To Lindsey she said, "Leroy McKinney wasn't leading High and Finnerty anywhere. But McKinney or Abu Shabazz was Latasha Greene's grandfather and they shared a house. And Hasan Rahsaan Rasheed, a.k.a. Luther Jones, sent a hitman to kill a little kid who was on the lookout at Latasha Greene's house. Rasheed's meeting you at Fuzzy's and using you as an alibi is one of those gorgeous ironies."

"I'm not amused," Lindsey said. "There's our exit."
"Mom, I have to pee," Jamie said urgently.
Marvia said, "There's a gas station."
They reached it in time.

Fifteen

Marvia pulled the Mustang onto the blacktop beside Eric Coffman's Mercury Topaz station wagon. Jamie brought his Flying Fortress inside with him. Coffman met them at the door. When Jamie was introduced, Coffman bent despite his more than sufficient belly and solemnly shook his hand.

The house was a modern split-level with flagstone floors and shag rugs. A mezuza was mounted on the doorpost.

Lindsey knew Coffman's wife, Miriam, but Coffman insisted on a complete set of introductions. Miriam was taller than Marvia, and ample figured with honey-blond hair that she wore in braids. An old-fashioned, middle-aged woman.

The Coffmans' daughters were Sarah and Rebecca. One was taller than Jamie and the other shorter. Rebecca was holding a Barbie doll. Or maybe it was Barbie's friend, the dark-haired one. Rebecca had dark hair. The three children looked at each other shyly. Jamie leaned against Marvia, one hand on her hip and the other holding his Flying Fortress.

Sarah Coffman broke the silence. "We have a Nintendo. You want to play?"

"You have Captain Skyhawk?" Jamie asked.

Sarah shook her head, no.

"You have Aquaman?"

"I have Mickey Mousecapade. Bugs Bunny Crazy Castle. I have Athena. That's my favorite. We can play Athena."

Jamie whined. "Athena's for girls. Don't you have any boy games?"

Marvia said, "Jamie, why don't you just try Athena. You might like it."

"But," Jamie whined and looked up at Marvia. She scowled. "All right," he grumbled.

With Sarah in the lead, Jamie following reluctantly and Rebecca trailing, they moved into the house.

Miriam said, "Girls, dinner in fifteen minutes."

Coffman led the way into the sunken living room. Polished mahogany bookcases occupied strategic positions and were separated by elaborately framed paintings. The cases were crammed. Most of the shelves were open; a few were protected by glass covers.

"I didn't know you were a book collector, Eric. Are these law books?" Marvia asked.

Coffman shook his head. "Those are in my office. These are my hobby. History. Especially Northern California history. The closer to home the better I like it."

Marvia looked at the books and asked "Isn't that a whole section on World War Two?"

Eric grunted and walked away and fiddled with the controls of a CD player. The music had a lot of violins in it. Lindsey had been hearing lots of music lately that he had never heard at home. Everything from Joseph Haydn to Bessie Smith. Compared to them, Coffman's choice seemed bland and uninteresting. Whatever it was, at least it wasn't abrasive.

Coffman served drinks. Miriam excused herself. "I'll join you in a little while."

Lindsey said, "Thanks again for getting me out of jail, Eric. What an experience that was. What a day."

Coffman said, "I had a talk with your friend Hartley. And—Marvia, do you know this? Did your lunkheaded friend tell you about his scrape with the law?"

"He did."

"I talked with Detective Hartley. I also had an interesting chat with a Contra Costa County assistant DA and another with some federal personages. They kept trying to connect you with Luther Jones and his well-managed commercial enterprises."

"But I'm not connected with him."

"My dear friend, *I* know that. I had to convince *them* of it."

"Well, I hope you succeeded."

"Your conversation with Luther in the jail cell didn't help."

"But all we talked about was old nightclubs and World War Two and jazz musicians. Mostly people I'd never heard of."

"Right. Now, you and Mr. Jones have just been in the middle of a shootout, you get hauled into the pokey, locked in a cell . . . and you talk about defunct nightclubs and military history. Seems to me somebody suspected that the cell was bugged—it was—and that someone had something that he didn't want to talk about."

"Makes sense to me," Marvia said.

Lindsey was astounded. "So if we talked about gangs and drugs and killing people that would prove we were criminals, and if we *didn't* talk about those things it still proves we're criminals!"

"That's why I prefer civil practice. Let me refresh those drinks, Bart, Marvia. How about a Wheat Thin? I'm really trying to lose weight, but the more of this diet stuff I eat the rounder I get."

Lindsey told Coffman the story of the *Bessie Blue* project, the death of Leroy McKinney and Lindsey's interview with Lawton Crump in Holy City.

Miriam returned from the kitchen. "Thank you for setting the table, Eric. Now would you check on the children? The food is almost ready and besides they're being quiet."

Coffman pushed himself out of his easy chair with a soft *oof*. "She never trusts the girls when they're quiet. She's convinced that they've murdered each other or been kidnapped by Hezbollah agents. As if the latest Ayatollah is going to send Hezbollah agents 9,000 miles to kidnap two Jewish girls in Concord, California."

After a couple of minutes, he returned. He was beaming. "Marvia." He held his finger to his lips and gestured with his other hand. She followed him.

They came back giggling, Coffman's arm around Marvia's shoulders. "Completely absorbed," she said. "Sarah and Jamie are playing Nintendo. Rebecca has her Barbie doll riding

Jamie's B-17. This is the first time I've seen it out of his possession since Mr. Crump gave it to him."

Miriam called, "Dinner. Everybody wash your hands before you come to the table."

Lindsey stood over the sink, watching it fill with hot water. His jacket hung from a hook on the bathroom door. He splashed water on his face, reached for a towel and locked onto his own eyes in the mirror. "Reserve," he whispered. So much had happened in the past twenty-four hours, the encounter with Detective Hartley in Richmond, the conversations with Desmond Richelieu and Eric Coffman, that he had left Reserve, Louisiana, somewhere in longterm parking. It was time to do something with it.

He ran from the bathroom and grabbed Marvia. She was already in the dining room, helping to settle the children. "Marvia," he gasped.

She looked up, startled. "What's the matter? Where's your jacket?"

"Never mind. It's in the bathroom. Never mind."

"Your face is all wet."

"I said never mind. Listen, Hasan Rasheed—Luther Jones—told me that Leroy McKinney was from Reserve, Louisiana. At first he couldn't remember the town, then he said Preserve, then he got it right."

"Never heard of it." Coffman said.

"Neither have I," Marvia added.

Lindsey stood there.

Miriam brought in a huge teakwood bowl with matching serving implements and set it in the middle of the table. The bowl was filled with green, leafy stuff. Miriam said, "Salad is good for you. Children, full of minerals. Eric, help you stay slim."

Lindsey went back to the bathroom, floating like a man dazed. He dried his face and hands and ran a comb through his hair. Then he rinsed his hands again, dried them and slipped into his jacket. He stared in the mirror and shambled back to the dining room like a zombie.

Jamie was describing his experience with Athena. He had revised his attitude. "It was great. They had all these neat creatures. They had this killer tree and a fire octopus and a lobster and a neat spider. The spider spits rocks and you have to shoot arrows at it. But the octopus was the neatest. It can spit fireballs. But the goomum can throw its head at you."

"What's a goomum?" Marvia asked.

"It's something like Frankenstein. Like Ben Grimm, the Thing."

Coffman cleared his throat. "I think he means the Golem."

Sarah said, "I don't like the Golem."

Miriam said, "Eric is quite the Nintendo expert."

Behind his beard, Coffman blushed. "I just bought a couple of games to see what it was like."

Marvia grinned. "Really. What were they, Eric?"

He wiped his lips with his napkin. Miriam reached over and picked a tiny speck of green from his beard. She clucked. He said, "Well, *1942* and *1943*. Just because I'm interested in history. I was telling Marvia about that just a little while ago."

Miriam said, "So that's why you play with the Three Stooges so much?"

"Sometimes I can't sleep at night. It helps me sleep. It's better than a glass of whiskey."

Miriam said, "I suppose so."

Lindsey had opened his pocket notebook and written in it.

Marvia put her hand on his leg. "You're acting very strange, Bart. You said Leroy McKinney was from Reserve, Louisiana. So what?"

"Lawton Crump is from Reserve, Louisiana."

Marvia whistled.

Miriam Coffman said, "Pardon me, I didn't hear the earlier part. These two men are from the same town?"

"Yes."

"You said, Reserve, Louisiana?"

"Yes."

"That doesn't exactly sound like a metropolis. They must know each other, yes?"

"Not anymore. One of them is dead."

Miriam nodded. "So, they're not even talking to each other in heaven."

Coffman said, "I doubt that Leroy McKinney is in heaven."

"What makes you think that?" Miriam asked.

"You're right," Coffman conceded. "He was a murder victim. We don't know anything about him. Not for sure. Or do we." His eyes flashed. "Bart?"

Lindsey said, "In fact, we know a lot about him. We just don't know how much of it's true. His granddaughter says he was a ballplayer, a pitcher. Reverend Johnson gave me some old scorecards. It looks as if that's true, anyway. Latasha says he was in the Marine Corps. I've put in a request through International Surety to verify that. Luther Jones says he was a nightclub manager and songwriter. I don't think that will be so easy to follow up. I doubt if any of those clubs are still open after forty years, but maybe we can find something out."

"He hardly sounds like a mystery man," Miriam said.

Lindsey nodded. "If the stories are true."

"But from Lawton Crump's home town. Miriam, Eric, I don't think you know my boss, Lieutenant Yamura. Dorothy Yamura. I know Bart has met her. She always says that coincidences make her nervous. She says she knows there are coincidences in life, but she just doesn't like them. She says when things are connected, she likes to know why they're connected."

Coffman pointed a fork full of salad at Lindsey. "What does that mean to you, old friend?"

Lindsey looked back at Coffman. He didn't say anything.

Coffman said, "I think it means you're going to Louisiana."

Lindsey said, "I don't know."

Marvia said, "You're in that new job now. In SPUDS. Doesn't that mean you have more freedom? Can't you just jump on a plane and go somewhere on I.S. business?"

Lindsey said, "Yes."

Lindsey expected the house to be quiet and Mother to be asleep when he got home. Instead he found her sitting in front of the TV watching *Royal Wedding*.

In color.

Lindsey stood beneath the archway, watching her watching Fred Astaire and Jane Powell.

Mother sensed his presence. "Did you enjoy yourself? You took Marvia home? Is she all right?"

"She's fine, Mother. I may have to leave town for a while. Will you be okay by yourself? Should I ask Joanie Schorr to stay with you?"

She smiled at him. "I'm going to see about a job. I'm going down to that training place. I guess they don't need anybody who can cut stencils on a Royal Upright these days. Maybe I can learn to work a word processor."

"I'm sure you can, Mother. How's the movie?"

"I still like the ones with Ginger Rogers the best, but that Astaire, he's some dancer. Is he still alive?"

Lindsey shook his head. "He died years ago."

"A pity. How old was he?"

"I don't know. He was an old man. I think he was in his eighties."

She turned back to the screen. "He could still dance."

Mother never watched movies in color. She never watched anything in color except occasionally cartoons. Sometimes Lindsey would reset the controls for color when he watched the late news and forget to reset them to black and white. Then Mother got upset. More than once, she had been close to hysterics.

Now she was watching *Royal Wedding* in color.

Lindsey planned to phone Richelieu first thing Monday, but Richelieu beat him to the punch. Lindsey was happy to see Ms. Wilbur at her desk when he arrived at International Surety and equally happy not to see Elmer Mueller.

"Adjusting a claim?"

"Investigating a case."

"Assessing an account."

"Surveying a site."

They laughed together.

"I've put in my papers." Ms. Wilbur said. "Thirty days and I'm out. I'll have my retirement."

Lindsey sat at a desk that Elmer Mueller had grudgingly authorized for his use on SPUDS business.

"Coffee's made. Mueller doesn't like that, either. Says there's a perfectly adequate machine downstairs. Of course if I use that, he complains that I'm abandoning my post. 'Leaving your desk unmanned.' I told him I've never been a man in my life, he'd better have his vision checked."

Lindsey filled his coffee mug. The mug's finish was black and glossy. It said SPUDS in gold leaf superimposed over the potato logo. The opposite side had an International Surety crest and read *Bart Lindsey* in fancy script. The coffee was tollable good.

Ms. Wilbur said, "You'd better call Ducky in Denver. Apparently Elmer's been putting a bug in Harden's ear again. And Harden's been passing the dirt along to Ducky. Have you been in jail lately, Hobart?"

"It was all a mistake. I was just in the wrong place at the wrong time. I wasn't charged with anything. They even apologized for the whole thing."

"Who's they?"

"Richmond P.D. I was gathering some data up in Richmond on this *Bessie Blue* case."

"Right. Anyhow, you'd better call Ducky back."

Sixteen

"YOU KNOW WHY I LOVE YOU?" Marvia looked at Lindsey across the table. They had finished their meal at a Thai seafood house on the Oakland Estuary. Spotlights illuminated the cabin cruisers moored a few yards beyond the window. A gray cat strolled down the gangplank from the rocky embankment to the wooden pier. It looked extremely well fed. It waved its tail as if it were setting off on an after-dark cruise around the Bay.

"You promised you'd tell me. I know why I love you. Because you're beautiful and kind and because you made me alive. All the years I was like a dead man. Go to work, process cases, go home, eat dinner, watch TV, go to sleep. It wasn't life. Everybody I knew was just like me. My world was the size of a—I don't know—it wasn't a world. It was nothing. You made me alive. But what have I given you?"

"You aren't spoiled. I don't know, maybe we can't have one without the other. Everybody I know is so damned cynical. Maybe that's 'cause they're all cops, or almost all of them. It's a way of life. We see everybody at his worst. Maybe that's why cops drink so much. And get so many divorces. And kill themselves. You know the suicide rate in law enforcement?"

"I'm in the insurance business, remember?"

"Oh, yes." She smiled and put her hand on his. "See, you could have been unfair about this. You could have asked me when we were in bed. You just asked me once and when I said I'd tell you sometime, you waited until I was ready to tell you."

He nodded. He waited for her to go on.

"You let me be black, but you don't make me be black, you see?"

"I don't have anything to do with that. But I'll admit, I was surprised you stuck with me. Nobody can pick his color."

"Some of us can. Some of us can cross the line if we want to. More used to than do nowadays. There's less of a price to pay than there used to be. Besides, Mother Nature made the decision for me." She laid her dark hand on the white linen tablecloth. Even the amber candlelight did not diminish the contrast.

"You have nothing sour inside, Bart. There's no poison in you. You missed a lot of the good stuff, sure, but the germs didn't get into you either. The ugly viruses of life. I'm so lucky. I got in there first. I promise I'll never poison you. And I'll try to keep anybody else from poisoning you, but I don't know if I can do that."

Lindsey settled the check. It was his turn.

They strolled on the pier afterwards, arms around each other. A gray shadow leaped from the prow of a cabin cruiser to the deck of a sailboat and turned to stare at them with eyes like amber candlelight.

Marvia nestled her head against Lindsey. "That's why I'm so frightened."

He halted and placed his hands on her shoulders. "Frightened?"

"For Jamie."

"I don't understand. Is it his father again?"

She nodded. There was no moonlight, but the floodlights provided as much illumination as a bright moon would have. Maybe more. From here they could see beyond the Estuary across San Francisco Bay to the lights of the city.

"I had another letter."

"I thought we'd been over this. I thought Wilkerson had given up custody. He must have some visitation rights . . . "

"He has nothing. He blew us off. Good riddance."

"Then he can't take Jamie from you."

"That isn't the point, Bart." She sounded angry and turned away. Lindsey caught a glimpse of the gray cat. Startled, it scurried up the gangplank and disappeared into a scrubby bush that had somehow survived the pounding of the bay and clung

131

to the rocky bank. More softly, Marvia repeated, "That isn't the point. I said we can't choose our color. We can choose each other, you and I, but Jamie can't choose. He's a little boy. His dad offers him a black home, a black family. You and I can't. It isn't your fault, it isn't my fault. We can't change ourselves. I can't do that to him."

He turned her toward him, she let him, and pulled her close as they walked back on the pier. "You want to go back to the restaurant? You want a brandy or a cup of coffee?"

She shook her head. "I want you to take me home. I want to lie in bed with you and hold on to you."

"You'll make the right decision. It will work out. I know it will."

In bed, she said, "Talk to me about something else."

"Ducky Richelieu. He's backing me. He wants me to go to Reserve and see what the hell this is all about. I talked to Doc High and he's keeping hands off, but I could tell he was pretty pleased. I talked to Eric about it again and he just gave me his lawyer stuff. Be careful, don't sign anything, don't tread on the cops' toes down there."

Marvia rubbed her forehead on his chest. He could have stayed like that forever. "Tell me some more."

"I've got some homework to do before I go down there. See if I can get a lead on McKinney. Start with something totally simple. See if there's a phone number for anybody named McKinney in Reserve, Louisiana. Not a very common name, but I think I'll find a few. But even if there are a platoon of them, I can do some work on the phone and narrow it down."

"How about Crumps?"

"You bet. If I can find some McKinneys and some Crumps in the phone book, I can start checking. And all the other things. High-school yearbooks, local church records. Whatever."

"You think you'll get a friendly reception?"

"Why not?"

"God is really watching out for you, you know that?"

Lindsey couldn't think of anything to say.

"I don't know. You did all right in Richmond. Latasha Greene, Reverend Johnson, Luther Jones. They all talked to you," Marvia said.

"You mean because I'm white."

"White and from out of town. You'll talk funny. You'll represent a big institution. You might not get very far."

"Someone black would do better."

"I thought you'd never ask."

"You're from out of town, and they'll think you talk funny."

"I can't talk piney woods black but at least I won't look alien."

"What about Jamie?"

"He'll be heartbroken. He reads aquarium magazines and he saw an article about the new aquarium in New Orleans. I can promise to bring him a souvenir. And we'll have to take him to Monterey as soon as we get back. He doesn't know much geography yet. He'll just know that he's on a trip and he can sleep away."

Lindsey ran his hands down her back. "You're willing to go with me? You can't be a cop down there, can you?"

"I'll take my badge. I won't take a gun. I won't be there officially. But if we talk to local cops, I can show my badge and they'll probably be courteous."

"Not like Rod Steiger and Sidney Poitier?"

"More like Carroll O'Connor and Howard Rollins. Huh, or Alan Autry and Anne-Marie Johnson."

She shifted her body so her weight was entirely on him. "You're losing me," he said.

"I mean, it isn't 1925 down there or even 1965. I don't think we'd have much trouble in New Orleans or Baton Rouge. We'll have to watch ourselves, watch out for some neighborhoods." She laughed. "That's no different from anyplace. But some little town down in the bayous or out in the piney woods—do you even know where Reserve, Louisiana, is?"

"I checked. It's thirty miles north-west of New Orleans. In Saint John the Baptist Parish."

"Well, I don't know much Southern geography. Sounds like sugar-cane country. A town like that. You and I together."

"You think there'll be good old boys ready to tar and feather us?"

"No. I just don't want to take any foolish risks."

"I could ask Aurora Delano to handle it. She was in my SPUDS class in Denver. Worked in the Eugene, Oregon, branch but she went back to New Orleans for SPUDS. Riche-lieu mentioned having her check out Reserve. Save on airfare. Then he changed his mind. It's my case, and I told him I was going to do it. But I don't want to ask you to come along if it's going to be dangerous for you. If you think it means taking foolish risks."

She put her face against his, her mouth close to his. "A cop risks her life everyday. We'll be careful. We have to be careful, but we can't let the haters win, either."

The Southwest 737 touched down at New Orleans Interna-tional in late afternoon. Lindsey leaned across Marvia to peer out the airliner's window. The airport looked just like the airports in Oakland, San Francisco, Denver, Los Angeles. Some were bigger, some had mountains around them, but air-ports were all the same.

The difference hit him like a giant boxing glove when he stepped out of the air-conditioned cabin into the steamy air. He had traveled light, as had Marvia, so they were able to avoid the nightmare of baggage carousels and indifferent airport person-nel.

They had planned to take a cab into the city, but Lindsey spotted Aurora Delano waiting for them. She smiled. "Nice to see you again." She made an all-inclusive gesture. "Not much like Colorado is it?"

"I'll wait till I see the city." He introduced Aurora and Marvia. He watched them smile and shake hands and size each other up.

That was something that would remain forever a mystery to the male race: the sizing-up that women gave each other at first encounter. Mothers must start giving their daughters secret lessons somewhere between toilet training and learning to feed themselves. For girls only. Boys need not apply.

"I've got you a room in the French Quarter," Aurora said. "Might as well see some local color while you're here. We need to go over this case before we go out to Reserve. You brought the file with you?"

"Right here." Lindsey raised his attaché case.

"Marvia." Woman to woman now. More female stuff. "I don't mean to pry, but are you along purely on social grounds?"

"Did Bart tell you I'm a homicide officer?"

Aurora raised her eyebrows. Lindsey knew she had good reaction time. "Is this a police case?"

"I'm not here officially. Bart and I have cooperated a couple of times and it's worked out well."

"We don't need to keep anything confidential," Lindsey said.

"All right. I just didn't want to spread this outside the company."

"Right. One of Desmond Richelieu's dicta."

"It's in the Operations Manual."

"And if it's in the Ops Man, we all stand and salute." Lindsey restrained himself from making the gesture.

Their hotel was on Rue Bienville, an old building with whitewashed walls and wrought-iron balconies. They had a third-floor suite. They settled in quickly, then convened over a stylish table in the sitting room. Room service had sent up a pot of chicory flavored coffee and biscuits with powdered sugar.

Lindsey laid out the papers relating to *Bessie Blue*. He showed Aurora a photo of Leroy McKinney and another of Lawton Crump that he had got from Ina Chandler at Double Bee. It took him almost an hour to get thorugh the details about Crump and McKinney, the information he had got from Latasha Greene and Reverend Johnson and the Fuzzy's #3 incident.

Aurora leaned back in an elegant Louis XIV chair, or maybe a good imitation of one. She pursed her lips and managed a low whistle. "Okay. Lawton Crump, our small town boy, made good. He's Mister Clean. War hero, successful career, big house, nice wife, gives toy airplanes to little children."

"That's him," Lindsey said.

"And Leroy McKinney is Mister Dirty. Leroy McKinney, a.k.a. Abu Shabazz. Ex-ballplayer, nightclub manager, questionable associations with your friend Hasan Rasheed, a.k.a. Luther Jones, shady character and reputed criminal bigshot. Who just happened to use you, Bart, as his alibi during a turf war shootout. Very nice people."

She sipped her chicory flavored coffee.

Lindsey watched Aurora and Marvia exchange glances. Marvia dipped her head almost imperceptibly. Maybe she was giving Aurora Delano the nod of approval. Maybe not. Lindsey was a mere male; he couldn't know.

"And Leroy McKinney is also from Reserve," Aurora Delano said.

"Yes."

"And thousands of miles away and decades after they left Reserve, Louisiana, the paths of these two men cross once more when Mister Clean stumbles across the corpse of Mister Dirty."

"Right."

"I don't like it."

"Neither do I. That's why we're here."

Aurora held her hands over her eyes for thirty seconds. When she lowered her hands she asked, "Did they know each other? I mean, did Crump say that he knew McKinney? Did he say that he recognized him?"

Lindsey shook his head.

"That doesn't mean anything," Marvia added. Lindsey watched as Aurora Delano studied Marvia Plum again. "If they never knew each other, you'd get that reaction. If they knew each other forty or fifty years ago and hadn't seen each other for all the intervening years, you'd get the same reaction. Or if Crump *did* recognize McKinney and didn't want us to know, for some reason, you'd *still* get the same reaction."

Aurora said, "So . . . what does that mean?"

"It means that we might as well ignore Crump's denial. His denial of knowing McKinney. It doesn't mean that he did know McKinney, either. It's just a non-starter."

"Thanks a lot," Aurora said.

"Anyway . . ." Lindsey picked up a sugar-covered biscuit, nibbled a corner, then popped the whole thing in his mouth. It melted. Through the remnants of the biscuit, he repeated, "Anyway . . . I want to go out to Reserve and talk to the McKinneys. You did check that out for me, Aurora?"

She unfolded a sheet of computer paper and spread it on the table. "I put everything into the machine. Only eight McKinneys in Reserve. I checked it through Tony Leroux."

Now it was Lindsey's turn to raise an eyebrow.

"Local insurance agent," Aurora said. "Antoine Napoleon Leroux. Very old Creole family."

Marvia said, "Creole."

"Caramel brown. Could pass for white if he wanted to or claim to be Panamanian or whatever. Chooses black," Aurora explained.

"Ah."

"Handles International Surety business in Reserve. He knows everybody in that town. Everybody. Immediately eliminated five McKinneys. They're white. Now, if you want to take this alone, Bart, it's your baby. But I think Marvia would get farther than you would. Reserve, however, is not named lightly. It's a conservative town. And a mixed couple might meet some resistance. You won't be lynched or anything, but you would probably not get any cooperation. I mean from the blacks as well as the whites."

Marvia nodded.

Lindsey said, "So . . . ?"

"So I'm going to suggest that the four of us go. You, Marvia, myself . . . and Tony Leroux."

Lindsey walked away from the table. He stood looking out the tall window. Bienville was a narrow street. The sky was darkening and old-fashioned gaslights flickered on. Horse-drawn carriages moved down the cobbled roadway. Tourists in Hawaiian shirts and baseball caps with Bourbon Street logos snapped pictures of each other.

"I don't know." Lindsey turned back toward the others. "Four people is an awful lot. I've done a lot of interviewing, and one-on-one usually works best. Not that I'm the only one who thinks so. It's another Desmond Richelieu rule."

"Right. But you can't have everything. Do the best you can with the resources you have. And Tony knows everybody in town."

"You said that."

"They're more likely to trust him than they are a stranger."

"Ducky Richelieu strikes again."

Seventeen

AURORA STEERED THEM TO A RESTAURANT in the Garden District, out of the French Quarter, away from the crush of tourists. Inside, the silver glimmered, the linen dazzled and the crystal tinkled. Aurora ordered poached salmon. Lindsey ordered jambalaya. When in New Orleans, he thought, do as the locals do. Marvia chose a dish of chicken prepared with an array of spices and cloves of garlic, spread to look like tarantulas, and sautéed in blackened butter.

"I'll be safe from vampires, but you won't want to get near me."

The maître d' assumed that Lindsey and Aurora Delano were a couple, Marvia a mutual friend. They let him think that. After they had finished the meal, mandatory bread pudding and chicory flavored coffee, they strolled past the mansions on St. Charles Avenue, the heart of the Garden District.

"I think our waiter caught on," Marvia said. "The captain didn't have the foggiest, but the waiter knew. I could see it."

"We got good service."

"They know me there," Aurora Delano said.

"It could have been the opposite."

They went to a club on Carondelet that looked like a hangout for graduate students. Tulane and Loyola T-shirts were everywhere. A pianist, a stand-up bassist and a drummer played standards. Lindsey and Marvia drank wine. Aurora Delano drank grapefruit juice. They played a game of naming songs and composers.

Aurora scored with "Ding Dong the Witch Is Dead" by

Harold Arlen and E.Y. Harberg. "Everybody knows Harold Arlen. Nobody remembers Yip Harberg, but I do."

Marvia countered with "U.M.M.G." by Billy Strayhorn. She won bonus points for knowing that the letters meant Upper Manhattan Medical Group. "He was dying. He decided if he had some time left he might as well do something useful with it."

Lindsey pronounced the contest a tie, with himself a poor third, and picked up the tab.

Aurora drove them back to Rue Bienville and beat Lindsey to the punch. "You must be wiped out after flying all day. I'll be by in the morning."

Outside their room, Lindsey felt his heart pounding. He held Marvia and said, "I feel like a honeymooner."

She gave him a squeeze and said, "Sounds good to me."

They showered the day's heat and perspiration from their bodies and made love in the four-poster bed. Lindsey kissed Marvia between her breasts and tasted her with his tongue. "Garlic. You were right about vampires. We can sleep with the window open." They slept in each other's arms.

The telephone wakened them. Lindsey planted a kiss on the side of Marvia's neck and picked up the phone. His head was still spinning from the city and from having Marvia in his bed.

They met Aurora at the Café du Monde for coffee and beignets, then got in the car and headed out I-10 toward Reserve. Aurora drove a Saab that still had Oregon license plates. "Good for winter starting in a cold, damp climate. If we ever get a freeze in New Orleans, I'll be sitting pretty."

The sugar mill still loomed over Reserve, but not much else to identify the town. A sickly sweet smell hung in the warm, close air. A row of franchise stores, a laundromat, a couple of gasoline stations, a boarded-up movie theater.

Lindsey said, "I feel like a character in *The Last Picture Show*. Maybe Randy Quaid."

"Right. And I'm Cybill Shepherd," Marvia said.

A storefront bore faded gilt lettering: ANTOINE LEROUX—REAL ESTATE AND INSURANCE. Aurora pulled the Saab to the curb and led the way inside. A black receptionist sat at a battered wooden desk studying a computer screen. There was no escaping the modern world.

"Good morning, Martha. Morning, Antoine. You able to help us with that problem we talked about?" Aurora asked.

Leroux stood up. He had khaki-colored skin, black wavy hair, a smile that showed off his brilliant white teeth and an Adolph Menjou moustache. He wore a light tan suit, a shirt as white as fresh snow and a narrow, black knitted tie. He nodded and said. "Of course. Won't you come into my private office."

The office was about the size of Lindsey's kitchen and shabby but neat and clean. Aurora Delano introduced Marvia and Lindsey. Leroux extended his hand and touched his fingertips to Lindsey's. Then he took Marvia's hand in both of his and held it longer than he needed to. "Please do seat yourselves."

He opened a manila folder that lay on his desk neatly squared with the desk's edges. "I have made a list of all the McKinneys in Reserve. As I told you previously, Ms. Delano, there are but eight McKinneys in this small town."

He looked around, showing his teeth. Pearly white, dear, thought Lindsey. And from somewhere came the source, Bertold Brecht. "And since you tell me the McKinney you are investigating is black, there is no need to bother with the five white McKinney households. That is correct?" He raised an eyebrow.

"I saw McKinney. Leroy McKinney. He was definitely black," Lindsey said.

"He could not have been of mixed blood? A white McKinney to give the name, a black mother to give the pigmentation?"

Lindsey shook his head. "I don't think so. But in any case I think we should check the black McKinneys first."

Leroux nodded. "Agreed." He must use the same hair tonic as Gladstone Gander, Lindsey mused. Did they still publish those comics with Donald Duck's smarmy cousin? Brecht and Disney, what a parlay.

"Very well," Leroux continued. I have here the addresses. Might I suggest that we take my vehicle? It will draw less attention than Ms. Delano's. Citizens of Reserve prefer American automobiles and Louisiana license tags."

As they left *Antoine Leroux—Real Estate and Insurance,* Leroux paused at the receptionist's desk. "You'll hold down the fort, Miss Washington."

Martha Washington nodded.

Leroux drove a Chevy Caprice. Unlike his office it was neither old nor shabby, but like his desk it was immaculately kept. He pulled up in front of a wooden house that looked as if it belonged in the poorer section of an Erskine Caldwell novel. The four walked onto the porch. Leroux rapped his knuckles gently on the dry, gray wood.

A black man opened the door a few inches then waited for Leroux to speak. They exchanged a few words that Lindsey could not make out. Then the man opened the door wider, and Leroux gestured the others to follow him inside.

It took Lindsey a minute to figure out why the man looked so odd. He had only one arm; the other had been neatly removed and the sleeve of his shirt stitched in place. It took a little longer to realize that he also had only one natural leg, that the other was a prosthetic.

"This is Mr. Floyd McKinney. Miss Plum, Mrs. Delano, Mr. Lindsey." They all exchanged nods. Floyd McKinney wore bib overalls, what looked like an old, yellowed long johns top and heavy shoes. He pointed to chairs and grunted. They sat.

Lindsey explained that they were looking for information on a Leroy McKinney who had once lived in Reserve.

"I don't know him," Floyd McKinney said. He had a deep voice but spoke softly. He sounded like a very distant thunderstorm.

Lindsey continued, "He left Reserve many years ago. He might or might not have returned. Are you sure you never met him? Might you even have heard of him? Could he be a relative, however distant?"

Floyd McKinney said, "Possibly, possibly. I haven't lived in Reserve all my life. Worked at the mill from age fourteen until I had my accident. Been on pension ever since. Missed the war because of it. I never heard of any Leroy McKinney."

Lindsey didn't have a good feeling about this. Maybe they were intimidating Floyd. Four people barging into his home, three of them strangers, two of them white. Maybe he should have come alone with Marvia. Maybe he should have come alone without Marvia.

"Do you know the other McKinneys in Reserve? In any town nearby? Could there be McKinneys who have moved away—I mean, other than Leroy?"

"What did Leroy do? Why do you want to find him?" Floyd McKinney asked.

"We don't need to find him. I know where he is. He's dead. I'm sorry. But there's an insurance matter. If I could find out some facts about Mr. McKinney's background—Leroy McKinney's background." Sure, it was an insurance matter. It was also a murder case, but he didn't need to talk about that.

"You don't want the white McKinneys, then. You just want us. Well, well." He rubbed his face with his hand, first one cheek, then the other. He hadn't shaved today and a gray stubble bristled his cheeks. "Well, they're a few McKinneys hereabouts. Couple in Edgard. Two, no, three families of McKinneys in Lutcher. We're all distant cousins."

"What about right here in Reserve?"

"I tried to get something out of the old school records, but I couldn't find anything. Apparently when the courts made the local schools integrate, they just absorbed the black schools into the white schools," Aurora said.

"I remember that," said Floyd McKinney. "I definitely remember that."

"Nobody knows what happened to all the old records from the black schools."

Floyd McKinney made a fist and pounded it softly on his knee. His real knee. "Everybody here knows what happened. They burned them up. Threw away the sports trophies, burned up the old records, everything."

Antoine Leroux started to stand up. "Well, I think we've taken too much of Mr. McKinney's time, perhaps, and we might . . . "

Floyd McKinney said, "Sit down, you." He pointed a thick forefinger at Antoine Leroux. "You going to bother everybody else about this?"

Lindsey said, "If we could possibly . . . "

"Well, my boy is working at the oil refinery. Sugar mill wasn't good enough for him. Don't know that there would be any point in your talking to him."

Leroux said softly, "That would be Claude William McKinney, Mr. Lindsey. Goes by C.W."

Lindsey nodded.

Floyd McKinney said, "If I don't know this Leroy McKinney, Claude surely wouldn't either. You might want to talk to his Aunt Willa, though. That's my sister-in-law. The William in Claude William is in her honor."

Lindsey said, "Yes, if we could, please."

Floyd Lindsey said, "That would be Miz Willa McKinney. She's an old lady now. I don't mean old like me, I mean really old. My brother G.B. was her third husband. Or maybe her second. No, third, she still uses his name. G.B. was nineteen years older than I was. We came from a large family. He was the oldest and I was the youngest. We had six sisters and seven brothers in between us and I'm the only one left. My mama bore fifteen children in nineteen years."

He took a deep breath. Antoine Leroux started to get up again. Floyd McKinney said, "Sit down, you."

Leroux did.

Floyd McKinney continued, "G.B. married Willa before I was born. He was younger than she was, a good deal younger. She had children from her other husbands, too. And I think she might had one with G.B. before I was born."

Lindsey was trying to keep up with this. He wasn't taking notes. He didn't want to inhibit Floyd McKinney. He would remember it now and write it down afterwards.

McKinney said, "I never knew my mama. Everybody said it killed her, having all those children and having to work to feed them. She had fourteen children in fourteen years and then she didn't have anymore children for five years and then she had me. Everyone said that killed her, having that fifteenth child. I don't know if it's true. Might could be. Once Mama died, we all got parceled out, the ones too little to take care of themselves. I was raised in Napoleonville. There are no McKinneys left in that town."

He patted his knee with his hand, nervously. "I got married and my wife had one child. Then she ran away, so I never knew if it would have hurt her to have more."

"If we could talk with Mrs. McKinney. Is she able to carry on a conversation?" Lindsey asked.

Floyd McKinney said, "Oh, yes. Sure she is. She lives next door to me." He jerked his thumb toward a window. A warm breeze stirred a thin curtain.

Lindsey said, "Maybe we shouldn't bother her with so many people. Maybe if just Marvia and I visit her."

Floyd McKinney grinned. "You go right on. She'll be up and around, cleaning her house and working. She says she'll never stop working till she dies, and maybe not then. She hasn't made up her mind about that. Just talk loud to her, that's all."

Lindsey stood up, took Marvia's hand and helped her to her feet. Just like a proper lady and gentleman. Lindsey shook Floyd McKinney's hand. "Thank you," Lindsey said.

McKinney pointed at Antoine Leroux and Aurora Delano. "You two stay right here. I'll entertain you while they visit my sister-in-law."

Lindsey and Marvia went outside. "What do you think?" Lindsey asked.

"It didn't go the way a police interrogation would have. But I guess you got what there was to get. It took him a little while to warm up, but once he got going it was like a history lesson."

"Did they do that with many schools? I mean, burn records, trash trophies?"

"I don't know about burning the records. That's a new one to me, but I can believe it. There was a lot of resistance here, and a lot of resentment when the courts insisted. I never lived in the South. But I've heard of destroying trophies, so the other might be true too. And then the whites who could afford it started pulling their kids out and sending them to private schools. So the public schools are for poor whites and poor blacks. Ain't it grand?"

"Just like the rest of the country," Lindsey said. He stopped

145

to take a breath. "Well, I guess we'd better try Willa McKinney."

Marvia grinned at him. "Sure. We're de-teck-a-tiffs, ain't we?"

Lindsey stood behind Marvia so she would be seen first when Willa McKinney opened her front door. Lindsey knocked. They waited. "Do you think she heard us?" He raised his knuckles again, but the door swung back before he could knock again.

Willa McKinney had a face like a walnut shell, brown and seamed. She was less than five feet tall, and she was thin. Her wispy hair was the color of a gray cat. It was pulled into a bun at the nape of her neck. She wore a faded cotton housedress and had tied an even more faded apron over it. She wore tennis shoes with the toes cut out.

In one hand she held a broom.

She peered at Marvia Plum, then past her at Hobart Lindsey. Her eyes were very black and very bright. She nodded and made a little crooning sound that might have been a word. She backed away from the door and made a vague gesture.

Marvia stepped through the worn doorframe. Lindsey followed. He thought, if Floyd McKinney's furnishings hadn't been changed in forty years, Willa McKinney's house had stood untouched for sixty. The furniture was mostly wooden, the little material that was visible had achieved a uniform shade of pale not-quite-white, not-quite-gray, not-quite-yellow.

Lindsey started to introduce himself.

Willa McKinney said, "You'll have to speak up. I am hard of hearing."

Lindsey had heard that deaf people speak loudly. They get in the habit because they have to hear themselves. But Willa McKinney spoke in a voice so soft that Lindsey had to strain to hear her. If Floyd McKinney spoke like a distant thunderstorm, his Aunt Willa spoke like a distant breeze whispering through dry grass.

Willa McKinney set her broom aside. She made a gesture as if she were patting the air and said, "Sit down, sit down." When they complied she said, "Tea. I have iced tea and lemonade in my house. Would you like some iced tea or lemonade?"

Lindsey felt Marvia's hand on his knee. There was a message in the touch. "That's lovely, Grandmother. Whichever is easier would be lovely," She said.

Willa McKinney made her crooning sound again. She turned and moved through a doorway. Lindsey could see that the next room was a kitchen. Willa seemed hardly to move her small feet as she walked; she glided like a ghost.

Marvia murmured, "Let me, Bart. Let me."

He assented silently.

Willa returned carrying a tray with a sweating pitcher of lemonade and two unmatched glasses. She set the tray on a wooden table with a crocheted cover. Slowly, she filled the glasses with lemonade, set down the pitcher and handed a glass to Lindsey and one to Marvia. Slowly, she lowered herself onto an ancient chair.

Marvia sipped her lemonade, then set the glass down. "Thank you, Grandmother. That's wonderful. Do you mind if I call you Grandmother?"

Willa turned her head from side to side.

Marvia told Willa her own name and then introduced Lindsey.

Willa leaned forward, her elbows on her knees, and took Marvia's hands. She peered into Marvia's face. She said, "You may call me Grandmother."

Marvia said, "We're trying to find information about Leroy McKinney. Does that name mean anything to you? Is he a relative of yours?"

Willa McKinney said, "My daddy was born in slavery. He was born in the year of 1844. He remembered slavery very clearly, and he told me many horrible stories of his life in slavery. Things that he experienced and things to which he was witness. My granddaddy, whose name I have never learned, was born in Africa and brought to this continent in the hold of a slave ship, as was my grandmother. My father lived through the War Between the States and through Reconstruction. He lived under the carpetbaggers and the scalawags. He was a strong man. He was sixty-four years of age when I was born. That was in the year of 1908."

Lindsey felt that he was in another world. He had fallen into a time tunnel, like James Darren on the old television series. Soon Whit Bissell and Lee Meriwether would snatch him back to 1966.

Willa said, "I was married to my first husband in the year of 1921. I was thirteen years of age. I had one child, born prior to my wedding. I was married to my second husband in the year of 1922. I had one child with my second husband as well. I was married to my third husband in 1926. I had one child with my third husband. All three of my children were boys. I always wished I had a girl, but I only had but my three boys."

Marvia said, "Would you tell us their names?"

Willa nodded slowly. Lindsey wasn't in her world, only Marvia Plum had been admitted, and the two of them were separated from him and from the universe of today. Lindsey could watch them and listen to their conversation, but he could not participate. Willa peered into the past and captured images of husbands and babies and of her life in a gone-away world.

With an odd motion, like a tape of a bird advancing one frame at a time, Willa cocked her gray head. "My first husband was Mr. James Crump. Our child's name was Lawton. James Crump. Lawton Crump. All of my children were talented. Lawton was mechanically talented." She nodded, smiling to herself, seeing the distant past more clearly than the drab present.

"My second husband was Jefferson King, Junior," she resumed. "Our child's name was also Jefferson King. He was musically talented. He played the organ for our church at the age of seven. He was blessed with a gift from the Almighty. He was Jefferson King the third. But his father was my second husband."

Lindsey waited for the story to go on.

"My third husband was Mr. G. B. McKinney. Our child's name was Leroy. Leroy was athletically gifted. He became a professional baseball player at a very early age. G.B. McKinney. Leroy McKinney."

Lindsey felt a shock. Before he could speak, Willa McKinney continued. She was still holding Marvia's hands. She said, "You are very dark. Very dark." She shook her head sadly. "Still, you're pretty enough. I always wanted a girl."

Lindsey started to try to speak again, but Marvia turned away from Willa and hissed at him. All in a fraction of a second. He held off.

"Are any of them still alive, Grandmother?" Marvia asked.

"All of my husbands are in the ground. All of my sons served their country. My oldest boy served in the Army. He learned to fly an airplane from Mr. Joseph Wagner right here in Reserve. Mr. Wagner is in the ground. My son flew an airplane in the war and dropped bombs on Adolf Hitler. He has been to visit with his wife. My younger sons were in the United States Navy. One of them was killed in the war. I do not know if the other is alive or in the ground."

"Lawton Crump is your son?"

"He is."

"And your second son, Jefferson King, was killed in the Navy?"

"No," Willa said. She shook her head. "No, not Jefferson. I don't know where Jefferson is."

"I don't understand," Marvia said.

Lindsey was taking it all in, like a witness at a fantastic ceremony, an audience of one at a play he only remotely understood.

Willa said. "Leroy McKinney died in the Navy. I received a telegram from the government. Mr. Joseph Wagner came to my house and read the telegram to me. I have never learned to read or write. I never attended school, you see. The telegram said that the Secretary of the Navy regretted to inform me that my son Leroy McKinney had been killed in the service of his country."

"You're sure? You're sure it was Leroy?" Lindsey asked.

Willa ignored him. She said to Marvia, "Leroy and Jefferson were both members of the United States Navy. Leroy gave his life in the service of his country."

"Do you know the date?" Marvia asked.

"Mr. Joseph Wagner told me that the date of the telegram was the eighteenth day of July in the year of 1944."

"You're sure of that," Marvia said.

"I am absolutely sure. I received a check from the United States of America, and Mr. Joseph Wagner helped me to deposit it in the Dixie Savings Bank of Reserve, Louisiana. It is still there."

Without moving from his chair, Lindsey looked out the window. Across the road from Willa McKinney's house was a row of similar houses. A spotted dog walked by, nose to the earth, patiently following some scent. Beyond the houses he could see the tops of pine trees and a sky turned gray by smoke from the sugar mill and the oil refinery.

He was on another planet. He felt the time waves drawing him back, but they weren't strong enough, and he stayed where he was.

"Do you have any papers, Grandmother? The telegram, anything? Do you have your bankbook?"

Willa McKinney released Marvia's hands and slowly stood. She walked to an ancient chest of drawers. An oval mirror was mounted on top of the chest. Lindsey could see Willa's patient walnut face in the mirror. She opened a drawer, rooted through things that Lindsey could not see, removed a small envelope from the drawer, closed the drawer, turned and glided with her ghost-like walk back to Marvia. All in silence, all in slow motion.

Marvia opened the bankbook. She said, so Lindsey could hear, "This hasn't been updated since 1949. Does your brother-in-law Floyd know about this?"

"I don't know. We seldom discuss financial matters. I do not think it would be seemly."

"I'll take this to him, if I may. Is that all right, Grandmother?"

Willa considered for a while. "I suppose it will be all right."

"Can Floyd read and write, Grandmother?"

With pride in her soft voice, Willa said, "Floyd and Claude William can both read and write and do sums. Claude William was named for me, you know."

Marvia said, "I know that. Floyd told me that." She stood up. "Thank you, Grandmother."

Willa took Marvia's face in her hands. Lindsey watched. He saw Willa look into Marvia's face. She kissed her on one cheek, then on the other and said, "You are very dark, but you are still a pretty child."

Outside on the porch, Marvia turned away. Lindsey waited, saying nothing. After a minute Marvia turned back and took Lindsey's hand. He saw that she had Willa's bankbook in the other.

During the very short walk back to Floyd McKinney's house, Marvia said, "Forty-eight years worth of compound interest. What do you think this thing is worth?"

Lindsey said, "Floyd will have to track down the bank. Chances are it's long since disappeared into some giant 'glom."

Marvia said, "I'll have Aurora Delano stay in touch with Floyd and Willa. I don't trust Mr. Antoine Leroux."

Eighteen

BACK AT *ANTOINE LEROUX—REAL ESTATE AND INSURANCE*, Lindsey checked his Seiko against the digital clock mounted on the wall. No wonder his stomach was sending up empty signals. Willa McKinney's lemonade had been tasty, but he hadn't eaten since the coffee and beignets at Café du Monde.

Martha Washington looked up from her keyboard and said, "Your appointment is waiting, Mr. Leroux."

Antoine Leroux looked up at the clock. He shook his head. "They're early. If I can move that old boarding house I'll buy champagne for all." He shook hands hastily with Lindsey, Marvia and Aurora Delano.

Martha Washington grimaced behind Leroux's back and said, "I'll put up the closed sign when I take my lunch."

"Is there anyplace here to get a light meal?" Lindsey asked.

Martha Washington surveyed the group. Lindsey tried to read her mind. When she narrowed her eyes, he almost could. "Nothing fancy," he said.

She nodded. "I'm just going for a sandwich."

Lindsey looked at the others. "That's all right with me. That all right with you?"

Marvia and Aurora agreed.

Martha Washington led them to a luncheonette. Hanging over the restaurant was a sign with faded red and green lettering and soft-drink logos. The lettering had once read WALTER'S FINE FOOD GRILLE. Inside, half the red leatherette seats at the counter were occupied. They found a booth and slid into it, Lindsey facing Marvia, Aurora Delano beside him facing Martha Washington. It had not been planned. At least no one had spoken of the arrangement.

The menu could have come from any luncheonette in the fifty states and had prices that hadn't changed in a decade or two. Lindsey ordered a club sandwich and a soft drink. The women ordered salads. Walter's Fine Food Grille had one waitress. Stitched on the pocket of her uniform was the name Rita. She set out water glasses, exchanging a few words with Martha Washington. Clearly, Martha was a regular at Walter's.

By the time the food arrived Lindsey was talking about the Double Bee project. Aurora Delano was interested from a SPUDS perspective and was quoting Ducky Richelieu at every opportunity. Martha Washington knew enough about International Surety to offer a comment from time to time.

Rita set Lindsey's sandwich on the wooden tabletop. Walter's Fine Food Grille wasn't only pre-McDonald's, it was pre-Formica. Amazing. Lindsey was talking about *Bessie Blue* and about the Tuskegee Airmen and Double Bee Enterprises. Rita had no qualms about joining the conversation. "I'll bet little Walter knows all about that," she said.

"Who's little Walter?" Lindsey asked.

"Little Walter Scoggins. This place has been in the Scoggins family for four generations. Little Walter studies at Southern U up in Baton Rouge, but he's home now for a break. He always comes in to help out. He's in the kitchen now."

"And he knows about the Tuskegee Airmen?"

"He's studying our people's history. He says he's going to be a teacher. Big Walter says he'll have to take over the business. I don't know what he'll do."

Lindsey nodded. He took a bite of his sandwich.

"You really making a movie about the Airmen?" Rita asked.

Lindsey swallowed toast and bacon and tomato and lettuce and turkey. "Well, I'm working with the people making the movie," he said.

"Little Walter would like to hear about that. Okay I send him out?"

"Sure."

Rita disappeared.

Lindsey took another bite of his sandwich.

Little Walter Scoggins was big. He wiped his hands on his white apron before he shook hands with Lindsey. He made a little bow to Aurora and to Marvia. He gave Martha Washington a kiss on the cheek, his white paper cap making a faint sound against her hair. She moved sideways and Walter slid into the booth beside her. The booth was now a little crowded, but no one complained.

Walter said, "You know about the Airmen?" His look was skeptical.

Lindsey said, "I've been talking with one of them. Lawton Crump. He comes from Reserve."

"I'd like to meet Lawton, but we don't see him around here. He tell you some stories?"

"He says it was the best time in his life. He was taught to fly by a man here in Reserve. A Joseph Wagner," Lindsey said.

"I can see you've been doing your homework. And I can see why Crump would feel that way. I've come across quite a lot of that. As an historian, that is." He actually said, *an historian.* He looked at his white apron and laughed. "This is all the rage in academia nowadays."

Lindsey asked what Walter meant by coming across a lot of that.

"They keep telling me I'll understand in thirty or forty years. I'm twenty-two now. I'll have my master's in six months and my doctorate in two years. But one poor old fellow—he must have been nearly fifty—told me that he'd saved two little girls from drowning in the Mississippi when he was fourteen. He got a gold medal for it, the mayor shook his hand, his picture was in the newspaper. He said it ruined his life."

"Why?" Lindsey asked.

"He said it was all downhill from there. Seemed to me he had everything. Finished school, got a job, a house, a family. But he never recaptured the thrill of saving those two little girls. That and the glory, the recognition. It ate away at him. He started drinking, started fooling around. He lost his job. His wife divorced him. I see him hanging around the campus. He's a wino now. He does odd jobs for drink money. It's sad."

154

"What about the Airmen?" Lindsey asked.

Walter smiled. "Right. Well, they really were heroes. They fought against all the odds to get the training they needed and to get into combat. I'm no supermind, but I happened to study the Airmen and I do have a good memory for numbers." He paused to take a drink of water from Martha Washington's glass.

"They graduated 992 pilots. They flew 1,578 missions in North Africa and Europe, destroyed 261 enemy aircraft and damaged or destroyed gun emplacements, radar installations, trains, ammunition dumps. Even sank a German destroyer in the Mediterranean. They won a Legion of Merit, a Silver Star and hundreds of other medals. And 147 of them gave their lives for their country."

"Okay, you do have a good memory for numbers," Lindsey conceded.

"It's about time they were remembered. I'll see your *Bessie Blue* film, Mr. Lindsey," Walter Scoggins said.

"Not really my film," Lindsey said.

Scoggins slid from the booth. "I have to get back to work. Pop will skin me if the gumbo isn't ready by dinner time."

Martha Washington waited until Scoggins had disappeared into the kitchen. Then she said, "I'm going to marry that man."

"Does he know that?" Marvia asked.

Martha Washington smiled and said, "I haven't told him yet."

The drive back to New Orleans took half an hour. When they arrived, Aurora Delano said, "I have desk space at the I.S. office on Tchoupitoulas. You can use that, use the phone, fax, whatever. It's just mid-afternoon in Denver."

"No thanks," Lindsey said.

"Don't you want to report in to Richelieu?"

"I'm not ready," Lindsey replied. Then to Marvia, "The trip was worth it. Marvia, you saved the day. As far as Willa was concerned, I was nobody. I wasn't even there. She only talked to you."

"I'm glad I met her. Did you hear, she was the daughter of a slave. It was that long ago, her father grew up in slavery."

"I'll have to sit down and work this out when I get back to California. It's very peculiar," Lindsey said.

Aurora shook her head. She had permed her hair since Denver. New job, new hairdo, new life. She had parked the Saab and walked with Lindsey and Marvia into the hotel. They were sitting in the hotel's brick courtyard surrounded by fantastically colored flowers. A fountain that could have come from France in Napoleon's day threw water into the air. The afternoon sunlight turned the spray into a miniature rainbow.

Lindsey had still not come to terms with his tour of worlds. Mother might travel among the decades, but Lindsey was enduring his own dislocations. Denver, Walnut Creek, Berkeley, Richmond, New Orleans, Reserve. Sitting in Willa McKinney's parlor, he had voyaged a century into the past.

"Are you headed back to California, then? I mean, right away?" Aurora asked.

"If I can get Marvia to stay another day or two, I will. I'll need to phone home, but if Mother is all right and if Marvia can stay, that's what I want."

"Well, call me if you need anything. At I.S. or at home. Enjoy your stay. *Laissez les bon temps rouler.* The Chamber of Commerce pays me to tell people that," Aurora said.

They got some advice from Aurora. After she left, they strolled through the French Quarter along Decatur Street and made their way to the old French Market. Marvia bought a black T-shirt with a golden saxophone on it for her brother, a purse for her mother and an alligator-skin belt for her dad.

They wandered back to Rue Chartres and ordered cool drinks in the Napoleon House. Marvia dropped her purchases at the hotel on Bienville, and they took a taxi out of the Quarter to another restaurant that Aurora had recommended.

Midway through the meal Lindsey asked, "You notice anything about this place?"

"They serve the best glazed ham I've tasted in years. How do you like your fish?"

"I don't mean the food. The food is fine. I mean the people here. The customers and the staff."

"No." She looked around. "They're just folks."

"I'm the only white person in the place," Lindsey said.

"No kidding!" She scanned the dining room again. "Don't say anything about it. I won't give you away."

She had phoned Berkeley from their hotel. Although she was on vacation, she wanted to check in. Lieutenant Yamura said that things were under control. No more problems than usual in Berkeley. There hadn't been a riot on Telegraph Avenue in weeks and the homicide rate had not skyrocketed in Marvia's absence.

"You were crying, weren't you?" Lindsey asked.

Marvia looked at him.

"On Mrs. McKinney's porch. When you turned away."

She nodded.

"I didn't do anything to help. I'm sorry. I didn't understand. I'm still not sure I understand."

"It's the history, Bart. It wasn't your fault. But being that close to it . . . it must be like Eric Coffman. He says his interest in history is casual. He pretends it's just a hobby. But those games. Why would he want 1942, 1943? And those books on World War Two. You must have seen how he changed the subject when I asked him about them. If I were Jewish, I'd feel that way about the Holocaust, the way I feel about slavery and everything that came after. It still isn't over."

She shook her head as if she could shake off the feeling. "Some vacation! Tomorrow's our last day. Can we go to the aquarium?"

"Sure."

"I want to get some souvenirs for Jamie."

"Maybe we can come here again. To New Orleans. And bring Jamie. He'd love this town. We could go to the aquarium, to the zoo . . . " Lindsey said.

Marvia reached across the table and put her hand on his.

"Like a real family," he said. "I don't think you should let his father take him, Marvia. I understand what you told me about his having a black home. But there are a lot of mixed

157

families today. I think I could be a good father to him. I want to try."

"Where would we live? What about your mother?"

"She's getting better. That's the fantastic thing. All the years that I had no one else, no outside life, she still believed I was her little boy. I think I was part of what was making her crazy. The more I took care of her, the more I helped her . . . I think I was harming her."

She frowned. "I doubt that."

"Ever since I've been with you, been away from her a lot of the time, she's been getting better. She's taking a course now for older women who want to get back into the job market."

Marvia pressed her hand against her eyes. "I don't know, Bart. I'm confused."

They took a cab back to Rue Bienville and sat by the fountain for an hour, then went to bed.

In the morning, they rode a streetcar along the waterfront to the aquarium and spent half the day there.

"We can't just take him to Monterey. Maybe for a treat, maybe for his next birthday. But we have to bring him here. The rain forest was wonderful and those white alligators were just astonishing. Did you get a good look at them?" Marvia asked.

"I got eye to eye with one fellow."

"Not like the dolphins in the Steinhart, are they? We could take Jamie there. It's just across the Bay Bridge. If one of those dolphins makes eye contact with you, it's like some big friendly uncle who thinks you're funny."

"I've never known a dolphin."

"You ought to try it. But those alligators, brrr! Did you get the same feeling I did?"

"They're not from our world, and we don't belong in theirs. They're prehistoric creatures. That guy was looking at me. I could almost read his mind. He was thinking: That thing would make a nice meal. If only I could get through this glass, it would make a lovely little meal."

Willa McKinney would not leave them in peace.

"I keep thinking about her," Marvia said. They were back at

Decatur Street, sipping cold concoctions at an outdoor bistro while a jazz trio serenaded the tourists. Lindsey was feeling acclimated and more akin to the city's residents than to the travelers from Chicago and Toronto and Philadelphia. It was time to go home.

Marvia gazed into her glass distractedly. Lindsey watched her in silence, then asked, "Is it the history again?"

"No. Well, yes, but not the way you mean. It's what Willa said about her sons."

"I've got that in my notebook now. I'll follow it up when we get home."

Marvia spoke into the bottom of her glass. "Why did Lawton Crump say that Leroy McKinney was a stranger to him if they were brothers? Half-brothers anyway. If Willa McKinney is really Lawton Crump's mother . . . "

"I believe that," Lindsey said. "Crump told me the same story about Mr. Wagner and the flying lessons that Mrs. McKinney told us. Told you. It was a wild shot but it wasn't completely nuts. Crump admitted that he was from Reserve. Huh, maybe I shouldn't put it that way. There was nothing to admit. It's just part of his biography. The whole story about Joseph Wagner and the flying lessons. But why did he leave out the McKinney family and his connection to them? He must have known we'd find out."

Marvia shook her head. "Maybe, maybe not. Did he say he didn't know Leroy McKinney, or that he didn't know the dead man at North Field?"

"I don't see what you mean. What's the difference? Leroy McKinney was the dead man." Someone tapped Lindsey on the shoulder. He turned. A heavyset woman with a camera in her hand smiled at him.

"Would you do me a favor?" She held the camera toward him. "It's one of those point-and-shoot kind. Would you take a picture of us with the piano player?" She waved at her table. Two other women sat there. They all wore flowered dresses and souvenir baseball caps with dancing alligators and Blackened Voodoo Beer logos on them.

They surrounded the piano player. He wore a straw hat but

pushed it off his forehead and grinned at the three women while they posed. Lindsey snapped the picture. The camera advanced the film automatically, and Lindsey shot another for good measure.

The woman took back her camera. "Would you like one with your friend?"

Lindsey grinned and put his arm around Marvia.

The woman in the flowered dress snapped the picture. Lindsey handed her his International Surety card and she slipped it into her wallet. "I'll send it to you as soon as I get my film developed."

"The South is not what it used to be," Marvia said. "What about Crump and Leroy McKinney?"

"I'm trying to remember," Lindsey said. "As far as I can recall, he just said that he didn't know the dead man. He didn't say the name, Leroy McKinney. But so what?"

"Willa McKinney said that Leroy was killed in 1944. Joseph Wagner brought the telegram to her house and read it to her because she didn't know how to read."

"Right."

"So how could Leroy McKinney have died last week at North Field in Oakland if he died in 1944? In the war. In the Navy."

They spent a last night in New Orleans, a last night in the four-poster bed in the hotel on Rue Bienville. They promised each other not to think about the McKinneys, about murder, about International Surety. Marvia was playful. Lindsey asked her again to marry him and even that failed to dispel her good humor.

When the 737 was an hour from Oakland, Lindsey used the in-flight telephone to call Eric Coffman. Their plan was Marvia's idea, and Coffman agreed. They would bring Jamie again so he could play with Sarah and Rebecca. Marvia and Lindsey would consult Coffman not about law but about history. Coffman said he had promised Miriam dinner out tonight, but they could come tomorrow.

When the plane touched down, Lindsey phoned Mother, or

he tried to. Mrs. Hernandez answered the phone. True to her word, Mother was out of the house.

He spent the next day catching up on SPUDS work, including Double Bee. Ina Chandler had given him some background information on the project. They had decided to shoot in Oakland because the terrain was suitable, the airport management was cooperative and the foundation funding the project had pressed them to use Oakland. Moreover, they didn't have the budget to shoot in North Africa, Italy or Germany.

Lindsey had balked at that point. "If the planes are based in Texas, and the action took place in Alabama and then in Europe and North Africa, it still doesn't make sense to me. I mean, that they are shooting this film here."

Ina Chandler's response had been brief. "Money talks."

Lindsey asked how Double Bee had persuaded the Knights of the Air to relinquish control of its precious airplanes.

"They flew the planes up from Texas, and they'll fly them back when the shooting is finished. They'll do all the flying except when we're actually shooting Lawton Crump. And when he takes up the *Bessie Blue* there will be a flight crew of Knights with him."

Doc High took Lindsey's call at Oakland Police Headquarters. He told Lindsey that he had contacted the Pentagon for verification of Leroy McKinney's identity. Lindsey sat up straight and grabbed a pencil. Ms. Wilbur and Elmer Mueller were both in the office, and they both stared at Lindsey.

"We got our reply this morning," High said.

"All right, what did they say?" He could hear High fumbling with something, maybe searching for his forbidden pipe and tobacco, maybe for a case folder with Leroy McKinney's name on the tab and a faxed report on top of the papers inside.

"Well, first of all, they couldn't verify Mr. McKinney's fingerprints. The military services fingerprint all new inductees nowadays. They have for many years. But back during World War Two things were not so well organized, and a lot of records have got lost or destroyed over the years. Warehouse fires, floods, packing and moving records."

"Okay, that's the bad news." Lindsey tried to concentrate on the lined pad in front of him, but he could still feel the eyes on him. Would SPUDS spring for a private office for him? he wondered. "What's the good news?"

"Well, I'm not sure that I'd call any of this good news, Bart. But it is information."

"Okay. What?"

"Well, they did have a record of a Leroy McKinney. I thought there might be more than one person with that name. Maybe you can help me with that angle."

"Was he born in Reserve, Louisiana?" Lindsey asked.

He could almost hear Doc High smile. "That's what the Pentagon says. All right. Then we've probably got the right man. Ah . . . or maybe not. You see, the Pentagon says that their Leroy McKinney was killed in 1944. And our Leroy McKinney just died. How could that be? Father and son, do you think?"

Before Lindsey could say anything, High said, "No, scrub that. The medical examiner indicated that our victim was a man of about seventy. That would jibe with a young serviceman in World War Two. But how could a young man, maybe even a teenager, die in 1944 and die again half a century later?"

"I thought you folks were going to soft-pedal this case. Sergeant Finnerty said you were concentrating on the drug gangs and the turf wars," Lindsey said.

"Well, yes. I heard about your little escapade in Richmond, you see. You certainly have a way of putting your foot into it, Lindsey. So I'll say that my interest in McKinney has picked up once again. Just a bit, don't you see."

"What was McKinney's date of death? His first date of death," Lindsey said.

"That was July 17, 1944. He was a Navy man, a seaman first class, assigned to the U.S. Naval Barracks, Port Chicago, California. You've heard of that? Little town up where the Sacramento River flows into San Francisco Bay. Don't look on your map, Lindsey. The town doesn't even exist anymore. But it was up near Concord, right where the Concord Naval Weapons Station is."

Lindsey was writing fast.

"How does that sound to you? You have any information that would jibe with?" High asked.

Lindsey gave High a rundown of his interview with Willa McKinney. Of Marvia's interview. He finished with Willa's account of the telegram from the Secretary of the Navy that Joseph Wagner had read to her.

High whistled. "Sounds like our man, all right. But we've got a bigger mystery now than we had before. And the part about Lawton Crump being the half-brother of Leroy McKinney. I'm going to review Sergeant Finnerty's file on Mr. Crump and then have a chat with Mr. Crump myself."

"Keep me posted, will you?"

"Now I'm not so sure," High said. "You know how we feel about private eyes messing around in homicides."

"Doc, you know I'm not a P.I."

"Right, thanks for reminding me. If you were, I could threaten you with having your license lifted. Well, what about your pistol permit?"

"Don't have a permit. Don't have a pistol. Don't know how to use one. Don't want to learn."

"That's the trouble with you minimalists. Nothing we can threaten to take away from you. How are we supposed to keep you in line?"

"Not in line. Don't want to get in line. So I can't get out of line."

"You're very funny. *Not.* As the kids are saying nowadays. Just be careful, Lindsey."

Nineteen

MARVIA PLUM PARKED HER MUSTANG at Lindsey's house in Walnut Creek. Lindsey opened the car door for her. This lady and gentleman thing could be addictive. She climbed out of the car. He put his arms around her and gave her a warm kiss.

She looked at him, startled. "Wow! You're turning into a real Romeo."

"You do that to me." Jamie swung open the passenger door and bounded out, the Flying Fortress still in his hand. He had progressed from a formal handshake to letting Lindsey pick him up and set him down again as a form of greeting. "I flew in the Flying Fortress. Mr. Crump took me up," he said.

Lindsey looked at Marvia. "Is that true?"

She nodded. "They're doing footage of Lawton Crump flying the B-17. Mrs. Chandler said they could have blue-screened the windows, whatever that is, then shot him sitting at the controls and supered in the exteriors. But he wouldn't do it. He said he'd been trained to fly a Seventeen and by God he was going to fly one. He's been up almost every day. Out over the ocean, out to the Farralones and back."

"But . . . was he really a bomber pilot?"

"You might want to talk to him about that," Marvia said. "Did he show you the book? I went to the library. There's a book on the Tuskegee Airmen. Flying fighters in North Africa and Europe. Must be the same book little Walter Scoggins memorized. Has all that info in it that Walter was quoting. You think Martha Washington is really going to get him?"

"The poor sap doesn't have a chance."

"I don't think so either." She didn't even pause to shift gears. "They were training to fly four-engine bombers. Once the war ended in Europe, the Army brought them home and started training them for bombing missions in the Pacific."

"I don't recall Crump's mentioning that."

"He might not have. The war ended before they got into combat in the Pacific. But they'd had training. Crump knows how to fly a B-17. And remember, he was in the airline business for another thirty years. He knows about big airplanes."

"And he took Jamie up?"

"Sure he did. Mom said I could go," Jamie said.

Marvia nodded. "Jamie was so excited, he took his toy . . . "

"It's not a toy, Mom. It's an authentic scale model." He enunciated every syllable carefully, as if he had been practicing. Au-then-tic.

Marvia said, "Sorry. Jamie brought his authentic scale model to school and showed everybody. His teacher phoned Double Bee, and they took the whole class out to North Field. Everybody loved it."

"And all the kids got to ride in the Fortress?"

"Just me!" Jamie was circling Lindsey and Marvia, flying his B-17 and making engine sounds.

"Come on in the house for a minute," Lindsey said.

"Good idea, Jamie can use a pit stop. So can his mom." Marvia said.

Lindsey's mother was home from her class. She told Marvia about learning to use a computer. "We have the loveliest teacher. She's a wonderful colored girl—no, we don't say that anymore. I have to remember. She's a wonderful young woman who works for one of those computer companies, and they give her time off to teach our class."

"I'm glad you're enjoying it," Marvia said. "You didn't have any trouble getting accustomed to the computer?"

Mother hesitated. "I was frightened of it. At first. I didn't know how to turn it on, and I was embarrassed to ask. It's been so many years, you see. But she won't let anyone feel embarrassed. And I'm catching on. I won't go back." She made a gesture with her head. The meaning was clear. "It's hard to learn, but I will not go back."

Lindsey took Mother's hand. "I'm proud of you."

Mother said, "Miss Riley—that's her name, Doris Riley— she says we all come from someplace and she won't let any of us go back. She's such a wonderful girl. Funny and smart as a whip. She says she's black Irish. That's why her name is Riley."

Jamie came back from the bathroom and Marvia excused herself. Jamie spotted Lindsey's computer. "Do you have any games, Mr. Lindsey?" he asked.

"You can call me Bart, Jamie."

Jamie looked embarrassed. "Okay."

"I'm sorry. I only use it for business. No games. But we'll be at Sarah and Rebecca's house in a little while."

"Nintendo!" Jamie said.

Mother took Lindsey by the hand and led him into the kitchen. She nodded toward the living room. "He's just a little boy," she said.

"Of course he is. He's seven years old."

"But I see them on the news. These gangs. All the killing." She made an anguished gesture with both her hands. "And your friend Marvia is his mother. And Miss Riley, my teacher. They're so nice. What makes them change?"

"I don't know, Mother. Or maybe I do. Look, why don't you come alone with us? You know Eric Coffman. You've met his wife, Miriam. You're invited for dinner, too."

"No." Her voice was abrupt, frightened.

"All right. I mean . . . "

"Not yet. Please, Hobart. Later."

Lindsey said, "I understand, Mother. When you're ready. All right."

"Bart?" Marvia called from the living room. "Let's not be late to the Coffmans."

They left the Mustang in the driveway in Walnut Creek and took the Hyundai to Concord.

This time, Sarah and Rebecca did not have to drag Jamie off to play Nintendo. Even before they left the foyer, they were negotiating over which game to play. It sounded as if they were going to settle on The Magic of Scheherazade. Jamie was fighting a rear-guard action, complaining again that Sarah and Rebecca only liked girl games.

Lindsey told Eric about the McKinney family of Reserve, Louisiana and the story of the 1944 telegram. Then he said, "Doc High at OPD got a fax from the Pentagon confirming Leroy McKinney's Navy service at Port Chicago and his death in July of 1944. So we still have to figure out who really died in the hangar at North Field. If it was Leroy McKinney, then who died in 1944? Or if McKinney really died in '44, who got bashed in the forehead in Oakland?"

Coffman chewed his lips. He walked to a bookcase. Reached into his pocket for a pair of gold-rimmed glasses. He pulled down a couple of books. "Marvia, how much do you know about the Port Chicago explosion and the mutiny that followed?"

"Some. It's a painful chapter," Marvia said.

Coffman cleared a platter of cheese and crackers from the cocktail table and laid out the books. "You can borrow these, Bart, if you want to. I'll need them back, of course."

Marvia said, "I know those books. Pearson blames the mutineers. Allen exonerates them and blames the Navy."

Coffman nodded. "You want to give Bart a fill-in, Marvia, or shall I?"

"I'd like to hear your take on it. You go ahead."

Coffman plumped his bulk into an overstuffed chair, then leaned forward, elbows on his knees, hands upraised. Lindsey looked at him. They had been friends for years, but for the first time Lindsey decided that he knew who Coffman looked like. If Sidney Greenstreet in The Maltese Falcon had been twenty years younger and had grown a reddish-brown beard, he would have been Eric Coffman.

"Very well." Coffman nodded. He even sounded like Greenstreet, or maybe like Caspar Gutman. "During the second World War, the armed services were under pressure to grant equal treatment to racial minorities, particularly to blacks. Negroes, that was the accepted term then."

Lindsey said, "Right. I've heard some of this from Lawton Crump, about the Tuskegee Airmen."

Coffman nodded. "The Navy was by far the most hidebound service—they would say, tradition-bound—on that score. There was a lot of ethnic harassment. Those old war movies about the tough Italian kid and the Iowa farmboy and the scholarly Chinese fellow with the glasses getting together in the name of freedom and democracy . . . "

"I've seen a hundred of those," Lindsey said.

" . . . they were more propaganda than reality." Light glinted off Coffman's glasses. "That was the ideal. There were more barrack tussles and teeth knocked loose than you can imagine. I've studied this. I know what went on. The blacks had it the worst. All they could do in the Navy was work as mess boys. Waiters and dishwashers for the brass. And the Jews didn't have it much better. We were fighting to stop Hitler's Holocaust, but we weren't much better off right here. But the blacks had it the worst." Coffman paused to catch his breath. Then he continued.

"Okay. Port Chicago was the major supply depot for the Pacific Theater. Right here in Contra Costa County. You could walk there. Thousands of tons of supplies and ammunition went through there. The Navy would bring in Liberty ships or Victory ships, a lot of them were built right here in Richmond. Big, slow-moving freighters. The ammunition came in by rail. They had a rail spur running right out onto the pier. They'd bring empty ships up to the pier, sometimes two at a time, one on each side of the pier, and start winching ammunition onto the ships and filling the holds."

Shrieks erupted from the Coffman Nintendo parlor. Eric turned his head. Once more, lamplight glinted off the metal frames of his glasses. "Apparently the Navy had more Negroes than they needed for mess duty, and there was this heavy stevedoring work to be done, so they formed up labor battalions and set them to work at Port Chicago. Marvia, do I have it right?"

"That's the version I've learned."

"All right. Now, Allen's book is the more recent and seems

to be the better informed of the two. He says these stevedores had no special training. They worked twenty-four hours a day, seven days a week. They were handling dangerous materials. Most of the men were black, some of the petty officers were black. The higher the rank the more whites, and all of the commissioned officers were white."

Lindsey said, "I've heard something like this before. About the Army back then."

Coffman said, "There were some pretty vicious, pretty nasty individuals involved."

He leaned over the books on the table as if he had never seen them before. He picked up a cracker and munched on it. Crumbs lodged in his beard.

"On the night of July 17, 1944, there was a disaster. Something set off a huge explosion. There were two ships tied up at the pier, one nearly full, one completely empty. They were vaporized. There was an ammunition train on the pier. The pier was completely demolished. The train disappeared. Later on they found the locomotive sunk in the mud where the pier had been. The engineer was still in the cab."

Lindsey shivered.

"If you read the newspapers from 1944, they saw the flash and felt the tremor for miles around. There are still old-timers around who'll tell you what it was like. You know the landscape over in Concord? River on one side, then some flatland, then rolling hills. Think of the air currents that were set up when those ships blew. Nobody knew what had happened. At the time, that is. Some people thought it was an earthquake, some thought it was a Japanese attack. The explosion was huge. Nobody knows exactly how many people were killed but it was at least 320. They confirmed that many. Most of them were black stevedores. The explosion was estimated at ten megatons. Ten million tons of TNT."

"Wait a minute. That's atom-bomb size. That's impossible," Lindsey said.

"Yes and no. Yes, it's nuclear detonation size. Ten megatons would be half the power of the Hiroshima bomb. And no, it's not impossible. Some people have suggested that the Port Chicago explosion was nuclear. That there was a small A-bomb loaded in the *E.A. Bryan*. That was one of the ships that blew up, the fully loaded one. Allen discounts that, but the question is still open. There's even a paranoid theory that the explosion was deliberate, a damage test."

"No way," Marvia said.

"I don't buy it either," Coffman said.

"What a tragedy," Lindsey said.

"That was just the beginning," Marvia said.

"You take over for a while, Marvia. I'm getting dry," Coffman said. "I'm going to see if Miriam needs a hand in the kitchen. And I want to check on the kids. They're being suspiciously quiet."

Marvia was sitting on the couch beside Lindsey. She turned to face him. "After the explosion came the mutiny. The surviving sailors claimed they hadn't been trained in loading explosives. They had a lot of other grievances, too. Do you know Tommy Morris, Bart?"

He shook his head.

"I'll introduce you to him. He's a friend of my dad's. He was at Port Chicago. He was a sailor. He told me there was a little mutiny even before the explosion. The white officers were pretty hard on the sailors. There were some black petty officers in charge of work crews. One white officer, in particular, was really riding them. He started chewing out the petty officer. Tommy Morris told me this officer said, 'I'd rather have Japs working this job than niggers.' "

Eric Coffman popped his head into the room. "Dinner's just about ready." He disappeared again. Shrill voices rose in protest, complaining about the interruption of the Nintendo game.

Marvia continued. "The crew chief said, 'Okay, go ahead and get the Japs to do it.' And he pulled his men off the job. They settled that one, smoothed it over. But after the explosion, some of the men refused to load ammunition again."

Lindsey said, "In wartime? They'd be court-martialed."

"Technically, they could. And were. Hundreds of men were involved. The whole situation was an awful muddle. The Navy picked out fifty black sailors and tried them for mutiny. They were convicted, but there was such a scandal that the brass didn't dare impose serious penalties. So they kind of shuffled them around for a while, held some of them on ships but didn't give them any work to do. It was like *The Man Without a Country*. Times fifty. Finally they discharged them."

"Were they guilty? I mean, *weren't* they guilty?"

Marvia shrugged.

Miriam Coffman called them to dinner. She served pasta and a green salad.

Over the meal, Lindsey said, "And Leroy McKinney was one of the 320 men who were killed."

"That would jibe with Willa's story," Marvia said.

"And it would jibe with Doc High's Pentagon fax."

"But it wouldn't jibe with the body at the airport," Coffman said.

"No, it wouldn't. I think I'd better talk with Lawton Crump again. I want to find out more about the Tuskegee Airmen," Lindsey said.

Coffman offered, "I've got a book on them, too."

"Right. But there's no substitute for talking to somebody who was there. Who was part of it. Marvia, I might want to meet Tommy Morris, too. If you can arrange that. But I really want to talk with Mr. Crump."

He looked at Marvia, at Miriam and Eric, at the three children. The children seemed uninterested in the adult conversation, but somehow the topic had seeped across the generational barrier. Jamie was telling Sarah and Rebecca about his flight on the *Bessie Blue*. At first, the girls reacted with angry disbelief. But when Jamie persisted, adding detail after detail, they gradually swung around to admiration and then envy.

Sarah tugged at her father's sleeve until he focused on her. "Daddy, Jamie got a ride on a bomber. Can we go? Can he take me and Rebecca?"

"Rebecca and me," Coffman corrected. "Place the other person first in your sentence."

Sarah managed to look contrite and exasperated at the same time.

Miriam added, "May we go. Not can we, may we. You're asking permission."

"Mother! Father! May Rebecca and I go on the airplane with Jamie and his friend Mr. Crump?"

Coffman said, "I don't know. We'll have to look into it. Marvia, Hobart, what do you think?"

"I'll have to see about that. If it's all right with you and Miriam, we'll see about it," Lindsey said.

Coffman said, "Bart, I want to get back to this McKinney killing. If you think the answer lies in the Port Chicago disaster, why do you need to talk with Crump again? Wasn't he at Tuskegee? Or, by the summer of '44, he would have been in North Africa or Italy flying fighter escort missions."

"I'm not sure. Well, yes I am. Crump and McKinney were both from Reserve, they were half-brothers. I want to talk to Crump about that. But I think there's more to it than that. I think it involves the Tuskegee Airmen and the Port Chicago Mutineers."

Jamie had exhausted his supply of details about the B-17, or maybe Sarah and Rebecca had heard all that they wanted to hear about it. Now they were discussing The Magic of Scheherazade. Jamie was complaining that it wasn't fair that somebody named Supica only spoke Peke Peke instead of English and that it was hard to find Gun Meca, the robot, to translate what Supica was saying.

"You think there's a connection between Tuskegee and Port Chicago?" Marvia asked.

Lindsey shrugged. "I don't know if there is or not. It's more of a feeling. Look, these Negro servicemen were trying to serve their country and to improve their lot at the same time. Somehow the Army gave them a chance."

"Grudgingly."

"No quarrel there. Talk about dragging your heels. But they did get a chance. And they won their share of glory. To say the least." He looked around. He had the attention of everyone at the table whose age was in double digits.

He said, "And the Navy stuck their black recruits in Port

Chicago doing stevedore work. Then came the explosion and then the mutiny. It was tragic."

Marvia said, "So far, I follow you. But where does this lead us? What does it mean? And what does it have to do with North Field?"

"What does it mean? I don't really know. It just seems to me that we're looking at two sides of the same coin. One group got a chance to prove themselves and wound up as decorated heroes, and the other group were squashed down and wound up branded as mutineers."

He looked around. "And now, fifty years later, these two . . . two, I don't know, roads that were created fifty years ago . . . " He drew twin paths in the air. "Somehow, for some reason, they've crossed. Crossed again. Lawton Crump and Leroy McKinney were half-brothers. Born in Louisiana, when, what did Willa tell us? Anyway, in the 1920s. By the 1940s, they're young men. Crump becomes a Tuskegee Airman and gets to fly in Africa and Europe. He comes home a hero. McKinney becomes a Port Chicago stevedore and . . . what?"

"Yes," Miriam Coffman said, "And what?"

"And he dies. But did he die in 1944 or just last month? Death by violence in either case. Was his head smashed with a monkey wrench? Or was he vaporized by the explosion in 1944? The Navy says he was killed at Port Chicago. Doc High queried the Pentagon and they confirmed Leroy McKinney's death in the explosion. If McKinney died in 1944, whose murder are we investigating?"

"You're leaving someone out of this, Bart," Marvia said.

Lindsey waited for her to continue.

"What happened to Jefferson King the third? Willa McKinney's middle son?"

It was getting late and the children were getting cranky. Lindsey and Marvia and Jamie took their leave.

Nellie Crump answered the phone. She told Lindsey her husband was taking a nap but she would have him call back when he woke up. Or, if Lindsey preferred, he could just see him at North Field the next day. Double Bee was shooting more footage, and he was going to be there in his leather flying helmet and heated flight suit.

Lindsey had called from Marvia's apartment. After talking with Nellie Crump, he flipped the pages of the two books dealing with the Port Chicago mutiny. He found a list of the 320 men killed in the explosion, black and white, civilian and military. The list was broken down by status and assignment. He pointed to the page and said, "Marvia, look at this."

She whistled. "Leroy McKinney. Listed under bodies recovered and identified."

Lindsey nodded.

"Willa told the truth. Not that I doubted her, but now we know for certain," Marvia said.

"And that's why he never tried for veteran's benefits, why he was so evasive about his service record," Lindsey said.

Marvia gave him a questioning look.

He said, "Reverend Johnson told me that Leroy never wanted to pursue any kind of government claim, even though everybody thought he was entitled to something. He wouldn't do it. He couldn't. Not if he was dead."

Marvia snorted.

"Wait. If Leroy McKinney was dead, then who was living under his name all these years? Who died at North Field and was buried under the name Leroy McKinney?"

"Let me have a look at that book," Marvia said. She ran her finger down the page, turned the leaf, stopped. With her free hand she dug into Lindsey's wrist. "Look at that."

The heading ran: UNIDENTIFIED DEAD—MEN WHO WERE ON THE SHIPS AND PIER AND PRESUMED DEAD AFTER THE EXPLOSION. The list was four pages long, broken down by naval officers, enlisted men, Coast Guard, civilian employees and Maritime Service. The biggest group was headed: ENLISTED PERSONNEL—U.S. NAVAL BARRACKS. Lindsey ran his finger down the list. Names number 108, 109, and 110 were KING, CALVIN, KING, CLIFTON, and KING, JEFFERSON III.

"What do you think?" Marvia asked.

"I think Jefferson King the third was not killed in the explosion. I've suspected that for a while, but I thought he might have been one of the mutineers. Now I don't think so. I think he became Leroy McKinney. He didn't like the Navy, he didn't want to go back to loading ammunition. Who can blame him? But if he deserted from the Navy and then turned up later under his own name, they'd drag him back and throw him in the brig," Lindsey said.

Outside Marvia's apartment, somewhere in the night, a Berkeley police car sounded its siren.

Lindsey continued. "He could just have made up a name, but he took Leroy McKinney's instead. His half-brother. Not a bad idea. If anybody ever questioned him, ever checked out his story, he knew all about Leroy McKinney. They had the same background. They even had the same mother. They were both from Reserve. They both went through Navy boot camp. Nobody would bother to find out if McKinney was alive or dead. Not if he was standing there talking to them."

Marvia took over. "But he could never apply for benefits. Of course he couldn't. If he ever did, they would discover that he wasn't who he claimed he was. He'd be claiming to be a dead man. They'd already identified the real Leroy McKinney and buried him. In 1944. King's real identity would come out, and then they'd have him for desertion."

Lindsey rubbed his chin. "So that accounts for the baseball story and the music story. Leroy was really a ballplayer, you know. Johnson showed me the scorecards. And Jefferson—Jefferson King who became the false Leroy McKinney—really was a musician. If his hand was ruined in the Port Chicago explosion . . . "

He shook his head sadly. "Damn!" he whispered.

Marvia said, "What's the matter?"

"The damned fool! When the explosion happened, back in July of 1944, if Jefferson King's hand was so badly injured, he could have gone to the hospital. He should have gone to the hospital! He couldn't possibly have reported for duty. He wouldn't have had to join the mutiny, and he didn't have to run away."

Outside, several more sirens had joined the first. Maybe a cop had rousted a drug dealer in People's Park. The usual suspects would be setting fires and smashing windows. The cavalry was on its way, sirens wailing.

"If King had just had the sense to stay put, he would have been all right. But he ran away instead, and he spent the rest of his life hiding out under his half-brother's name. He didn't have to end up in a janitor's coveralls with a hole in his forehead," Lindsey said.

He slid the two Port Chicago books away, picked up the book on the Tuskegee Airmen and looked for Lawton Crump in the index.

Twenty

THE B-17'S ENGINES FIRED UP, one by one, each coughing a cloud of black smoke before settling down to a steady drone. The morning fog had burned away and the sun glinted off the airplane's aluminum skin. The only paint on the Flying Fortress's exterior was its identifying data, its World War II Air Force insignia and the huge portrait of Bessie Smith with the BESSIE BLUE logo in intense cobalt lettering on the airplane's nose.

The airplane stood on the North Field runway. A camera crew rode on a motorized dolly near the airplane's wing tip, slowly rolling past the engines and toward the cockpit.

Lindsey stood in the mouth of the Double Bee hangar with Ina Chandler and Lawton Crump. Crump sipped from a steaming paper cup. Lindsey caught the odor of coffee. Behind them a catering table had been set up. Columns of steam rose from silvery beverage urns. Plates of finger food stood half empty. Obviously the aircrew and the Double Bee staff had been at them. Lindsey watched the camera crew at work. "I hope they know those propellers are dangerous."

Ina Chandler laughed. "Botheration, Mr. Lindsey. You are ever the insurance man, aren't you?"

Botheration. She actually said *botheration.* If there was a Mr. Chandler, he must have stepped out of a Grant Wood painting. Or maybe disappeared back into one.

"I guess I can't help it," Lindsey said. "There have been cases, you know. I never handled one myself, but there have been cases of people not watching themselves, stepping into a propeller. What a mess. And what a claim."

The camera dolly rolled safely past the outboard engine.

"Not that jets are any safer." He smiled. "We've had to pay a couple of those. Instead of getting chopped up, you get sucked in. Whoosh! And sometimes when they get airborne, a window blows out or a door opens or a hole rips open in the roof. People zoom out of the aircraft. Remember that one in Hawaii? Never found the body. And then you get a case like D.B. Cooper. Remember D.B. Cooper? Of course that wasn't an accident so there was no claim to pay, but what a story!"

"You're certainly tuned in to disasters today, Mr. Lindsey," Lawton Crump said.

"Just my job. I heard about your giving young Jamie Wilkerson a ride."

Crump smiled broadly. "Great kid. Put him in the copilot's seat and took him for a little excursion. Ina had a cameraman with us, of course."

"I thought there had to be a Knights of the Air crew on every flight," Lindsey said.

"We got around that. By gosh, the old Fort is a great plane. One man can fly it. They had to, sometimes, coming home from missions full of flak and fighter fire."

"You should see the dailies," Ina Chandler said. "That kid has a million-dollar face. The airplane shots were fine, but we've got lots of those now. But that boy will have offers from every producer in Hollywood. Not that he'll be in our film, just in the outtakes. But what a face."

"Did you say anything about that to his mother?"

"Not yet. She'll hear."

"Mr. Crump, there are a couple of things I'd like to talk over with you. If you don't mind," Lindsey said.

Crump frowned. "You were down in Holy City. I thought you got what you needed."

"Pretty much. There were just a few more questions, though. I did phone your home yesterday, but Mrs. Crump said you were taking a nap."

Crump looked good in his flying gear. Somehow the leather jacket and the soft helmet—even dangling from his fingers—made him look twenty years younger and thirty pounds lighter.

Once he put on the helmet and covered his gray hair, he could pass for a young man.

Lindsey continued. "I want to ask you a little more about Tuskegee and your experiences in the Army. And a couple of other questions." He would get to Reserve in time. Reserve and Willa Crump and her three talented sons.

Ina Chandler had a clipboard in her hand and a walkie-talkie attached to her belt. Lindsey thought that she'd had them surgically attached. Crump looked at Ina. "How soon you going to want me again?"

Ina studied the clipboard, put the walkie-talkie to her mouth and muttered into it. She jotted something on the board. "Be about forty minutes. Don't go far."

Crump inclined his head toward the catering table. "Come on, then. Help yourself to some java. Treat's on Mrs. Chandler." He strolled into the hangar.

Lindsey helped himself to a cup. He didn't really want any coffee, but he had found that people talk better over shared food and drinks.

"Come on, let's borrow an office. It won't be fancy but it sure beats standing," Crump said.

They sat in the room where Lindsey had seen Crump and Ina Chandler being interviewed by Sergeant Finnerty on the day of the murder. Lindsey gazed back into the hangar.

His eye found a stain on the floor where he thought Leroy McKinney had lain. It might be grease, long since soaked into the concrete flooring. Or it might be McKinney's blood. Somebody had tried to clean away the stain. A greasy copy of the *Oakland Trib* lay where it had been abandoned.

"Little Jamie really enjoyed his flight," Lindsey said.

Crump merely nodded.

"You sure it was completely safe? I mean, our coverage is only intended for the movie. Taking passengers up for joy rides doesn't sound very responsible to me."

Crump made a sound low in his throat. "I'll tell you something, Mr. Lindsey. The B-17 was one of the safest aircraft ever built. She was one of the first airplanes that ever had a redundant control system. Do you know what that means?"

179

Lindsey started to answer, but Crump didn't wait. "You know the other heavy bomber that was used in Europe—the B-24, the Liberator—no redundancy. Piece of flak or enemy fighter fire clipped a control line, that was it. Those things went down like ducks. Fortresses were forgiving airplanes. Some of 'em came home with holes in 'em, engines gone, pieces knocked off the tail. It was remarkable."

"Even so, do you think a little boy . . . "

"Or are you challenging my ability as a pilot? I'm still FAA certified, you know. I can show you my ticket." He fumbled for his wallet, but Lindsey stopped him with a gesture.

"Nothing like that. No. But there's always a risk. The crowded skies and so forth."

"Oh." Crump had set his coffee cup on the battered desk. He picked it up again and took a sip. "We've got splendid cooperation from the tower. Outstanding. And I'll tell you something else. That B-17 is safer with Lawton Crump at the controls than a car is on the freeway in the hands of an expert driver. Has young Wilkerson ever ridden in your car? What kind of car do you drive, anyway?"

"A Hyundai."

"Hyundai!" Crump roared. "Asian-built tin cans, that's what those cars are! Why don't you buy American? What's the matter with people nowadays? Japanese are buying up the whole country. Germans are the boss of Europe. What did we fight that war for?"

"Uh, I see your point." This interview was not going the way Lindsey had intended. He sipped his coffee and tried to think fast, to get back out ahead of Lawton Crump.

Crump was still rolling. "That's what this picture is going to do, if I have anything to say about it. Get some pride back in our people, get some backbone back in America. We were strong in my day. We had to struggle for everything we got. I was a poor boy fresh out of a very small town. You know that already. I got nothing for nothing. I . . . "

Lindsey held up his hand. "That was what I meant to ask you about."

Crump looked puzzled. He had laid his soft leather helmet

on the desk near his coffee cup. He picked it up and studied it as if he had never seen it before. "What was that?"

"Well, you flew fighters in Europe, right?"

"North Africa and Europe."

"Yes. Single-engine aircraft."

"Some twins. The P-38 was a twin-engine. You know how they taught us to fly those? Of course we'd qualified in single-engine fighters, everything from the old Thirty-nines and Forties up through the Fifty-ones. So when some Thirty-eights came in—you never knew what was coming in, you might be flying Warhawks on Monday and Thunderbolts on Tuesday—when the Thirty-eights came in, they led us out to the flightline and handed us each a manual. They said, 'Climb in the cockpit. Read the manual. Handle the controls. When you figure you've got it under your helmet, start the engines and fly.' "

He nodded vigorously, agreeing with himself.

Lindsey looked at him, astonished.

"That was how we did it." Lawton Crump continued. "Lost a lot of pilots and a lot of aircraft, but by golly we learned to fly. I'm the living proof of that."

"I understand, yes. Yes. But how did you learn to fly the B-17? And what's the story of *Bessie Blue?*"

Crump swung around in his chair. Lindsey peered through the hangar door and saw the Flying Fortress still on the flightline, its propellers turning, its engines idling. Obviously, Crump could see it too. That showed in his eyes. He was dreaming of 1944, reliving his glory days. Lindsey expected to see Dean Jagger stride into the hangar with a clipboard in his hand, but it was only Ina Chandler.

She stuck her head into the little office.

"Everything okay?"

Crump said, "Just fine."

"Few more minutes, then." Chandler exited.

Crump stared into his coffee. Lindsey could see him, half a century younger, not long after Joseph Wagner's makeshift landing field in Reserve, Louisiana, elevated to the grade of an Army officer and flying a sleek Mustang or a twin-boomed Lightning at 400 miles per hour over Berlin.

"Once Hitler was whipped," Crump said, "they sent us back home. Loaded us on ships. The Atlantic was safe then. It was frightening, shipping over there. Subs all around us, or so they warned us. Could be torpedoed at any moment. Lot of ships were. Lot of boys went down to Davy Jones without ever seeing a Wehrmacht soldier or a Messerschmitt."

Maybe that was what he saw in his coffee cup. A convoy of troop ships crossing the Atlantic, lights doused, voices hushed, thousands of frightened young men praying to reach England safely. What happened after that would be in their own hands. Maybe. At least they would have a chance. But until they arrived, they were in God's.

"We got back to Tuskegee, nobody knew what was going to happen. They were still turning out new pilots and gunners and mechanics. Then they set up conversion training to turn us into bomber crews. Eased us through some AT-10s, that was a twin trainer, then B-25s. Meanwhile we're moving around. Mather Field, Elgin Field, Hondo Field."

He looked up from his coffee at last. "You know the Twenty-five? Billy Mitchell bomber. That was the plane Jimmie Doolittle used to sock old Tojo on the kisser. You know there were only sixteen B-25s in that flight? Right off the *Hornet* and straight on to Tokyo. Must have been quite a shock for those Nips to look up and see the Yankee Star on the wings and then bombs falling. Yes sir, that must have been something to behold."

"But the B-17?"

"Now pipe down, young fella! I'm coming to that! We trained in the Mitchell for a while. That was a sweet plane to fly. Noisy son of a gun, but it handled beautifully. Those big Wright Cyclones sat practically up against the cockpit. Mitchell was a lot of fun, yes sir."

"But the B-17?"

"I was in the 332nd fighter group, 99th squadron. Those were the Tuskegee Airmen. Man, were we ever proud. Then they sent us home and formed up the 447th bombardment group. That was going to be a B-17 unit out in the Pacific. Matter of fact, by the time we got there the Seventeen would have been ready for retirement." Crump's eyes had a faraway look.

"Boys were flying the Twenty-nine by then. The Superfortress. Pressurized fuselage, warm air. Not like the little Fort. You know we had to wear electric suits in there, and breath through oxygen masks. We keep it low now, so it doesn't get too cold, air doesn't get too rarified. But up high, those suits were a must. Not in the Superfort, though. No, sir."

Ina Chandler was back. She stood in the doorway with her clipboard in hand.

"We got to name our planes, of course. I was designated pilot and aircraft commander of a B-17F. Even as a Seventeen, she was kind of old and outmoded. They changed the design a little with the G model. Put the Cheyenne tail turret on 'em and put an extra gun mount under the bombardier's station. Called it a chin turret. A few F's had that, but old *Bessie Blue* didn't."

"Time to get airborne, Lawton," Ina Chandler said.

Crump pushed himself to his feet. To Lindsey he said, "The B-17 was the greatest bomber ever built. Don't let anyone tell you otherwise, sonny. You know they flew in Korea? You know the Israelis used 'em in '48 in their war of independence? You know Uncle Sam even painted some of them flat black and used 'em for secret night missions in Vietnam? No sir, don't you tell me about the wonders of the jet age, the wonders of the stealth age. B-17 was the greatest bomber ever built."

Twenty-One

LINDSEY STARTED TO FOLLOW LAWTON CRUMP and Ina Chandler back toward the runway, but the phone on the borrowed desk rang. Lindsey hesitated. Probably it was for someone in Double Bee, maybe for the caterer. Still, something made him pick it up.

"High here. That you, Lindsey?"

"How did you know where I was?"

"An old Gypsy woman gave me the power to divine your whereabouts. I hear you're still pushing the McKinney thing. What have you got to share with me? Think we ought to get together? I've got a craving for tacos if you want to buy me lunch."

Lindsey said okay. Outside the hangar he could see the silvery B-17 still in position. The Double Bee people and the Knights of the Air had sent up a couple of camera craft. A new-looking Bell helicopter was hovering above the B-17, a daredevil camera jockey standing on the Bell's landing skid, pointing a camera straight down at the bomber. A silver-bodied P-51 with its tail painted in a black-and-yellow checkerboard pattern swooped past, circled back toward the City of Alameda, then banked for another overflight.

Lawton Crump was visible through the cockpit window of the B-17. He had donned his soft leather helmet and looked like a youngster barely out of his teens. Ina Chandler stood just beyond the 17's wing tip. Crump gave her the thumbs-up sign. Four Wright Cyclones roared and the plane rolled forward.

As Lindsey drove up Hegenberger Road toward the freeway, he heard a droning and looked up. There was the *Bessie Blue*.

The old bomber climbed and banked back toward North Field. Inside the Hyundai, an announcer on an all-news station was explaining the nation's economic outlook for the coming year. Lindsey wondered what year it was for Lawton Crump.

At Oakland Police Headquarters, Lieutenant High was slumped behind his desk, wearing his usual houndstooth check jacket, rumpled shirt and narrow tie. He held a telephone wedged between his jaw and his shoulder. He was muttering unintelligibly into the phone. He waved Lindsey to a chair, finished his call and hung up.

"Where have you been?" he asked.

"I thought you were going to buy me lunch," Lindsey said.

"Oh, is that the way it is? I think this would be a good time for the bright lights and the rubber hose."

"Not very long ago you were talking about tacos," Lindsey said.

High raised his hands. "All right. I guess I can catch more flies with a Rawlings mitt than with a cat o' nine tails."

"You're getting awfully frisky for an old geezer."

High stood up. "Yep. I guess you reach a certain point and everything starts to look different. How different, deponent sayeth not."

They walked around the corner to a Mexican restaurant and settled into a booth. Lindsey looked at the customers. He had been in this joint before. As usual, the booths were filled with assorted off-duty cops, bail bondsmen, civil servants on lunch breaks and a few women who looked like hookers who had just made bond and were stopping off for some quick refreshment before reporting back to work.

High kept his word and ordered a plate of tacos. Lindsey asked for *gallina en caldo*.

They both pulled out pocket notebooks and pencils. "All right, what have you got for me? Bring me up to date," High said.

"I'm going to start billing you for services rendered," Lindsey replied.

"Help yourself. It'll go with the rest of the city's unpaid bills.

This is Oakland, California, sonny, not Bel Air. Or hadn't you noticed?"

"Okay, I surrender. Maybe International Surety will pay for the grub." Lindsey then proceeded to describe his visit to Reserve and repeated the information from Marvia's interview with Willa McKinney.

High jotted notes, gesturing with his free hand for Lindsey to keep the facts flowing. When Lindsey finished, High said, "That's wonderful. That's really terrific. If I had an expense account, I'd buy you lunch to celebrate. As it is, I will be delighted to accept your kind offer to pay the señorita."

"That isn't all," Lindsey said. "I was out at Eric Coffman's house, Marvia and I were out there, and . . . "

The waitress brought their food. Lindsey hadn't realized how hungry he was until he saw the colors and savored the scents. Red beets, golden broth, pale green celery, orange carrots, white potatoes, boiled chicken that would have made Mollie Goldberg do something Yiddish with envy. Do what? What was the word? Eric Coffman had used it a hundred times. Plotz, that was it. Plotz with envy.

He tasted the soup. Superb. Mollie would definitely plotz.

High crunched a taco. Around it he said, "Yep. I know Coffman. Didn't he rescue you from my clutches once or twice?"

"You put it so elegantly."

"Pardonez moi, m'sieu. Continuez, s'il vous plaît."

"You know, Coffman is a history buff. Strictly amateur, but he knows his stuff and he's got an impressive reference library."

"So what?"

"So he heard the story of Willa McKinney's three talented sons and their exploits in World War Two, and he put them together so they almost make sense."

"Almost?"

"Well, they *do* make sense. I just think it'll take a little more work to sift out the truth from the lies. Or not exactly lies. Distortions, revisions and the like. Eric loaned me his reference books, and I spent some time with them. I think I need to talk

186

with Latasha Greene again. And maybe with Mr. Luther Jones."

"Yep." High loaded his fork with rice and refried beans and shovelled the mess into his mouth. Lindsey waited while High chewed and swallowed. "Yep, I've been following your exploits in the wonderful City of Richmond," High said. "You certainly get around, Hobart. I love having Richmond nearby. No matter how bad things get in Oakland, anytime I want to I can step outside Headquarters and stand there gazing up at the beautiful freeway and say to myself, It ain't so bad, Doc, it ain't so bad. You could always be working in Richmond."

"Do you know if Jones is still in jail?" Lindsey asked.

"Or back on the street, bond posted all nice and legal?"

"That's what I meant."

"I can check. But if gambling were legal, I'd lay about squeenteen to zip that he's out."

"That's what I meant."

"You want me to phone up to Richmond and ask 'em? Who was the 'tec you talked to up there?"

"Hartley."

"Right."

"Okay. Soon as we get back to the shop. No point in using a pay phone when I can charge it to the taxpayers." He downed another bite of taco. "So what do you make of the three McKinney brothers? Well, only one McKinney, right? One mom, three dads, so we have a McKinney, a Crump and a King. How do you put them together?"

"The thing that tripped us up was the connection between Leroy McKinney and Jefferson King," Lindsey said. "Apparently they joined the Navy together and were both serving at Port Chicago in 1944. From the books on the subject, that wouldn't have been unusual. There were several pairs of brothers there."

"Okay," High nodded.

"Now follow me on this," Lindsey said. "Leroy McKinney was a minor-league ballplayer before the war. Not minor-league, Negro League. That's what I meant."

"I've got that."

"And Jefferson King was a musician. Had been a church organist and was getting started as a professional."

"Yep."

"It's the night of the explosion, July 17, '44. Leroy McKinney and Jefferson King are both at Port Chicago. Leroy is on duty, loading the *Bryan*. His half-brother, Jefferson King, is off duty, sound asleep in his bunk. When the ships go up, Leroy is killed outright. Jefferson King survives, but he's injured, maybe badly burned. Again, the books say that the men actually on the ships or working on the pier were wiped out. Those a little farther away from the explosion received varying degrees of damage. Some of the men were in the barracks or sitting on their bunks looking out the window, and the blast shattered the window glass and sent slivers all through the barracks. The unlucky ones were blinded for life."

High winced.

"All right." Lindsey took a sip of water. "Jefferson King's right hand was ruined. I don't know what happened. Maybe it was burned, maybe crushed, maybe the tendons were severed by flying glass. Your coroner's report might give us a clue to that. But the point is, he was finished as a musician. And he deserted. He could have reported to sick bay, he probably would have been hospitalized until they could discharge him and send him home with a disability pension. But instead he panicked."

"Poor guy."

Lindsey looked into High's face. Was High being sarcastic or did he really feel sympathy for the man? "Once King calmed down, he had to figure out what to do. He didn't want to turn himself in. He could be charged with AWOL or even desertion. Not a light matter in wartime. He couldn't keep his own identity because he'd already been listed as missing, presumed dead, in the explosion. There were stories in all the local newspapers, in the Oakland and San Francisco papers. But King's half-brother, Leroy McKinney, had been identified as dead. His body had been found. So King took McKinney's name. He was safe as long as he kept his head down, but if he applied for any kind of benefits they'd nab him. And that was how he lived for the next fifty years."

"Let's go back upstairs," High said. "Don't forget to pick up the check."

Once at Homicide, High phoned Richmond. He put his call to Detective Hartley on the speaker phone. Lindsey identified himself and asked, "Do you still have Luther Jones there?"

"Sorry, Mr. Lindsey. He's long gone."

"Bailed?"

"Nope. We had to release him. Thanks to you, sir. You furnished him with an ironclad alibi. Not that it was your fault. We understand that, sir. But it would have been nice to pin him for the Ahmad Hope killing."

"Did you get an identity for the man who was shot at Fuzzy's #3?" Lindsey asked.

"Oh, that was very unusual. These gangs usually stay organized pretty well on family lines. There's a lot of respect for family. But the dead man was Andrew Hope. Young Ahmad's uncle. Really tough on Mrs. Hope, losing her nephew and her son the same day. But at least she won't have to see 'em go to trial."

Lindsey heard a ringing in his ears. His hands felt cold. He sat down quickly and waited for the feeling to pass. He heard Lieutenant High say, "You okay, Lindsey?"

He managed to say, "Just . . . just give me a minute." He heard Detective Hartley's voice coming over the speakerphone from Richmond.

"Lieutenant High, you still there?"

"Everything's all right. Mr. Lindsey just felt a little faint," High said.

"I'll bet. Tell him that he'll get used to it."

Lindsey managed to say, "No I won't."

An hour later he was in the Hyundai, heading up the freeway to Richmond. High had forced a cup of his evil coffee on him. Lindsey decided that the coffee was designed to push the human system to its limit. If you could survive it, mere bullets should not frighten you.

But Lindsey felt frightened.

He parked on Twenty-third Street and walked to Fuzzy's #3. The shattered half-moon glass in the padded door had been covered with brown cardboard. Inside the saloon, Lindsey swayed for a moment while his eyes adjusted to the darkness and his ears to the blues blasting from the jukebox.

When he could see again, he recognized Fuzzy behind the bar. On the TV set over Fuzzy's head a black version of June Cleaver was telling a black version of Ward Cleaver that her new detergent was going to make the rest of her life a living paradise. Her voice blended with the male voice of the blues singer.

Fuzzy stared at Lindsey.

The saloon was more full than empty. Every bar stool was occupied, as were the majority of the tables. The place reeked of cigarette smoke. Lindsey pulled his handkerchief from his trouser pocket and wiped his eyes.

"Look-a here, if it isn't Mister Lindsey-Hobart-Lindsey," said a familiar voice.

Luther Jones was seated at a table. An open bottle of beer sweated in front of him. A cigar smoldered in an ashtray. Jones wore a black shirt closed with shining black buttons. A fine gold chain supporting a golden religious ornament circled his neck. He gestured to an empty chair. "Won't you deign to honor me?"

Lindsey edged toward the table and slid gingerly into the chair. "Hello, Luther."

Jones looked at him. "What's that?"

"I said, 'Hello, Luther.' Luther Jones, isn't it?"

The only sign of displeasure was a momentary narrowing of the eyes. "I prefer my name as a free man. I don't like to use my slave name."

Lindsey waited for him to say more.

"Luther was a preacher, anyhow, and I'm no preacher. And a Jones is a bad habit. Maybe you didn't know that. But a Jones is a bad thing. So you see, I don't like Luther and I don't like Jones. Preaching a bad habit. Heh-heh." He said it just like that. Heh-heh.

"But you can call me Hasan or you can call me Rahsaan or

you can call me Mister Rasheed, whatever you need, Rasheed of Richmond, sitting here, having a beer."

Lindsey said, "I need some more information about Leroy McKinney."

"You don't scare easy, do you, Lindsey-Hobart-Lindsey? Would you like a brew courtesy of Rasheed?"

Lindsey waited.

Rasheed signaled Fuzzy.

Lindsey waited. The jukebox went silent for a moment. Then another song began. The minority Cleavers had disappeared from the TV screen and been replaced by a boxing match. Lindsey's eyes flicked to the screen long enough to realize that he didn't recognize either fighter and to guess that the match was on tape anyhow.

The customers of Fuzzy's #3 glanced casually at Lindsey and Rasheed/Jones, then looked away, returning to their own interests.

Fuzzy brought Lindsey a beer. He didn't wait to be paid, just set the bottle on the table and walked away.

"You stood up okay there, Lindsey," Rasheed said. "You helped Rasheed in an hour of need. Enjoy your brew and what can I do?"

"I need some more information about Leroy McKinney," Lindsey repeated.

"You said that before, when you came in the door." *Befo' Do'*

"I still need it."

"You sure act like a cop. For an insurance man, Lindsey, you sure act a lot like a cop."

"I'm not."

"What do you want to know about Leroy?"

"Was that his real identity?"

"Abu Shabazz. Or you talkin' 'bout his slave name?"

"That's not what I mean."

"That will still be seen. Tell me what you mean."

"I mean I have reason to believe that he was really someone else. That Leroy McKinney has been dead for many years, and the man you knew as Leroy McKinney took his identity."

Rasheed shook his head. He lifted his cigar from the ashtray. The cigar had gone out. "You do not mind if I smoke, do you, sir?" He extracted a box of wooden matches from his trousers, struck one and puffed the cigar back to life. In the dim saloon, its tip glowed like a smoky sunset.

Lindsey picked up his beer, examined the lip of the bottle and sipped.

"Far as I know, Abu Shabazz was Abu Shabazz and Leroy McKinney was Leroy McKinney and they was all jes' one man and he wasn't no nother man," Rasheed said.

"How long did you know him?"

"Long, long time."

"What year did you meet him?"

Rasheed removed the cigar from his mouth and studied its glowing end. Lindsey could see him sliding back through the decades. "Christmastime. I remember it clearly. All the news was coming from Europe. Our boys thought the war was all won. Ike was the big noise over there. Then the Germans started to push back. Caught our side by surprise."

Lindsey nodded, willing Rasheed to continue.

"They called it the Battle of the Bulge. I 'member. I was working in the shipyard, all the stores was full of Christmas decorations, radio was playing that sappy Christmas music and the newspapers was all full of the Battle of the Bulge. I met Leroy in a saloon. I 'member I took one look at that awful claw hand of his and I couldn't look at it no more. I was a young, young man at that time. A blade."

"And his name was definitely Leroy McKinney?"

"He was just out of the Marine Corps."

Lindsey tried not to say anything, but an involuntary grunt escaped him. Rasheed's eyes flicked open. That was all it took. "That's what he told me," Rasheed said. "I wasn't gone ask him no difference. He told me he'd got that claw out in King Solomon Islands, something like that. Picked up a white phosphorus grenade, he told me. Throwed it out a bunker. Saved his whole platoon, but it burned the shit out that hand. Ruined his career. He been a musician afores the war."

"So he spent the rest of his life managing nightclubs," Lindsey said.

Rasheed nodded.

"Then why was he working as a janitor?"

Rasheed leaned forward. Lindsey could smell the cigar smoke and the beer fumes coming from him. His eyes were bloodshot, but he did not appear to be drunk.

"You know what, Lindsey? Abu Shabazz one big shitter."

Lindsey waited.

"He wasn't never no club manager. He wasn't never no nothing but jes' a janitor. He worked in those places, all right. He saw those greats. Bird and Miles and Monk. But not from behind no microphone. No. He saw them from behind a wet mop. Leroy wasn't no Goddamned big shot. Wasn't nothing but a Goddamned floor-swamper, toilet-swabber, puke-scrubber janitor. And he was a Goddamned liar. Probably wasn't no Goddamned war hero neither."

Twenty-Two

THE FADED STUCCO FRONT OF LATASHA GREENE'S house had fresh bullet holes in it. Scraps of yellow plastic fluttered from the house or lay in the overgrown front yard. Lindsey tried to figure out what they were. He picked up a strip that had wrapped itself around a brown weed. The black lettering read IME SCENE—DO NOT CRO. . . .

There was no evidence of kids with water pistols or other kinds of weapons. Lindsey felt an absurd pang of loss.

He knocked on the door. The man who opened it very nearly filled the doorway. His skin was very black, as were his trousers and narrow bow tie. His shirt was white, the sleeves rolled above his elbows. The wooden grip of a black metal revolver protruded from his trousers. It made a dent in his belly.

"I came to talk with Latasha Greene. Is she at home?" Lindsey asked.

The huge man looked down at Lindsey. He did not speak or move.

Starting at 100, Lindsey began counting silently down toward one.

The huge man might have been doing the same. It was hard to tell.

When Lindsey had passed his age and was approaching the number of days in the month, the huge man blinked. He said, "Why?"

Lindsey reached for his pocket. He could see the huge man's eyes follow his hand and heavy muscles tense beneath his skin. Lindsey extended his card. The huge man looked at it without moving to take it. He said, "Why?"

"My company is insurance carrier for the *Bessie Blue* project out at Oakland Airport. Latasha's grandfather worked there and he died."

The huge man blinked when Lindsey said the word *died*.

"I'm trying to learn about Mr. McKinney and the circumstances of his death. I am not a police officer. I am concerned solely with the insurance aspects of the event. We may be able to pay some benefits in Mr. McKinney's death, which would presumably accrue to Ms. Greene."

The huge man wrinkled his brow. Lindsey wondered whether he should resume counting where he left off or reset the counter and start over at 100. The huge man stepped aside. Lindsey heard him close the door and felt his presence as he crossed the living room.

Latasha Greene sat on the tattered couch wearing what seemed to be the same T-shirt and jeans she had worn the last time Lindsey was in the house. She was nursing her baby. The TV set was turned on, once again tuned silently to a rap video. Lindsey wondered if the sound was broken on her TV, or if she just didn't like to listen to rap.

Lindsey laid his attaché case across his knees. When he unsnapped the clasps, he heard a sound behind him. He didn't turn around. It was probably just the huge man pulling his revolver, an appropriate precaution in case Lindsey had a weapon. He didn't. He extracted the old *Call-Bulletin* clipping.

"I've made a couple of photocopies for you on good paper. That old newsprint tends to dry out, and you want something that will last."

Latasha extended a long slim hand and took the papers. She didn't say anything. Lindsey had studied the photo and its caption. It showed a group of American Marines in combat gear, brandishing their weapons. They were surrounded by tropical vegetation. The caption indicated that they were celebrating a victory over Japanese defenders on Tarawa. No names were given, and the faces were blurred and faded. Somebody, long ago, had crayoned a heavy circle around one of the Marines. The Marine Corps wasn't integrated during World War

II. Not according to everything Lindsey had been told about that war. But it wasn't for him to judge.

Look, it could have been Latasha's grandpa.

Or the Good Humor man.

"I'm sorry if this is painful for you, Latasha, but please try to answer my questions. You could be a big help," Lindsey said.

She looked from her baby's face to Lindsey's.

"Do you know if your grandfather had any dealings with a man named Luther Jones, also known as Hasan Rahsaan Rasheed?"

Latasha shook her head.

"The little boy who was killed, Ahmad Hope . . . "

"I knowed Ahmad." Well, at least he had got a response.

"The police say that he was killed by his own uncle, Andrew Hope. Then Andrew was killed in a running shoot-out with the police. The same day. Do you . . . "

"I know Ahmad. I din' know Andrew. He killed Ahmad. It's a good thing he's dead. Ahmad." She turned her face away, lifted the edge of her T-shirt and used it to wipe her eyes. When she turned back her cheeks and her upper lip were wet. Lindsey decided to try another tack.

"Your grandfather was Leroy McKinney. Do you know if he ever used any other name? Would you remember a name such as Abu Shabazz? Jefferson King? Or Lawton Crump?"

Latasha shook her head very slowly from side to side.

"Did your grandfather ever speak of his childhood? Did he ever mention a town named Reserve, Louisiana?"

Latasha turned her face from Lindsey, bending down to her baby. She smiled softly at the baby. She moved the baby from one breast to the other, pulling one side of her T-shirt down and the other up. Lindsey noticed several wet spots and dried stains on the front of her T-shirt.

He studied the contents of his attaché case. Was Latasha another one? Another person whose soul lived on some other planet, while her body occupied space on Earth? Had his questions even registered? Or was Latasha's unresponsiveness the product of intimidation by the huge man?

Before Lindsey could ask another question, he felt a vise close on his shoulder. The lid of his attaché case slapped shut, as the big man lifted him to his feet and steered him toward the front door. The door slamming behind him sounded like a howitzer.

Lindsey left his car in front of Latasha's house on Twenty-third Street. If anything was going to happen to it, it would happen. He retraced the path he had taken with the Reverend Johnson the day of his first interview with Latasha. He might as well return the Negro League scorecards while he was at it. And he might learn something more from the minister. He certainly couldn't accomplish any less than he had with Latasha.

The Reverend Johnson's church appeared deserted when Lindsey arrived. The front door was unlocked, so Lindsey let himself in. The building was quiet and the lighting, filtering through from the street, was dim. Lindsey heard low-pitched voices and followed the sound to the door of the Reverend's study. The door stood open a crack.

The sound of chairs scraping signaled the end of a conversation. The study door opened wide and a young couple emerged, followed by the Reverend Johnson's bulk.

The boy couldn't have been more than sixteen, probably less. He made eye contact with Lindsey for a fraction of second. Lindsey wasn't sure, but the boy might have been one of Ahmad Hope's former playmates. He was very skinny and very dark. His head was covered with a thin black stubble.

The girl looked even younger than the boy and even skinnier. She was obviously pregnant. She avoided Lindsey's eyes.

The Reverend Johnson walked behind the young couple, his hands on their shoulders. As he passed Lindsey, his eyes flashed an unambiguous message.

Lindsey watched the minister guide the youngsters to the door. He embraced the girl, shook hands solemnly with the boy and watched them leave the church. He closed the door behind them and walked back toward Lindsey, shaking his head.

"Did you know that our school district actually went bankrupt a few years ago?"

"I read about it," Lindsey said.

"No money for sex education. And half the community doesn't want it anyway. Claims it will lead to the deterioration of the morals of our youth."

"What are they going to do?"

Johnson shook his head. "I don't want to depress you, Mr. Lindsey." He squeezed his eyes shut and bit his lip. Then he said, more to himself than to Lindsey, "I will not think that way. No, sir. I am going to save them, with God's help."

He shook himself like a wet dog and said, "Come into my study and sit down, sir. What can I do for you today?"

In Johnson's study Lindsey found a seat and opened his attaché case. He looked up to see Johnson lifting a bottle from a lower drawer in his desk. A couple of glasses followed.

Lindsey returned the Negro League scorecards to Johnson. "I've been able to learn a good deal about Leroy McKinney, Reverend. Maybe some things that will be useful. At least, I hope so. Some that are merely puzzling. I thought I'd share them with you to see if you could offer any help."

Johnson nodded. He held up a glass in one hand, the bottle in the other. "Some mineral water, Mr. Lindsey? Seems to benefit both the body and the soul."

Lindsey accepted a glass. It was room temperature but at least it wasn't flat. Win one, lose one.

"I buried Mr. McKinney. I've tried to counsel his grand-daughter. There seems to be no other family, at least in the area. Latasha's mother was Mr. McKinney's daughter. She has been deceased for a decade at least. No one seems to know anything about Latasha's father, only that his name was Greene. Even for that, we have only the word of Latasha. What more can I do, Mr. Lindsey?"

"I hope you didn't spend too much for the tombstone," Lindsey said.

Johnson's eyebrows flew up. "What an odd comment. In fact, there was no money to pay for a monument. There was no money to pay for the funeral. The church paid for everything. If you're that concerned, perhaps you could see your way clear to making a contribution."

Lindsey closed his eyes. He opened them and dug his wallet out of his trousers. He had a hundred fifty dollars in cash. He took a breath, extracted the hundred dollars and laid it on Johnson's desk.

Johnson gave Lindsey a long appraising look, then picked up the bills and dropped them into the top drawer of his desk. He laid a book of business forms on the blotter and painstakingly made out a receipt. He handed it to Lindsey.

"Thank you very much, sir."

"If you erected a marker with McKinney on it, you might have to take it back down," Lindsey said.

"Please." Johnson held up one hand, palm forward. He looked like an old-fashioned traffic cop. "Don't tell me that his name was Abu Shabazz. I've had enough of that. You're becoming a quite a notorious character in our community, Mr. Lindsey. I appreciate the contribution but please don't come in here and try to tell us how to live. We don't need advice, for all that I'm sure you mean well."

Lindsey shook his head. "That's not what I'm talking about at all. I don't care whether he called himself Leroy McKinney or Abu Shabazz or Babe Ruth. His name was Jefferson King the third."

"What?" Johnson twitched. With the movement, a drop of mineral water flew from his glass all the way to Lindsey's coat. Johnson looked at the spot, seemed ready to comment on it, then changed his mind. All he said was, "What are you talking about?"

"I'm talking about two young sailors from Louisiana. Two half-brothers who served at Port Chicago. One was Leroy McKinney, the other was Jefferson King. McKinney was killed in the disastrous explosion of July 1944. King was injured in the same explosion. King ran away. He deserted. He took his half-brother's identity. The man you buried as Leroy McKinney was actually Jefferson King. The real Leroy McKinney has been dead since 1944. He was killed instantaneously when the *Bryan* went up."

Johnson tossed off his mineral water and refilled his glass. "What did you say about Louisiana?"

"Both McKinney and King were from a small town in Louisiana. There was a third brother. Half-brother. He's the only one still alive. His name is Lawton Crump and he is a retired airline employee. He lives near San Jose."

Johnson leaned forward eagerly, his bulk covering most of the desk. "Perhaps he could help Latasha and her child. What is his financial condition? He would be Latasha's, ah, I'll have to check the rules of genealogy. The Mormons are the authorities on that, but we don't have the best relations with them. I think he would be her half-great-uncle. Or perhaps a cousin. At any rate, I shall impress upon him the nature of his obligations as Latasha's only possible hope in this cruel world."

He found a sheaf of scratch paper and picked up his pen. "You say this Crump lives in San Jose?"

"Actually, Holy City," Lindsey said.

"An aptly named community, I pray."

"I don't know that he'll be able to help much. He was on the retired role of Pan American, and they went belly up. I don't know what becomes of their pensioners. I'm sure he gets Social Security and maybe some veteran's benefit."

Johnson pursed his lips. "We'll have to look into this."

"Did Jefferson King—Abu Shabazz—your Leroy McKinney—did he ever say or do anything that made you think there was something odd going on? Something that he kept concealed?" Lindsey asked.

Johnson shook his head. "Leroy was not a regular churchgoer. In fact, he was not a member of my congregation nor of any that I know of. But I consider it my duty to visit the homes of all those in the community who are in need, even the unchurched, and I visited his home from time to time. Mainly, I worked with Miss Greene. She did attend services now and then, and I was blessed to be able to baptize both her and her baby."

"Did King ever travel? Disappear for a few days at a time? Or longer? Did he ever turn up with large amounts of unexplained cash?"

Johnson pushed himself to his feet. He picked up the bottle of mineral water and walked around the desk and refilled Lindsey's glass and put the bottle back on his desk. He went to the window and stood with his back to Lindsey. For all his weight, he did not have the waddle of a fat man.

Beyond Johnson, Lindsey could see an overgrown lot. It was late afternoon but the sunlight was still strong. A stickball game was in progress. Even the poorest kids could turn up a tennis ball and a broom handle. Lindsey wasn't sure of it, but he thought he recognized a few of the players as Ahmad Hope's companions, including the boy who had left the church with the pregnant girl.

"I recall a few such incidents," Johnson said. He started speaking to the glass, so his words were almost inaudible. Then he turned around with a look of concern. "Just once I can recall Latasha coming to see me. She must have been little more than six years old. I remember she was just learning to read. She could read her name and a few other words." He stood next to his desk, leaning one fist on the scarred wood like a defensive lineman ready to tear into the opponent's backfield.

"She showed me a postcard. She had read the name on it. It was addressed to her. She asked me to help her read the rest of it. I asked why she didn't show it to her mother and ask her to help. She told me that she was afraid of her mother and afraid to show her the postcard. I thought that was a shame. I wish I had intervened at the time, but you know we try to regard family relationships as sacrosanct. Still, I wish I had intervened."

"What did the postcard say?" Lindsey asked.

Johnson shook his head. "I really can't recall. It was just a greeting, a typical greeting. You know, to the effect of, 'Having fun down here, but I miss my girl.' Really, it was quite innocuous. I can't imagine Latasha's mother disapproving. And it was from Leroy. That is, it was signed, 'Grandpa.'"

"Certainly sounds harmless. It was a picture postcard? What was the picture?"

"This was a long time ago, Mr. Lindsey. As I recall, it was a Mardi-Gras scene. A picture of a black marcher made up as some exotic figure with sequins and feathers and such folderol."

"Did you notice the postmark?"

"I did not, but if the card was from New Orleans, I imagine it was postmarked there. Or somewhere in Louisiana. At any rate, when Leroy returned, he seemed to have some extra money. Yes, I believe he actually made a contribution to the church, even though he was not a member. As you are aware, we have no prohibition on receiving contributions from persons who are not members of the church. We believe that doing good works in this world is as worthy an act as that of prayer or praise."

He sent a message with his eyes.

Lindsey sighed and reached for his wallet and his remaining fifty dollars.

Twenty-Three

MOTHER WAS SEATED AT LINDSEY'S COMPUTER demonstrating the skills she had picked up at Miss Riley's class. Lindsey watched her insert a disk, boot up the system and access a file. He still couldn't get over her improvement. A year ago, Mother had been lost in time, wandering mental corridors lined with doors that opened into 1953, 1936, 1895. That opened to San Francisco, Korea, Hollywood, Tibet. That opened to the North Pole or to Fairyland.

She didn't know how close Lindsey had come to making the anguishing decision to place her in a nursing home or a mental hospital from which she would probably not have emerged.

And now she was shopping and cooking meals, attending classes, using a computer and preparing to apply for a job. Lindsey put his arm around her shoulders and said, "I'm really proud of you."

The phone rang. Lindsey picked it up and heard Marvia Plum say, "He's here."

Lindsey didn't have to ask who she was talking about. Nor did she give him time.

"James is here. With his bride. They just checked into their hotel and he wants to have a meeting and he wants to see Jamie."

"When? When does he want this meeting? What did you tell him?" He didn't comment on the venomous way she said the word *bride*. He had heard her speak with compassion, or at least objectivity, of murderers, extortionists, hold-up artists. She was horrified of crimes that humiliated or degraded the victim. She despised rapists. She hated child molesters. But he had never heard her speak a word the way she spoke this one: *bride.*

"Tomorrow. Tomorrow after work. I'm back at work now and I'm not going to let the taxpayers down and the killers go on killing. I'm not going to take another vacation day to talk to those two."

"Where are they staying?" Lindsey asked.

"Nothing but the best for Major and Mrs. James Wilkerson. The Parc Oakland, my dear."

"Oh, boy. I wonder if they'll run into the Double Bee gang. Don't see how they can miss them, the way they've taken over that hotel."

"I expect that's why they picked it. James can strut around and tell his Desert Storm stories. You know, 'How I won the Battle of Basra single-handed,' while wifey worships him from a respectful distance and the movie people beg for his autograph."

"Isn't Desert Storm getting a little bit old?" Lindsey asked.

"Maybe so," Marvia conceded. "But it's his war and he's sticking with it. And he wants to go out to North Field to see what they've got."

"You're going to see him, then. You're not going to stonewall him."

"I can't. Not Jamie's father." Her anger was a tangible presence. "But I haven't promised he could see Jamie. I haven't decided how I'm going to handle that."

"Is there anything you want me to do?" Lindsey asked.

"I want you to come with me."

He held the phone. From where he stood, he could see Mother. She had an exercise book open beside the computer. She had keyed in a sample letter, and he could hear the printer rattling as it printed out.

"Bart, will you?"

"Absolutely. I'll pick you up at your house. What time are you going to meet him? What time should I come by? Uh, how are you going to dress? How do you want me to dress?"

She filled him in. "Okay, I'll see you then. Tomorrow night," he said.

He talked with Mother for a while, then settled into his

recliner and watched the late news on television. He couldn't contemplate going to bed yet. Maybe there would be some exciting footage of jets from the *Abraham Lincoln* repelling a fierce onslaught by the ghosts of Admiral Yamamoto and the Imperial Navy.

Instead, the local news led with a story from right here in Contra Costa County. Someone in Richmond had set a fire or planted a bomb or thrown a grenade. Or maybe a gas line had developed a leak, or the Saturnian Squid People had switched on their Interplanetary Explode-O Ray. Nobody was quite sure.

There had been an explosion in a neighborhood in Richmond. Nobody mentioned the racial composition of the neighborhood. That information wasn't included in news stories anymore. Besides, the tapes told the story better than words could.

The blast had flattened a neighborhood tavern, a long-time community institution called Fuzzy's #3. Dead were the popular proprietor, Fuzzy Quinn, and several customers, including a self-styled community leader and reputed gang figure, one Luther Jones, a.k.a. Hasan Rahsaan Rasheed.

The Richmond explosion story was followed by a teaser of *Abraham Lincoln* footage—aircraft carriers and jets always made good video—but Lindsey couldn't take any more news. He hit the mute button, leaned back and stared at the ceiling. When he couldn't tolerate looking at the ceiling anymore, he looked back at the screen and browsed the silent channels. The most interesting program was a faded videotape of the 1972 Olympic hockey finals. He had watched the U.S. team in its unlikely upset of the powerhouse U.S.S.R. a dozen times before. He watched it again, wondering what had happened to the Soviet coach when he got home and where all the athletes were today. Some of them must have lived longer than their country had.

At last he gave it up and turned off the TV and climbed into bed and stared at the ceiling some more. Eventually, God sent morning to make things better.

*   *   *

Marvia was in a sweatshirt and jeans when Lindsey arrived at her apartment. He wore a suit. She peeled off her shirt and jeans and said, "Do I look so bad?"

"You look wonderful. You look beautiful. Come on, let's fly to Reno and get married and phone the s.o.b. from the honeymoon suite."

She jumped on his chest and toppled him onto her bed. For a crazy instant, he found himself eye to eye with one of the bright Raggedy Anns on the bedspread. Marvia held him with her arms and legs. She grabbed a pillow and jammed it onto his shoulder and shoved her face into it and shook.

Then she got up. "What if I said yes?"

He didn't hesitate. "Let's do it."

"You really mean it. You do."

"I do."

"I have to do this but thank you for saying that and thank you for going with me. I don't want to go up one against two and I didn't want to bring my daddy or my brother."

She opened the mirrored door of her wardrobe and pulled out a dark-green dress. She slipped it over her shoulders. Lindsey pulled up the zipper for her. That actually made her laugh. She looked in the mirror, then turned. "What do you think?"

"Looks good on you."

She looked in the mirror again. "Dowdy. Dowdy dowdy dowdy." She opened the zipper unassisted and threw the dress into a wastebasket. She opened a dresser drawer and pulled out a pair of slacks and pulled them on. They were black and tight. From another drawer came a filmy gold-orange blouse. She pulled it on and adjusted the bodice to expose her cleavage.

"Nice," Lindsey said.

"This will show the bastard!" She put on a thin golden chain with a tiny, vaguely Egyptian charm.

"Are you sure you wouldn't rather fly to Reno?" Lindsey asked.

On the short drive to Oakland he asked, "Where are we supposed to meet them? Their room?"

"We're going to have dinner. There's a fancy restaurant right in the hotel. White linen and waiters in tuxedoes and sky-high prices. All the good stuff.''

"Okay."

When they got to the hotel, he let the top-hatted and gloved valet take his Hyundai. The valet's sneer was almost audible. Walking into the lobby, Lindsey felt Marvia grab his hand.

The Wilkersons had arrived first. Lindsey asked for their table, but he spotted them at once. At least only one man in the room wore an Army officer's uniform. It wasn't like one of those World War II dramas where nightclubs and restaurants were full of men—and occasionally women—with metal ornaments on their collars and chevrons on their sleeves.

Wilkerson stood up when Marvia and Lindsey approached. He looked like Billy Dee Williams with a short haircut and a thin moustache. He smiled and twitched forward about an inch, enough to suggest a bow without looking silly. His wife sat next to him. She didn't move.

Lindsey felt Marvia's fingernails dig into his wrist.

Wilkerson reached across the table toward Marvia. She offered him her free hand. He captured it in both of his. The metal on his uniform glittered. Major's oak leaves on his epaulets; the gleaming U.S. and branch insignia on his lapels; a combat infantryman's badge; a paratrooper's badge; pilot's wings. Among the ribbons over his pocket, Lindsey recognized an Air Medal and the colors of Desert Storm. The only thing missing was a wound stripe above the officer's band on his cuffs.

"Marvia, you look wonderful!" Lindsey saw Wilkerson's eyes dart to the cleavage unconcealed by Marvia's orange blouse. "You look younger and more lovely than ever."

"James," Marvia said.

Wilkerson released one hand from Marvia's. He took his companion's hand and raised it a few inches, like a referee raising the hand of the winner and new champ. "My darling wife, Claudia. My ex, Marvia."

Lindsey smelled the ozone that crackled between the women.

Marvia got her hand back from Wilkerson. Claudia got hers back and extended it a few inches toward Marvia. They touched fingertips. "This is my friend, Hobart Lindsey," Marvia said.

Lindsey shook hands with Wilkerson. "Major." He nodded. "Mrs. Wilkerson."

"Ferré. Ms. Claudia E. Ferré. I exchanged vows with Major Wilkinson and rings. Not names."

Waiters swirled around the table. Lindsey watched as one of them pulled back a chair for Marvia. Then he felt a pressure on the back of his knees and found himself seated beside her.

"It's been a long time," Wilkerson said.

"Six years."

"And you've been a police officer all this time. Well, good for you. I'm just a trifle disappointed that you didn't bring James Junior along. But I suppose it's a little late for him."

"Jamie has homework."

Lindsey watched Claudia Ferré taking in the conversation. She wore a maroon suit with huge white buttons. The jacket closed at her neck. Her skin was lighter than Marvia's, closer to the color of her husband's. She wore her hair long. She looked a lot like Jasmine Guy. A tiny rectangular purse lay on the linen near her wrist.

A hovering waiter asked if they would like a beverage before dinner. Four mineral waters. Uh-oh! Trouble, Lindsey thought. Maybe some small talk would help. "Uh, have you and Major Wilkerson been married very long, Mrs., uh, Ms. Ferré?"

"Three months."

"Well, ah, congratulations. You're practically on your honeymoon."

"Hardly. I'm visiting my firm's local affiliate." When he didn't respond she said, "Ferré, Borden, Squires, Ferré, Quaid. Corporate and estate work."

Lindsey was impressed. "You're a partner already? Pardon me, but you look very young."

"The first Ferré was my grandfather. Founder of the firm. We keep his name for its historical value. He was the first attorney in our county of African descent. The second Ferré is my father."

Lindsey shot a look at Marvia. He wanted to see if she needed any help. He wasn't sure whether she did or not. Major Wilkerson was telling a Desert Storm story.

"Right after Basra. The Saudis and Kuwaitis did as much as they could. I mean, what do you expect of people who live under feudal monarchies? But they did all right. We gave 'em some training and leadership. The Brits were in there too. They did a good job."

Ms. Claudia E. Ferré was gazing at her husband as if she had never heard the story before, as if she were suffering the vertigo of love at first sight. Any minute now Major Wilkerson would start flying with his hands.

"Anyway, the ground troops had retaken Basra and there was this wacky Iraqi Army just standing there in the desert. Their officers had jumped in the vehicles, mostly air-conditioned Mercedes that they'd stolen from the Kuwaitis, and headed back for Baghdad. And here were these wacky Iraqis sitting in bunkers or standing around. Their officers had taken away all the valuables they could carry, but there were still all these goods lying around. You never saw anything like it."

That was for sure.

The waiter hovered behind Major Wilkerson, oversized menus tucked under his arm, waiting for his chance to pass them around. But Wilkerson was busy.

"We came over in our choppers. We were flying late model Apaches specially fitted for desert use. At least we learned something from that moron Carter's fiasco in Iran. I was in the lead Apache, my unit v'd out behind me. We came in low, expecting ground fire, but all these wacky Iraqis started waving anything white they could find. Old undershirts, bedsheets, pillow cases. They just wanted to surrender."

Zoom, whoosh, whiz.

"So we made a pass overhead, then came up behind them. We were driving them like cowboys driving a herd of cattle. And they kept waving their surrender flags. We drove 'em all the way to the border, right into the POW stockade. Two battalions of wacky Iraqis. We didn't lose a man or a ship. I'll tell you."

It was there in his eyes. It was 1991 again, and he was flying his Apache over Basra, herding those wacky Iraqis like a cowpoke herding cattle. Just like he said.

Ms. Claudia E. Ferré was still gazing at her husband. At last, Lindsey identified the look. It was the Politician's Spouse's Stare. Major James Wilkerson, Senior, was running for office.

When the Major paused, the waiter inserted menus into their hands. Wilkerson asked for a recommendation. The waiter suggested the sea bass. Wilkerson ordered a steak. His wife ordered Coquilles St. Jacques. Lindsey ordered sea bass. Marvia ordered an endive salad.

Wilkerson started comparing General Schwartzkopf and General Powell. "Tell me, Mr. Lindsey, what do you do?" Claudia E. Ferré asked.

Lindsey told her.

"Oh, how fascinating. And how do you find International Surety as an employer?"

"They're all right. They could pay more, but they're all right."

When the food was half consumed, Wilkerson brought up the topic of Jamie again. "I know you mean well for him, Marvia, but do you really think this is the best environment? Living with an invalid grandfather and a grandmother who is out of the house all day earning a living?"

"Invalid? What gave you that idea?"

"I thought you told me your father had a disability retirement."

"He caught asbestosis from his work. He's going to die of it someday. But for now he's still strong and capable. He does a wonderful job."

Claudia put her hand on Marvia's wrist. Lindsey saw Marvia flinch. Claudia said, "But don't you think Jamie would be better off with a real father and mother than living with grandparents? And what happens when your father . . . " The sentence faded into the air like a hint of subtle perfume.

"I see him every chance I get. I see him two or three times a week."

"Whenever your police duties permit, I'm sure. But is that truly as good as having a real home?"

"He has a real home."

"Don't you see, Marvia, what would be best for Jamie? And he's my son, too. Don't forget that," Wilkerson said.

Angrily, Marvia said, "You signed away those rights. Or don't you remember? An officer getting a little female MP pregnant! I did everything for you, everything to save your career. And you were thrilled to be rid of us. Of Jamie and me. Get us out of Germany, get me out of the Army, get us both out of your life. And now you're remarried. Well good for you. I hope you're both very happy. But you're not getting Jamie back."

Claudia said, "But the child needs . . . "

Clenching his fists beneath the sparkling tablecloth, Lindsey managed to say, "Marvia and I are going to be married." His heart raced and his chest was tight. "We're going to make a home for Jamie. He is going to be our son."

No one said a word. Lindsey could feel the couple's eyes shifting from his face to Marvia's. Marvia grabbed his hand. Her touch was like ice.

Finally, Claudia Ferré said, "I guess that's that. James, call for the check." She started to stand but Wilkerson pulled her back into her chair. He was furious. Lindsey wasn't sure with whom.

"I'll be out at the airport the next few days," Wilkerson said. "I've already talked with the Double Bee people, with that Chandler woman. And with some of the pilots handling those old aircraft. They're from Texas. I'm at Fort Hood now, near home. It doesn't hurt to have connections like that for later on."

"What later on is that?" Marvia asked.

"James is planning to resign his commission," Claudia said. "He is going to be a congressman."

"Now I see," Marvia said.

"You see nothing," Wilkerson said. "Most of those airplane people are from Texas, except for the old geezer."

"You mean Lawton Crump? He was one of the original Tuskegee Airmen," Lindsey said.

"How remarkable, Mr. Lindsey. Have you been studying African-American history?" Claudia asked.

"I've been studying American history."

"At your stage of life? It must be rather like taking religious instruction prior to converting. Do you have something like that in mind?"

Wilkerson interrupted. "I'll be flying a P-38 this week, Marvia. The least you could do is let James Junior see me, let him know who his father is and what he's accomplished in this world."

On the way back to Oxford Street, Marvia said, "Thank you."

"For what?"

"What a horrible encounter. What a horrible woman. 'Grandfather was our founder. James is going to be our next congressman. Do you think that's truly best for the child?' "

"At least it stopped short of a food fight," Lindsey said.

Marvia managed a feeble laugh. "Not by much," she said. "I was really, really close. If I'd had a plate of spaghetti, I think I would have let her have it."

She reached over and touched his face with her hand. "Anyway, thank you."

"Well then, what about it?" Lindsey asked.

"About what?"

"Getting married."

She inhaled sharply and leaned her head on his shoulder.

"But you know, they were using the same arguments you've used. For why you can't marry me. They're the same arguments they used for why they should take Jamie."

"I know that. Hearing it from them . . . hearing it from them was a good thing. It made me understand better."

"You don't think she'll make trouble? She's a lawyer."

"I don't know. I just don't know. But I'll never give Jamie up. They can't make me and I won't do it."

212

Twenty-Four

SOMETIMES YOU PHONE AHEAD. Usually you phone ahead. It's good business practice. It's in the International Surety Operations Manual. But as Ducky Richelieu had told the SPUDS class in Denver, as far as violating policy was concerned, you only get in trouble when you get in trouble. The middle of the pack is full of rule followers. The big winners, and the big losers, are the rule breakers.

Lindsey drove to Holy City first thing in the morning. The dark-green Oldsmobile stood clean and sparkling on the black-top. There was plenty of room beside it, where the Jeep Grand Wagoneer had stood during Lindsey's last visit.

Nellie Crump was kneeling in front of a rose bush. When Lindsey climbed from his Hyundai and closed the door, she stood up and turned around. She could have been posing for a magazine ad. She wore a bonnet, overalls and thick gloves. She held a pair of pruning shears.

Buy Burpee's gardening products.

Frowning, Nellie Crump said, "Mr. . . . . Lindsey, isn't it?"

"Yes, ma'am."

"What can I do for you, Mr. Lindsey? Mr. Crump isn't home. He's up in Oakland working on the movie. You really should have telephoned."

"Yes, ma'am. But I just thought I'd drop in. Since Mr. Crump isn't here, I thought maybe you could help me out a little." Where had he picked that up? From Doc High, most likely, who seemed to have got it from watching television. Still, you use what you have and you use what works. In

Lindsey's mind, Ducky Richelieu whispered his ghostly approval.

Nellie Crump put her hands on her hips. "I can't imagine what I could possibly tell you. You know my husband found that poor man at the airport. He answered all your questions. What more can you want to ask? And why me?"

Lindsey looked in his pocket organizer. Nellie Crump knew he wasn't a cop so there was no point in trying to pull authority. And sometimes the indifferent bureaucrat got good results.

"We're still working on the insurance aspect, Mrs. Crump. I know you've been married to Mr. Crump for a very long time. Maybe you could provide the information I need and save me another trip down here or from pestering Mr. Crump out at the airport. It certainly was foolish of me to drive all the way down here without calling first. But as long as I'm here . . . "

He spread his hands helplessly.

She looked at her roses regretfully. "I suppose that would be all right."

"Can we go inside?"

She hesitated, then apparently decided that he wasn't an ax murderer after all. She opened the door—it wasn't locked—and followed him inside. She laid her pruning shears and gloves on a wooden stand, pulled off her bonnet and laid it on top, peered into a hallway mirror and adjusted a loose strand of hair.

"Suppose we sit in here." She led the way into the kitchen and gestured Lindsey to a chair. The kitchen was decorated cheerfully in yellow. Wallpaper with false wooden latticework, a sun-bright ceiling and chrome and lemon-peel Formica table and chairs. The kitchen was many shades brighter than the living room where Lawton Crump had answered Lindsey's questions.

"Would you like some tea, Mr. Lindsey? Some iced tea? I have some made in the refrigerator. I love a cold glass of tea after my gardening work. I'm afraid I'm greedy about it. I always make a full pitcher. We could share."

He nodded and she poured for them both.

"I'm trying to learn about Mr. Crump's life over the years. I suppose this may sound odd . . . how could it possibly be connected with the, ah, unfortunate death of Leroy McKinney, eh? But sometimes the most surprising connection turns up. I don't expect it will, but I have to do my job, don't you see."

Nellie Crump frowned and shook her head. "Well, you can ask away, I suppose, but I don't really grasp your point. Mr. Crump discovered this unfortunate person, this dead body. But he was a perfect stranger. How could there be any connection?"

Lindsey made an entreating gesture. A *help me, please* gesture. "If I could just get a few answers. If I don't . . . " He let that hang.

Nellie Crump let herself be coaxed. She was reluctant but not adamant. She heaved a sigh and waited for Lindsey's first question.

Lindsey studied his pocket organizer. "You met Mr. Crump during World War Two. Is that right?" he asked.

"That's right. I was a USO girl. I'd been a student at Tuskegee before the war, and I just stayed. I was what they called a townie-girl. You know, town and gown."

Lindsey nodded.

Nellie continued. "Well, when the Air Corps came, suddenly there were all these wonderful young men just flooding into Tuskegee. I suppose it was a dangerous situation. Of course, I'm looking at it from an older perspective now. But in 1942, 1943, why, we girls thought it was just ideal. We were outnumbered, oh, twenty or thirty to one. Nobody knew how all the young cadets were going to spend their free time. Not that they had very much, but when they got a weekend pass, what were they going to do?"

Lindsey smiled encouragingly.

"So our community leaders organized a USO and we gave parties and dances and the like. We got bands to come and play. The cadets looked so handsome in their uniforms. They looked very mature to us. I suppose they were mere boys, really, but we were just teenagers ourselves. And we knew they were going off to fight in the war, flying those big airplanes. And we knew that some of them would never come back. It was all very melodramatic. It was easy to get carried away."

She smiled distantly.

"The Army tried to discourage those training-camp marriages, but there were still quite a few of them. And some, well, let's say that some of the girls got into trouble. Without being married. It was sad. And a lot of romances blossomed with the promise that couples would be married after the war. Assuming that the young man came back after the war. I don't suppose you've ever been through anything like that. You couldn't understand if you haven't."

"My father was in the Korean War. My parents were married just before he left. My mother didn't know she was pregnant. My father was killed in the war. He was in the Navy. I never knew him," Lindsey said.

Mrs. Crump said, "I suppose you can understand, then. Well, Lawton and I were married. It's been nearly fifty years. We're looking forward to our Golden Wedding. A lot of those wartime romances came to tragic ends, but ours was a complete success."

"You were from Alabama and Mr. Crump was from Louisiana, is that right?" Lindsey asked.

"That's right."

"He visited your home, he met your family in Tuskegee?"

"Oh, yes. My parents were very concerned, very strict." She paused to consider. "Well, maybe not too strict. But they kept an eye on us. I had a brother and a sister. My brother served in the Army. He lived until two years ago. I have a niece and nephew, his children. And I have a sister. She never married. She stayed with our parents all their lives, and she still lives in our old house back in Alabama."

"What about Mr. Crump's family?"

"Would you like some more tea, Mr. Lindsey?" She refilled his glass. "What about Lawton's family?"

"Did he talk about them much? Did you ever meet them? Did you ever visit Reserve?"

She smiled. "Reserve, Louisiana. Oh my, yes. Don't we think of the old South as picturesque and beautiful, with magnolia blossoms and ladies in crinolines? Even slavery gets glamorized, doesn't it? But Reserve was just a dirt-poor, ugly, isolated place. But I loved Lawton's mother. What a strong woman. I don't think I could have done what she did. Willa McKinney . . . "

A look appeared on her face that sent a needle of icy terror through Lindsey.

"Leroy McKinney."

"That's right," Lindsey said. "Are you telling me that you never put that together, Mrs. Crump?"

"I didn't, no." She shook her head. Either she was telling the truth or she was a heck of an actress. "I'm so stupid! I never thought . . . "

"There's no reason you should have. You never saw the body. You had nothing to do with his death." He didn't want to call her on it. He couldn't prove she was lying, and if he held back from accusing, he might get more out of her. "You never met Leroy. Or did you? Was he in Reserve when your husband took you there to visit? Did Willa ever say anything about him to you? Or about her other son, Jefferson King?"

She held her hand over her mouth. The look that had so shocked Lindsey was gone from her face.

"He only took me to Reserve that once. To meet his mother. He thought she was a heroic woman, and she was. Still is, isn't she? She must be very old by now. He never talks about his family. He sends her money, but he never talks about his family. And we've never gone back to Reserve, not once in all these years. And since the Pan Am bankruptcy, I don't know what's going to happen. They'll be in court for years and in the meanwhile what becomes of Lawton's pension, I ask you. It just isn't fair."

He sends her money, Lindsey thought. Willa hadn't said anything about that, and neither had her crippled brother-in-law, Floyd McKinney. Leroy—the false Leroy—had returned to Louisiana at least once. Lindsey was certain of that. Leroy had sent a postcard to his granddaughter, Latasha Greene, and Latasha had brought it to the Reverend Johnson for help in

217

reading. But nobody ever said anything about Lawton Crump sending money home to Reserve.

"Did he send checks? Would there be cancelled checks or stubs?"

"Check stubs, yes."

"I hate to pry, but do you think I could have a look at those stubs?"

Nellie Crump stood up. She had still not recovered from the realization of who the dead man was—or was supposed to be—and was turning reluctant again.

"I'm not sure that you have any right to do that, Mr. Lindsey. To look at our check stubs. I don't see what it has to do with this. And you are not the police."

"No, ma'am. I'm not. But the police will want to know, eventually. And if you won't help me—and maybe I can help you—you'll have to show your records to them." The carrot and the stick. Let me help you or talk to the cops.

She looked at him angrily, opened her mouth, then closed it again. She took a moment, obviously counting her options. Finally she said, "Come along. Let's have a look."

The checkbook was kept in Lawton Crump's desk in his study. The room was even darker than the Crumps' living room. A green-shaded banker's lamp stood on a leather-topped desk. The walls were decorated with wartime aviation prints. Nellie Crump unlocked the desk and took out an oversized checkbook. It was the size of an old-fashioned photo album.

She opened the book, ran her finger down a page of check stubs, turned the page and stopped. "There it is."

Lindsey read Lawton Crump's strong writing. The stub was made out to the United States Postal Service for a money order. The amount was very substantial. He looked at Nellie Crump.

"Were the checks always that large? That's a lot of money." And it certainly hadn't shown up in Willa McKinney's way of life, Lindsey thought.

"They've increased over the years. At first, when we weren't making much money, they were smaller. As Lawton rose in the world and our income increased, so did the amounts he sent to his mother."

"He always did it that way? Never actually wrote a check to Willa McKinney?"

"Never. He always used money orders."

"Did you actually see the address on the envelopes when he sent the money orders?"

She shook her head. "He always kept that to himself."

"Did you know that Lawton had two half-brothers? Did Willa tell you that, or did Lawton ever talk about them? About their serving in the Navy, or that one of them died in the war?"

"He had such a big family. And he never liked to talk about them very much. Just his mother. He spoke of her from time to time. That was all."

She locked the checkbook in the desk and escorted Lindsey from the murky study back to the sunshine-filled kitchen. "I'll tell Lawton that you were here," she said. "Shall I have him telephone you?"

"Not just now. Thank you for helping me out. Mr. Crump needn't call me. I'll call him."

She pulled her bonnet over her hair, slipped on her gloves and picked up her pruning shears. Lindsey caught a glimpse of the rubber lining inside the heavy canvas. They would protect Nellie's hands well from the thorns on her rose bushes. "I'll get back to my gardening, then. I love my roses but they do require care."

Twenty-Five

LINDSEY PHONED MARVIA FROM THE INTERNATIONAL SURETY office in Walnut Creek. She was at her desk, catching up on paperwork. She told him that James Wilkerson, Senior, had called her at home.

"This morning?"

"Last night."

"That must have been pretty late."

"I asked him if he wasn't keeping his bride awake and he said he was calling from the hotel lobby."

Lindsey tried to whistle, started to laugh and wound up making the kind of sound he called a raspberry when he was a kid.

"Yeah, me too." Marvia didn't sound too upset. "He wants to take Jamie out to the airport today. After school."

"I'm not surprised."

"He wants to show off. Show Jamie what a wonderful dad he has. I don't like the idea, but I don't feel I can stop him."

"Sure you can. He signed away his parental rights, didn't he?"

Marvia sounded weary. "I know I can. I mean, I don't think it would be right. I'm not going to give him Jamie, and I don't really care about his paternal feelings or his thin skin. But I don't think it's fair to Jamie. He is entitled to know his dad."

Lindsey wanted to ask where he fit into this picture but didn't say anything.

"So I'm signing out early and I'm going to pick Jamie up after school. I don't want James picking him up. He doesn't even

220

know him. I don't want him going with strangers. And I just don't want the Major to play that role."

The Major.

"Okay. Do you want me to come along? You and Jamie and I?"

"Not with me. Us. I mean, it could be too confrontational. I don't think James liked you very much."

"I don't think Claudia liked me at all."

"Her!" Marvia took several breaths that were audible over the telephone. "Patronizing bitch. I don't really hate James, but if I did I would want to see him married to Ms. Claudia Ferré."

"Is she going to be at the airport?"

"No. She has to visit her daddy's firm in San Francisco. She'll probably spend an hour there, get some hotpants young associate to take her to lunch at the St. Francis and spend the afternoon at Saks."

Lindsey clucked his tongue.

"I'm sorry," Marvia said. "Hell hath no fury, has it? The woman who took my place in his bed, all of that. But she is a cold-blooded bitch."

"Don't look for a fight from me."

"If you could do this for me . . . It's a lot to ask, but I'm trying to work through this, Bart."

"If I could do what for you? I thought you didn't want me there."

"No, I just don't think you and Jamie and I should arrive together. And I don't want James picking him up at school or at his grandparents' house. But Jamie knows you. If you could pick him up at my house, maybe take him for a treat, stop at his favorite hot-dog stand. And then arrive at the airport together. I'll meet you there. Is that too much, Bart? Does it make any sense? Sometimes I think I'm going crazy."

Quickly, he said, "I'll be there. I'll meet you at Oxford Street. You and Jamie, right. Don't worry about it. We'll get through this." He didn't want to hear her say, "Please, Bart."

"Thank you, Bart."

Lindsey put down the telephone and breathed a sigh. Ms.

Wilbur said, "Pardon my long furry ears, Hobart, but that was very intense. Is everything all right?"

He rubbed his eyes. He hadn't been sleeping too well.

"How's your mother doing?" Ms. Wilbur asked.

"She's doing beautifully. Learning to run a computer. Watch out. She's going to look for a job."

"I'm going to leave a vacancy here. But I wouldn't wish this job on your mom. Not with . . . " She inclined her head toward Elmer Mueller.

Mueller had been scowling into a computer screen. He looked up. "Don't you two have any work to do? Can't you see I'm trying to concentrate here?"

"Sorry, Elmer. You know, International Surety tries to maintain the human touch."

Mueller growled. "What kind of company gives a man a job and then don't give him any authority to do it with?"

"I think you mean, 'don't give him *no* authority,' don't you, Elmer?" Lindsey said.

Mueller uttered a very vulgar oath.

"I'll be out of here the end of the month, Mr. Mueller. I hope you don't subject my successor to that kind of language. I don't think it fits in with modern ideas of the workplace."

Mueller jammed his hat on his head and headed for the exit. "End of the month can't come a day too soon. And as for you . . . " He glared at Lindsey, shook his head and slammed the door behind him.

"Aren't we awful to him? But I can't resist such an easy target. And I can't feel sorry for him," Ms. Wilbur said.

"Neither can I."

"That was Marvia, then?"

Lindsey nodded. "It's complicated."

"How long have you been together?"

"Depends on what you mean by together."

"You tell me."

He felt himself flush. "Okay. It's been almost five years. Since we first met. Since that comic-book murder in Berkeley."

Ms. Wilbur pursed her lips, screwed up her face into a Maurice Chevalier grimace. "Ah yes, I remember it well.

Hmm. Don't you think that's long enough to make up your mind? You're no spring chicken, Hobart. If you don't mind hearing that from a lady of a certain age."

"No. You're right." He looked at her. It was a hell of a relationship between an ex-boss, now an uneasy office guest, and the office manager. Sometimes Ms. Wilbur was more like a scolding aunt. And sometimes, when Mother was at her worst, Ms. Wilbur had been like a second mother.

"So?" she asked.

"I've asked her. She keeps putting me off."

"A nice gentile fellow like you, what's the matter? She isn't prejudiced is she?"

"She's worried about Jamie. Her little boy. And now his father's in town with a new wife and the whole thing is getting really tense."

"Let me know if there's anything I can do."

Lindsey said thanks. Ms. Wilbur returned to her work, whistling softly. It was that damned show stuff. She would never be Hermione Gingold. He picked up the phone and dialed Double Bee in Oakland. Someone might pick up the call at the Parc Oakland, or it might go through to North Field.

Before a word was spoken, Lindsey could tell from the echoing sounds of engines that someone had picked up the phone in the hangar at North Field. After a couple of minutes, he was able to get patched through to Ina Chandler.

"Everything's going wonderfully," she said. "The flying's been great, the shooting's been great. Looks like we're going to wrap in a couple of days. And what can I do for you?"

"I wondered if Lawton Crump is there today. And Major Wilkerson. Have you been in touch with Major Wilkerson?"

"In fact, Mr. Crump will be flying tonight. He isn't here yet, but I expect him any minute. I heard from Major Wilkerson. He's sitting in the P-38 now, getting the feel of the controls. He's quite an airman, isn't he? Must be the pride of the Air Force."

"Army," Lindsey said.

"Army? He isn't in the Air Force?"

"He flew a chopper in Kuwait. He was a big hero. I'm surprised he didn't tell you all about it."

Ina Chandler snorted. "He tried to. I couldn't get rid of him until I got him into the cockpit, then I just walked away. Is there anything else, Mr. Lindsey? I'm glad you called. I want to make sure that umbrella policy covers Major Wilkerson."

"Only if he's affiliated with Double Bee in some capacity. I suggest you write out a personal services contract. Make him a consultant and pay him a dollar a day. Don't let him fly until you do that."

"Right. Will do. Anything else?"

"I'll be out there in a few hours. Good idea if you make that agreement in triplicate. One for Wilkerson, one for Double Bee, one for International Surety."

He dropped the handset onto its base. "How's about lunch, Ms. Wilbur. On me. You can set that thing for voice mail until Uncle Elmer gets back."

Jamie and Marvia were in the living room when Lindsey arrived. He picked Jamie up and hugged Marvia. The boy was squeezed between them, but he didn't seem to mind. Jamie clutched his Flying Fortress in one hand. "Hello, Mr. Lindsey."

"Hello, Mr. Wilkerson. I thought we'd agreed to call each other Jamie and Bart."

Jamie said, "Okay."

A couple of Marvia's housemates were busily at work in the kitchen. There was an odor of stir-fried mushrooms and onions and peppers and sounds of cans clattering on a tile countertop and cupboard doors slamming. An angry voice said, "All right, I'll come back when you finish putting away your precious ingredients."

A round-bodied woman in a sweaty T-shirt and jeans flounced out of the kitchen and sat down noisily in an easy chair. She glared at Marvia and Jamie and Lindsey, muttered and began to drum her fingers on the chair's arm.

Marvia ushered Lindsey and Jamie onto the porch of the Victorian. "They've been together for years and they never fight, except when they get into the kitchen. Wait, now the veggies will char and they'll *really* get into it. That's true love there."

Jamie tugged at Lindsey's hand. "Can we go to Mr. Harry's?"

Lindsey looked at Marvia questioningly.

"Mr. Harry runs Kasper's," she said. "Original Kasper's. Go to no other."

Lindsey raised his eyebrows.

"Telegraph and Forty-fifth," Marvia said. "It's been there a million years. They have a varied menu. You can have a hot dog with or without tomatoes, with or without onions and with or without pickle relish."

"Okay with me," Lindsey said. "And then we'll head out to North Field. Then what?"

"I'll get there before you do. Take your cue from me, okay?" She gave Jamie a hug and kiss. Lindsey could see that she was shaky. He touched her, then took Jamie and led him to the Hyundai.

Kasper's was as Marvia had described it. A tiny triangular building stuck in an island where Shattuck Avenue merged with Telegraph. Its barn-red paint and signs bearing the logo of a white-hatted chef made it look like something taken brand new from another era and dumped into the present.

Jamie tugged Lindsey inside. An old man stood behind the counter, painstakingly slicing a fresh tomato for a young man who stood fidgeting impatiently. The old man had a white moustache and a fringe of white hair. The young man had crinkly hair, thin features and an intense, nervous energy about him. "Why doesn't he get things ready in advance?" Lindsey asked.

"He makes everything fresh. Harry's always done it that way," the young man explained.

A short-haired woman had her back to the counter, stocking a glass-fronted cooler. "Hello, Mrs. Harry," Jamie said.

The woman turned and said, "Hello, Jamie." She said something to the old man and gestured at Lindsey and Jamie.

The old man took a hot dog from a steamer, put it on a roll

and spread slices of tomato and onion on it. "No relish today?" he asked.

The young man took the hot dog. "Not today, Harry." He turned away and sat on a leatherette-covered stool at a counter facing Telegraph. He had a notepad and a fat textbook with him. He spread them on the counter and studied while he ate.

The old man gestured to Jamie and they engaged in a whispered conversation. He said something to the woman, and she picked up a telephone and dialed. The old man said, "Jamie says you're his friend, Mister . . . "

Lindsey introduced himself. The old man extended his hand. "Yaglijian," he said. "Harry Yaglijian. Everybody calls me Harry." His hand felt like tree bark over ironwood, until he closed down on Lindsey's fingers. Then it felt like steel cables.

The old man said, "What do you want? Same as Jamie?"

"Right." Sight unseen. A line formed behind them, while the old man sliced onions and tomatoes and put together hot dogs and condiments. Even the newcomers knew the drill. No one complained.

Lindsey and Jamie sat near the young man with the crinkly hair. Every time Lindsey looked back toward the counter, either the old man or the woman was watching him. The phone rang and the woman answered it. She gestured to Lindsey. He left Jamie munching his hot dog and took the phone from the woman. It was an old, heavy instrument. Kasper's had never heard of plastic.

To Lindsey's astonishment, he heard a familiar voice. "Mr. Lindsey?"

"Yes," Lindsey said.

"Bart, how's my grandson?" Marcus Plum asked.

"He's fine. He's eating a hot dog. Is something wrong?"

"Nothing wrong. Just put Norma back on."

"Who?"

"Mrs. Harry."

Lindsey complied.

The woman talked briefly, then she hung up the telephone. "Okay, you're okay. You take care of Jamie."

The old man laid down a huge kitchen knife. It looked like

226

it belonged on the cover of a mad-slasher paperback. "You're okay, Hobart. Mr. Plum says you're okay. You be good to Jamie."

They finished their hot dogs and slid off their stools. The young man was eating slowly, studying his textbook. As Lindsey and Jamie headed for the exit, the young man said, "Bye, Jamie."

"Bye, Ken."

"Nice to see you. Say hello to your Uncle Tyrone for me."

Outside, they climbed into the Hyundai. Lindsey had parked in front of Kasper's. A huge McDonald's was across the street. "You have a lot of friends, don't you, Jamie?"

"Yep."

"Mr. and Mrs. Harry always check up on you like that?"

Jamie shrugged. He was flying his B-17.

"Jamie, you love your mom a lot, don't you?"

"Yep."

"You like living with your grandma and grandpa?"

"Yep."

"But would you rather live with your mom?"

Jamie put the B-17 through a difficult bank-and-roll. Lindsey waited for him to answer. The silence was more frightening than being shot. Finally Jamie said, "I guess so."

Lindsey was sweating. "Would it be all right if I lived with you? I mean, with you and your mom?"

"Sure."

Lindsey's heart started to work again.

Lindsey pulled into the dirt parking lot at North Field. He recognized the Crumps' Jeep Grand Wagoneer parked among the airport vehicles and the Double Bee film vans. He would have thought that the Wagoneer was Nellie's and the Oldsmobile was Lawton's, but maybe he had got it backwards. Or maybe they used the vehicles interchangeably.

There was also a flashy, nail-polish-red Ford Probe parked at an angle that didn't block any of the vehicles but that would draw the attention of anyone arriving or leaving. The Probe had rental indicia on its dashboard. One guess whose car it was.

Marvia's Mustang was nowhere to be seen. Lindsey checked his Seiko. Marvia should have arrived by now. What would happen if Marvia arrived and found Lindsey and Jamie chatting amiably with James Senior?

Bessie Blue sat on the runway surrounded by smaller aircraft. She looked like a queen bee encircled by busy workers and idle drones. The Fortress's propellers were still and the sun glinted off her metal skin and glass eyes. She had the look of a creature eager to leap up and be gone.

Good as Ina Chandler's word, Lawton Crump had arrived before Lindsey. He was standing with Major James Wilkerson in front of the hangar. Ina Chandler hovered nervously nearby. The big hangar doors were open and the crew had rolled the P-47 Thunderbolt inside for servicing. Crump and Wilkerson were chatting like comrades in arms, fellow airmen whose shared experience spanned the forty-five years between their glory days.

Lindsey saw them swooping their hands in the air, before he heard a word. They were completely engrossed. Crump's elbows were raised, his hands palm-down at eye-level, as if he were going to take a sobriety test by touching his nose. But he was illustrating a bombing run. At closer range, Lindsey could hear his vocalizations. He was the B-17, he was its fighter escort, he was the Messerschmitt 262, a twin-jet fighter, the first ever to go operational.

The sound effects and gestures amounted to nothing less than a self-accompanied dance.

Ina Chandler jumped backwards, clipboard clutched to her chest, to avoid being rammed. Lindsey held Jamie Wilkerson tightly, although Jamie seemed more inclined to join the others.

James Wilkerson, Senior, was obviously more interested in telling his own Gulf War stories than in hearing of Lawton Crump's long-ago exploits. Lindsey imagined that Wilkerson could hardly care less about this relic.

Crump looked away from Wilkerson and locked eyes with Lindsey. Lindsey watched Crump gesture dismissively at Wilkerson. He stalked toward Lindsey, looking angry.

"I want to talk to you."

Lindsey was surprised. "Who, me?" He relaxed his grip on Jamie's hand and the boy slipped away. Lindsey saw Wilkerson Senior flash a look at Jamie and then at Lindsey. He moved toward Jamie. Jamie looked confused.

Before Lindsey could act, Crump reached him. He grabbed Lindsey by the lapel and steered him toward the hangar. Lindsey looked behind him. He could see Major Wilkerson and Mrs. Chandler and Jamie standing together. Mrs. Chandler squatted in front of Jamie and began to talk to him. Wilkerson watched Lindsey and Crump walk away and then rejoined Mrs. Chandler and Jamie.

Without missing a beat, Crump dragged Lindsey into the hangar and into the little office that seemed to have been designated a Double Bee conference room. He had to drag him past the P-47 to get there. Lindsey ducked his head under the P-47's metal wing tip. Lindsey tried to protest. Jamie seemed to be in no danger, but he didn't want to leave the boy with two strangers. And where was Marvia? Everything had been worked out so carefully, and now everything was turning into a shambles.

The P-47 had a huge, stubby engine cowling and a shiny four-bladed propeller. A brown-skinned woman with a gardenia in her hair was painted on the cowling, along with the name *Lady Day*.

Crump slammed Lindsey into a hard metal chair and plunged his own mass into the swivel chair behind the desk. Even seated, Crump was still inches taller than Lindsey. He must have outweighed him by forty pounds. Despite the difference in their ages, he was an intimidating presence.

"Why did you go to my house?"

"You can't do this to me. I'm responsible for that boy. I have to . . . "

"He's safe with Chandler and Wilkerson. You can go out there as soon as you answer my questions."

Lindsey judged Crump's size and strength against his own. "What? What questions?" He felt like a schoolboy called on the carpet and accused of cribbing on an exam. He didn't know whether to deny the charge, plead guilty with an explanation or simply refuse to discuss the matter. Lawton Crump didn't wait for an answer.

"My wife told me you went there to snoop. Who the hell do you think you are, mister? You're a puny little insurance adjuster, that's who you are. You are one of God's own pismires. I welcomed you into my home and treated you with courtesy, and as soon as I turn my back you sneak back there and harass my wife. You rifle my desk and stick your nose into my private papers."

Lindsey raised his hands. He wanted to get back to Jamie. He wanted to find out where Marvia Plum was. But Crump wasn't stopping.

"You've been spying on my family. You went to Reserve, didn't you? Don't deny it. I've been checking on you, too, mister. I still have connections in Louisiana. I have family and friends. How dare you intrude on my mother and torment her with questions? She's a weary old woman. She's suffered. She's lost most of her family. You think a long life is a blessing, don't you, insurance man? But it isn't when you have to bury your loved ones, one generation after another."

He shook his head like an angry bull, ready to lower his horns and charge. But he still wasn't finished.

"I want an explanation from you and I want it right now and it had better be good!"

Lindsey caught his breath. He thought, *A good offense is the best defense.* He hadn't harassed Nellie Crump, he had questioned her politely, almost diffidently. He hadn't rifled Crump's desk. Nellie Crump showed him the checkbook after only a little prodding. He hadn't tormented Willa McKinney. Marvia Plum had drawn her out gently, lovingly, and left the old woman happy.

But a good offense . . .

"Why did you lie to me?" Lindsey demanded. "More important, Mr. Crump, why did you lie to the police? Sergeant Finnerty and Lieutenant High are going to be very upset with you."

"Lie!" If Crump had been angry before, now he was furious. His eyes glowed red in the gloomy hangar. "You nobody! How can you call me a liar? I ought to thrash you within an inch of your life. What in hell are you talking about?"

"Leroy McKinney."

"What about him?"

"Or should I say, Jefferson King the third?"

Crump reached a massive hand across the desk and grabbed Lindsey by the lapel. "Tell me what you know!"

"I know that you had two half-brothers, Jefferson King and Leroy McKinney. Your mother had three husbands and she had a son with each. Hence the last names—Crump, King, McKinney."

Breath hissed like steam through Lawton Crump's nostrils. He grabbed Lindsey's other lapel and nodded to Lindsey to go on.

"I know that both of your brothers served in the Navy during World War Two. They served at the same time you were in the Air Corps." This time Crump didn't correct Lindsey's usage. "I know that both your brothers—half-brothers— were Navy stevedores involved in the Port Chicago disaster. One of them was killed outright. The other was injured—his hand was ruined—but he recovered. He ran away. And to avoid getting picked up as a deserter, he took his dead brother's name."

"More," Crump said.

"Leroy McKinney was the brother who was killed in Port Chicago. Jefferson King took his name and used that name—or Abu Shabazz—until he was murdered in this hangar. As Abu Shabazz, he was mixed up with Luther Jones's drug ring in Richmond. Did you have anything to do with that? I don't know. But I think you were paying your half-brother all these years to avoid a family scandal."

Each time Lindsey paused for breath, Lawton Crump shook him by the lapels until Lindsey started up again.

"All those check stubs that you used to buy money orders— they weren't for Willa McKinney. They were for Jefferson King. Why was it so important to keep King's desertion secret, Lawton? Tell me that."

"Figure it out," Crump said.

"You were a poor kid from the South in a time when a Negro hardly had a chance in this country. But you'd gone against all odds. With Joe Wagner's help, you'd made it in the Air Corps. You didn't want to be dragged back down. You were afraid that if they knew your brother was a deserter it would smear you as well. You couldn't bear to give up your rank, your officer's uniform. After the war, you made a good career with the airline. But you were always afraid. Always afraid. So you kept on paying. You didn't want a family scandal. You didn't want your brother to go down and drag you with him."

"And what did Jeff do with the money?" Crump asked.

"I don't know. Lived on it. He didn't live well, but he got along."

Crump had released one of Lindsey's lapels but was still clutching the other.

"I thought he was living on it. Sometimes I guess he was. But he wanted a big payoff. I wormed it out of him. I found out why he needed the big payoff. It was that Richmond business. It was that Rasheed gang. I doubt that I would have paid him anyway. But with Pan Am belly up, I was frightened. That's a nice house we have, two big cars. You don't know what that means. I couldn't risk losing that. So I said I'd meet him here and pay him off."

Lindsey started to ask what Crump planned to do now. He even started to reach for the telephone to call Oakland Homicide. He glanced toward the telephone and so he barely saw Lawton Crump's fist, his onetime sugar mill hand's, onetime fighter's, onetime mechanic's iron fist, fill the world.

The impact sent a flash of blinding white light through Lindsey's brain. He felt himself tilt backwards as his lapel pulled free of Crump's hand. He rotated toward the cement floor and saw a final shower of sparks as his head smashed against the cement. Then came the blackness.

Twenty-Six

LINDSEY'S BLACK-AND-WHITE DREAM was a formless morass of licorice syrup and molten marshmallow. It was hot and sticky, and it felt bad. He opened his eyes and the world was still black and white. But now it was mostly black, with only an edge of light forcing its way through a narrow crack.

He was crumpled up like an empty sack. He scrambled to his feet, or tried to, and found that he was in a metallic enclosure that smelled of oil and was full of heavy machine parts. One of the parts was digging into Lindsey's back. In the absence of messages from his other senses, he concentrated on the pain.

Managing to brace his elbows against the sides of the enclosure, he made another attempt to stand up. This time he succeeded. Some of the hot, sticky substance from his dream had stayed with him. His face was smeared with it.

He felt toward the edge of light and discovered that it was seeping between a pair of metal doors. There was no latch inside the enclosure. He tried to call for help but his voice was so feeble he doubted that anyone could hear him.

He tried pounding on the doors, then kicking. Every so often he would pause, then try again. He yelled for help. With each attempt his voice grew stronger.

When he heard someone say, "What the heck's going on in there?" he renewed his kicking and banging.

The metal doors swung open and Ina Chandler gaped at him. He slumped forward. She dropped her clipboard, caught him and helped him to a chair—the same one Lawton Crump had put him in, the same one he had been sitting in when Crump's fist crashed into his face.

Lindsey's eyes ached and it hurt to open them. When he did, he could see the stubby, single-engined *Lady Day* gleaming under brilliant work lamps. Permanent hangar lights illuminated the rest of the building.

"Somebody get the first-aid kit!" Ina Chandler yelled. She looked at Lindsey. "What happened to you? Did Lawton Crump do this to you?"

" . . . hit me." He didn't want to say Crump's name. He thought he might be nearby and had the irrational fear that if he tattled Crump would come after him again. But if he didn't say who had hit him, he thought, Crump would leave him alone.

"He's the only one who could have done it. I saw you come in here together, then he came out alone." She reached toward his face, then drew back her hand. "Mercy, how could that gentle person . . . "

Lindsey said, " . . . hit me."

Somebody in a Double Bee jacket clattered a first-aid kit onto a workbench and opened it. Ina Chandler reached for a sterile package of gauze pads. Over her shoulder she commanded, "Go fetch Marvia Plum."

She opened a bottle of hydrogen peroxide, soaked the gauze and swabbed Lindsey's face. Lindsey sat in a daze. Helping hands and concerned faces moved in and out of his field of vision, seemingly at random. Beyond the hands and faces, beyond the massive P-47, he could see that the big doors had been rolled back. Cold night air crept into the hangar.

Outside, the runway was illuminated by huge electric lights. The sky was black. A heavy mist had moved in from San Francisco Bay, and the exterior lights were surrounded by ghostly halos. Even the bright moon looked as if its edges were blurred.

Lindsey didn't know how long he had lain unconscious in the metal enclosure. It seemed that he had been banging and calling for hours but it was probably only minutes. He remembered it was full daylight when Lawton Crump dragged him into the hangar, so it must have been two or three hours at least. Where was Marvia? And what had happened to Jamie? He tried to stand up but hands held him in the chair. He started to shake his head but the pain nearly made him pass out again so he held still.

Marvia ran toward him.

"Bart! What happened to you? Where have you been?"

He pushed the restraining hands aside and staggered to his feet. He stumbled toward Marvia. As he wobbled forward, he caught a glimpse of his reflection in *Lady Day*'s polished metal skin. He looked like Robert DeNiro in his Jake LaMotta makeup, after taking a thrashing from Rocky Graziano. He tried to talk but only gagging noises came from his throat.

Marvia touched him. He winced away from the pain.

He was getting his equilibrium back and his eyes and mind into focus. "Where's Jamie? Where's Wilkerson?" he asked.

"Jamie is with Lawton Crump," Marvia said.

"Crump? No. Crump killed McKinney. Only he wasn't really McKinney. He was Jefferson King." Marvia had been with him in Reserve and knew the story of Willa's sons. She understood what he was saying.

She yelled at Ina Chandler. "Get OPD. Dial 911. Try to get High or Finnerty here. Whatever you do, get somebody from Homicide." She drew her breath and clapped her hands to her cheeks. "Jamie. Jamie's in the B-17 with Crump."

Behind her, the runway was empty. The fighters had been towed to the edges of the tarmac, clearing a takeoff path for *Bessie Blue*. The Flying Fortress was gone.

Lindsey could see James Wilkerson, Senior, trotting toward him and Marvia. He was decked out in full flying regalia. Except for his burnished skin, he looked like a Chesterfield ad on the back cover of a 1943 *Life* magazine.

"Lawton Crump took Jamie," Marvia said.

Wilkerson nodded. "I know that."

"He killed McKinney. He knows he's been found out. He clouted Bart and he's taken Jamie."

"This doesn't make sense. It's a night sequence. There are choppers up there with the Fort. The plane has extra lights on it for filming. It's a thrill for Jamie. He was excited about it. I let him go with Crump. It's just the two of them in the bomber."

"No," Lindsey shouted. "There has to be a full crew from the Knights on every flight."

"Nobody told me that." Wilkerson frowned petulantly.

Lindsey moaned. "Crump smashed a man's forehead in with a wrench. He'd been paying him for years and the man wanted a final payoff and Crump killed him. I confronted him and he did this to me." He knew his face was a ruin.

Before Wilkerson could reply, Ina Chandler came running from the hangar. "He won't come down. They finished the scene and the copters are heading back . . . "

Lindsey could already hear the helicopters' engines and their thrashing rotors. They sounded like the movements of herculean watches.

" . . . but Mr. Crump won't come back."

Through a curtain of pain, Lindsey said, "But how can one man can fly that giant plane? It must take nine or ten people. The movies about them . . . "

"It's not a giant plane. Maybe the old movies made it seem big, but it actually isn't much bigger than a DC-3. Those crews were mainly gunners and bombardiers. The actual flight crew was only three or four people—pilot and copilot, navigator and flight engineer. One man can fly a B-17. Crump can and he's doing it."

Lindsey's breath hissed between his teeth. "Did Crump say anything? Did he talk to you or to the control tower?"

Ina Chandler shook her head. "I couldn't understand what he was saying. Something about making history. Something about the war. He didn't say which war."

"I'm going after him," Wilkerson said. He turned and ran toward the P-38.

Lindsey shuffled after him. But Marvia easily caught up and said, "That plane holds two. I'm Jamie's mother. I'm going."

"You're not going. Crump and I know each other. I'm going to talk him out of it. I'm going to talk him down."

"But you're not a hostage negotiator. We need . . . "

Lindsey took her by the arms and glared at her. He knew that

236

his eyes were crimson with broken blood vessels from Lawton Crump's smashing blow. He knew that his face was bloody and swollen, that his nose was broken and that huge blue bruises were appearing over his cheekbones.

He knew that he had to be calm, to make a rational appeal to Marvia. He was in control of himself and yet he had no control, as if a higher self had stepped in and whispered to him, *Just this once, Lindsey, and just for this moment . . .*

"There's no time to get a hostage negotiator here. I'm Jamie's dad, and he needs me. My life for my boy's. It's an easy trade."

Marvia looked stunned. She reached toward him but drew back her hand. An electrical field had sprung up around Lindsey, inviolate, impenetrable.

He sprinted after Wilkerson. Alone.

Wilkerson scrambled onto the short wing beside the P-38's cockpit. The Plexiglas canopy was open and Wilkerson slipped inside as if he had done it a hundred times. The area behind the pilot had been cleared of hardware and fitted with a cramped jump seat.

Lindsey crawled onto the wing. He caught a glimpse of the P-38's name and bright nose art. Neither meant anything to him. To Wilkerson, he said, "I can talk to Crump." Wilkerson nodded and shoved Lindsey into the jump seat. It was painfully constricted and Lindsey's face felt as if it had been ground in a gravel pit.

Wilkerson hit the starter. The Lightning's twin Allison in-lines coughed to life. Wilkerson was already on the radio, talking to Oakland International Control. They cleared the P-38 for takeoff. Wilkerson muttered, "Damned Air Force stand-down. They should have scrambled by now but all of a sudden it's love thine enemy and cut the budget time."

"Can we catch them? Can we find them?" Lindsey asked.

"Let's just hope. If there's radio contact, we can home on them. And there's radar. Everybody's looking for them."

"Where are they going?"

Wilkerson muttered into the cockpit radio. The jump seat was also fitted with a headset, a pair of modern-looking earphones and a bead mike. He slipped into the rig. Now he could hear Wilkerson and the tower.

"P-38, subject plane has headed due west. They're in radio contact with us. They've passed the Farralones and they're still going," a tower controller said.

"How far can they fly?" Lindsey asked.

"We've got a log here on 17Fs. The book says they had a range of four-four-two-oh miles at one-six-oh mph cruising speed and a top speed of three-two-five mph. The pilot seems to be proceeding at cruising speed. You should have no problem overtaking."

"That's for sure." Wilkerson made a humming noise. "Lightning could hit four-two-five max. We don't need to do that. We can cruise at three hundred and catch them okay. Tower, what's the traffic?"

"We're clearing everything. Commercial flights to and from Hawaii have been either delayed or diverted. We think he's headed for Hawaii."

"Why the hell would he do that? He could have bought a ticket," Wilkerson said.

"P-38, we've alerted Alameda Naval Air Station. They're going to patch *Abraham Lincoln* into our net. There's a naval flotilla out there. If they can match *Bessie Blue*'s route, they might be able to lend some help."

"What can they do?" Wilkerson asked.

"Alameda's not sure. Listen, my contact is Commander Jarrold. Let's get him on here."

A new voice came over Lindsey's earphones. "Jarrold here. Who's up there in that Thirty-eight? ID yourselves."

Wilkerson and Lindsey gave their names.

"What's Crump up to? You have any idea, Major? Mr. Lindsey?" Jarrold asked.

"I think he's fighting World War Two. He was a fighter pilot in Europe, he came back to the U.S. and he was training to fly bombers in the Pacific when the war ended," Lindsey said.

Wilkerson muttered, "The old fool. He's flipped out."

"It was his glory time. It was his Desert Storm, Major. He never let go of it. Now he's afraid. He's killed a man, and he wants it to be 1945 again so he can be a war hero instead of a murderer."

Jarrold cut in. He had the authoritative manner of a career officer. "We've got the *Abraham Lincoln* steaming to intersect *Bessie Blue*'s course. We can send up aircraft to escort *Bessie Blue* ahead to Hawaii."

"I don't think *Bessie Blue* can make it," Wilkerson said. "That range was based on maximum fuel load. I think they kept her light for those filming flights."

Jarrold uttered a sailor's oath.

"Can Crump land that bomber on the *Abraham Lincoln?*" Lindsey asked.

"Impossible," Jarrold said.

"Didn't Jimmy Doolittle take off from an aircraft carrier to bomb Tokyo in 1942?" Eric Coffman would be proud of him for remembering that, Lindsey thought.

"He did. But those were B-25s, Mr. Lindsey. It's a famous piece of carrier history. Crump is in a B-17. Twice the size of a Twenty-five. And landing is a different proposition from launching. Still . . . " Jarrold paused. Lindsey could imagine him searching for a pencil and scribbling numbers on a yellow pad.

"It might just . . . " Jarrold made a contemplative sound. "Major Wilkerson, what's the landing speed of a Seventeen?"

Lindsey wondered if Wilkerson had researched the old aircraft. It didn't seem in character with his today-and-tomorrow orientation. But . . .

"Seventeens didn't stall out till about fifty knots, Commander."

Jarrold moaned. "If we can put the *Lincoln* under *Bessie Blue*, headed upwind at top speed . . . Flight deck is almost exactly one thousand feet . . . It might be possible. Just barely possible. Take a hell of a pilot to keep his wing tip over the edge of the flight deck and land with his wheels barely on deck. Otherwise, he'll clip the island and buy a farm."

"It's worth a try," Wilkerson said.

"What kind of brakes does the Seventeen have, Major?" Jarrold asked.

"Wing-mounted air brakes and wheel brakes."

"Trouble is, he should still use the arrestor cables to stop his aircraft. But he wouldn't have a tailhook."

"No, sir."

"Hard enough even with one. Without, he's in big trouble." Jarrold paused. "Still, it's his only chance. *Lincoln* can launch rescue choppers in case Crump has to ditch."

"Let's try it, sir."

"One other thing might help a little, Major."

"What's that, sir?"

"Never hurts to pray, Major. Oakland Tower tells me Crump has your boy with him. It never hurts to pray."

"We're following you on radar, P-38. And we've got a fix on B-17. Here's your course." The tower controller read Wilkerson a course correction. Lindsey squinted over Wilkerson's shoulder. He could see the illuminated instruments and feel the plane respond when Wilkerson adjusted her course.

The plane banked. Lindsey was shoved sideways in the jump seat. Through the Plexiglas canopy, he could see the stars and the bright moon. The P-38 had climbed quickly above the clouds. They were already past the Golden Gate and over the Pacific. It was nothing like flying in a commercial jet. There was no sense of enclosure in a machine. Lindsey felt like one with the Lightning. Wilkerson and Lindsey were separated from sky by only a layer of curved plastic. Lindsey was suddenly aware that they were several miles off the ground. Without warning, he was trembling with the cold.

The radio crackled again. Oakland Control said, "You're going to have more company, P-38. The rest of the National Knights squadron is following you."

"What do they think they can do?" Wilkerson asked.

"They say that *Bessie Blue* is their aircraft and they're going after her. Maybe they can force the pilot to turn around. I can order them back, Major."

"No, let them follow. They might be some help," Wilkerson said.

Lindsey wiped his forehead. He was shivering and sweating

at once. It was the combination of the cold and the P-38's movement.

Wilkerson read his mind. "These planes didn't have much in the way of creature comforts, Hobart. Just hang on." He said, "Tower, can you patch me through to *Bessie Blue?*"

A few seconds later, Lindsey heard Lawton Crump's gruff, old-man's voice. "What is it?"

"*Bessie Blue*, this is *Rainy Mama*. This is your fighter escort. How are you doing?" Wilkerson asked.

"Everything's under control," Crump said. "No bandits. No flak. Pure milk run." His voice sounded strange to Lindsey. It had changed in a matter of seconds. Crump sounded like a young man. He even pronounced his words differently. He sounded eerily like Willa McKinney's younger brother, Floyd.

"*Bessie Blue*, I think you should turn back to Oakland International. This flight is dangerous and unnecessary," Wilkerson said.

"Dangerous, yes. But it *is* necessary, brother. The wide-blue yonder is no place for the fainthearted."

Good God, he was starting to sound like John Wayne.

"Captain Crump?"

There was a pause and Crump asked, "Who is this, please?"

Lindsey's mind raced. Who was the top commander of the Tuskegee Airmen? Crump had spoken about him in Holy City, and he had been mentioned throughout Eric Coffman's book.

"Captain Crump, this is General Davis. Do you . . . " What was that slang they used in all the war movies? " . . . do you read me?"

Crump sounded startled. "General Davis?"

"General Benjamin Davis, Senior. Do you read me, Captain Crump?"

"Captain? It's Lieutenant Crump, sir."

"It's Captain now."

"Yes, sir." He sounded happy. Lindsey thought, *He's snapped. He's all the way back there now. He wants to be a hero.*

"Captain Crump, I want you to check your aircraft for a stowaway," Lindsey said.

"Yes, sir," Crump said.

Wilkerson moved his hand on the controls. "Radio off, Lindsey. What's going on? That's my son he's got on that plane. He . . . "

"Look, look, is that *Bessie Blue?*" Ahead and beneath them, brilliant lights flaring against its polished skin, the four-engined bomber glowed like a phantom in the moonlight.

"That's it," Wilkerson said.

A new voice crackled in Lindsey's headphones. "*Chippie's Hips* here, *Rainy Mama. Chippie's Hips.* Do you read me?"

"I read you, *Chippie.* Position?"

"Five o'clock high and climbing."

Wilkerson turned. Hobart Lindsey followed his glance. Above and behind the P-38, he saw a streamlined, silvery, single-engined monoplane. It gleamed in the moonlight like a Christmas decoration.

"We're all here, *Mama.* Do you have visual?"

"With *Bessie Blue* and with you, *Chippie,*" Wilkerson said.

"The rest are strung out behind me. Form up, Knights!"

Wilkerson had turned back to the controls. Lindsey turned to watch *Chippie.* Now he could see a formation assembling in an unbalanced V with *Chippie's Hips* at its point. Lindsey tried to identify the other planes. They were calling in. *Lovely Lena. Ella Fitz. Lady Day.* He recognized the stubby, powerful P-47 that had been in the hangar when Crump landed his one-punch knockout. That was *Lady Day.* Strung out behind her were the P-39, P-40, P-51.

"*Bessie Blue,* do you visual us? We are your escort. We're at six o'clock, high," Wilkerson said.

"I visual you, *Rainy Mama.*"

"*Bessie Blue,* please indicate your destination and fuel situation."

"We're headed for Hickam Field, Hawaii. Glad to have you along, escort! I don't imagine we'll meet any Zekes or Tonys, but you can never tell."

"Repeat, what is your fuel situation?"

Lindsey and Wilkerson waited for Crump's reply. Finally, it came.

"There must be something wrong with my instruments, *Mama*. They indicate low tanks. That can't be right."

"Listen, *Bessie*, you only have a little fuel. Do you have your classified orders with you?"

There was a long silence.

"Do you read me, *Bessie Blue?*"

A pause. Then, "I don't have any classified orders here, *Rainy Mama*."

"That's correct, *Bessie Blue*. You are under my personal command. I want you to drop below the cloud layer. We have a surface rendezvous to keep," Wilkerson said.

Crump's old-young voice said, "Is it safe to use open radio transmissions, General?"

"Not to worry, Captain. These are scrambled channels. All our planes have been retrofitted. Including *Bessie Blue*."

What happened when you played into another person's fantasy? Lindsey had never tried it with Mother. He had always worked to get her to connect with reality. It seemed wrong to reinforce her delusions. But maybe Wilkerson could make this work. Maybe . . . Lindsey sensed that Wilkerson was sweating as much as he was.

Wilkerson had geared back the Lightning, trying to hold its speed to that of the lumbering B-17. He banked the Lightning. Lindsey watch the B-17 dip and disappear into the clouds.

Over his earphones, Lindsey heard Crump's voice. "What's that?" He sounded excited.

"Hold on," Wilkerson said. He banked and circled, then dropped the Lightning's nose.

Whiteness swept around the Plexiglas dome. To Lindsey it seemed that the plane had dipped into a giant wad of soft, opaque cotton. He became conscious once more of his perspiration. Then, suddenly, the fluffy cotton was overhead, beyond the Plexiglas. Beneath the Lightning, Lindsey could see *Bessie Blue*'s lights, and beneath and beyond *Bessie Blue*, a huge illuminated football field.

Abraham Lincoln.

It took a few seconds for Lindsey's eyes to adjust. Then he became aware of the tiny lights hovering near the aircraft carrier. Those must be the helicopters Commander Jarrold had promised.

Still another new voice came over Lindsey's earphones. "*Abraham Lincoln* Flight Control. *Bessie Blue,* we have your special cargo ready for loading. You are cleared for landing. Approach at landing speed and welcome."

Crump's voice. "Roger. Wilco."

Roger Wilco. What was going on in the man's confused brain? He might be imagining anything. If he had snapped back to 1945, he might think that *Abraham Lincoln* was carrying the world's first nuclear weapon. Maybe he believed that *Bessie Blue* would pick up the bomb and continue on. In this time line there was no Trinity test and no *Enola Gay.* There was only *Bessie Blue.* The war would end, and Lawton Crump would end it.

More voices crackled over Lindsey's earphones. He looked over his shoulder and saw a *V* of lights drop through the cloud layer.

Lawton Crump's youthful voice sounded in Lindsey's headphones. "Nice to see you boys. Nice to see the Ninety-ninth again. I've missed all you fellows." A moment later Crump asked, "Who's flying today? That you, Linson? Linson Blackney?"

Lindsey sent up a silent prayer that the Knights were as quick on their mental toes as they were at the controls of their aircraft.

One of them said, "I'm here, Lawton."

Over his shoulder, Lindsey saw the Curtiss P-40 waggle its wings.

"Who else? Clemenceau Givings? You there, Clem?" Crump asked.

"Here, Lawton."

The sleek North American P-51 waggled its wings.

"Len Willette?"

The Bell P-39, its nose shaped like a ballistic missile, waggled its wings.

"Norvell? Stoudmire? Stoudie, you there?"

"Here, Lawton."

The stubby-nosed Republic P-47 *Lady Day* waggled its wings.

At Wilkerson's touch, the P-38 leveled off. The four Knights held formation. The P-38 surged forward until it was parallel to the B-17.

Lindsey could see the external lights blazing on *Bessie Blue's* body. He could see through the bomber's windows into the cabin. Inside, he could see the tiny form of James Wilkerson, Junior. He even thought he could see the miniature Fortress in the boy's hand. He could definitely see Lawton Crump in the pilot's seat beside Jamie.

Crump turned and looked straight at *Rainy Mama.* Fleetingly, Lindsey thought that he had made eye contact with Lawton Crump. Then he realized that Crump had edited him out of his reality, just as Willa McKinney had edited him from hers. The old man was watching James Wilkerson, Senior, with something very much like hero worship. He raised his hand in a smart salute.

"Captain Crump, there's a special weapon awaiting your pickup. It's a single bomb that could end this war and bring victory to our country. I want you to land so that weapon can be stowed aboard your aircraft," Wilkerson said.

From this altitude, the *Abraham Lincoln* no longer resembled a football field but rather a large, illuminated parking lot. Maybe that was what it was. Lawton Crump's voice came over Lindsey's earphones. *"Bessie Blue* here. I'm lowering my wheels. I'm on my landing run."

The B-17 dropped toward *Abraham Lincoln.* Lindsey's body turned to ice. He sent out psychic waves to help Crump land the old bomber safely.

Crump brought the B-17 over the stern of the aircraft carrier. The flight deck was canted. Crump seemed to have slowed the Flying Fortress to a halt in midair. That was impossible. Without forward motion, the wings would lose their lift and the bomber would stall and fall into the sea.

Lindsey watched as the Flying Fortress swept along the carrier's deck. Crump kept the bomber near the edge of the ship. If he centered the B-17 over the flight deck, its wing tip would clip the carrier's island and spin the aircraft into a mass of flaming wreckage.

A moment earlier, *Bessie Blue* had appeared to hover above *Abraham Lincoln*'s wake. Now the bomber was racing along the deck.

The Fortress bounced visibly when its wheels first hit the carrier's deck. Then the plane settled and rolled forward. Smoke rushed from its engines as Lawton Crump reversed his props' pitch and gunned the Cyclones. *Bessie Blue* slowed. The bomber was approaching the forward end of the flight deck. If only it had been equipped with a tailhook—but that was a futile wish. How could the airplane be moving so slowly, yet approach the end of the deck so quickly? What was going through Lawton Crump's mind? What was going through Jamie's mind?

Closer to the end of the deck.

And slower.

And closer.

Bessie Blue rolled to the very edge of the flight deck, teetered, then tipped forward in agonizing slow motion and almost frame by frame plunged nose first into the Pacific.

Twenty-Seven

THE ANGLED FLIGHT DECK OF THE *Abraham Lincoln* meant that *Bessie Blue* splashed into the Pacific beside the prow of the carrier, rather than beneath it. The carrier swept past the drowning bomber.

Lindsey heard a moan. He couldn't tell whether it was his own voice or Wilkerson's. As Wilkerson banked the *Rainy Mama* above *Bessie Blue*, Lindsey could see the bomber settle onto the choppy ocean surface. The plane had dropped off the flight deck nose first, but once it hit the water had flopped back and wallowed on its belly.

"Wilkerson, how long can they float?" Lindsey asked.

"Ten minutes, maybe. Maybe only five. They couldn't have rigged to ditch, they didn't have time. There go the choppers."

Navy rescue helicopters raced toward *Bessie Blue*. Their spotlights shone on the bomber. The B-17, previously a symbol of strength, looked puny as it rocked on the waves. It looked like something old and tired. Something that belonged in the past. Something dying.

A big chopper hovered above the bomber. A speck began to descend from the helicopter. It had to be a man.

The speck reached the airplane.

Wilkerson circled lower. Lindsey could see waves washing over the ditched airplane's wings. It was settling lower in the water.

The speck from the helicopter was now balancing on the bomber's wing, still attached to his lifeline. A heavy wave rocked the airplane and knocked the man down. He slid to the edge of the wing, caught hold and hauled himself back.

He crawled along the wing to the fuselage and pulled himself onto the edge of the cockpit. The cockpit window had been slid open. Something black, something far smaller than the black shape that was a wet-suited rescuer, emerged from the window.

The airplane was settling faster now. The upper surfaces of the wings were awash.

The rescuer leaned into the cockpit. A moment passed. He pulled away. He held the smaller shape in his arms.

The helicopter lifted the two black specks dangling at the end of the lifeline.

A plume of green-white water rose and *Bessie Blue* was gone.

The lifeline shortened until the black specks disappeared into the helicopter.

Abraham Lincoln had moved away from the sinking *Bessie Blue*. The helicopter followed the carrier. Major Wilkerson brought the Lightning up to a safer altitude and followed the chopper until it landed on the carrier. Crewmen swarmed toward the chopper.

The voice of Flight Control crackled. *"Rainy Mama.* You and your flight will return to your land base. I hope you all have enough fuel. I don't want anymore attempted landings without tailhooks."

Wilkerson surveyed the Knights. They could all make it back to Oakland.

The Athletics were playing a night game at the Coliseum. Lindsey could see the banks of lights, the colorful clothing of 50,000 spectators. He thought he could see the players on the field, tiny white specks against the green. Or perhaps that, too, was a trick of his injured eyes and tired brain.

He wondered if the spectators or players could see the military planes in the night sky. If some bored fan or distracted outfielder heard the engines, he might turn his eyes upward like an air-raid warden in 1941 and watch the formation of fifty-year-old warplanes pass in the night.

Their flight path brought them back toward North Field.

Lincoln Flight Control had told them that Jamie Wilkerson was safe. He was drenched and half frozen and terrified, but he was being cared for on the carrier. Once he was checked out and fed, he would be ferried to Oakland by jet. Doc High offered to send Marvia to the air station in a police unit. She accepted. She would pick up her Mustang later.

Lindsey thanked God for the Navy. It had saved Jamie Wilkerson's life.

It had not saved Lawton Crump's. Crump must have been a hell of a pilot in his day. And his day had lasted until this final act. He had gone down with his airplane. Lindsey would wonder for the rest of his own life what thoughts had swirled through Lawton Crump's mind as *Bessie Blue* plunged to the bottom of the Pacific Ocean.

Maybe it wasn't the Navy's vigilance that had saved Jamie. At least, not that alone. Lawton Crump's skill, too, had saved Jamie Wilkerson. But Crump had also killed his own brother. Smashed his skull and spilled his brains. He had reenacted the first murder in the world.

"There's plenty of room. Here we go," Wilkerson said. He swung the P-38 into a banking approach, lowered its wheels, opened the air brakes and touched down on the tarmac. Riding high on its tricycle landing gear, the Lightning flashed past hangars, parked aircraft, police cruisers and emergency vehicles. It slowed, then halted 100 feet from the end of the runway. Major Wilkerson could never have landed this airplane on the *Abraham Lincoln*.

Wilkerson popped the canopy open. He climbed onto the Lightning's wing, hopped agilely to the ground and ran. Lindsey's face was a giant ache and his body stiff and sore from the cramped ride behind Wilkerson in the Lightning. Moving gingerly, he followed Wilkerson.

The moon provided some illumination but the runway was lighted mainly by ground lights and by the headlamps of police cruisers and emergency vehicles.

Lieutenant High and Sergeant Finnerty were waiting at the edge of the tarmac. The sight of them was a jolt to Lindsey. His return to earth after riding with Wilkerson and witnessing the events over the Pacific was as great a shock as any transition between worlds.

"Lindsey, are you all right?" High asked.

"I'm okay. I'm okay." He looked for Marvia, but the first woman he recognized was Ina Chandler. She had tears in her eyes.

"I heard. My Lawton is gone," she said.

Lindsey stood still.

Marvia had run up to him. She held him. "Jamie's safe," she said. "They radio'd. I heard his voice."

To no one in particular, Lindsey announced, "Crump was the killer. He was the monkey wrench man."

Ina Chandler was still there. She was red-eyed and wet-faced. "No, he wasn't," she cried.

Doc High whirled. "He wasn't? Wait a minute! You go first, Mr. Lindsey. Give me a thirty-second version. We'll take a full statement at Sixth Street."

Drawing Marvia to him, Lindsey complied.

Before High could say anything, Ina Chandler said, "No. No, he didn't. He couldn't have killed that man. I was with him when he found the body, don't you remember?"

Lindsey said, "He was alone in a room at the Parc Oakland. He left the hotel and went to the airport twice. The first time was very early in the morning, maybe a little after midnight. He had his meeting with Jefferson King. Not Leroy McKinney." Lindsey's face felt like an overripe melon. He paused to gather his strength and his thoughts.

"Wait a minute," Doc High said. "What's this about Jefferson King? Leroy McKinney was the dead man."

"No, he wasn't. I'll explain that when we get downtown, Lieutenant. Crump came to the airport and killed Jefferson King, then returned to the hotel, waited awhile, then met you, Mrs. Chandler. Then he came out here again, the second time, with you. And the second time, he found the body he'd left here the first time."

"No," Ina Chandler said. She caught her breath, then she said, "He couldn't have come out here in the middle of the night. He was with me."

"I thought he was in his room, all alone," High said.

"He was in his room, but I was with him. It was . . . it was

250

a one-night thing. I knew he was married. But he was so lonely. I could sense it. His stories, all the things he'd done, all the places he'd been, but he was still alone somehow. When we finished our day's work, we ate dinner and talked and talked. We went to his room and talked some more. He didn't want to be alone. Neither did I. We had a couple of nightcaps. And . . . "

She pulled a bandanna from her jeans, wiped her eyes, honked into the bandanna and said: "It wasn't anything cheap or evil. It was—suddenly we just—just needed each other. We were both adults and we knew what we were doing. No one would ever have to know. But we could remember that night forever. For all our lives."

High patted his pockets, fumbling for his long-forbidden pipe and tobacco. Instead, he came up with a notebook and pencil and jotted notes busily. "You'll have to come downtown, too, and give us your statement. Mr. Lindsey, you made a nice case. I don't know that we could have proved it, I'd need to talk it over with the DA and see what they have to say. But it was a nice theory. But if Mrs. Chandler alibis Crump, it all blows up. Unless we can shake her story."

He turned to Ina Chandler. "I've said too much already. We'll need your statement. We'll never get one from Mr. Crump, of course. More's the pity. And as for you, Mr. Lindsey, you've been keeping me informed, but we'll need to have another talk very soon, won't we?"

Lindsey nodded and turned away. Marvia was still in his arms. James Wilkerson, Senior, stood beside them. He looked baffled and useless.

"James, thank you for all you did," Marvia said.

Wilkerson mumbled.

Nearby, within earshot of Lindsey, Doc High said, "Sergeant Finnerty, will you take Mrs. Chandler downtown, please? She's not under arrest, she's not accused of anything, but before you take her statement, you'd better Mirandize her just to be on the safe side. Is that all right with you, Mrs. Chandler? Do you understand what we're doing and why we're doing it?"

Ina Chandler nodded. "He was a sweet man," she said. "He

could be a little stiff, even a little harsh, but he was a sweet person. And there was pain in him." She reached toward Lindsey's battered face. "I'm sorry for what he did to you. But if he killed that other poor man, if he killed his own half-brother, why didn't he kill you? He could have. Why didn't he kill you?"

Sergeant Finnerty led her away.

"She has a point, Lindsey," High said.

Lindsey shook his head. The pain had receded a little, or maybe he was just distracted. Now it came back, washing over him in a wave that buckled his knees. Now it was he who clung to Marvia until the wave receded. "I . . . let's sit down."

They walked to the office in the Double Bee hangar. Lindsey leaned on Marvia all the way. She helped him to a chair. A moment later, he had his hands wrapped around a steaming cup. He didn't drink its contents, didn't even taste them. He just held onto it.

"Can you handle this?" High asked. "Can you talk, or should we hold off 'til tomorrow?"

"Go on. Once I'm out, I'm really going to be out."

"What do you think of Chandler's story?"

Lindsey shrugged. "Could be. I mean, it fits together. You'd have to check it with the other Double Bee people or the Parc Oakland. But what if nobody saw them together? What if nobody saw him go to her room? Or was it his room?"

High moaned. "Whichever."

"Unless somebody saw them," Lindsey continued, "it's just a question of whether you want to believe her or not."

High said, "With Crump at the bottom of the ocean, there's no reason for her to lie for him. What difference does it make?"

Marvia said, "You're not a woman, Lieutenant. It makes all the difference. Will he be remembered as a murderer or a hero? Some kind of hero." She shook her head. "It makes all the difference to her."

"Accepted." High was jotting notes now, the way Lindsey so often did. "I've seen people come apart before. I'm sure you have also, Sergeant Plum. But this was like something out of *King Lear*."

252

"I thought there was something odd at the house in Holy City," Lindsey said. "As if there were all these Lawton Crumps: the boy in Louisiana; the young man in the Air Corps; the older man. He never had any children. I think that keeps people attached to the world. It keeps them connected to the present, to the changes of the world. Having children, I mean."

He closed his eyes to rest them. The light was like needles. "Not that I have any. But Crump never got over those peak experiences he had in the Tuskegee Airmen. When he killed Jefferson King . . . "

"Right. We'll have to go downtown and straighten *that* part out, once and for all. I'm still worried about the time of death in the coroner's report, but that's always a little shaky."

" . . . that knocked him loose from his bearings. He was really looking forward to flying bombers in the Pacific back in 1944, '45 . . . The war ended too soon for him, and he never got over it. Here was this seventy-year-old body with all of these minds in it. They were all Lawton Crump—he wasn't a multiple personality like the ones they make movies about. He was always Lawton Crump. But he was many Lawton Crumps, Lawton Crump at different times in his life."

"An interesting theory, Lindsey," High said. "I think you're nuts, but it's an interesting theory. I'll tell you one thing. If that alibi Mrs. Chandler gave him holds up—if Chandler doesn't wobble—we're back to square one on this thing. Maybe we go back to Richmond and try working through the Luther Jones connection. Nobody else knew about this alleged meeting that Crump was supposed to have with Leroy McKinney. And for all that Ina Chandler is trying to salvage Crump's reputation, that points the finger straight back at him." He looked around at the others and breathed in the cold night air. "And I've got so much other work to do," he added mournfully.

"Somebody else knew about the meeting," Lindsey said.

After a long silence, High asked, "Who?"

Lindsey told him. "Nellie Crump."

Twenty-Eight

LIEUTENANT HIGH PULLED THE POLICE CRUISER across the driveway on Call of the Wild Road. From the passenger seat, Lindsey could see Nellie Crump sitting in the shiny Oldsmobile. The engine was running. Despite the darkness, its exhaust was visible in the headlights of the cruiser.

Lindsey had drunk the coffee after all. He could have handled a juicy steak and stiff drink as well. His body was crying out for protein and his hands were trembling. But that would have to wait. He had cleaned up as much as he could without a thorough scrubbing and a complete change of clothes. He longed for a hot soak.

Somehow he felt he could function for a while longer.

He knew he would pay all the higher a price once he did crash.

Behind the wheel of the police cruiser, High whistled softly. "What do you think of that. It's a good thing we didn't wait for morning, isn't it?"

High and Lindsey walked to the Oldsmobile. Lindsey's body ached with every step. High tapped a coin against the driver's window. Nellie Crump turned her face toward the two men. She appeared composed. She wore a dark cloth coat and a tiny hat. She reached for a switch and the tinted glass window descended into dark-green metal, hissing like a spaceship door.

When the window was open, Lindsey could hear the Oldsmobile's radio. It was tuned to an all-news station. The announcer was talking about tule fog in the Central Valley.

"What do you want?" Nellie Crump asked.

"Mrs. Crump, this is Lieutenant High, Oakland Homicide," Lindsey said.

High touched a finger to the brim of an invisible fedora. Always the upholder of tradition.

"Mrs. Crump, we'll need to ask you some questions. If you don't mind."

She frowned. "I do mind. My husband needs me. At least, I'll have to identify the body. I'm going to him. Please get your car out of my way."

High shook his head. "I doubt that they'll ever recover his remains. I'm really very sorry. In any case, there's nothing you could do for him."

"You let me decide that." She glared at Lindsey. "You are a viper. You come around here with your polite questions, saying you just want to help. Now look what you've done."

Lindsey said, "But I haven't done anything, Mrs. Crump. I've . . . " High stopped him with a hand on his arm.

"If you'll just get out of the car, please," he said. "We contacted the San Jose PD and the San Mateo Sheriff's Department by radio. Everything is nice and orderly. We do need to speak with you, Mrs. Crump. Please."

She looked from High to Lindsey and back to High. She shut off the Oldsmobile's engine and lights. She got out of the car. "I expected Lawton to come home tonight, but I wasn't really worried. I know he stays late sometimes. I know he stays over in Oakland. I don't mind that."

"No, ma'am," High said.

Hobart Lindsey felt like Harry Morgan to High's Jack Webb. He wondered if Nellie Crump had seen enough episodes of *Dragnet* to fall into a role of her own.

"But I was watching the late news and they had this story about an airplane. I thought it was a hijacking, you know, some hijacker demanding money and a flight to Cuba, that sort of thing. Then they showed the tape. I saw it was a B-17. It was footage of the *Bessie Blue* from this movie they're making. Then I knew it had to be Lawton. What happened? What happened to him?"

Lindsey told her.

"I just wondered if you could help us out with this, ma'am. I'm sorry to disturb your bereavement. It's a terrible situation. Maybe you could help, and then we'll be on our way," High said.

Lindsey had seen this act before. He had even been on the receiving end of it. He waited to see how Nellie Crump would react.

"I don't follow you," she said. "Are you accusing Lawton of that awful killing at the airport? What are you saying to me? What kind of help do you want from me?" Nellie Crump shivered. Lindsey realized that all three of them were sending plumes of warm breath into the cold night.

High said nothing. Somewhere a cat yowled. Somewhere a motorcycle engine roared.

"If you're going to keep me here, at least let's go inside and be warm." She led the way into the house. High and Lindsey followed her docilely into the yellow kitchen. When Nellie hit the switch to light the fluorescent ceiling fixture, the room sprang to cheerful life. Lindsey was relieved that she had not led them into the dark living room or the still darker den, so infused with Lawton Crump's presence and the mementos of his career.

Lindsey sat in a wire-backed kitchen chair. High stood in the doorway. Nellie Crump busied herself with the coffee maker.

Always the proper hostess.

"We do have to resolve the murder charge. We have to find the person who killed Leroy McKinney or Jefferson King," High said.

Nellie dropped a measuring spoon on the tile counter. Coffee grinds rained onto the bright floor. She dampened a sponge and dropped to her knees. She had hung her coat on a mahogany coat tree in the foyer but still wore her little round hat. She wore a flowered dress and pumps with heels like the ones Lindsey's mother wore to attend her computer classes. She wiped up the scattered coffee grinds, brushed them into the sink, knelt and cleaned up a few that she had missed.

"Why do you keep saying that name? I never heard of Jefferson King. I doubt that Lawton did either. I'm sure this is all a misunderstanding of some sort. I don't know what we pay these taxes for. To get police protection? They can't prevent any crimes, and when they fail they turn around and make false accusations to make themselves look better."

Lindsey started to speak up, but High gestured again.

"You're absolutely right, Mrs. Crump. But we do our best. You didn't know that your husband found a body in the hangar at North Field? Didn't he tell you about that?"

"He didn't even know who that was."

"The man was carrying ID."

"Of course I remember that," Nellie said. "Lawton told me about it. Lawton always tells me everything. I want to see his body. I demand that the Navy recover his body. I want to see the responsible authorities in the Navy. You can't keep me here like this. Who do you think you are?"

"Please," High said. "Just a little longer. You have not been mistreated in any way. Mr. Lindsey is a witness to that. Please pay close attention, Lindsey. Mrs. Crump, you say that your husband *did* tell you about finding the body. Is that correct?"

"Of course he did. And it was in all the news. It was in the paper and on the TV. But that was Leroy McKinney."

"You knew all about this last time I was here," Lindsey said.

High gestured angrily. Lindsey shut up.

"Your husband killed Jefferson King. Or Leroy McKinney. At this point, they were the same person. King was using McKinney's name."

"Mr. Lindsey is right," Nellie Crump said. "I know who the McKinneys are. They were Lawton's family in Louisiana. But he couldn't have killed this man."

"I disagree, ma'am. It works out very nicely. He sneaked out of the Parc Oakland Hotel, drove to the airport for a meeting with King or McKinney, killed him and returned to the hotel. Later he drove to the airport again with Mrs. Chandler and pretended to find the body. We're very certain of this. He doesn't stand a chance. Now there's no way we can bring charges against a . . . against a deceased person. So we'll probably close the case. But we need to get the facts together before we do that."

Nellie Crump slid onto one of the wire-backed chairs. "It wasn't Lawton's fault," she said. "He had to do it. That man was draining him. Draining us. You think we're well-off, don't you, with this house and two cars? But we're in debt. We're deeply in debt. That man was draining Lawton for years. We could always keep up, but then he made a big demand. And Pan American is bankrupt. Lawton worked for them faithfully. He gave them his lifetime. We've been together all our lives. We made our way together in this world, Lawton and I. I wasn't . . . Lawton wasn't going to let him ruin it. He wasn't going to let that horrible man ruin us by taking our money or by dirtying our good name."

"Then he did kill McKinney?"

She reached for a roll of paper towels, tore one off and wiped her eyes. Lindsey saw that the towels had a colorful pattern printed on them, yellow ducks on a pale blue background.

"He did it. He told me. He made me promise not to tell anyone."

"What about the gloves?" High asked. "We found bits of canvas and rubber gloves burned in a stove at the site of the killing."

"He borrowed a pair of my gardening gloves. He was afraid of leaving fingerprints, so he took my gloves. Then he burned them after . . . after."

High pulled a Miranda card from his pocket. "Everything you've told us up to now, Mrs. Crump, concerns other people. Before we ask you any more questions, you must know what your rights are. You have the right to remain silent. You are not required to say anything to us at any time or to answer any questions . . . " He droned on until he came to the end of the Miranda warning. Then he said, "Lindsey, you are witness to this."

Lindsey nodded.

"Mrs. Crump, do you know Ina Chandler?"

"Why are you doing this? I thought you were accusing Lawton. I thought . . . "

"Do you know Ina Chandler?"

"I know who she is."

"You've never met her?"

"No."

"You wouldn't say she is an attractive woman?"

"I told you, I never met her. I know who she is."

"Mrs. Crump, do you and your husband have what . . . how shall I put this? Pardon me. Do you and your husband have what used to be called an open relationship?"

"You mean are we fornicators? Speak plainly, you dirty little man. Say what you mean."

High flushed. Lindsey watched him fumble for his pipe. It wasn't there. It was never there.

"Yes, ma'am. I don't mean to be indelicate, that's all. But that's exactly what I mean."

"Absolutely not," Nellie Crump said. She stood up and turned her back to High and Lindsey. High's hand slid toward his hip. Nellie Crump looked at the coffee maker. She opened a cupboard, took out cups and saucers and began to pour. She put cream and sugar on the table and placed a cup in front of High and one in front of Lindsey.

"Lawton and I have been married since the Second World War, and we have maintained a decent and moral relationship all these years. We are not fornicators."

"Your husband didn't kill Jefferson King or Leroy McKinney," High said. "He couldn't have. He spent the night with Ina Chandler in the Parc Oakland Hotel. They were in bed together when the killing took place. As far as I can determine, Mrs. Crump, you were the only other person who knew about the rendezvous."

"What rendezvous? I don't believe you, that my husband would just . . . that Lawton and this woman . . . that . . . " She sputtered into silence.

"I'm not talking about Lawton and Ina Chandler," High said. "I'm talking about Lawton and Leroy McKinney. Or Jefferson King."

"I met her once. I was at the hotel. She shook my hand."

"Who did"

"That woman."

"Chandler?"

Nellie Crump nodded.

"You told me you'd never met Mrs. Chandler," High said.

"Well I did. That once."

"All right."

"I should have made him come home every night. Or I should have stayed in that hotel with him. He was a weakling."

"Your husband was a weakling?"

"Such a hero, strutting around. Did you see that living room? Paintings of him, photos of him, all his war mementos. Did you know he kept his old uniforms in the closet and all his old newspaper clippings? Like nothing had happened since 1945. Like the world ended in 1945. Like nobody else ever sacrificed, nobody else ever worked or suffered. I knew he was sleeping with her. The way she buttered him up, played up to him, fluttered around him."

That wasn't Lindsey's impression of Ina Chandler, but maybe it was Nellie Crump's. Maybe it was all in the eye of the beholder.

"You knew he was supposed to meet Jefferson King?" High asked. "How did you know? And why didn't your husband keep the appointment with King? Did he know you were going in his place? Did the two of you arrange it together?"

"He didn't know about the meeting. He knew Leroy wanted a lot of money. Leroy used to call here and talk to Lawton. Or to me. He was always careful about what he said to me. But I keep the checkbook. I knew what was going on. He'd call, sometimes I'd answer, sometimes Lawton would answer. They'd talk. Then Lawton would buy a money order for his mother. But they weren't really for his mother. I knew they weren't for his mother."

She had been peering into the past. Now she looked up and said, "You're not touching your coffee. Is anything wrong? Did you want decaffeinated?" She was a well-bred young woman, the product of a hard struggle by Negroes to win respect in the old Alabama.

Lindsey dutifully sipped his coffee.

"What about that night?" High asked.

"I made the meeting for Lawton. I let him sleep at the hotel.

I knew he was sleeping with that harlot. I went to the airport in his place. Leroy didn't know who I was at first, but he recognized my voice. I told him I'd come in Lawton's place. I got there first. I had the wrench behind me. I'm a strong woman. He just looked surprised. I only had to hit him once."

"You've heard all this, Lindsey?" High asked.

"Yes," Lindsey said.

"You'll have to come with me, Mrs. Crump."

"I'd better disconnect the coffee maker first. It could be dangerous. It could start a fire."

"Yes, ma'am," High said. "You'd better take your warm coat, too."

"Yes, I think I'd better."

Twenty-Nine

FOR SOME REASON, IT SEEMED right to visit the Original Kasper's again. Harry greeted Marvia and Jamie like old friends. Then he said, "Nice to see you again, Mr. Lindsey. Nice to see you with Marvia and Jamie."

"Call me Bart, please." It was weird, a man twice his age calling him Mister.

"The usual?" Harry asked.

"For everyone. Yoo-hoos, too," Marvia said.

"Make it to go, though. Please," Lindsey said.

They put their food in the Mustang's luggage space and drove a few blocks to a tiny park hidden on a street just off Telegraph. Jamie took his hot dog and ate it sitting on a giant plastic frog. Marvia took Lindsey's hand, and they sat on a wooden bench, watching. For the moment, they were the only ones in the park.

A group of teenagers came out of a single-storey frame bungalow, tumbling from the stoop and roughhousing on the lawn. They walked off, shoving each other and laughing. They passed Marvia and Lindsey's bench, slowed and looked, mostly at Lindsey's face. Then they continued out of the park. They were black. They could have been Ahmad Hope and his friends in half-a-dozen years, if any of those kids in Richmond were still alive in half-a-dozen years.

"Jamie's getting over Lawton's death," Marvia said. "He loved him. He's too young to understand everything that happened. It was all a wonderful adventure for him, even when they went off the deck and *Bessie Blue* sank."

She looked at Jamie and waved. He rocked back and forth on

the green frog, munching his hot dog. He pretended not to see his mother's wave.

Lindsey took a bite of his hot dog. "I didn't know your father was sick, Marvia. This is the first chance I've had to talk to you about him."

"He isn't sick yet. His doctor's monitoring him. He'll get the best of care when he needs it."

"But there's nothing they can do for that, is there?" Lindsey asked.

She shook her head.

"You have any idea how long?"

"No." Her voice was almost inaudible. "Probably a couple of years, the doctor says. My mother has to get the information from the doctor and tell me on the sly. Daddy won't talk about it. Says he's healthy as a horse. He is. Or as strong as one, anyway."

"We had a good time, Jamie and I." Lindsey walked to a trash receptacle and deposited the napkins his hot dog had been wrapped in. "He said he wouldn't mind living with you and me."

She looked at him. She didn't say anything.

He looked at Jamie. There was the B-17 again in his hand. Today, he had showed it to Harry Yaglijian. Harry had amazed him by launching into his own stories of aerial warfare. He had been a flier fifty years ago, as well. An immigrant from Armenia. A new American fighting for his new country, just as Lawton Crump had done.

Jamie finished his hot dog and ran to Marvia, demanding his Yoo-hoo. "Where did you put your napkin?" She asked. Jamie produced it from a pocket. Marvia took it and wiped mustard from his chin. She stuffed the napkin back in his pocket, opened the bottle of chocolate drink and handed it to him.

He started back to his frog.

"Don't run with that in your hand," Marvia said.

Jamie slowed to a crawl.

Marvia looked at Lindsey. "We can keep on for a while. My father's all right. Tyrone helps out, too. We're okay."

Lindsey sat on the bench and took Marvia's hand. He felt

like the Phantom of the Opera, like Lon Chaney and a score of other Eriks, taking the hand of Mary Philbin and as many other frightened sopranos. "You're just putting it off, Marvia. You can keep it up for a while, but what happens when your dad can't handle Jamie anymore?"

Angrily, She replied, "I won't marry anyone just to get a father for my son. No way."

"I'm sorry. That would be the wrong reason, wouldn't it?"

"I could always contact his father. Eat a little crow. James would enjoy roasting me a little. Claudia would give him hell and love doing it. But they'd take him."

"Marvia, I want to be your husband and I want to be Jamie's dad. That's why I want to marry you."

"I'm on the late shift," She said. "I have to get Jamie to my parents' house."

Lindsey kicked the cement pediment of the bench. It hurt his foot but distracted him from what he was feeling. "All right. Let's go. Wilkerson and his wife are gone. Ina Chandler and Double Bee are cleaning up and getting ready to head back to Hollywood. The Knights of the Air have taken their airplanes back to Texas, all except the B-17. They sent me a bill for that."

He had to laugh.

Even Marvia smiled. "I'm sorry, Bart," she said. "I didn't mean to be cruel to you. Please give me a little more time."

Thirty

Mrs. Blomquist glanced up from her work and said, "Have a seat, Mr. Lindsey. Mr. Richelieu will see you as soon as he gets off the phone." She turned back to her work, then did a double take. "Mr. Lindsey! What happened to your face?"

Lindsey managed to smile, even though it cost him a twinge and a groan. "You wouldn't believe I ran into a doorknob, would you?"

Mrs. Blomquist laughed. Underneath her Gibson Girl hairdo and pale powder, she was beginning to seem almost human. "How 'bout them Rockies?" she asked.

A light on her phone winked off and she told him, "You can go in now."

Richelieu waved Lindsey to a chair. Richelieu wore a midnight-blue suit with barely visible pinstripes and a shirt and tie that must have been cut and tailored to his order. He had a way of making Lindsey feel as if his own clothing was straight from Goodwill.

"I don't know what to do with you, Lindsey." Richelieu looked sad rather than angry. Like a teacher whose star pupil had been caught in a cribbing scandal. Not angry. Just very disappointed and deeply, terribly hurt.

Lindsey felt like apologizing, but he said nothing. He was acutely aware of the sterile tape on his painfully set nose and his fading black eyes. At least he hadn't lost any teeth. The rest would heal. Lawton Crump had done all that with a single punch. What a wallop he must have packed when he was twenty rather than seventy.

"Aside from the media uproar, the first information I got on this matter came from Elmer Mueller," Richelieu said.

"I don't imagine Elmer was too kind, was he?"

"But you know, I got a very different report from Ms. Wilbur," Richelieu said. "Very different. I don't know what I'll do for information, now that she's retiring."

"Ms. Wilbur sent you a report?"

Richelieu leaned back in his heavy leather chair. Outside the office building, a puff of wind must have rippled the face of Cherry Creek. In turn, the ripples scattered the bright morning sunlight, creating a graceful pattern of light that cut through the crisp Colorado air, through a double pane of thermal glass and onto Desmond Richelieu's gold-rimmed glasses. The glasses sparkled, until Richelieu nodded in response to Lindsey's question.

"Surely you wouldn't expect me to rely on a fool like Mueller."

"I'm glad to hear that," Lindsey said.

"I'll find somebody else," Richelieu said. "Not to worry about that. In the meanwhile, I've had several conversations with Ms. Johansen at National about you. And a fax from World HQ." He said it the way a humble parish priest would have said that he had received a fax from the Pope. No. More than that. The way the mayor of a Japanese fishing village would say that he had got a fax from the Emperor. The very words set the air to vibrating with powers and portents.

World HQ.

"Now suppose you give me a very brief summation of the matter," Richelieu said. The teacher again, hoping that his favorite might somehow provide mitigation for his unforgiveable misconduct.

"I've been talking with Lieutenant High and with the Alameda County Prosecutor's Office regularly," Lindsey said. "Mrs. Chandler is sticking with her story about spending that last night with Lawton Crump. They've grilled her pretty hard, and she won't budge."

"That gets Mr. Crump off the hook," Richelieu said. "Not that it matters. You don't have posthumous prosecution in

266

California, do you? No, not even California would be that nutty. I want to know where this leaves International Surety. Legal's been getting into the act and they'll want to have a long meeting with you, you know."

"That's all right with me."

"Is your friend Lieutenant High still out to hang this on Mrs. Crump?"

"I wouldn't put it quite that way, Mr. Richelieu. But yes, that's the essence of it. The forensics lab has done a lot of work. They never did get anywhere with the murder weapon, but they were able to match the burned rubber and fabric in the hangar stove with the rubber and fabric of Mrs. Crump's gardening gloves. They're an unusual brand. Most gardeners don't like them because they make their hands too hot."

"Can't hang her on that, can they?"

"They took some scrapings off the chassis of the Oldsmobile and matched it with the oil and dirt from the North Field parking area. That particular combination was just about unique. And everybody agrees that Lawton never used the Oldsmobile. Never. Only Nellie drove it, and she'd been denying that she ever parked at North Field, so High has her on that. And all the financial records support the connection with Luther Jones via Leroy McKinney. That is, Jefferson King."

"So Crump was subsidizing his half-brother all those years, bleeding away month after month until the Pan Am bankruptcy threw a financial scare into him. What a pity. Uncle Sam has stepped in. Those pensioners will be all right. I wonder how many people are suffering."

"The Richmond police have been working on their end of it," Lindsey said. "Crump wasn't just supporting Jefferson King with those money orders. Crump was bankrolling him. He was never bleeding. Nellie thought he was bleeding, but Crump was a silent partner in the whole Hasan Rahsaan Rasheed operation. That was how he managed his lifestyle on his salary from Pan Am. You know, he earned a decent living. But that house, those furnishings, two new cars—he couldn't manage that on a mechanic's paycheck. There was no way."

Richelieu steepled his fingers. "Now there was a man I could

267

really admire." Richelieu's grin turned his silvery waves into a halo.

"Crump never did get over World War Two ending before he could fly a bomber in combat. And then he never got to be an airline pilot, just a mechanic," Lindsey said.

"Well, we could kick this around all day, couldn't we? What I need to determine is what it means to International Surety. The Legal kids tell me that Lawton Crump's stealing that plane and kidnapping the youngster constitute moral turpitude and since Crump was an agent of Double Bee, we're off the hook."

Lindsey shook his head. "I wouldn't be so sure. If Crump was legally insane when he stole the *Bessie Blue*, there's no moral turpitude. And we'll have to pay."

The jovial, almost paternal Richelieu disappeared. In his place, an ice-blooded fury glared out from behind gold-rimmed glasses. He leaned across his desk. He almost launched himself at Lindsey. "Whose side are you on? It's your job to save this corporation money, not throw it away."

"I think I can even work out a way to get something for Latasha Greene and her baby. Reverend Johnson and I have had a few more chats, and he's offered some wonderful suggestions," Lindsey said.

"Mr. Lindsey, I am prepared to accept your resignation from International Surety as of close of business today," Richelieu said.

"Mr. Richelieu, I am not prepared to tender my resignation. And after all the wonderful things I've said about this company to those reporters from *Time* and *Newsweek* and CNN, I don't think you'd want to tell them why you fired me."

"Out. Goodbye. I'll talk with Ms. Johansen and you'll have your next assignment."

Lindsey rose and headed for the door without shaking hands with Richelieu. As he reached for the door, he was stopped by Richelieu's voice. "I promise you, it will be one that you love."

"Thank you, sir."

He walked past Mrs. Blomquist. Her powdered face betrayed no identifiable expression. But as Lindsey strode toward the elevator he could not help but think he had seen a wink that lasted as long as a nanosecond.

No. Impossible.

Lindsey winced and groaned.

"Sorry. I'm sorry. I just wanted to touch you," Marvia said. She pulled a tissue from its box and wiped her eyes. "I don't know why I'm crying. I think it's because Jamie's all right. Or what I would have done if he hadn't been all right."

Lindsey put his hand on her cheek. He didn't say anything.

"Or maybe it's because you do look funny, Bart. At first you looked . . . I was frightened. I see some gruesome sights in my work, but when it's somebody you . . . somebody I love . . ." She looked at him and started to laugh. "But now you just look so ugly and so funny. I can't help it."

He said, "Come on, let's go get some dinner. It's our last night in Denver. Let's enjoy it. I guess I can stand the stares. Let 'em wonder what happened to me. Let 'em think I'm a boxer who lost one. Badly."

They wound up at Morton's, where parking cost more than Lindsey would have paid for most meals. Lindsey turned over the rented Thunderbird to the valet with a flourish. The valet only stared briefly at Lindsey's discolored and bandaged face. He spent more time admiring Marvia.

Marvia liked to dress down, Lindsey knew, and she carried that look well. But she also knew how to turn heads. He pitied Ms. Claudia Ferré. Lindsey pictured Marvia in her flame-colored blouse. Poor Major Wilkerson would never be the same. And, what the hell, if International Surety wouldn't buy Hobart Lindsey a new pair of pants, it was going to treat him to a superb evening with Marvia.

Tonight Marvia wore something that shimmered green in one light and blue in another and a strand of beads that drew eyes away from Lindsey's ravaged face. Over a shared chateaubriand, he proposed to her again. They had been drinking champagne, blessed by a waiter with tolerant ideas of what went with what.

"I can't say no anymore."

He felt the same jolt of electricity flash through his body that he had the first time he had touched her.

"Not after what happened at North Field," she said. "It wasn't what you said to James and Claudia at the Parc. That was sweet but that wasn't what won me. I knew you were saying that to help me, and it did. But it was when you said you were Jamie's father. When you said you'd exchange your life for your boy's. For Jamie's."

"I might not have said it, if I'd thought about it. I didn't have time to think. It just came out. After . . . after, I thought, How could I say that? Wilkerson was his father. I know you wanted a black father for him. I thought, What kind of role model would I make, anyway?"

"That's why I love you," she said. "We tell the truth, when we don't stop and calculate. When what we have inside just comes out. There's a truth teller inside that pushes everything out of the way and leaps up and speaks. It's stark naked and it doesn't hide anything. That was your truth teller. That was when I knew. If you felt that way about Jamie . . . I knew how you felt about me, but I had to know how you felt about Jamie. It won't be easy to be his father, but in your heart that's what you are."

He held her hand. "Is that your truth teller?"

"Yes." She slipped her other hand into his lap, beneath the linen tablecloth. She said, "Is that your truth teller?"

"Let's get out of here and get back to the Brown Palace and celebrate," he said. "You'll just have to be careful of my nose."

"I have to take care of you. Eat your dinner. Your body needs the protein. And married people don't have to hurry back to bed. They have all the time in the world."

Author's Note

READERS MAY WONDER HOW MUCH of *The Bessie Blue Killer* is fact and how much is fiction. The Tuskegee Airmen were quite real, a heroic group of aviators whose service in World War II included many combat missions in North Africa and Europe. Against overwhelming odds, they contributed not only to the victory over Nazism in Europe but also to the cause of justice in America.

The Port Chicago disaster of 1944 is also historical, and my references to this tragedy are as accurate as research permits. The town of Port Chicago, California, no longer exists; the ground upon which it once stood is now part of the Concord Naval Weapons Station.

My research was aided immeasurably by the personal reminiscences of Mr. Morris Soublet of Oakland, California, a survivor of the Port Chicago disaster; Mr. LeRoy Roberts, Jr., of Seattle, Washington, a veteran of the Tuskegee Airmen and a P-51 pilot; Mr. John Albanese of Castro Valley, California, a onetime bombardier in both B-17s and B-24s; Mr. Edward Rehbeck, Jr., of Poughkeepsie, New York, who knows the B-17 from the inside out; Mr. Alfred Coppel of Portola Valley, California, who rode the P-38 Lightning; and Mr. J. D. Tikalsky of the Concord Naval Weapons Station.

The standard sources for information on events at Port Chicago are *No Share of Glory*, by Robert E. Pearson (1964), and *The Port Chicago Mutiny*, by Robert L. Allen (1989). The standard reference work on the Tuskegee Airmen is *The Tuskegee Airmen*, by Charles E. Francis (1988). Also of interest is *Liberators: Fighting on Two Fronts in World War II*, by Lou Potter with

William Miles and Nina Rosenblum (1992). In addition to material concerning both the Tuskegee Airmen and Port Chicago, this book (and an associated PBS television series) provides further illumination of the role of black Americans in the Second World War.

Blues lyrics quoted in *The Bessie Blue Killer* were transcribed from 78 rpm period recordings as restored by Australian Robert Parker, Rosetta Reitz, Billy Altman, Don Jarvis and other dedicated electronic wizards. Many such recordings dating from the 1920s and '30s are now available on Compact Disc. The recordings' restored sound quality and clarity are often remarkable.

Incidents surrounding the death of Bessie Smith, as described in *The Bessie Blue Killer*, have become part of American folklore. They have been challenged, however, by biographer Chris Albertson in *Bessie* (1972) and by Donald Bogle in *Brown Sugar: Eighty Years of America's Black Female Superstars* (1980, 1992).

A number of books on Negro League baseball are available. The first, and still the definitive volume on the subject, is *Only the Ball Was White*, by Robert Peterson (1970, 1984). Additional research is incorporated in *Invisible Men: Life in Baseball's Negro Leagues*, by Donn Rogosin (1983). Many striking photographs as well as reproductions of Negro League memorabilia are included in *When the Game Was Black and White: The Illustrated History of Baseball's Negro Leagues*, by Bruce Chadwick (1992).

All of the above notwithstanding, *The Bessie Blue Killer* remains a work of fiction and all persons and events described in it, other than those included for purposes of historical background, are the product of the author's imagination.